RIVERDALE®

THE TIES THAT BIND

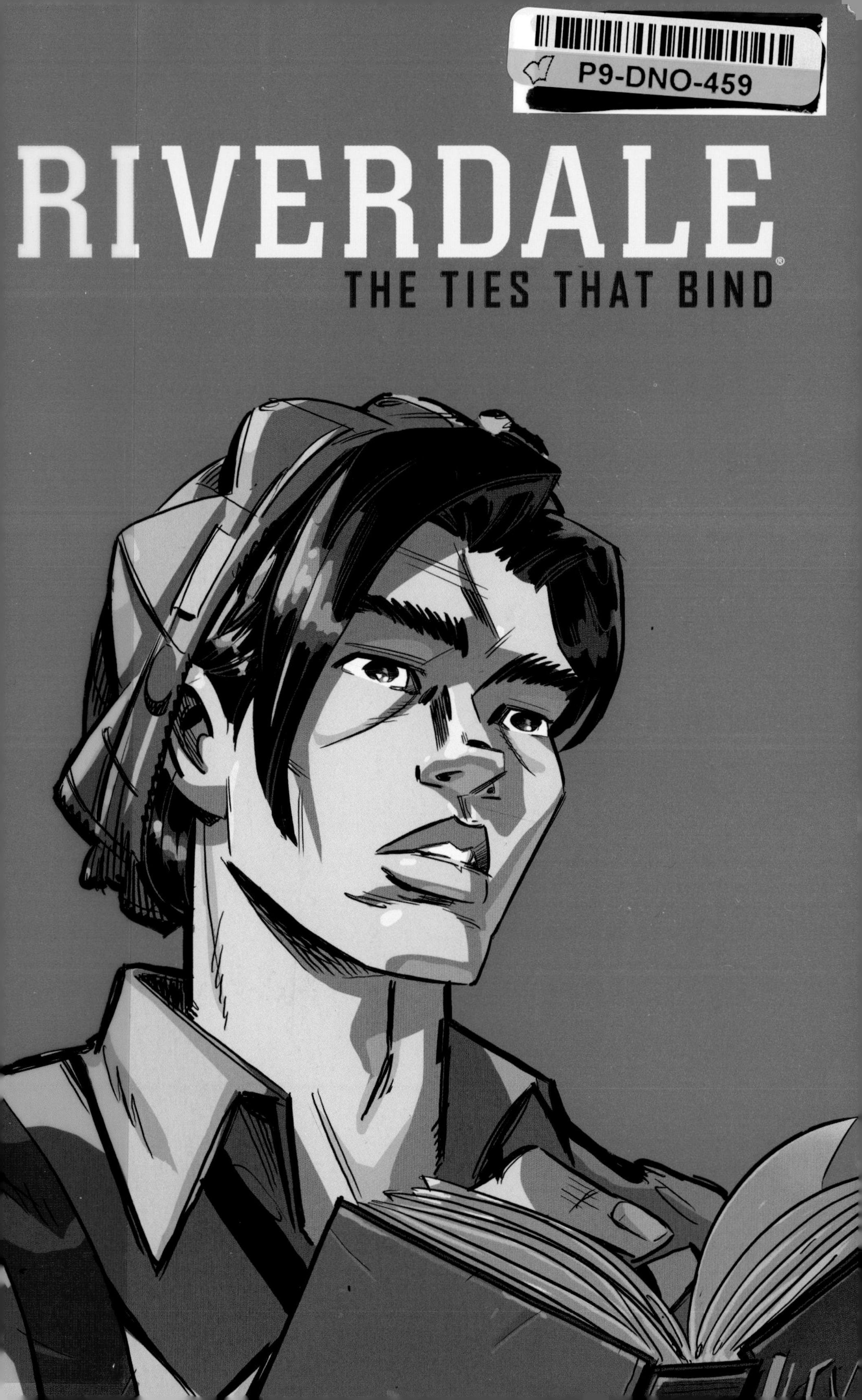

WRITTEN BY

MICOL OSTOW

ILLUSTRATED BY

THOMAS PITILLI

COLORS BY

ANDRE SZYMANOWICZ

LETTERS BY

JOHN WORKMAN

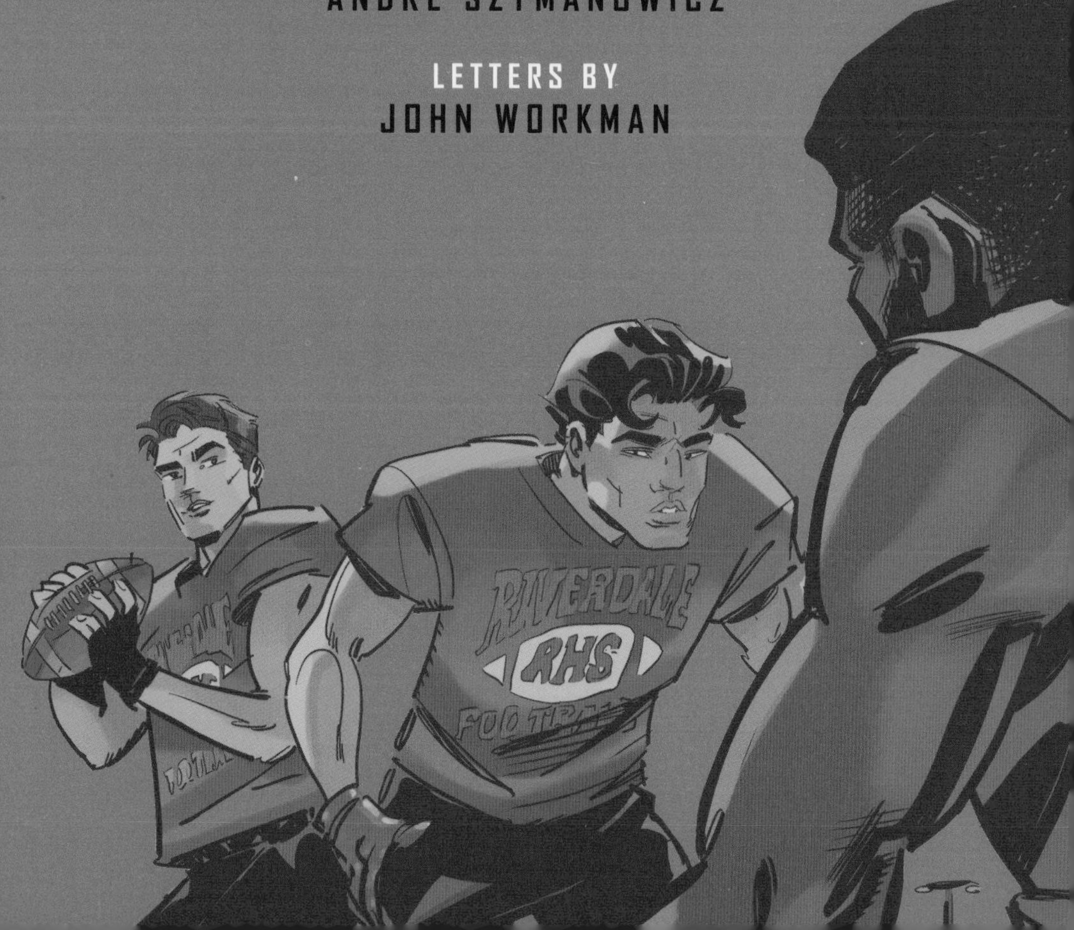
RIVERDALE
RHS

Cover by
Thomas Pitilli

Designer
Kari McLachlan

Editors
Alex Segura &
Jamie Lee Rotante

Associate Editor
Stephen Oswald

Assistant Editor
Vincent Lovallo

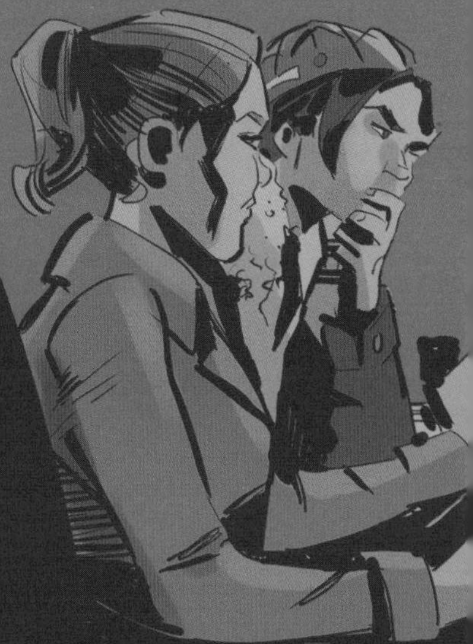

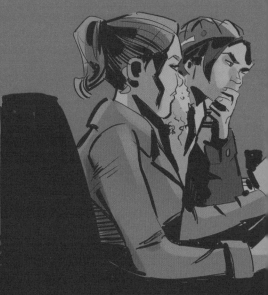

Publisher / Co-CEO: Jon Goldwater
Co-President / Editor-In-Chief: Victor Gorelick
Co-President: Mike Pellerito
Co-President: Alex Segura
Chief Creative Officer: Roberto Aguirre-Sacasa
Chief Operating Officer: William Mooar
Chief Financial Officer: Robert Wintle
Director: Jonathan Betancourt
Art Director: Vincent Lovallo
Production Manager: Stephen Oswald
Lead Designer: Kari McLachlan
Editor/Proofreader: Jamie Lee Rotante
Co-CEO: Nancy Silberkleit

ISBN: 978-1-64576-958-3

TABLE of CONTENTS

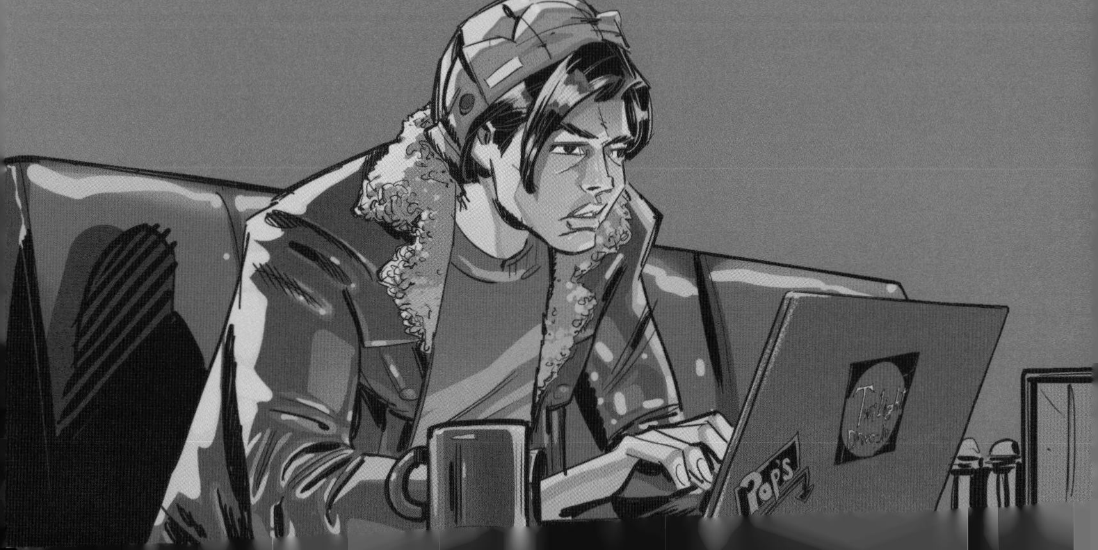

Pap's

PROLOGUE

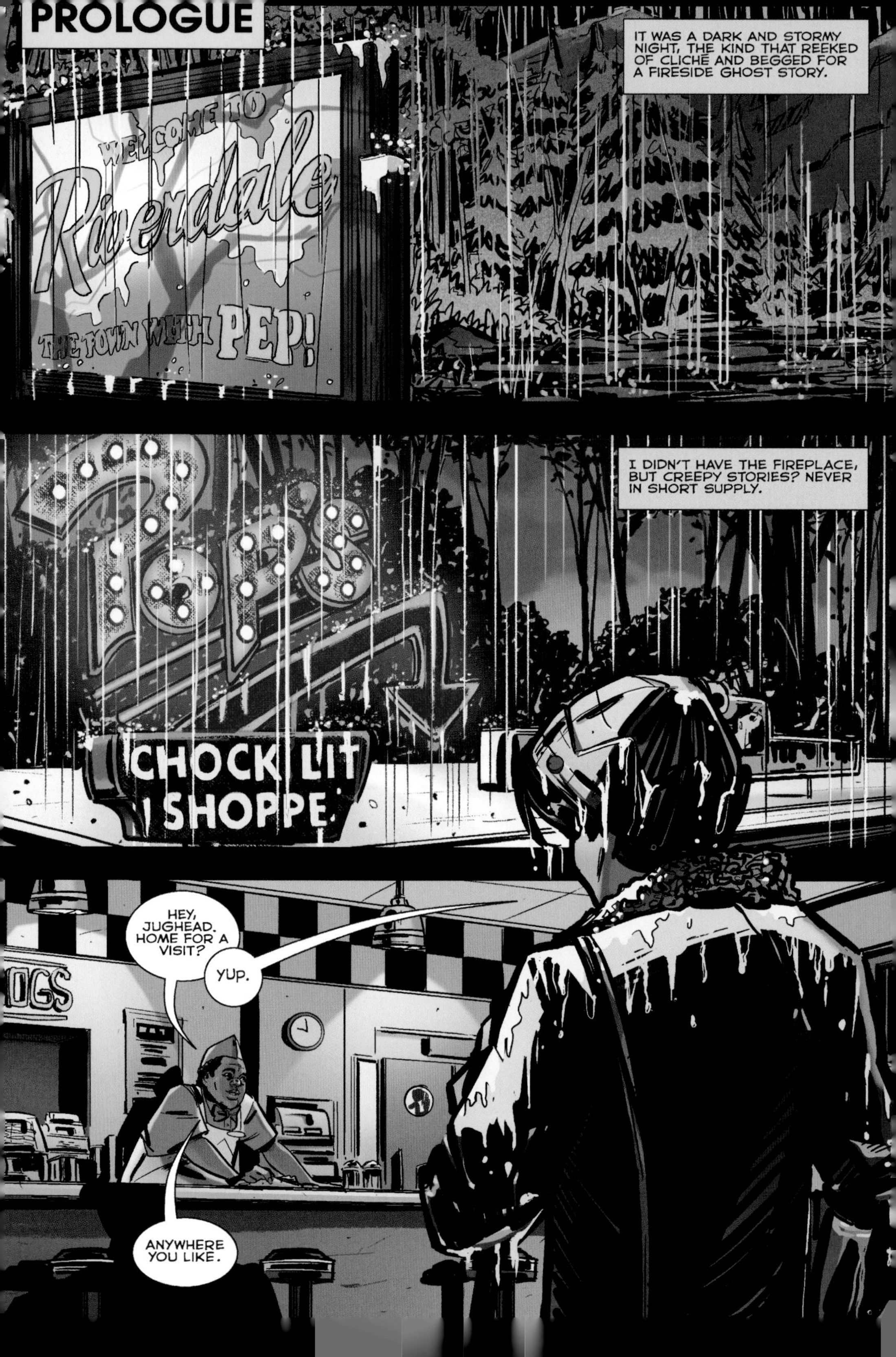
IT WAS A DARK AND STORMY NIGHT, THE KIND THAT REEKED OF CLICHÉ AND BEGGED FOR A FIRESIDE GHOST STORY.
WELCOME TO
Riverdale
THE TOWN WITH PEP!
I DIDN'T HAVE THE FIREPLACE, BUT CREEPY STORIES? NEVER IN SHORT SUPPLY.
POP'S
CHOCK LIT SHOPPE
HEY, JUGHEAD. HOME FOR A VISIT?
YUP.
ANYWHERE YOU LIKE.

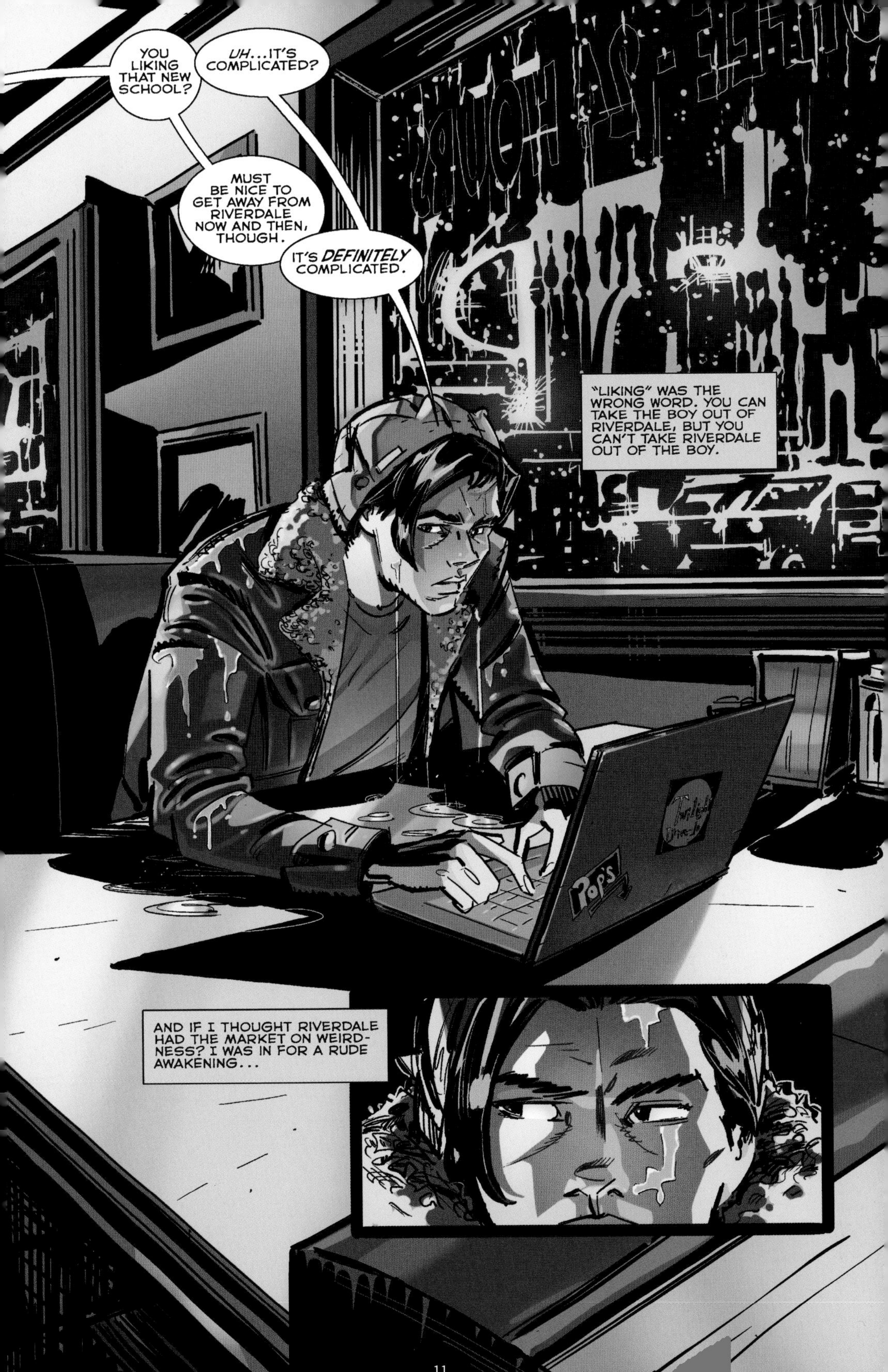
YOU LIKING THAT NEW SCHOOL?
UH...IT'S COMPLICATED?
MUST BE NICE TO GET AWAY FROM RIVERDALE NOW AND THEN, THOUGH.
IT'S DEFINITELY COMPLICATED.
"LIKING" WAS THE WRONG WORD. YOU CAN TAKE THE BOY OUT OF RIVERDALE, BUT YOU CAN'T TAKE RIVERDALE OUT OF THE BOY.
POP'S
AND IF I THOUGHT RIVERDALE HAD THE MARKET ON WEIRDNESS? I WAS IN FOR A RUDE AWAKENING...

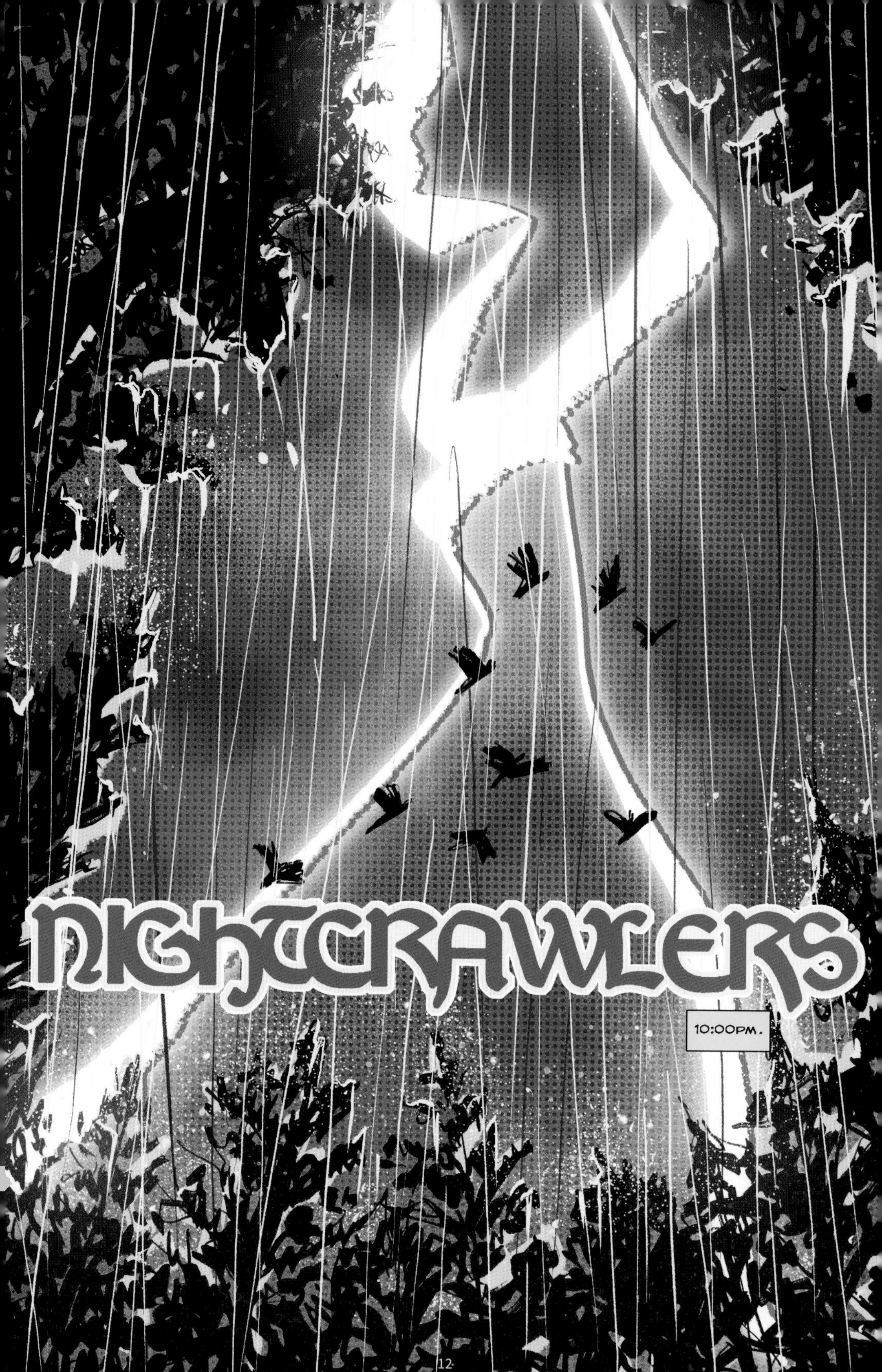
NIGHTCRAWLERS
10:00PM.

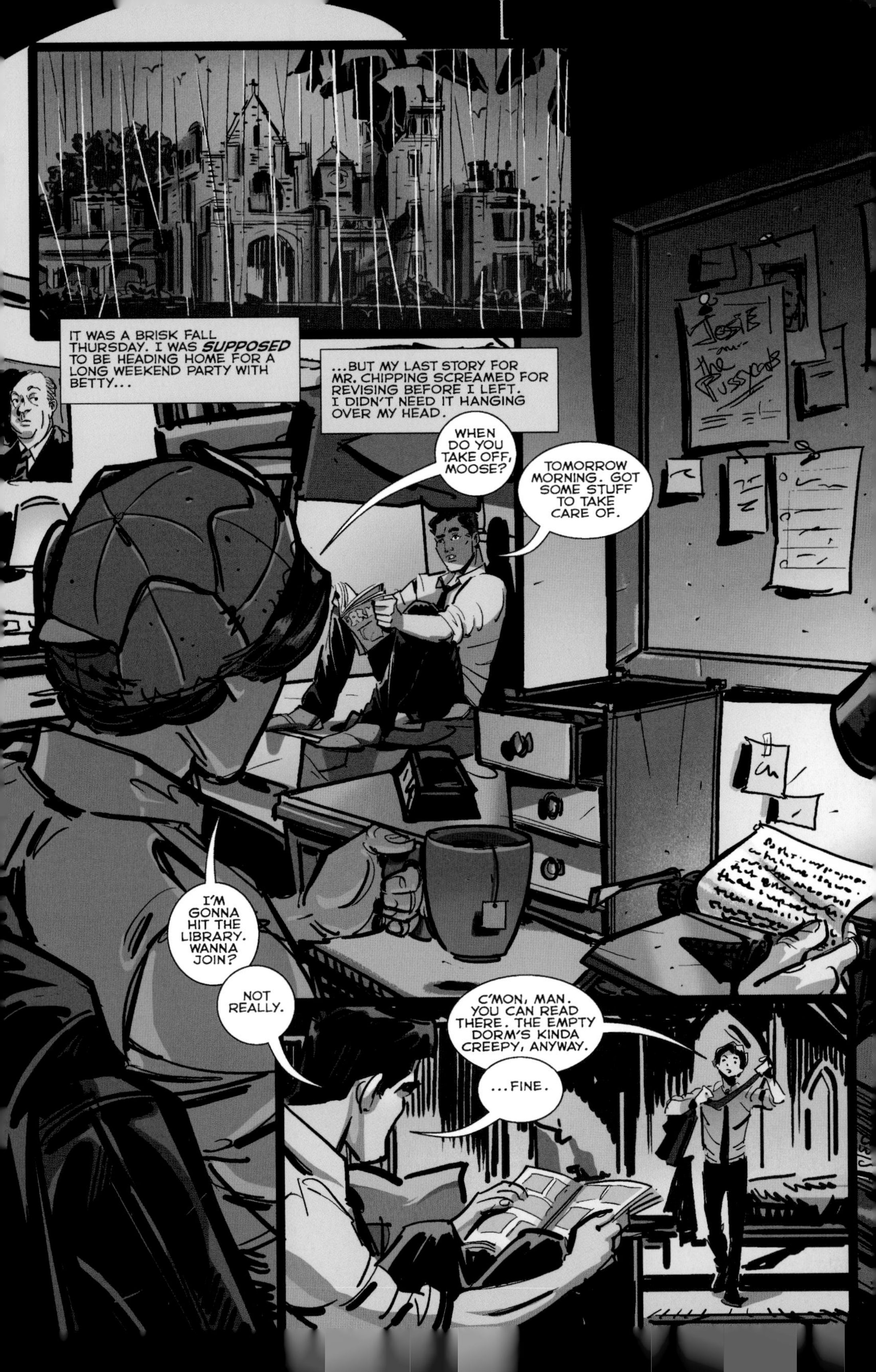

IT WAS A BRISK FALL THURSDAY. I WAS *SUPPOSED* TO BE HEADING HOME FOR A LONG WEEKEND PARTY WITH BETTY...
...BUT MY LAST STORY FOR MR. CHIPPING SCREAMED FOR REVISING BEFORE I LEFT. I DIDN'T NEED IT HANGING OVER MY HEAD.
WHEN DO YOU TAKE OFF, MOOSE?
TOMORROW MORNING. GOT SOME STUFF TO TAKE CARE OF.
JOSIE AND THE PUSSYCATS
I'M GONNA HIT THE LIBRARY. WANNA JOIN?
NOT REALLY.
C'MON, MAN. YOU CAN READ THERE. THE EMPTY DORM'S KINDA CREEPY, ANYWAY.
...FINE.

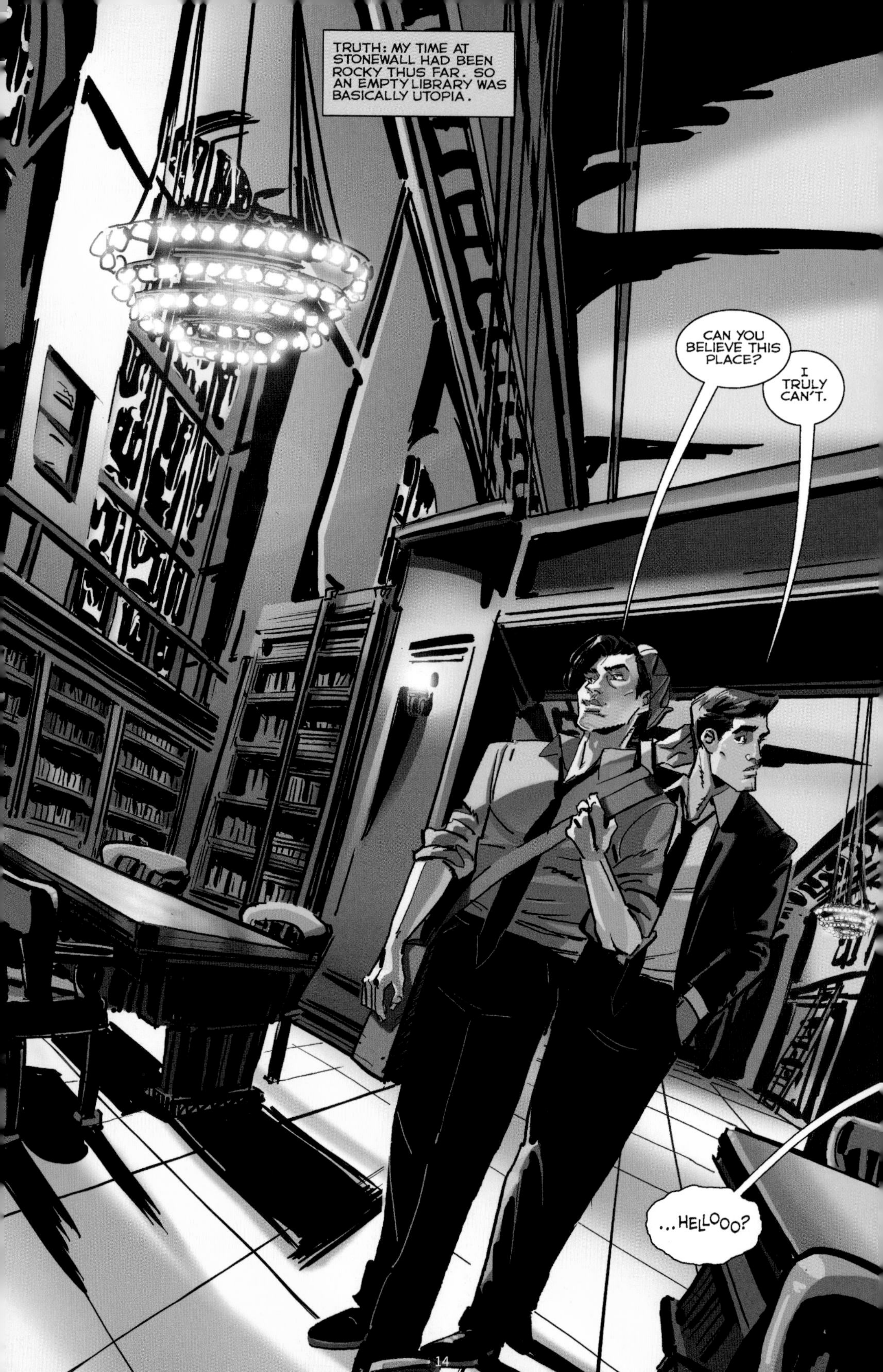
TRUTH: MY TIME AT STONEWALL HAD BEEN ROCKY THUS FAR. SO AN EMPTY LIBRARY WAS BASICALLY UTOPIA.
CAN YOU BELIEVE THIS PLACE?
I TRULY CAN'T.
...HELLOOO?

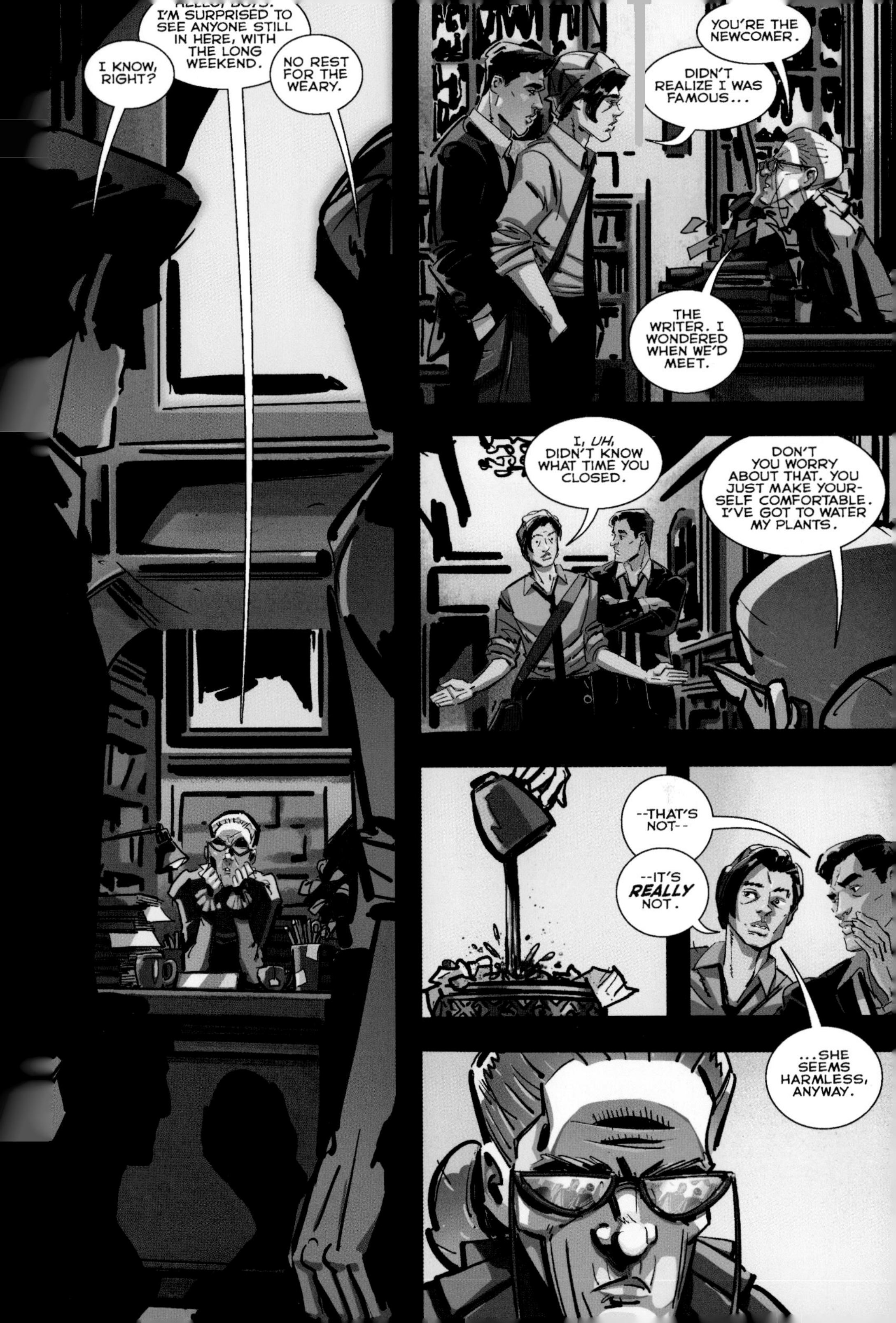
I'M SURPRISED TO SEE ANYONE STILL IN HERE, WITH THE LONG WEEKEND.
I KNOW, RIGHT?
NO REST FOR THE WEARY.
YOU'RE THE NEWCOMER.
DIDN'T REALIZE I WAS FAMOUS...
THE WRITER. I WONDERED WHEN WE'D MEET.
I, *UH*, DIDN'T KNOW WHAT TIME YOU CLOSED.
DON'T YOU WORRY ABOUT THAT. YOU JUST MAKE YOURSELF COMFORTABLE. I'VE GOT TO WATER MY PLANTS.
--THAT'S NOT--
--IT'S ***REALLY*** NOT.
...SHE SEEMS HARMLESS, ANYWAY.

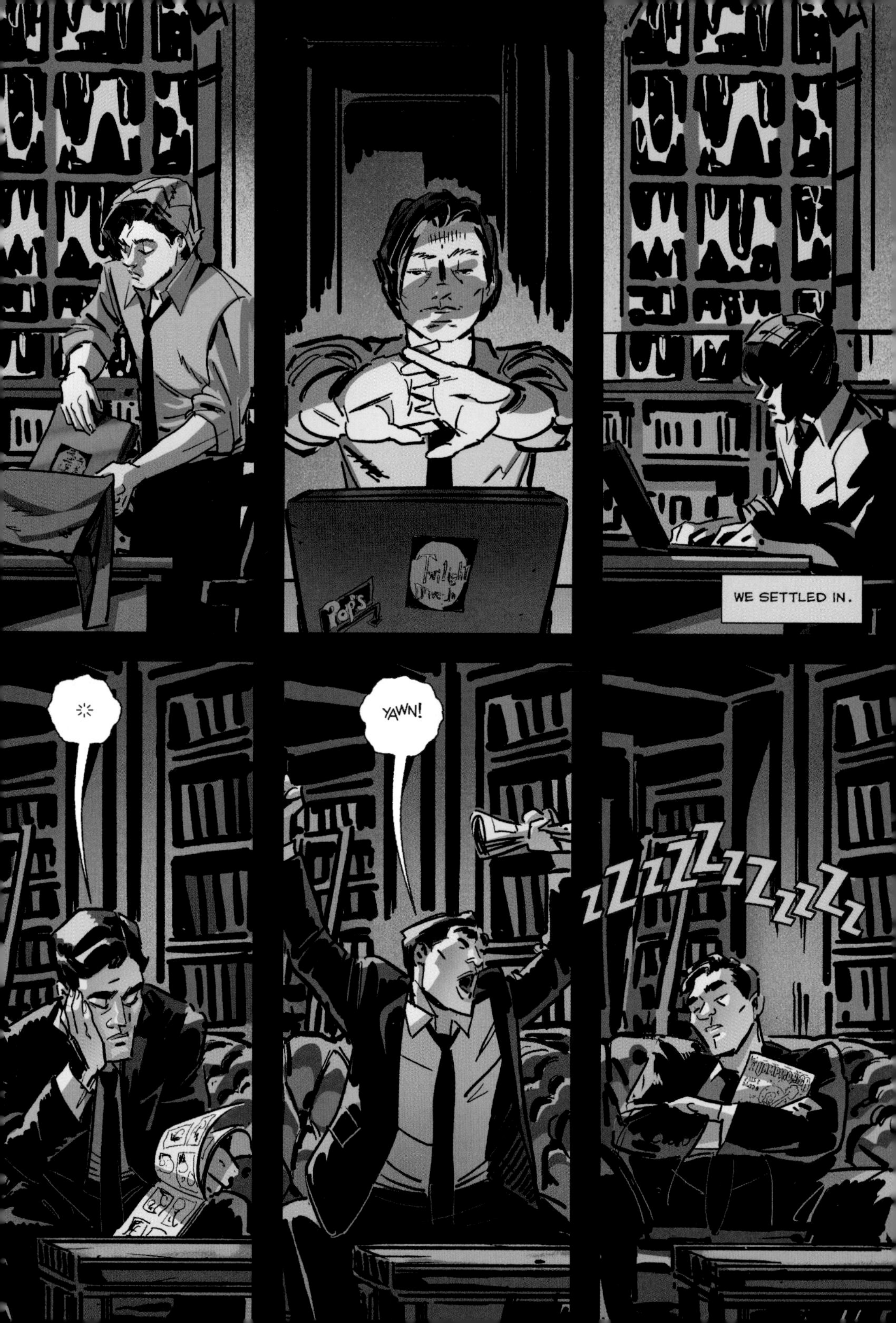
Twilight Drive-In
Pop's
WE SETTLED IN.
YAWN!

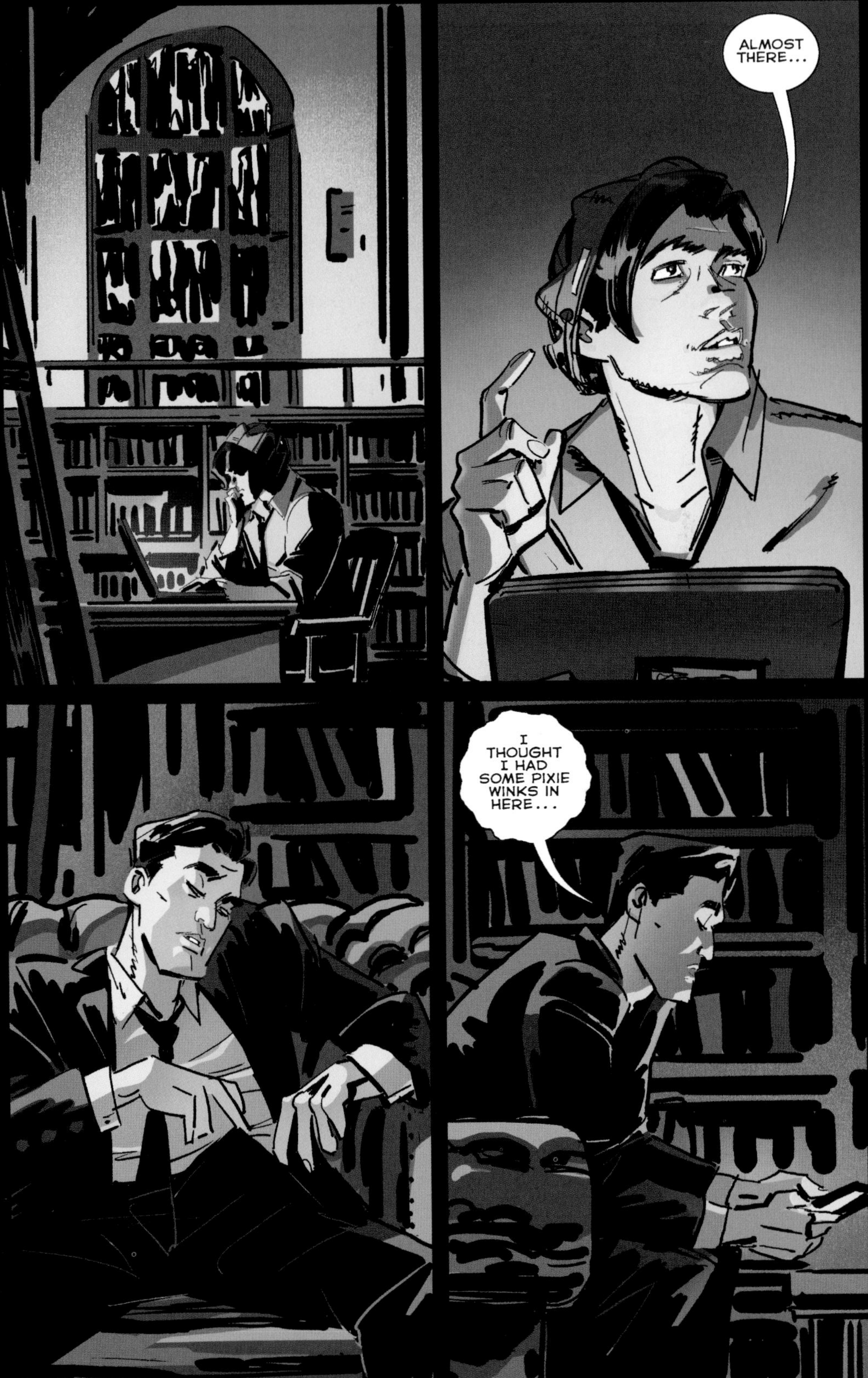
ALMOST THERE...
I THOUGHT I HAD SOME PIXIE WINKS IN HERE...

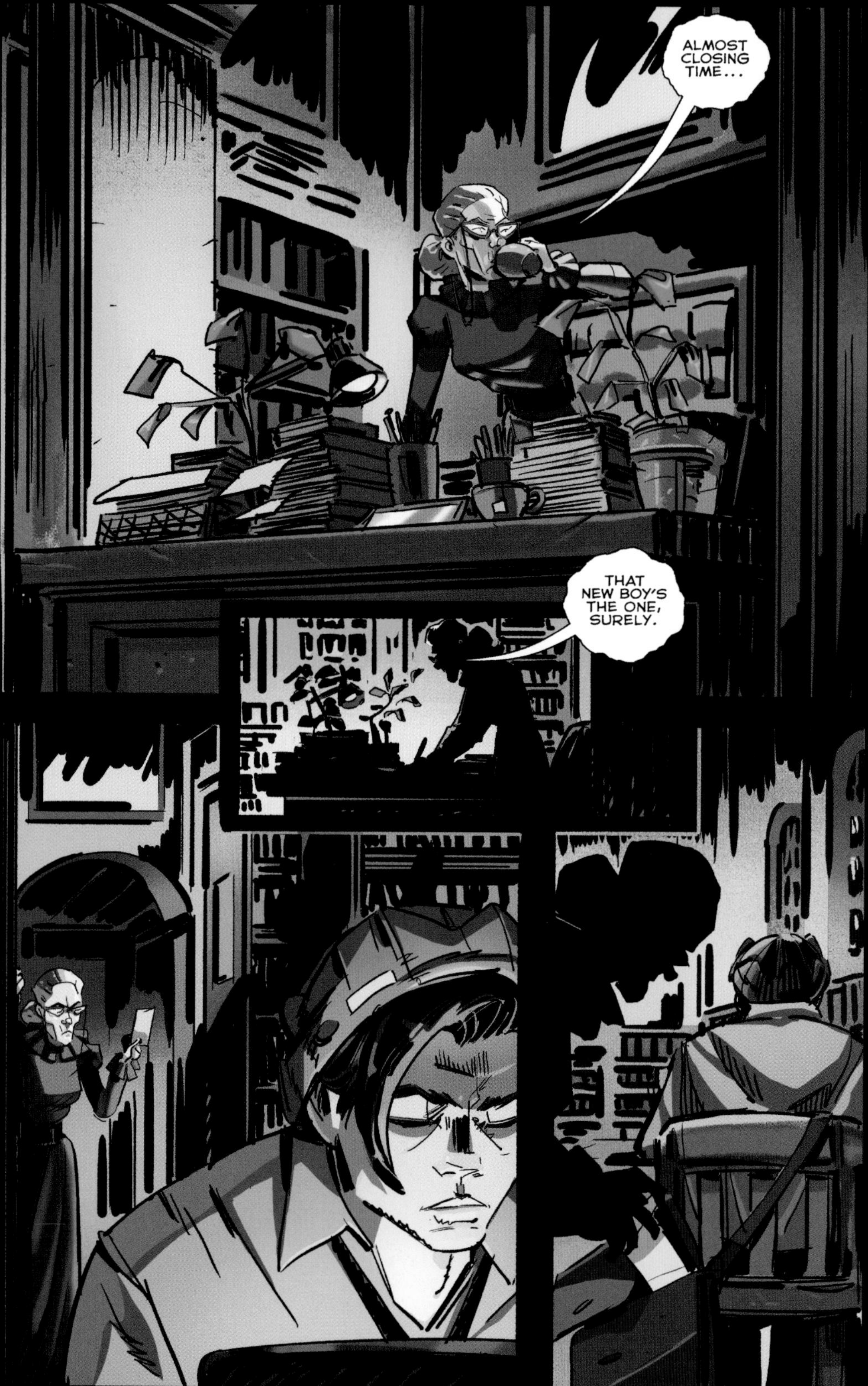
ALMOST CLOSING TIME...
THAT NEW BOY'S THE ONE, SURELY.

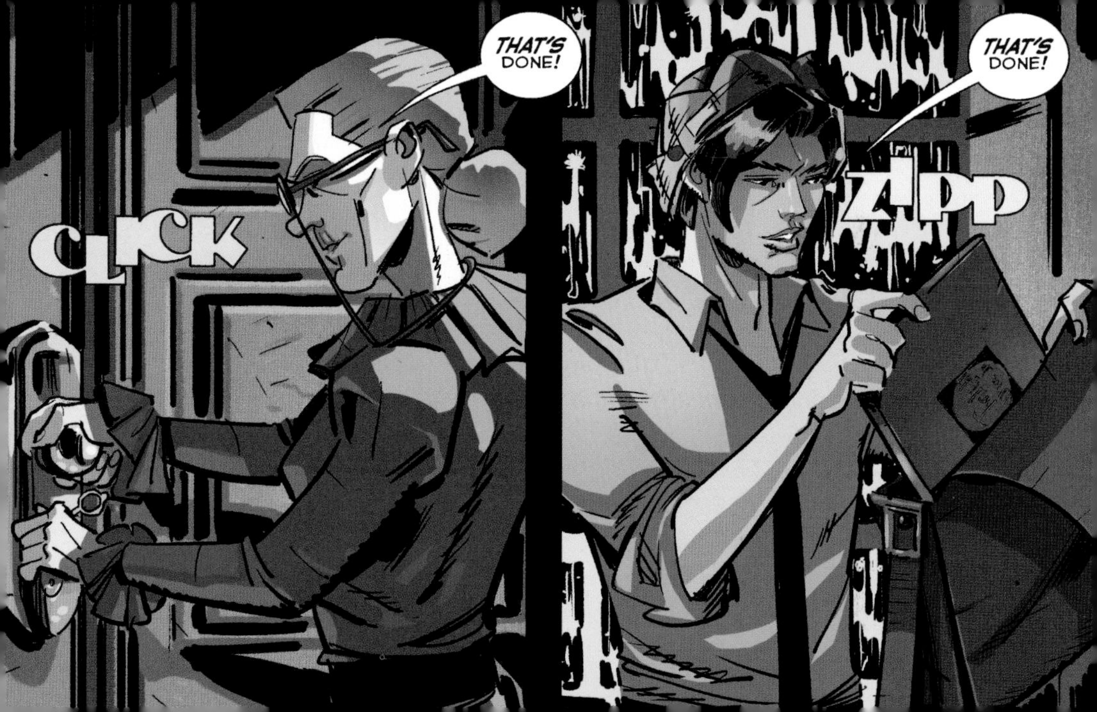
THAT'S DONE!
CLICK
THAT'S DONE!
ZIPP

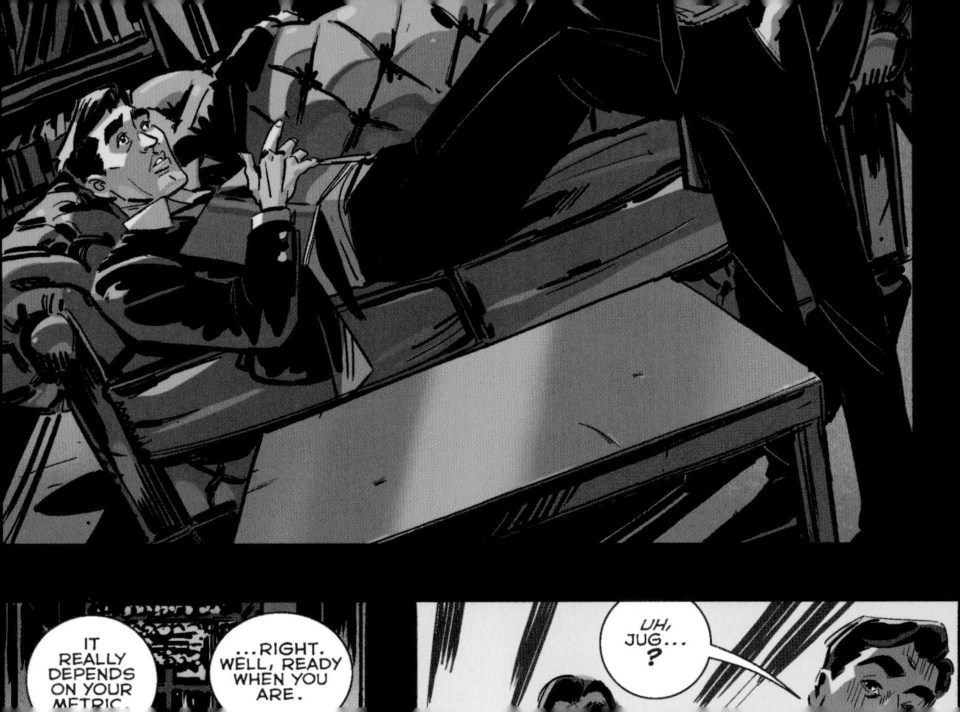
IT REALLY DEPENDS ON YOUR
...RIGHT. WELL, READY WHEN YOU ARE.
UH, JUG...?

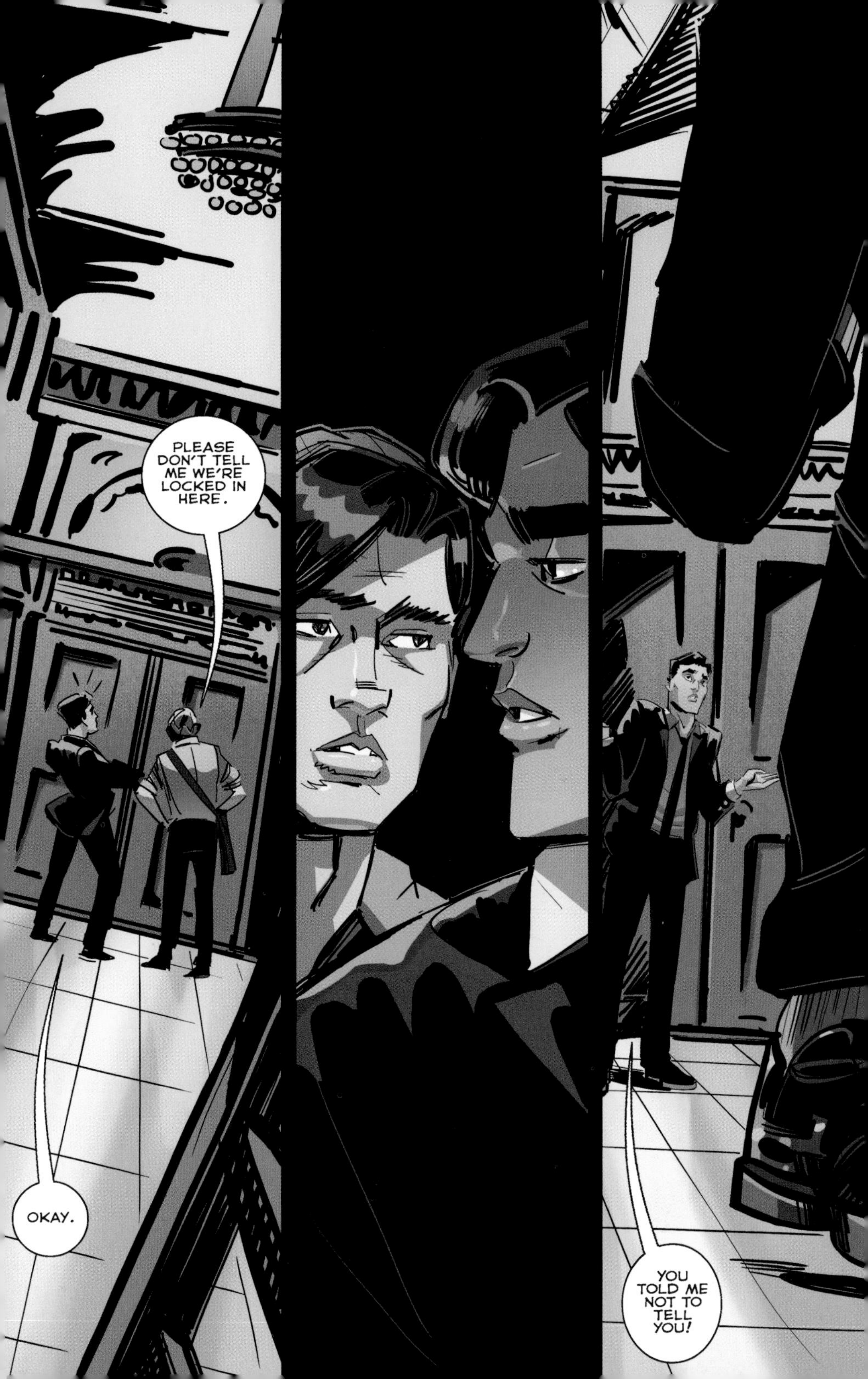
PLEASE DON'T TELL ME WE'RE LOCKED IN HERE.
OKAY.
YOU TOLD ME NOT TO TELL YOU!

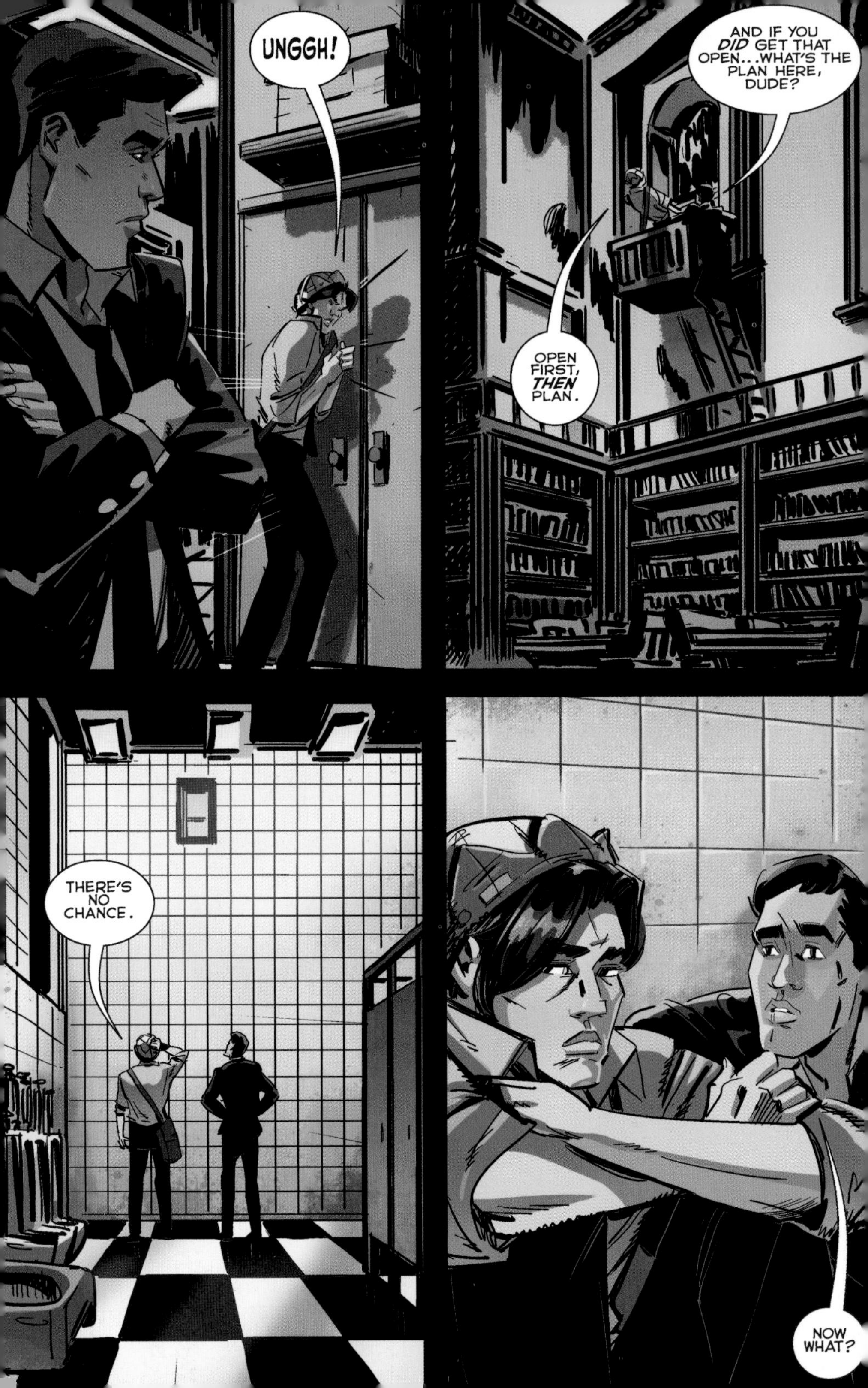
UNGGH!
AND IF YOU DID GET THAT OPEN...WHAT'S THE PLAN HERE, DUDE?
OPEN FIRST, THEN PLAN.
THERE'S NO CHANCE.
NOW WHAT?

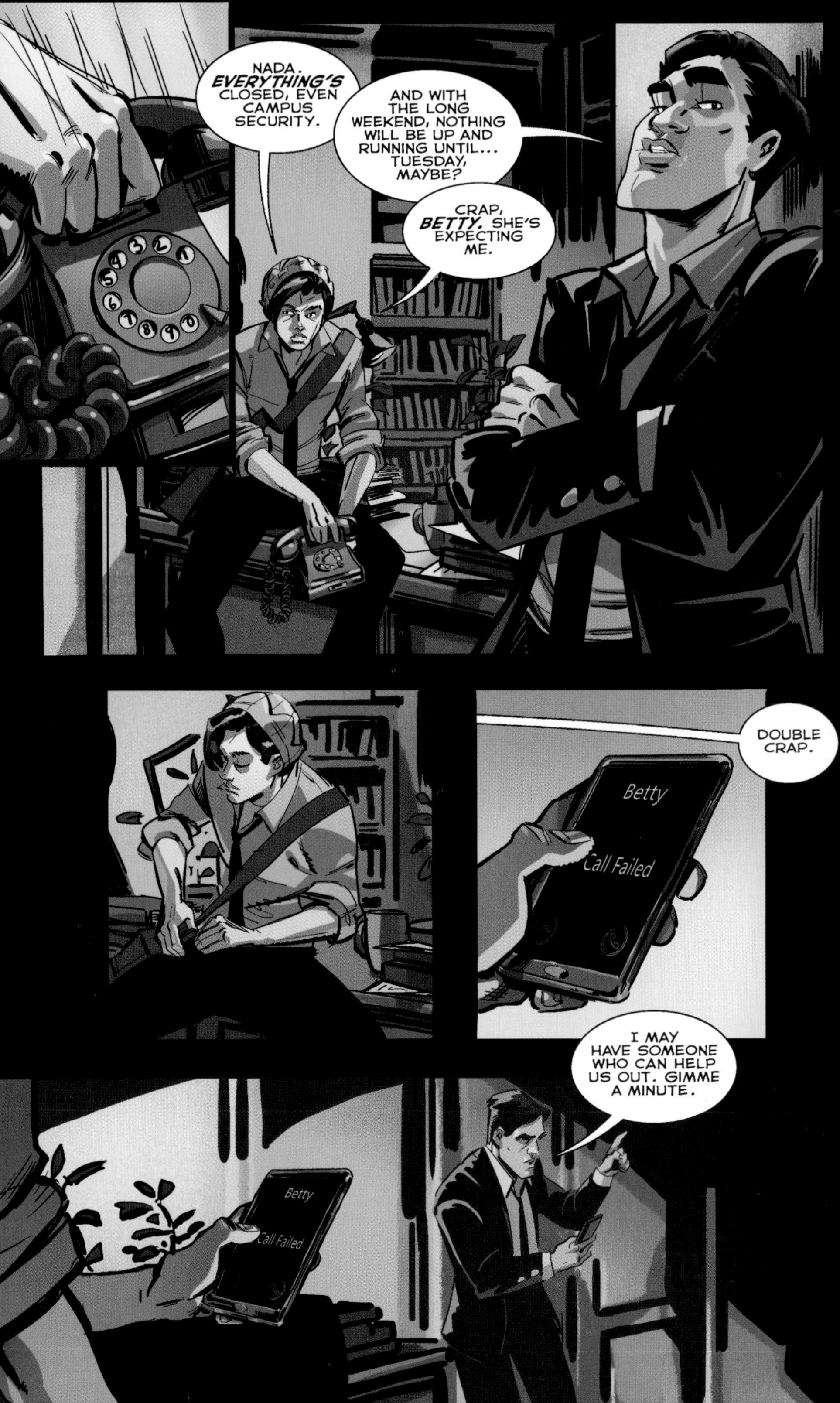
NADA. EVERYTHING'S CLOSED, EVEN CAMPUS SECURITY.
AND WITH THE LONG WEEKEND, NOTHING WILL BE UP AND RUNNING UNTIL... TUESDAY, MAYBE?
CRAP, BETTY. SHE'S EXPECTING ME.
DOUBLE CRAP.
Betty
Call Failed
I MAY HAVE SOMEONE WHO CAN HELP US OUT. GIMME A MINUTE.
Betty
Call Failed

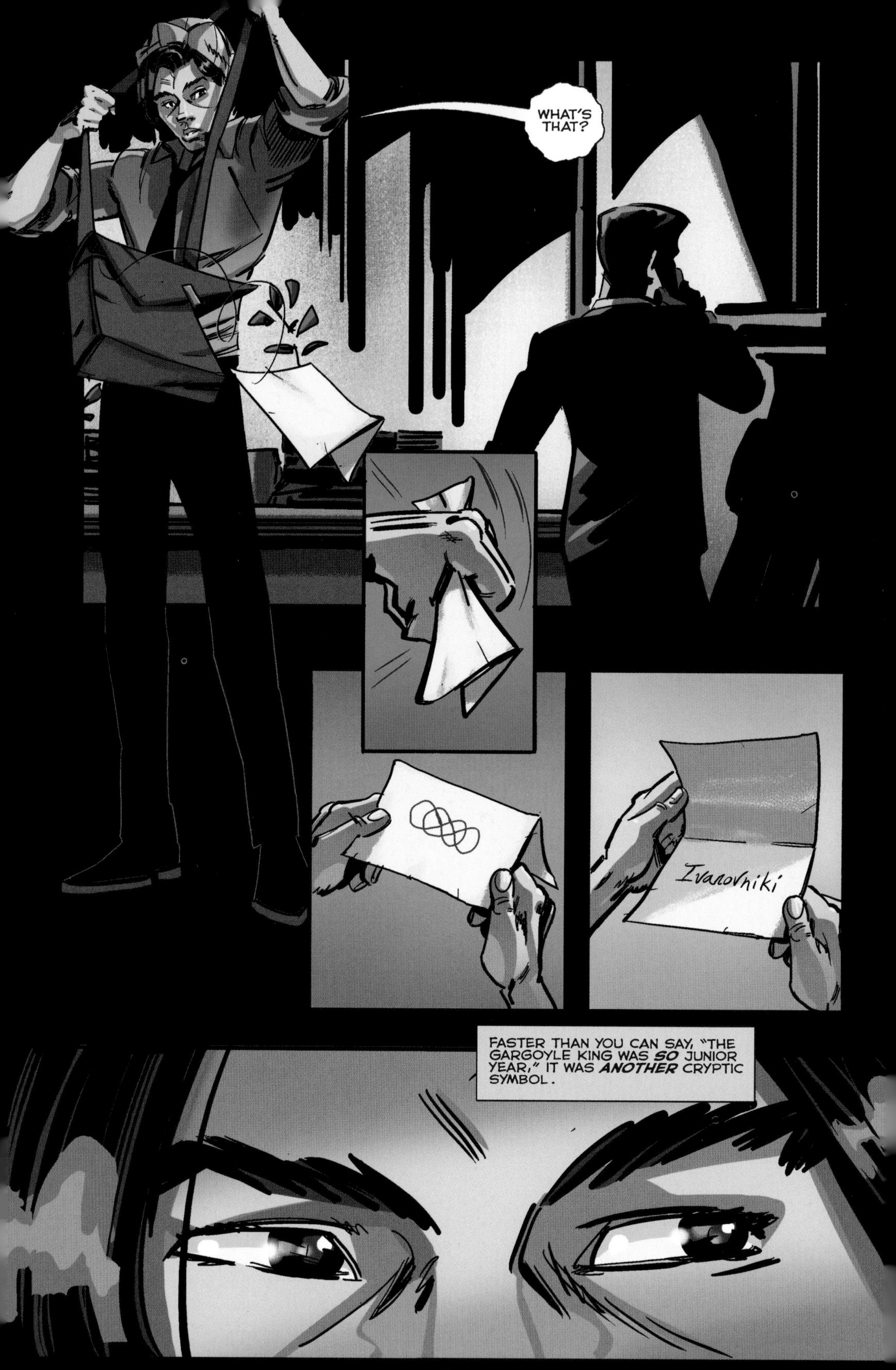
WHAT'S THAT?
Ivanovniki
FASTER THAN YOU CAN SAY, "THE GARGOYLE KING WAS *SO* JUNIOR YEAR," IT WAS *ANOTHER* CRYPTIC SYMBOL.

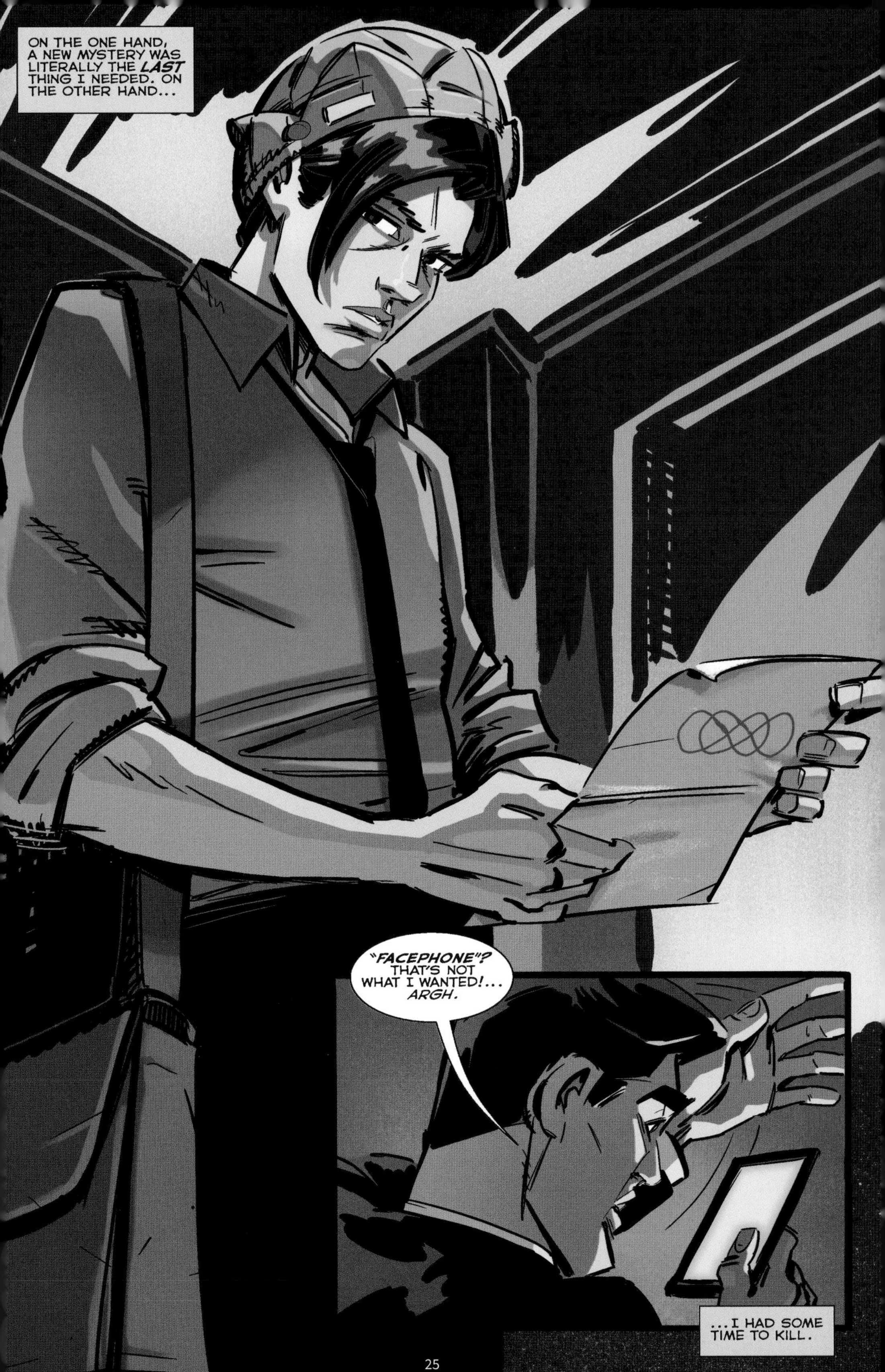
ON THE ONE HAND, A NEW MYSTERY WAS LITERALLY THE *LAST* THING I NEEDED. ON THE OTHER HAND...
"FACEPHONE"? THAT'S NOT WHAT I WANTED!... *ARGH.*
...I HAD SOME TIME TO KILL.

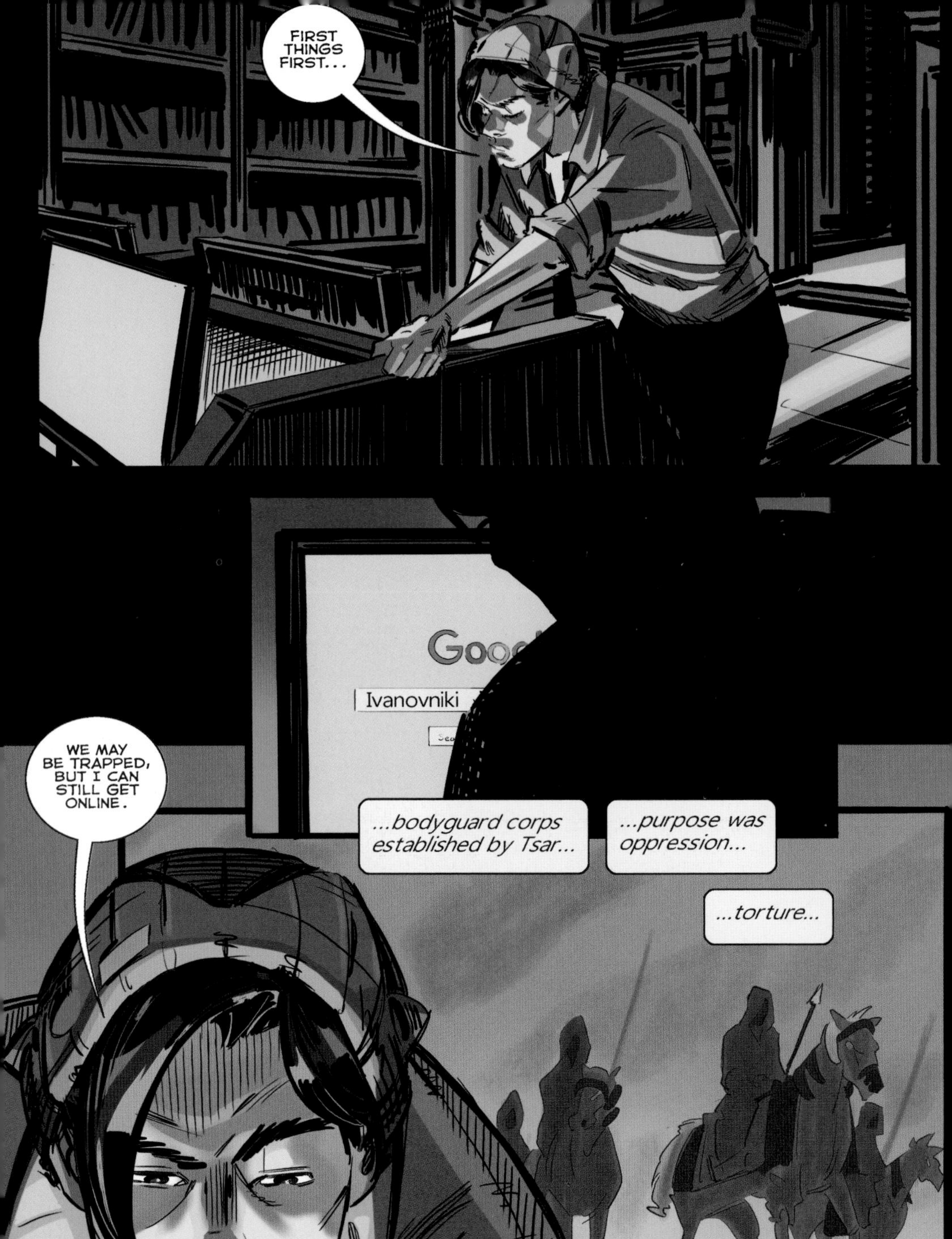
FIRST THINGS FIRST...
Google
Ivanovniki
WE MAY BE TRAPPED, BUT I CAN STILL GET ONLINE.
...bodyguard corps established by Tsar...
...purpose was oppression...
...torture...
THIS WAS ALL CHARMINGLY MORBID, BUT WHAT DID IT HAVE TO DO WITH *ME?* WHY *MY* BACKPACK?

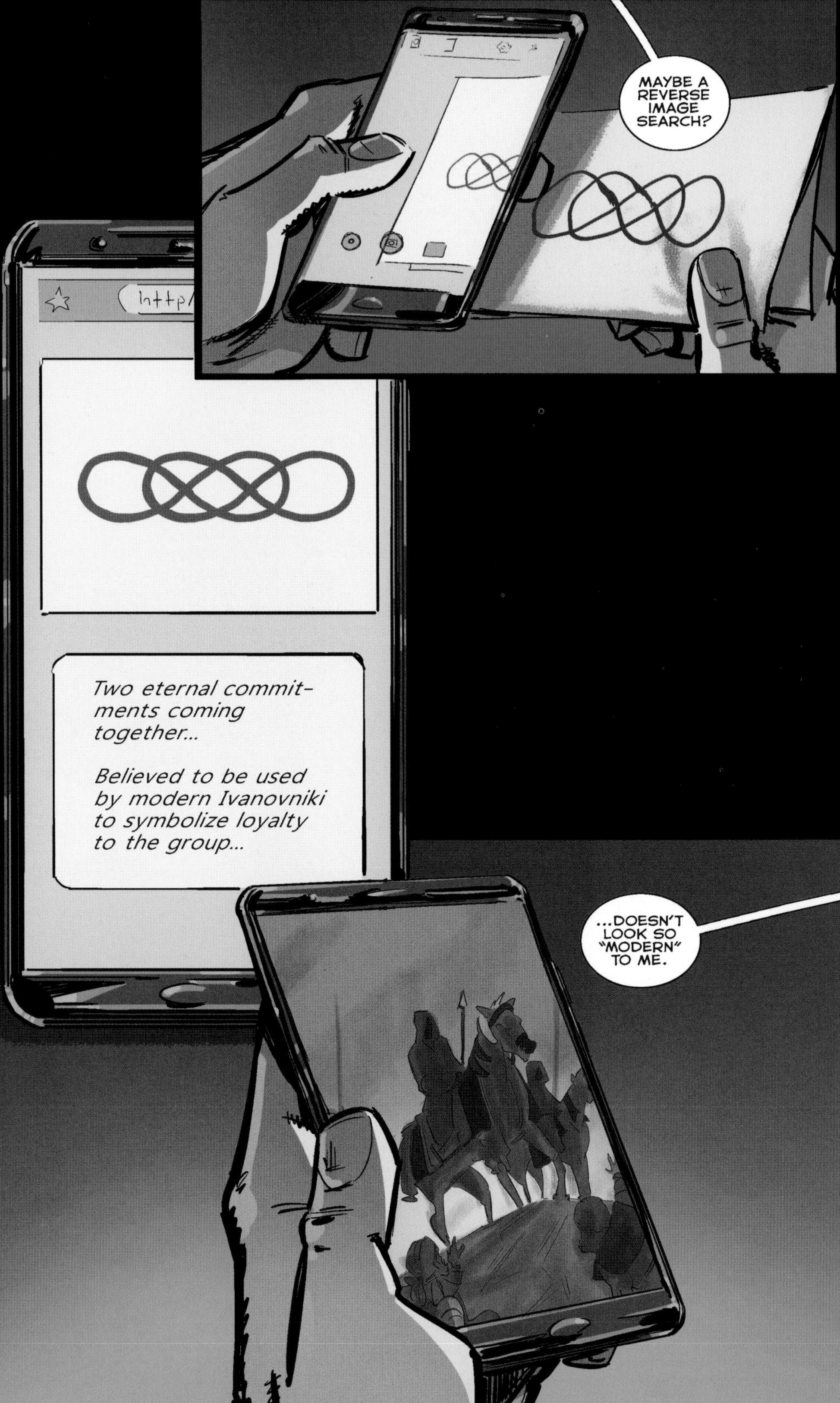
MAYBE A REVERSE IMAGE SEARCH?
http/
Two eternal commit-ments coming together...
Believed to be used by modern Ivanovniki to symbolize loyalty to the group...
...DOESN'T LOOK SO "MODERN" TO ME.

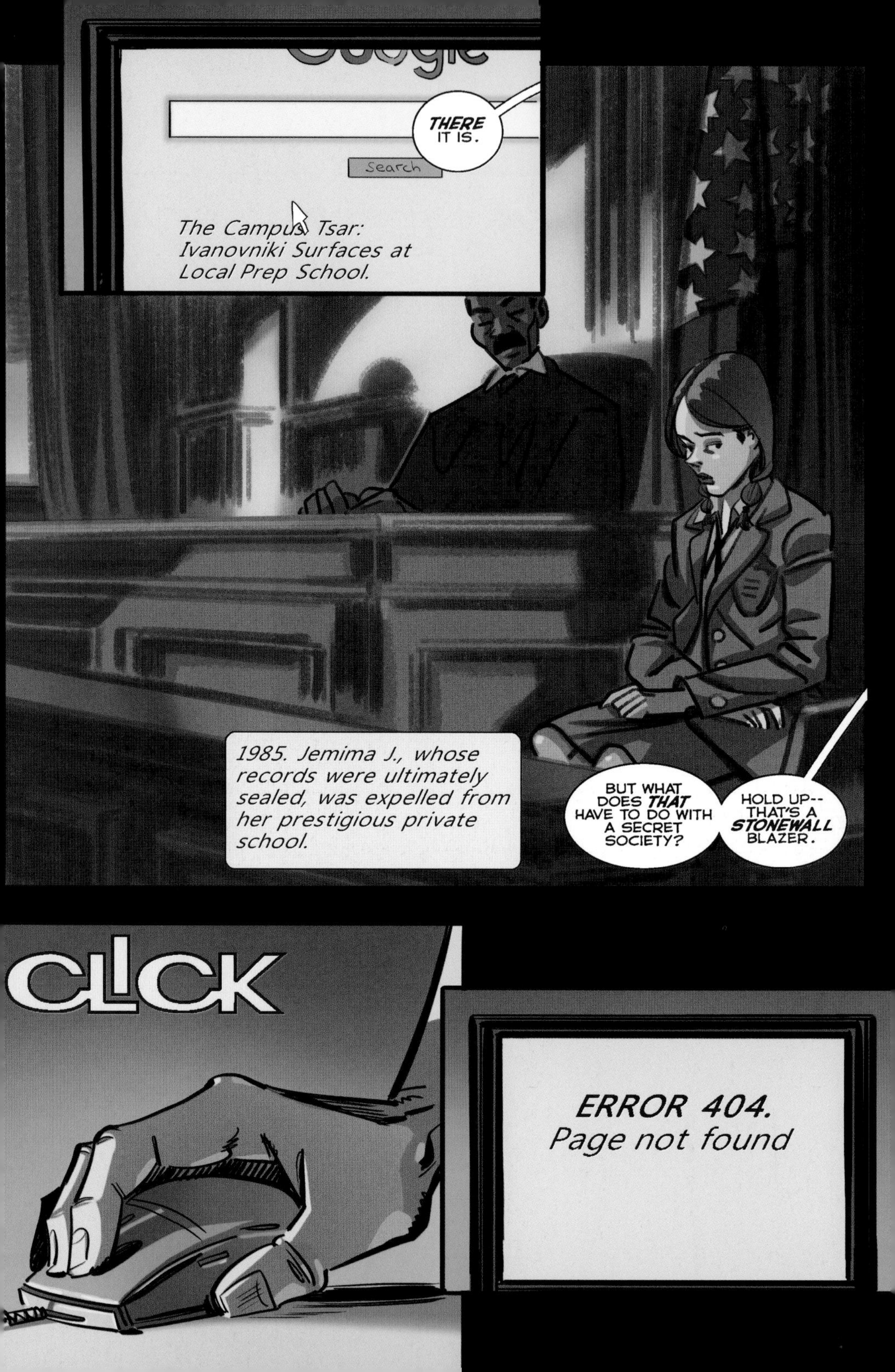
Google
Search
THERE IT IS.
The Campus Tsar: Ivanovniki Surfaces at Local Prep School.
1985. Jemima J., whose records were ultimately sealed, was expelled from her prestigious private school.
BUT WHAT DOES THAT HAVE TO DO WITH A SECRET SOCIETY?
HOLD UP-- THAT'S A STONEWALL BLAZER.
CLICK
ERROR 404.
Page not found

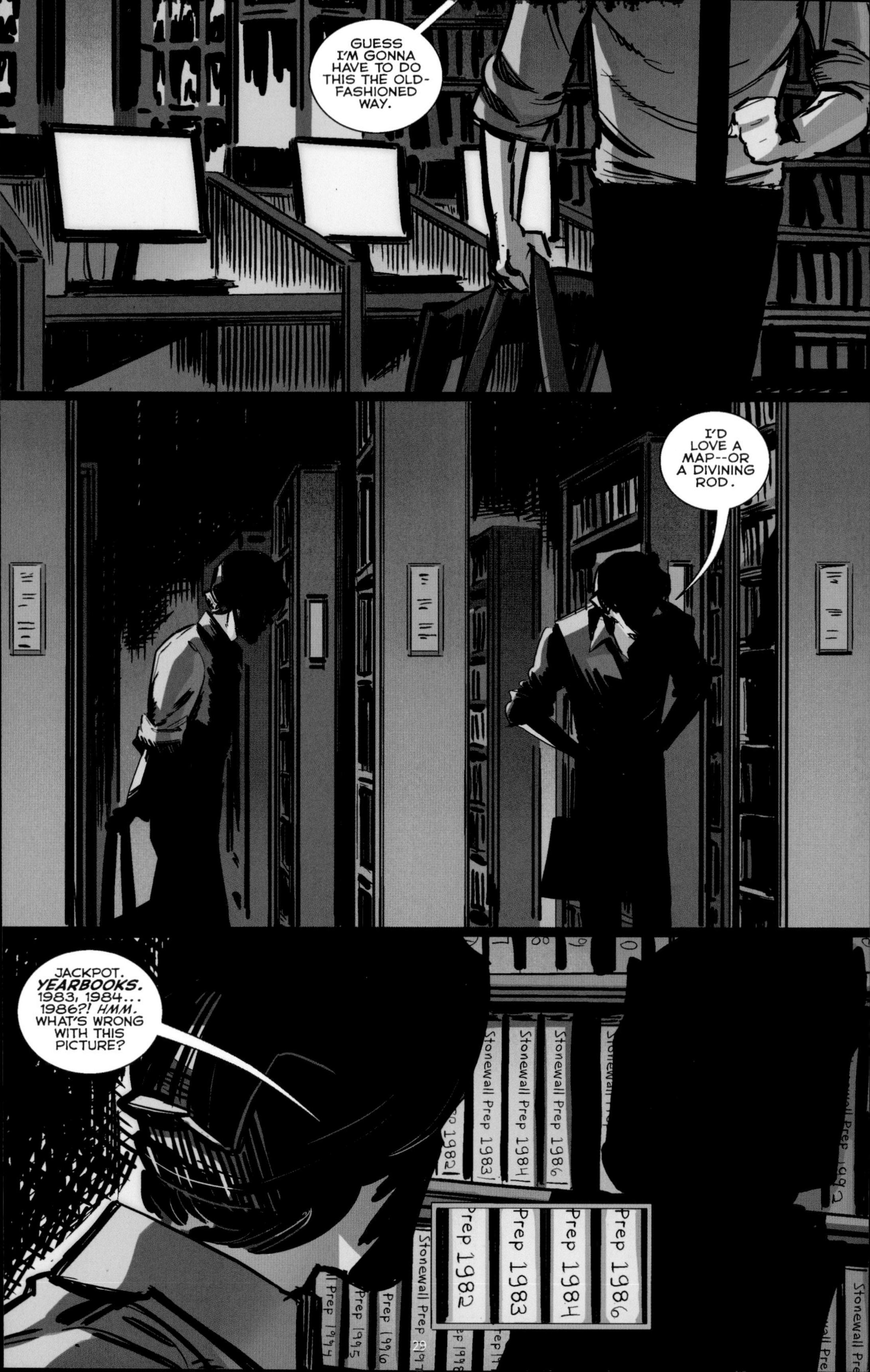
GUESS I'M GONNA HAVE TO DO THIS THE OLD-FASHIONED WAY.
I'D LOVE A MAP--OR A DIVINING ROD.
JACKPOT. *YEARBOOKS.* 1983, 1984... 1986?! *HMM.* WHAT'S WRONG WITH THIS PICTURE?
Stonewall Prep 1983
Stonewall Prep 1984
Stonewall Prep 1986
Prep 1982
Prep 1983
Prep 1984
Prep 1986

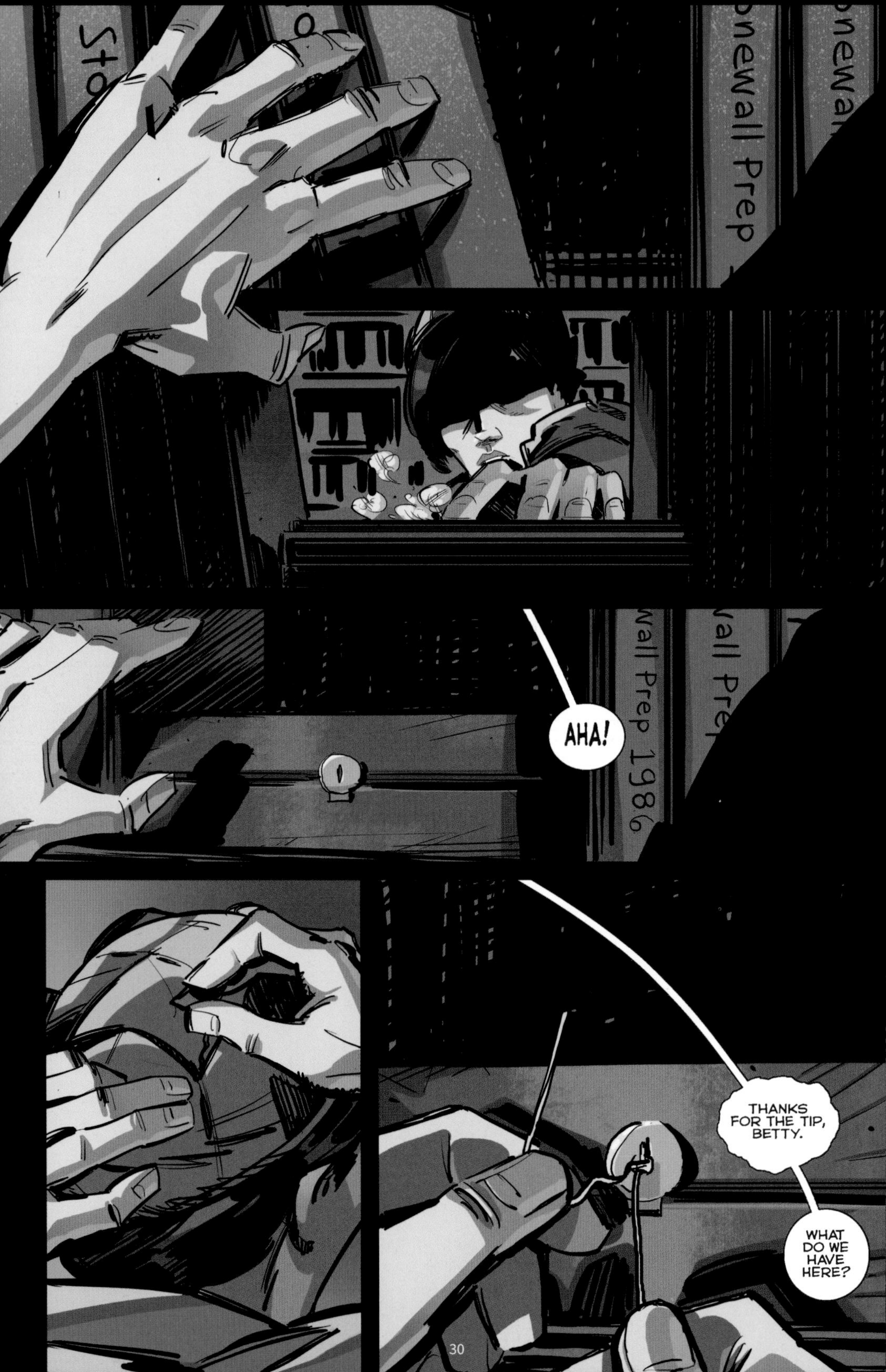
AHA!
THANKS FOR THE TIP, BETTY.
WHAT DO WE HAVE HERE?

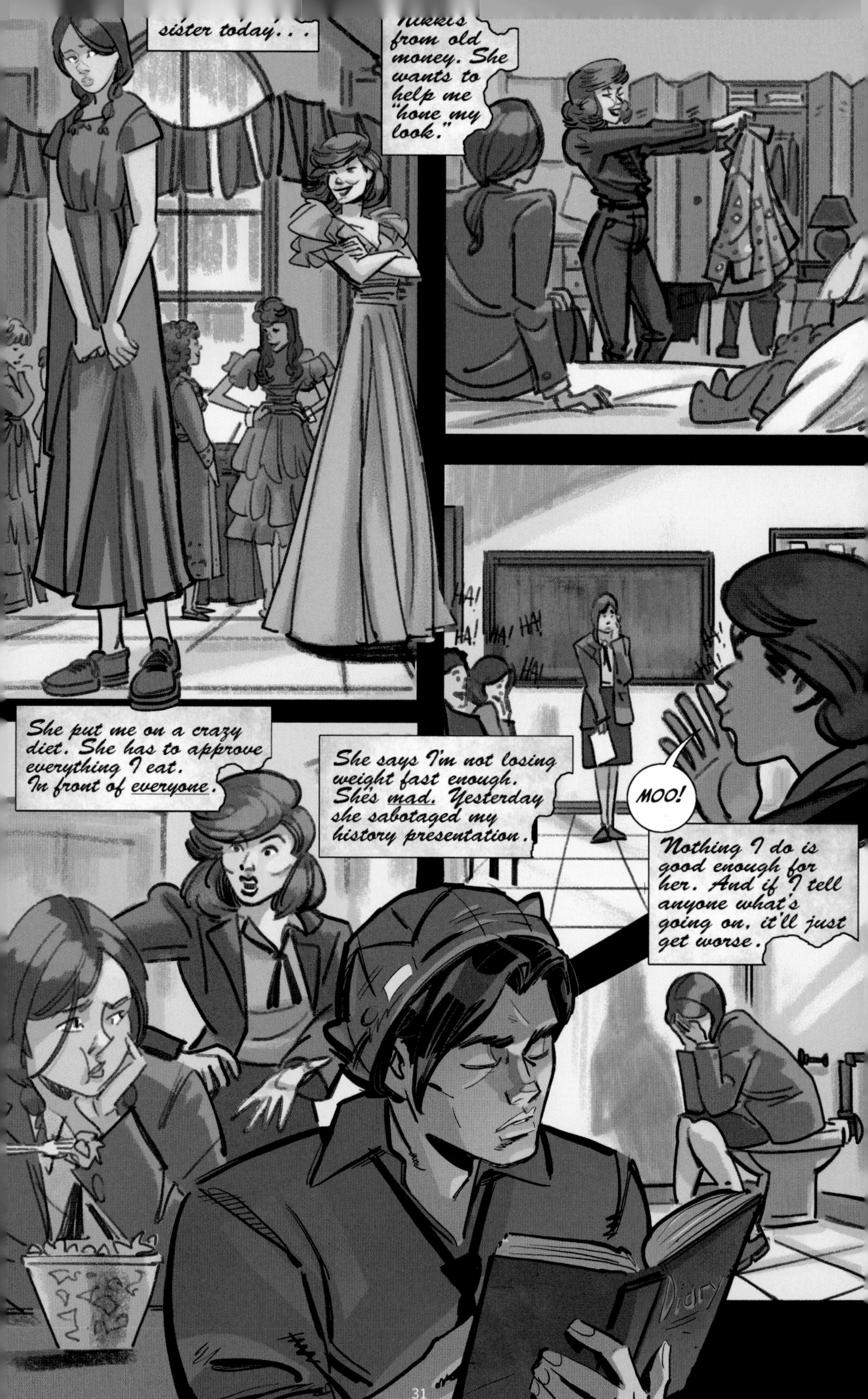
sister today. . .
from old money. She wants to help me "hone my look."
She put me on a crazy diet. She has to approve everything I eat. In front of everyone.
She says I'm not losing weight fast enough. She's mad. Yesterday she sabotaged my history presentation.
HA! HA! HA! HA! HA!
MOO!
Nothing I do is good enough for her. And if I tell anyone what's going on, it'll just get worse.
Diary

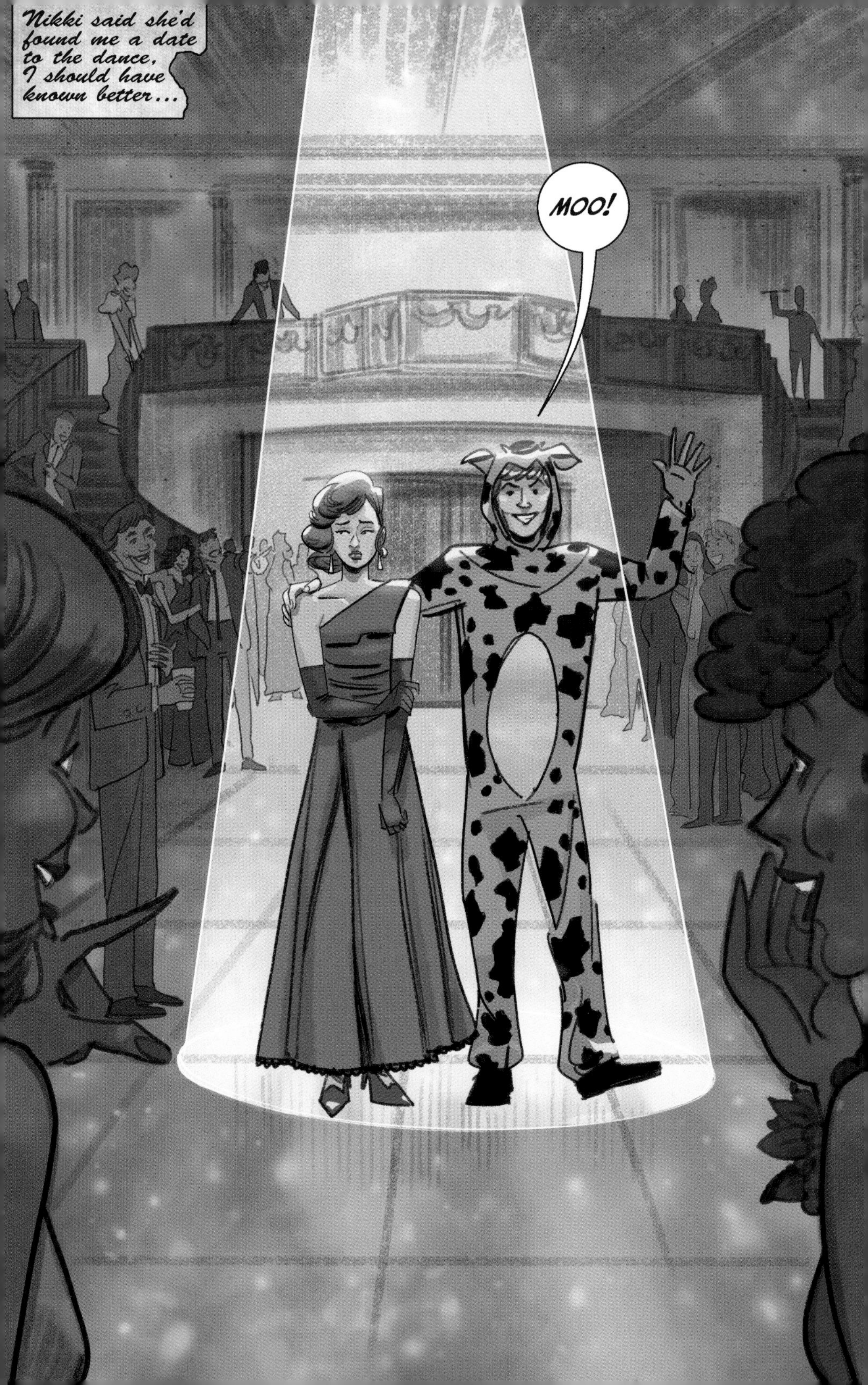
Nikki said she'd found me a date to the dance. I should have known better...
MOO!

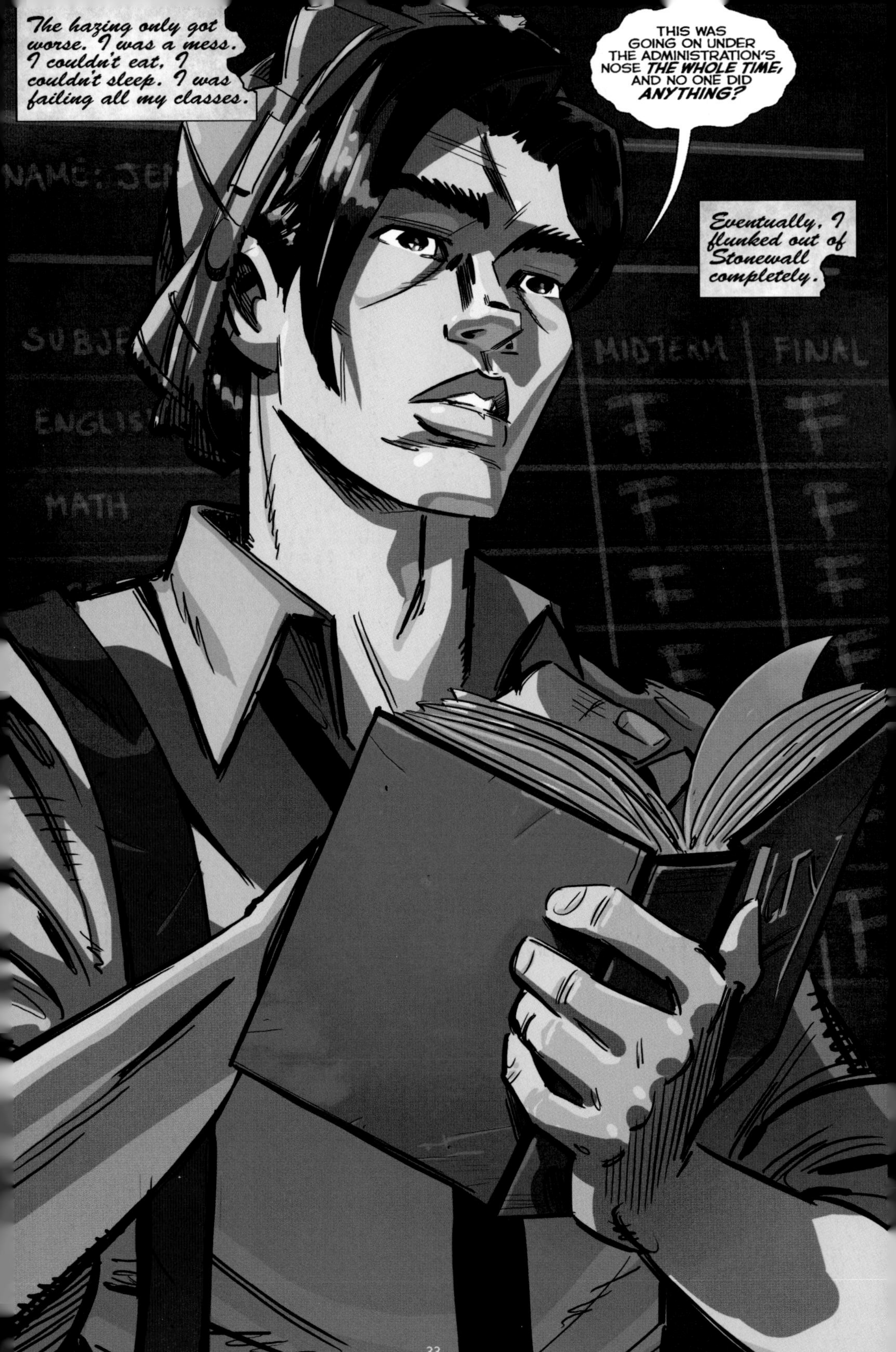
The hazing only got worse. I was a mess. I couldn't eat, I couldn't sleep. I was failing all my classes.
THIS WAS GOING ON UNDER THE ADMINISTRATION'S NOSE THE WHOLE TIME, AND NO ONE DID ANYTHING?
Eventually, I flunked out of Stonewall completely.
MIDTERM
FINAL
MATH

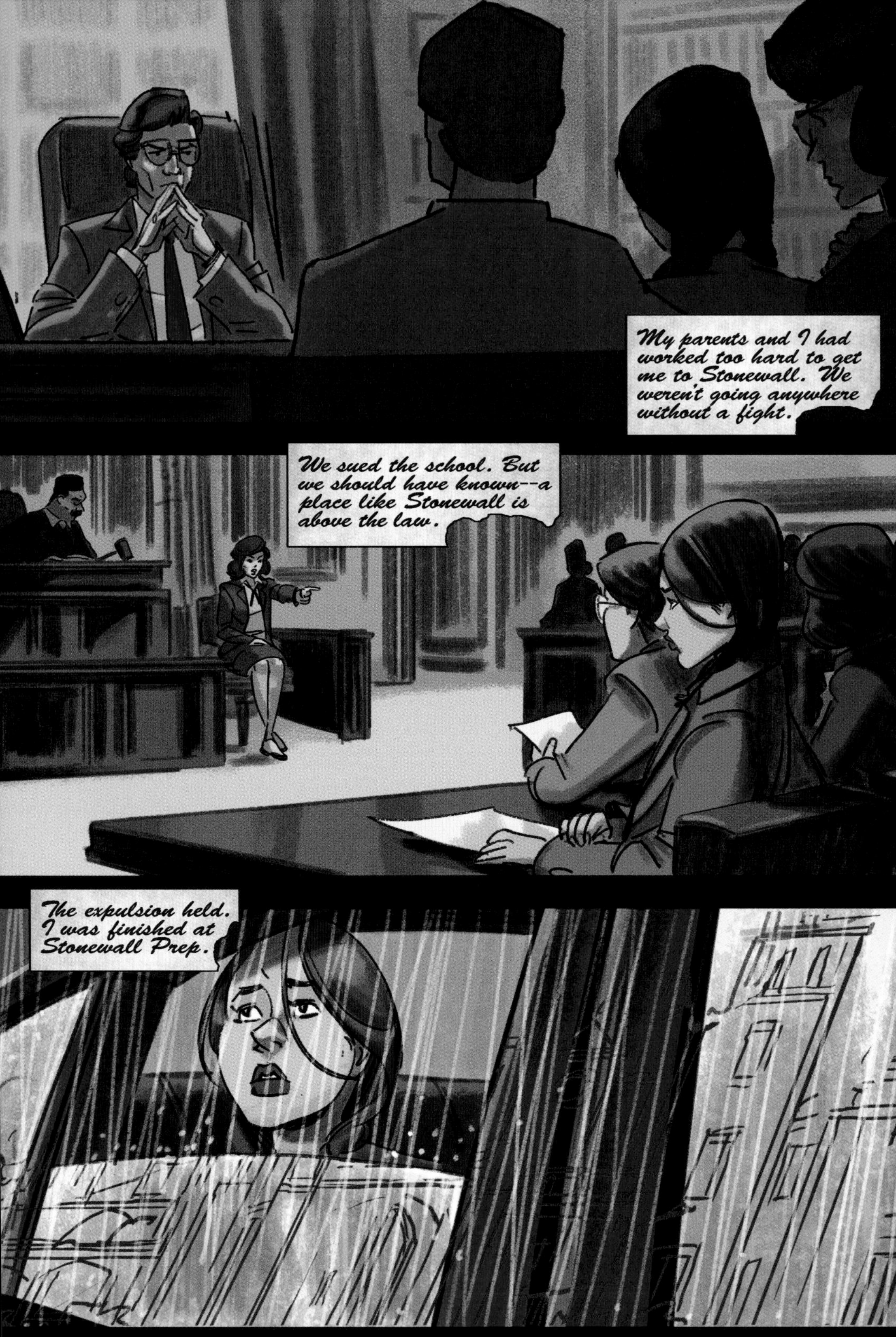
My parents and I had worked too hard to get me to Stonewall. We weren't going anywhere without a fight.
We sued the school. But we should have known--a place like Stonewall is above the law.
The expulsion held. I was finished at Stonewall Prep.

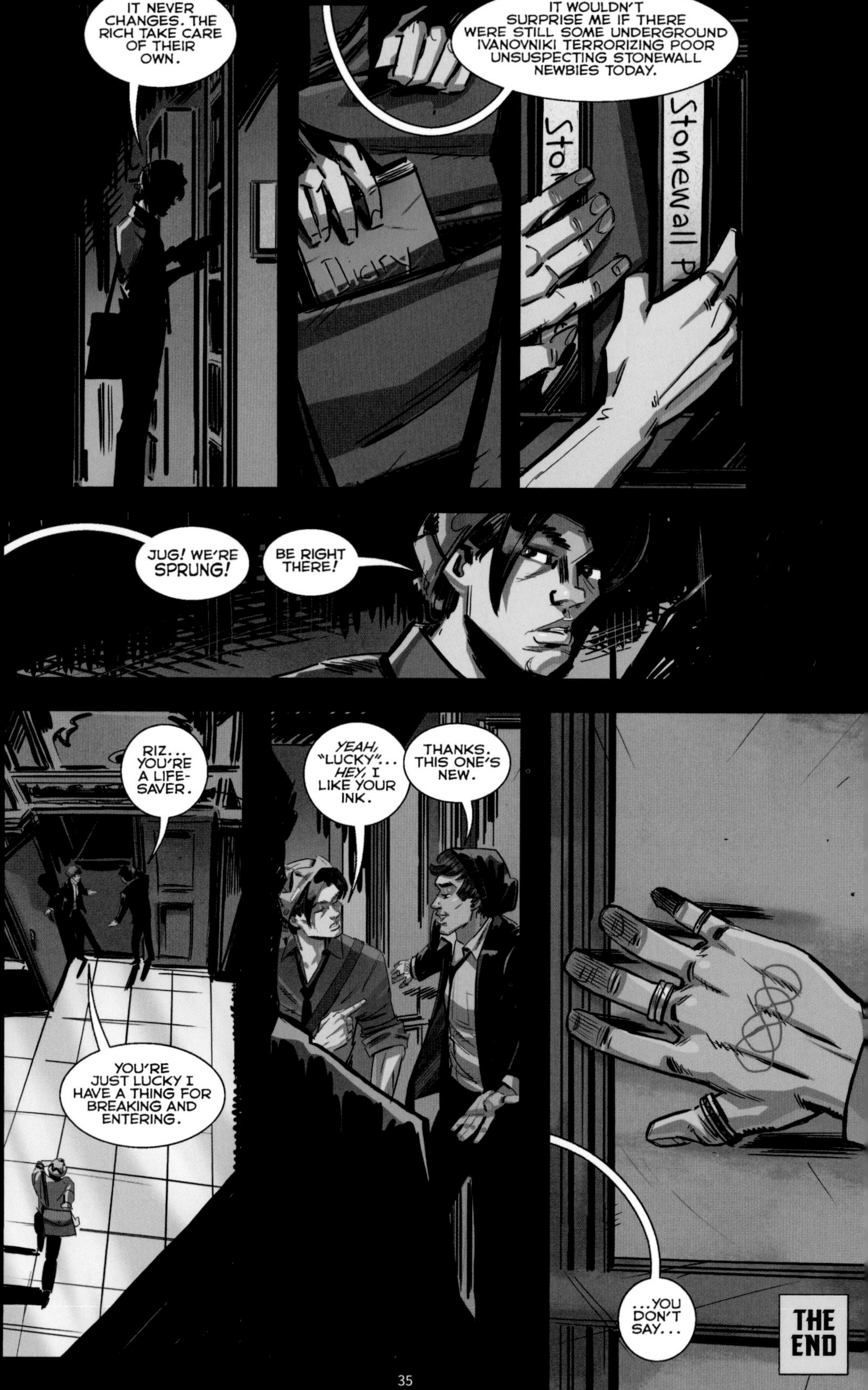
IT NEVER CHANGES. THE RICH TAKE CARE OF THEIR OWN.
IT WOULDN'T SURPRISE ME IF THERE WERE STILL SOME UNDERGROUND IVANOVNIKI TERRORIZING POOR UNSUSPECTING STONEWALL NEWBIES TODAY.
Stonewall
JUG! WE'RE SPRUNG!
BE RIGHT THERE!
RIZ... YOU'RE A LIFE-SAVER.
YOU'RE JUST LUCKY I HAVE A THING FOR BREAKING AND ENTERING.
YEAH, "LUCKY"... HEY, I LIKE YOUR INK.
THANKS. THIS ONE'S NEW.
...YOU DON'T SAY...
THE END

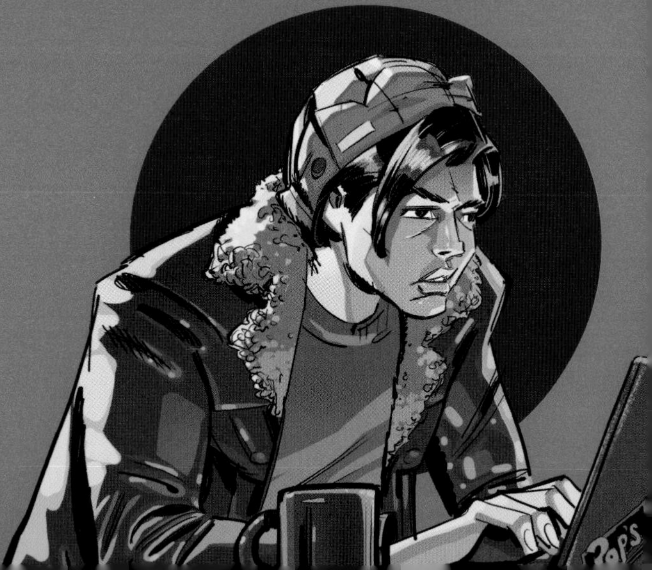
Pop's

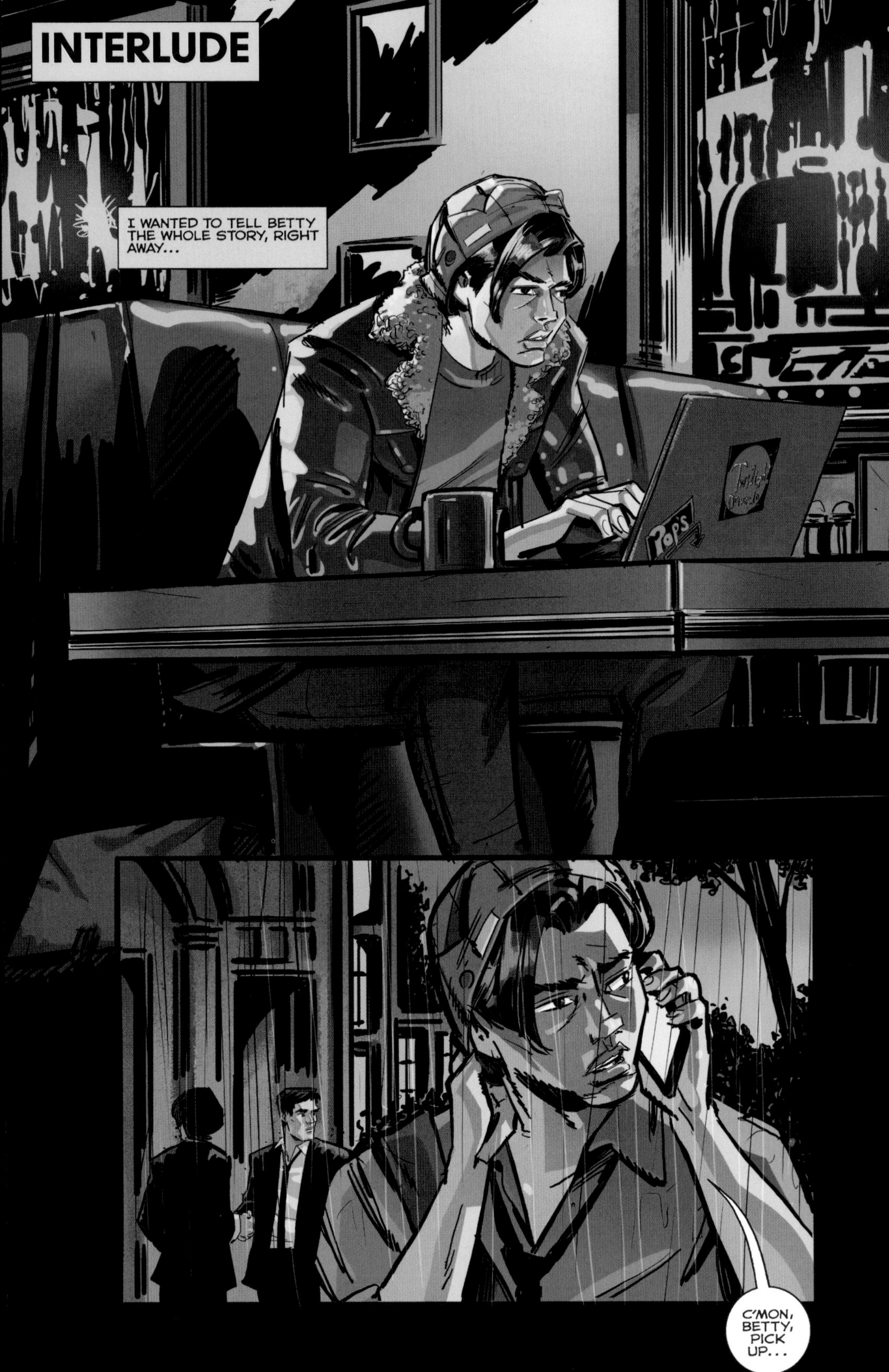
INTERLUDE
I WANTED TO TELL BETTY THE WHOLE STORY, RIGHT AWAY...
C'MON, BETTY, PICK UP...

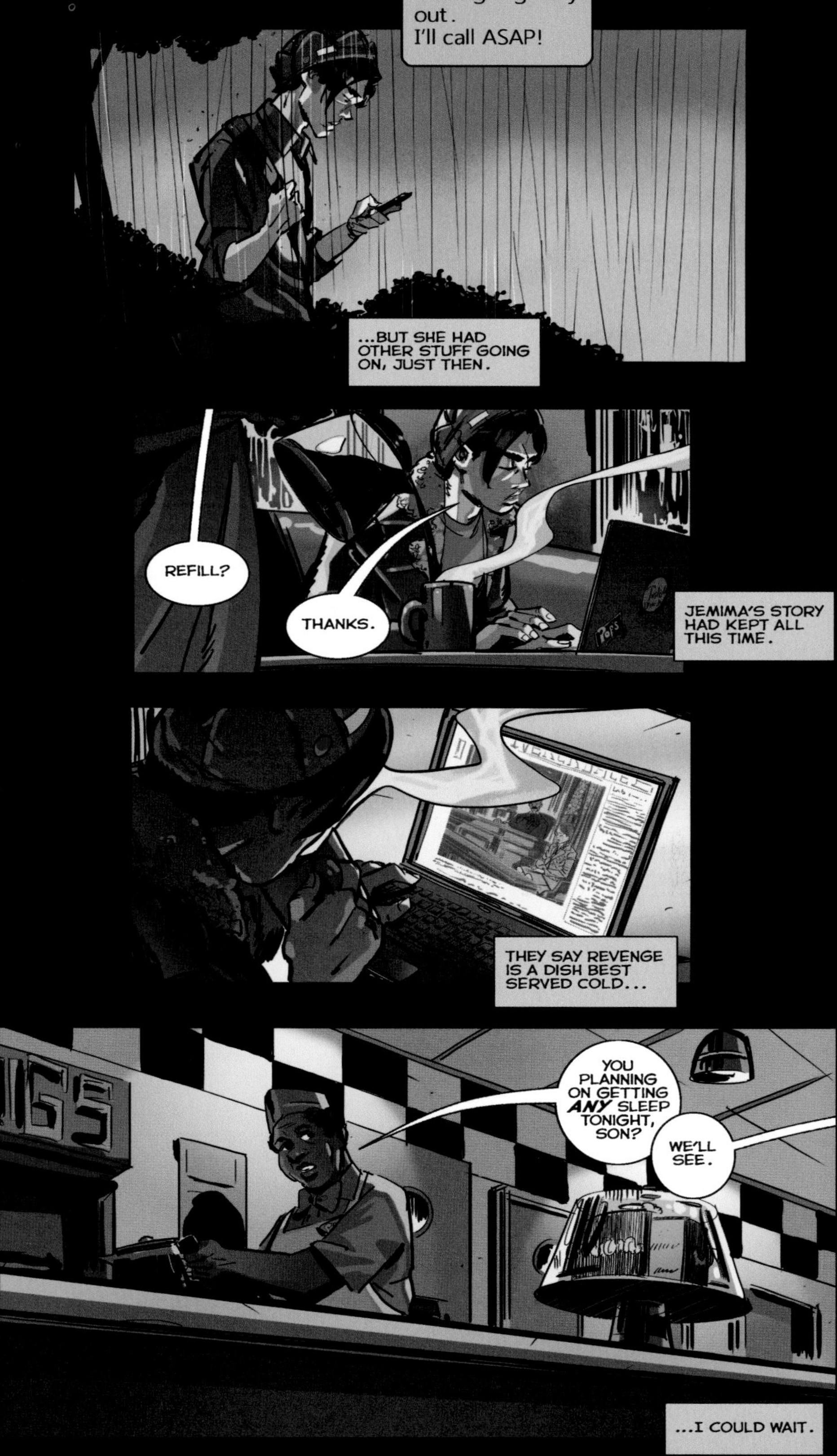
out.
I'll call ASAP!
...BUT SHE HAD OTHER STUFF GOING ON, JUST THEN.
REFILL?
THANKS.
JEMIMA'S STORY HAD KEPT ALL THIS TIME.
THEY SAY REVENGE IS A DISH BEST SERVED COLD...
YOU PLANNING ON GETTING ANY SLEEP TONIGHT, SON?
WE'LL SEE.
...I COULD WAIT.

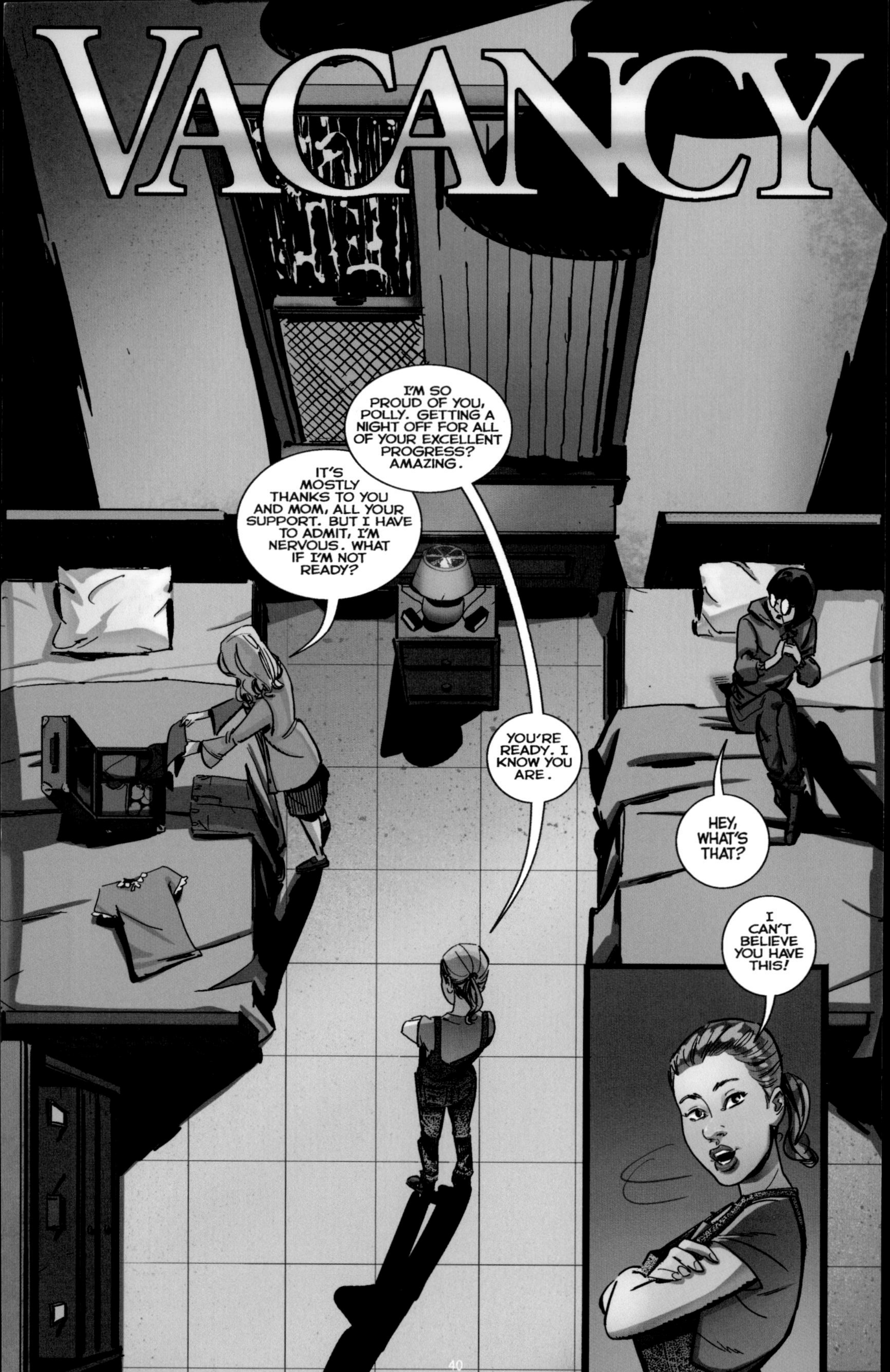
VACANCY
I'M SO PROUD OF YOU, POLLY. GETTING A NIGHT OFF FOR ALL OF YOUR EXCELLENT PROGRESS? AMAZING.
IT'S MOSTLY THANKS TO YOU AND MOM, ALL YOUR SUPPORT. BUT I HAVE TO ADMIT, I'M NERVOUS. WHAT IF I'M NOT READY?
YOU'RE READY. I KNOW YOU ARE.
HEY, WHAT'S THAT?
I CAN'T BELIEVE YOU HAVE THIS!

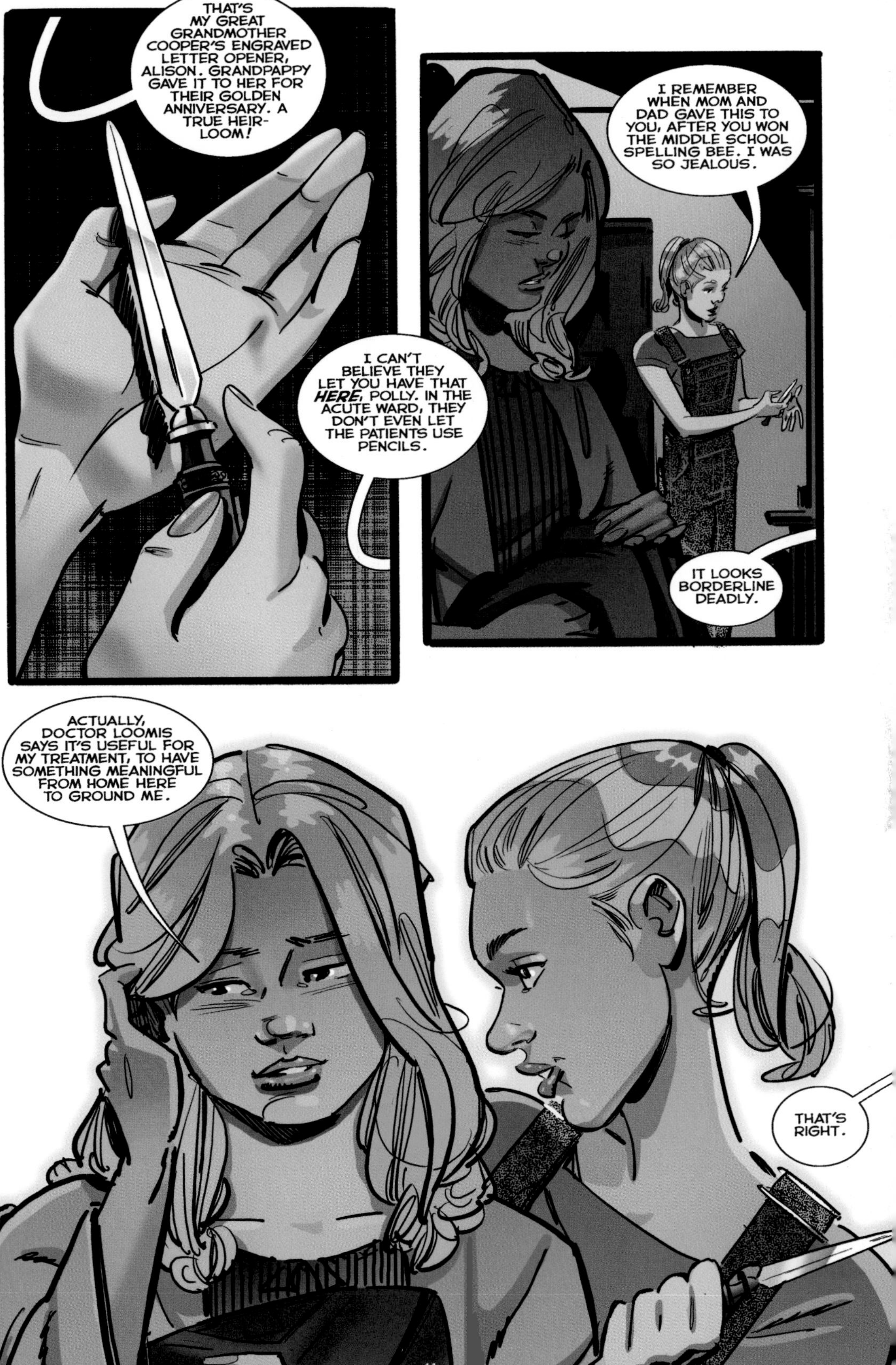
THAT'S MY GREAT GRANDMOTHER COOPER'S ENGRAVED LETTER OPENER, ALISON. GRANDPAPPY GAVE IT TO HER FOR THEIR GOLDEN ANNIVERSARY. A TRUE HEIR-LOOM!
I CAN'T BELIEVE THEY LET YOU HAVE THAT *HERE*, POLLY. IN THE ACUTE WARD, THEY DON'T EVEN LET THE PATIENTS USE PENCILS.
I REMEMBER WHEN MOM AND DAD GAVE THIS TO YOU, AFTER YOU WON THE MIDDLE SCHOOL SPELLING BEE. I WAS SO JEALOUS.
IT LOOKS BORDERLINE DEADLY.
ACTUALLY, DOCTOR LOOMIS SAYS IT'S USEFUL FOR MY TREATMENT, TO HAVE SOMETHING MEANINGFUL FROM HOME HERE TO GROUND ME.
THAT'S RIGHT.

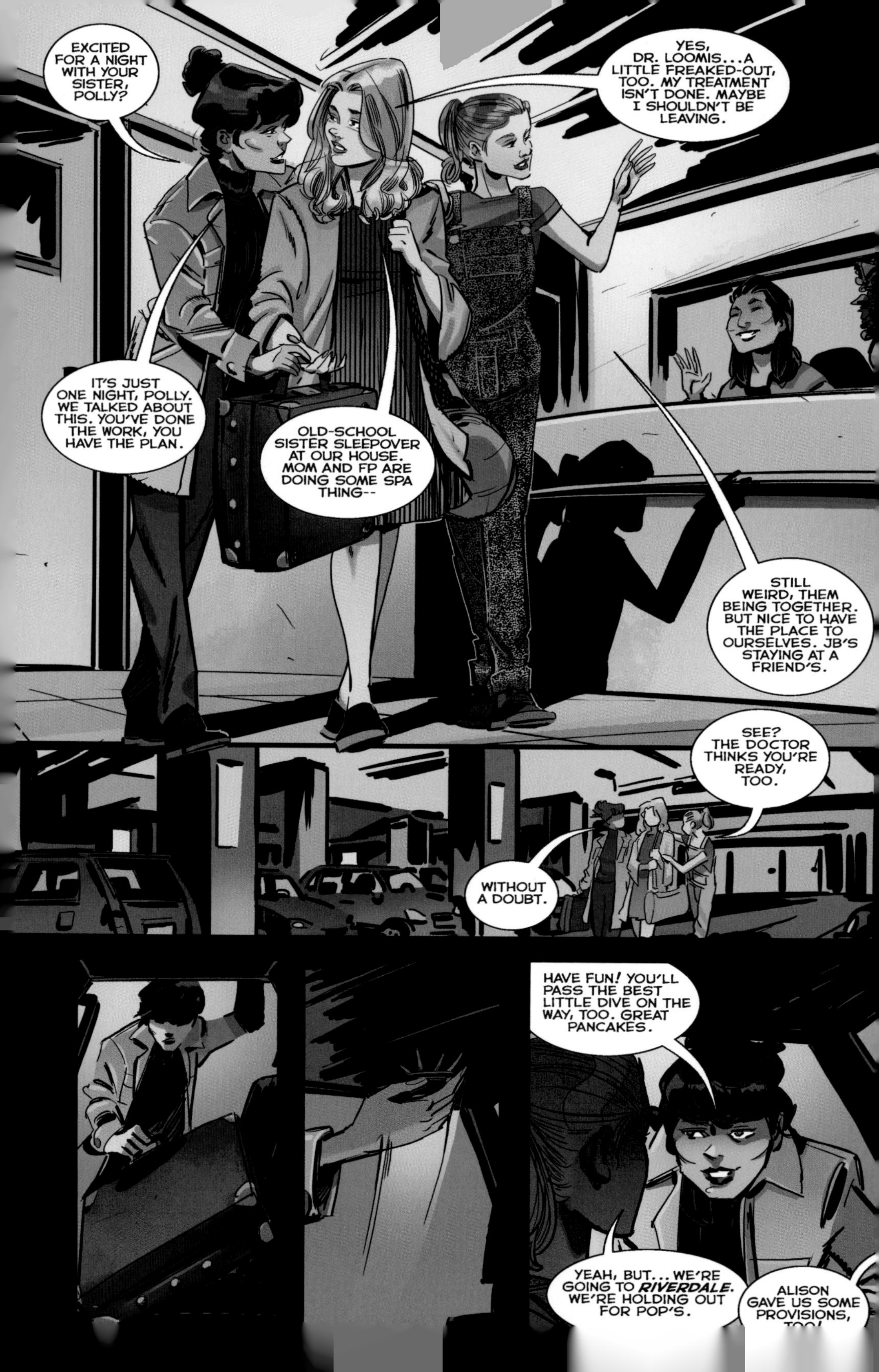
EXCITED FOR A NIGHT WITH YOUR SISTER, POLLY?
YES, DR. LOOMIS...A LITTLE FREAKED-OUT, TOO. MY TREATMENT ISN'T DONE. MAYBE I SHOULDN'T BE LEAVING.
IT'S JUST ONE NIGHT, POLLY. WE TALKED ABOUT THIS. YOU'VE DONE THE WORK, YOU HAVE THE PLAN.
OLD-SCHOOL SISTER SLEEPOVER AT OUR HOUSE. MOM AND FP ARE DOING SOME SPA THING--
STILL WEIRD, THEM BEING TOGETHER. BUT NICE TO HAVE THE PLACE TO OURSELVES. JB'S STAYING AT A FRIEND'S.
SEE? THE DOCTOR THINKS YOU'RE READY, TOO.
WITHOUT A DOUBT.
HAVE FUN! YOU'LL PASS THE BEST LITTLE DIVE ON THE WAY, TOO. GREAT PANCAKES.
YEAH, BUT... WE'RE GOING TO *RIVERDALE*. WE'RE HOLDING OUT FOR POP'S.
ALISON GAVE US SOME PROVISIONS,

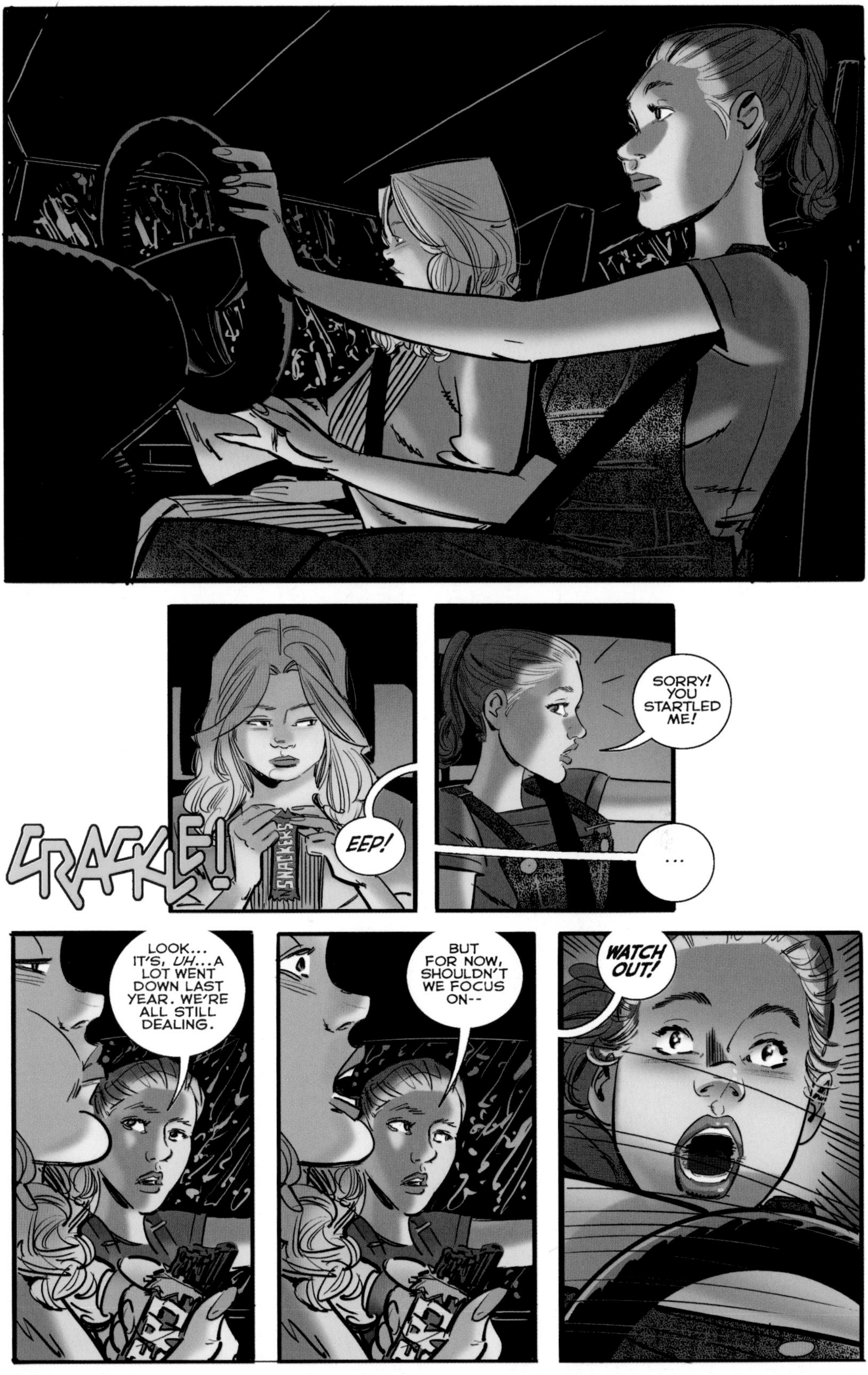
CRACKLE!
SNACKERS
EEP!
SORRY! YOU STARTLED ME!
...
LOOK... IT'S, *UH*...A LOT WENT DOWN LAST YEAR. WE'RE ALL STILL DEALING.
BUT FOR NOW, SHOULDN'T WE FOCUS ON--
WATCH OUT!

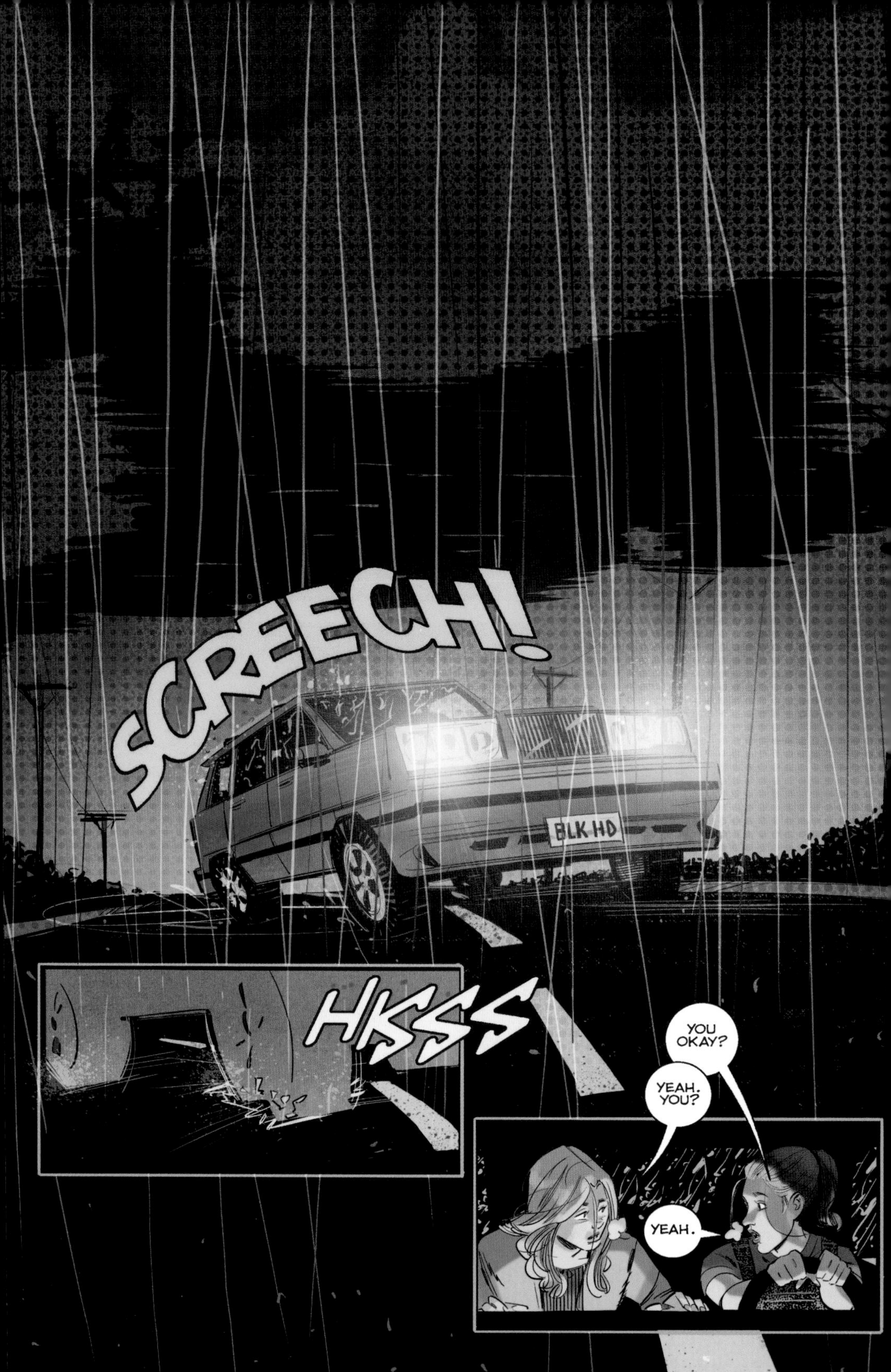
SCREECH!
BLK HD
HISSS
YOU OKAY?
YEAH. YOU?
YEAH.

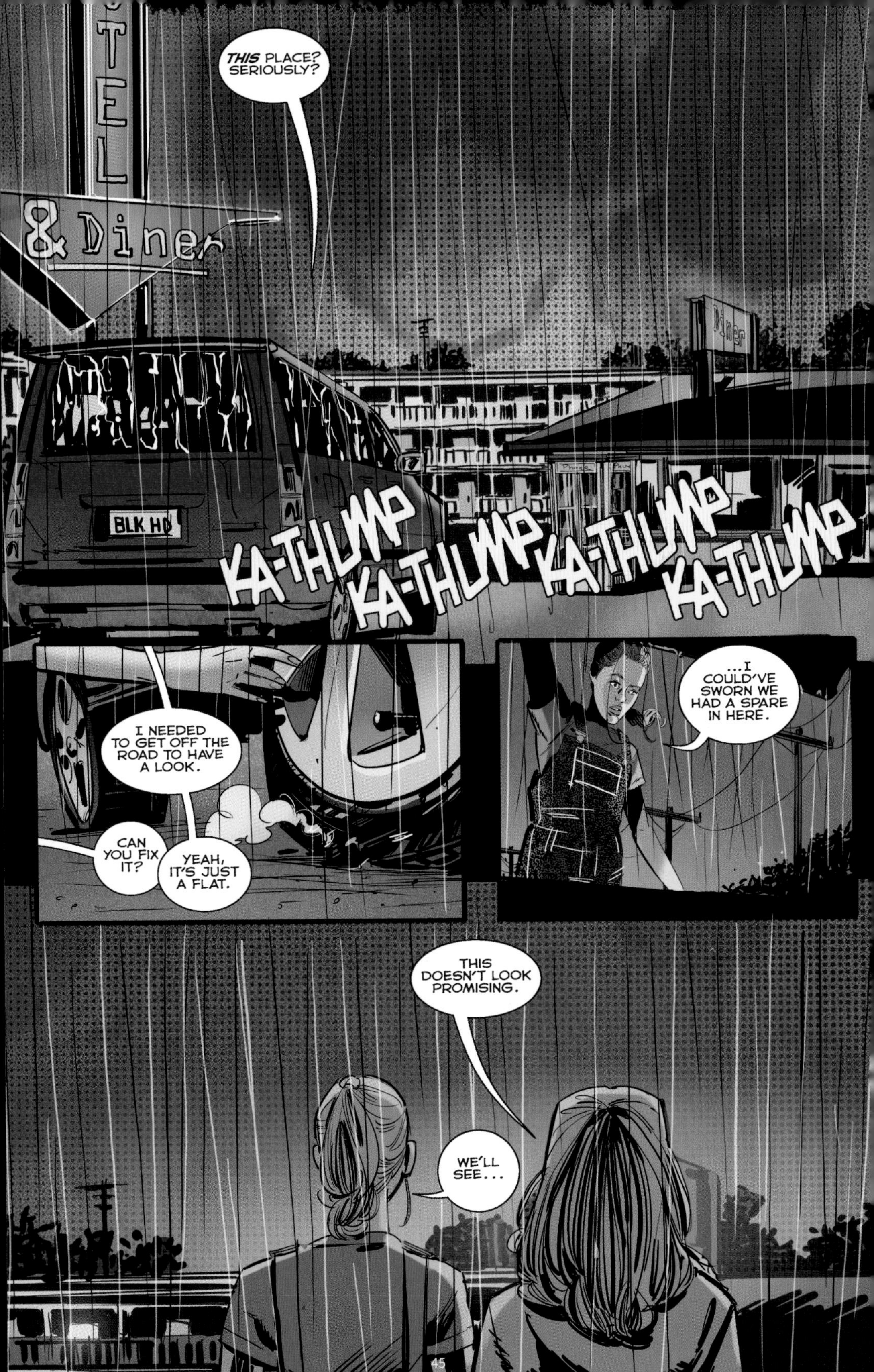

&TEL
& Diner
THIS PLACE? SERIOUSLY?
BLK HD
KA-THUMP KA-THUMP KA-THUMP KA-THUMP
I NEEDED TO GET OFF THE ROAD TO HAVE A LOOK.
CAN YOU FIX IT?
YEAH, IT'S JUST A FLAT.
...I COULD'VE SWORN WE HAD A SPARE IN HERE.
THIS DOESN'T LOOK PROMISING.
WE'LL SEE...

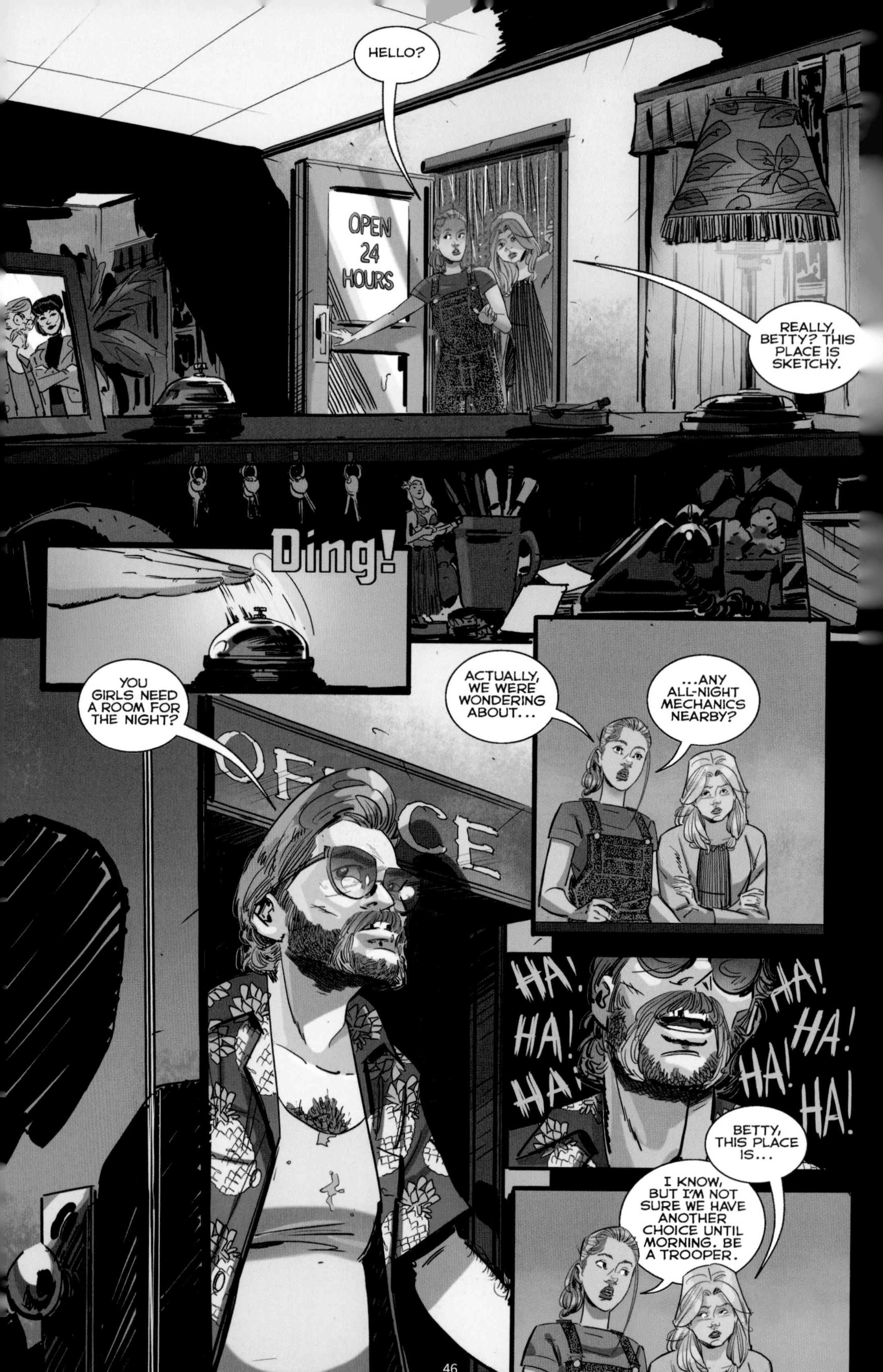
HELLO?
OPEN 24 HOURS
REALLY, BETTY? THIS PLACE IS SKETCHY.
Ding!
YOU GIRLS NEED A ROOM FOR THE NIGHT?
OFFICE
ACTUALLY, WE WERE WONDERING ABOUT...
...ANY ALL-NIGHT MECHANICS NEARBY?
HA! HA! HA! HA! HA! HA! HA!
BETTY, THIS PLACE IS...
I KNOW, BUT I'M NOT SURE WE HAVE ANOTHER CHOICE UNTIL MORNING. BE A TROOPER.

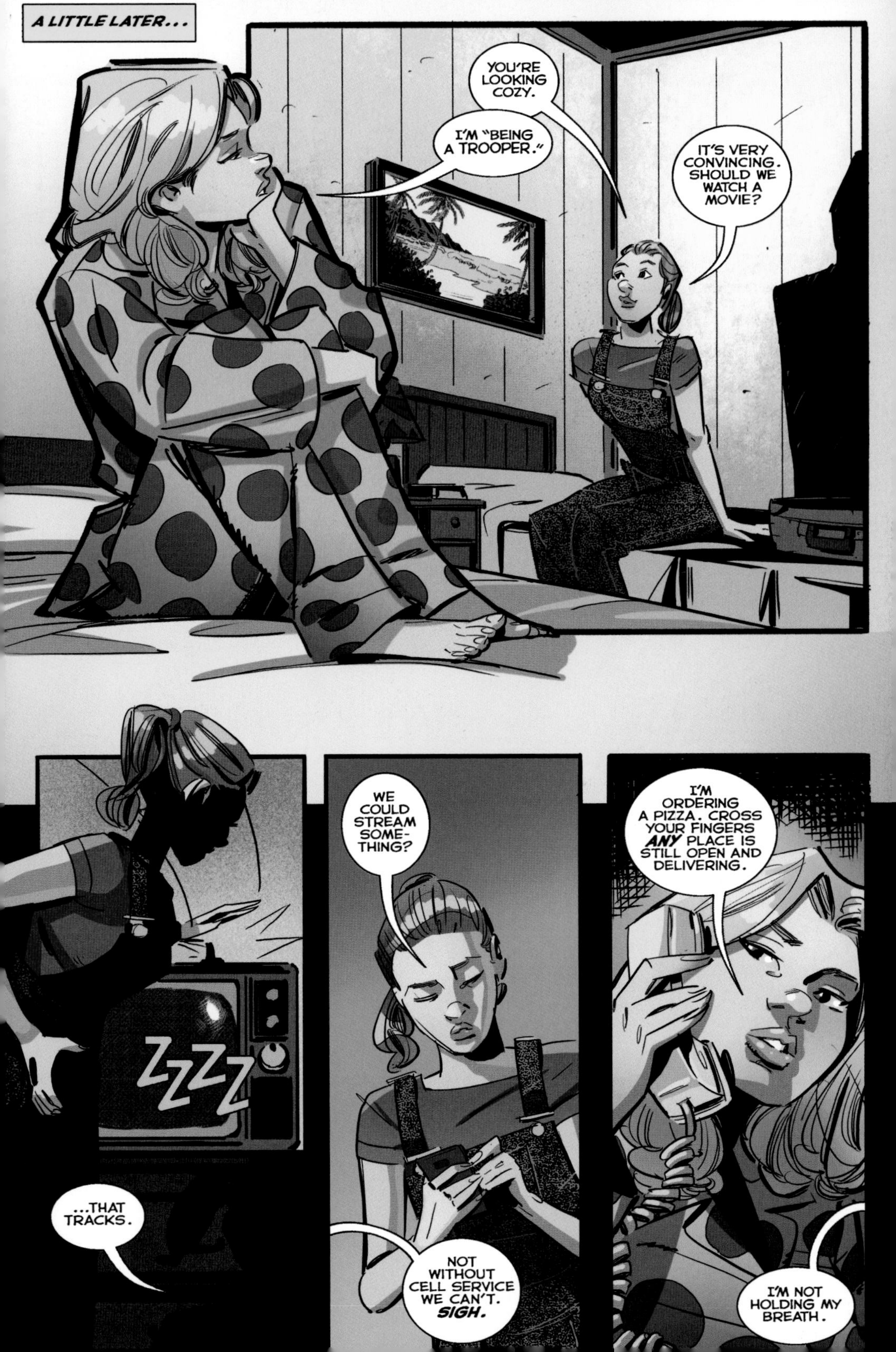
A LITTLE LATER...
YOU'RE LOOKING COZY.
I'M "BEING A TROOPER."
IT'S VERY CONVINCING. SHOULD WE WATCH A MOVIE?
ZZZZ
...THAT TRACKS.
WE COULD STREAM SOME-THING?
NOT WITHOUT CELL SERVICE WE CAN'T. SIGH.
I'M ORDERING A PIZZA. CROSS YOUR FINGERS ANY PLACE IS STILL OPEN AND DELIVERING.
I'M NOT HOLDING MY BREATH.

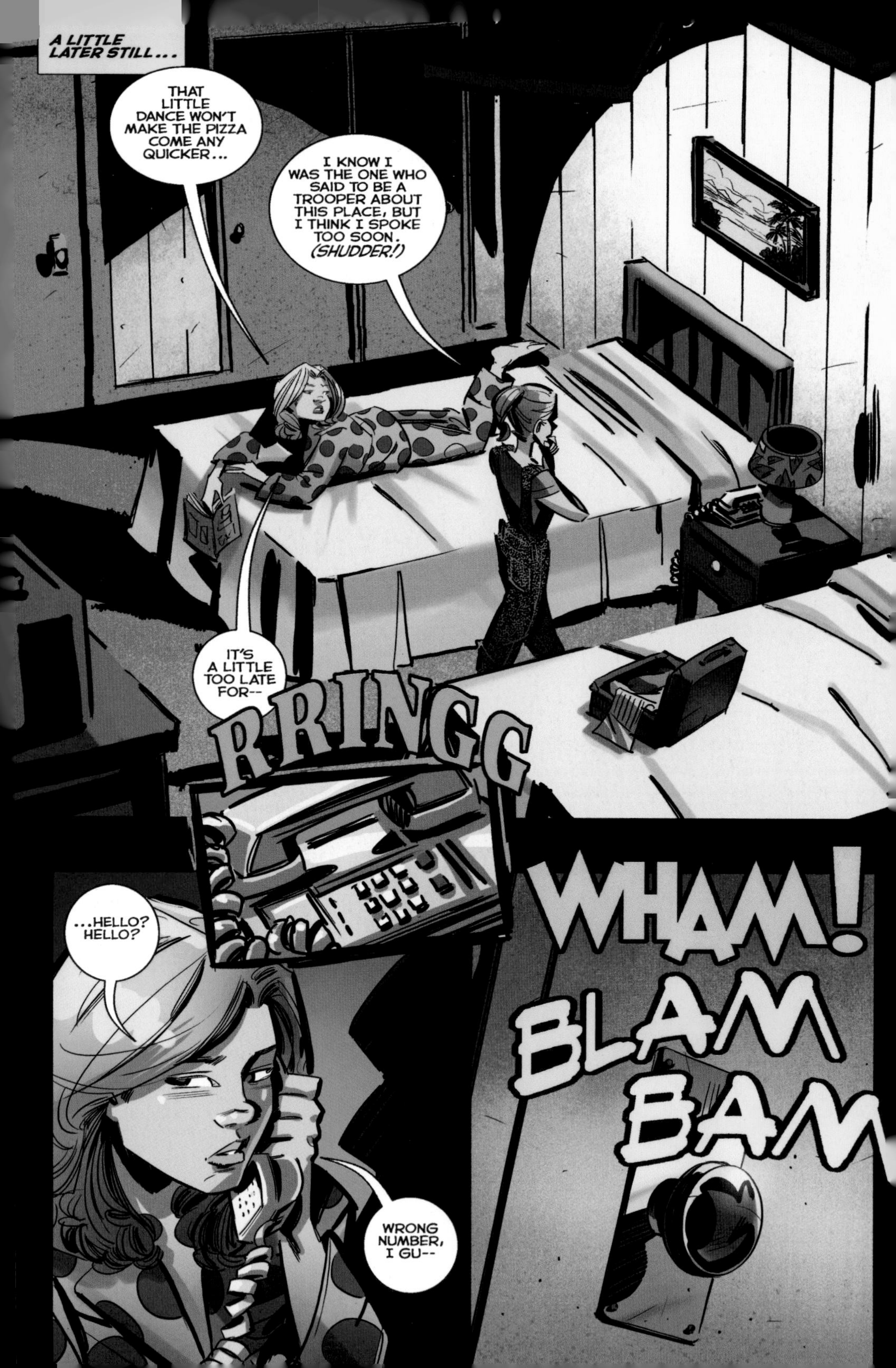
A LITTLE LATER STILL...
THAT LITTLE DANCE WON'T MAKE THE PIZZA COME ANY QUICKER...
I KNOW I WAS THE ONE WHO SAID TO BE A TROOPER ABOUT THIS PLACE, BUT I THINK I SPOKE TOO SOON. (SHUDDER!)
IT'S A LITTLE TOO LATE FOR--
RRINGG
...HELLO? HELLO?
WRONG NUMBER, I GU--
WHAM!
BLAM
BAM

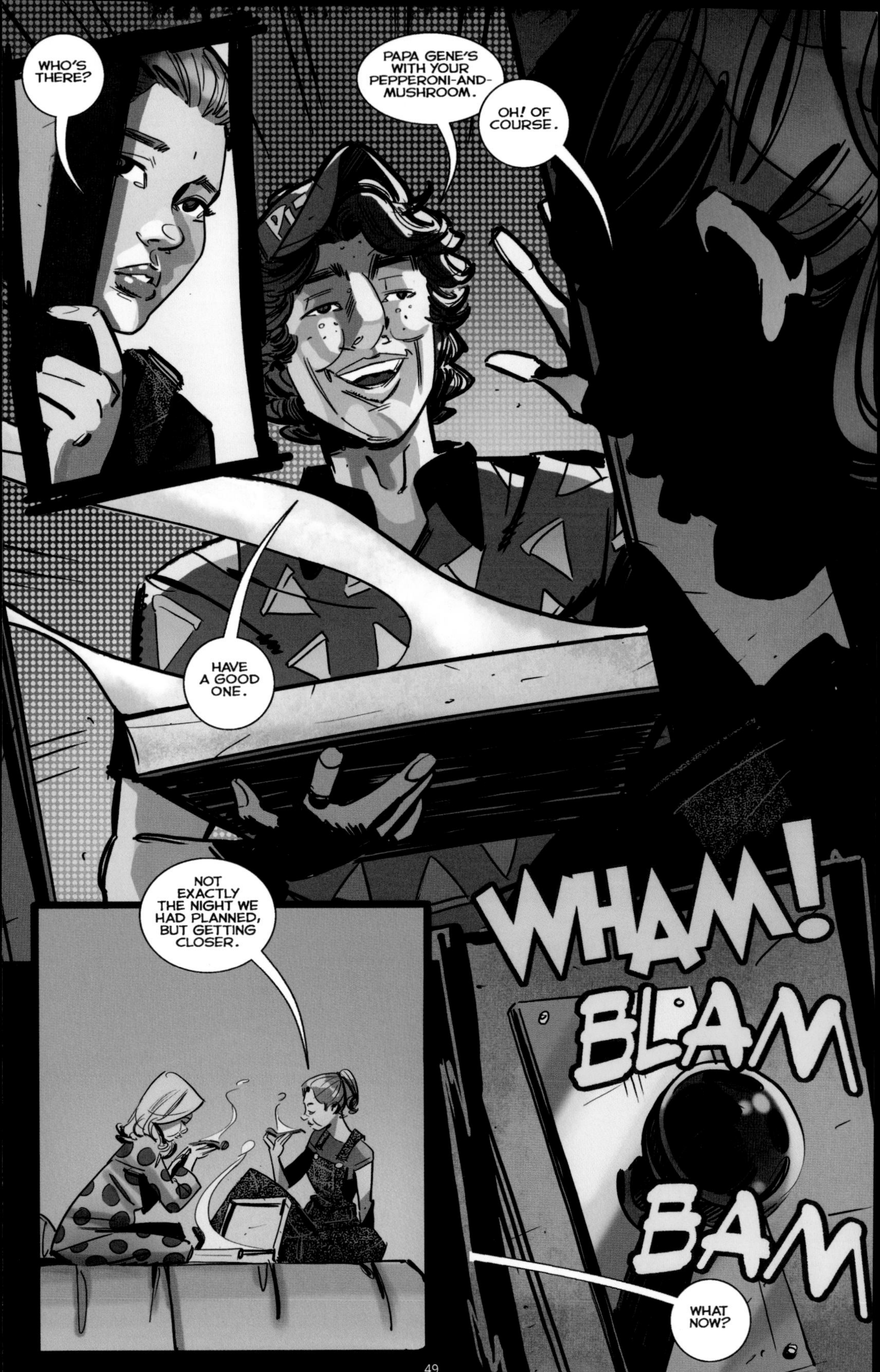
WHO'S THERE?
PAPA GENE'S WITH YOUR PEPPERONI-AND-MUSHROOM.
OH! OF COURSE.
HAVE A GOOD ONE.
WHAM!
BLAM
BAM
WHAT NOW?
NOT EXACTLY THE NIGHT WE HAD PLANNED, BUT GETTING CLOSER.

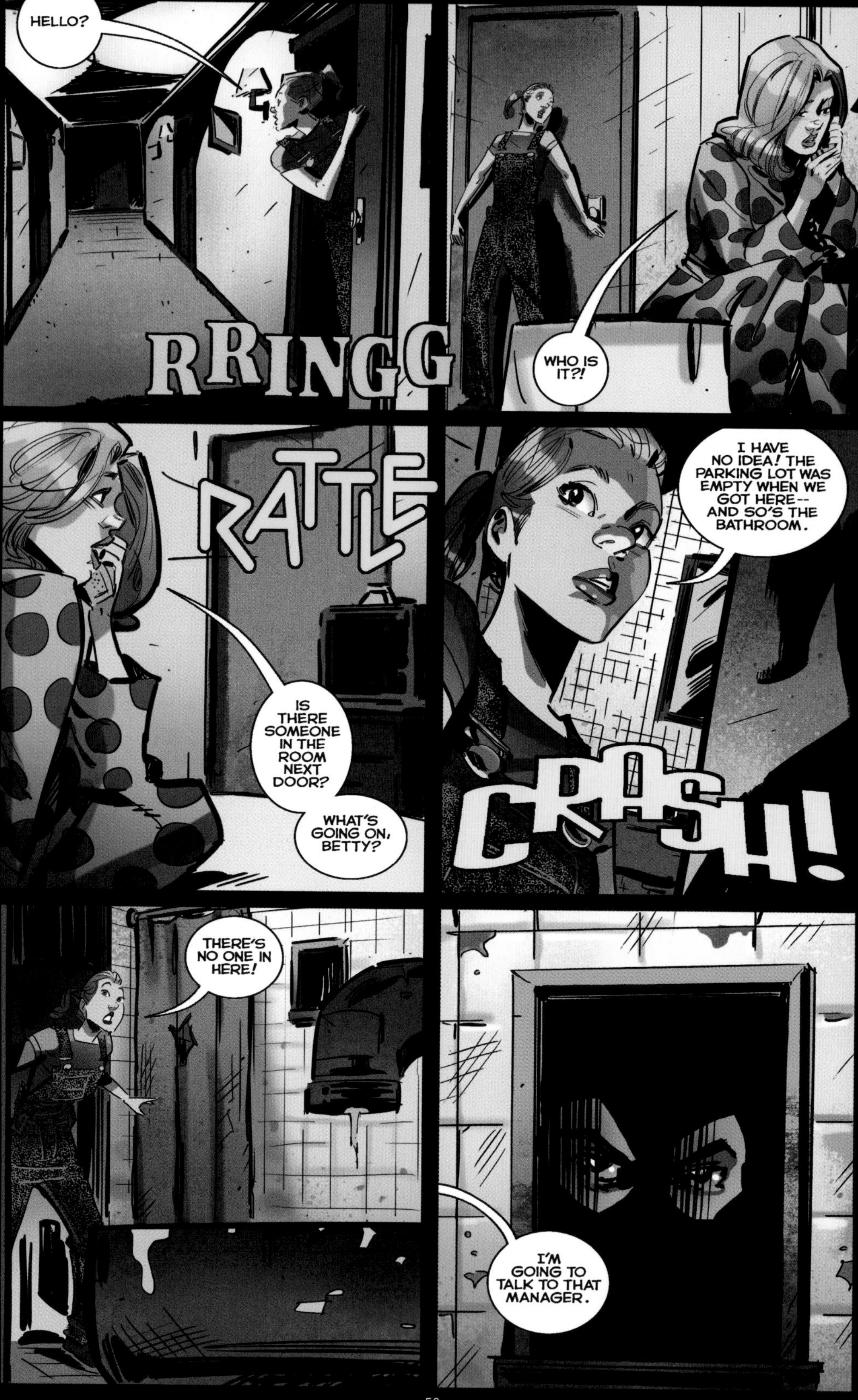
HELLO?
RRINGG
WHO IS IT?!
RATTLE
IS THERE SOMEONE IN THE ROOM NEXT DOOR?
WHAT'S GOING ON, BETTY?
I HAVE NO IDEA! THE PARKING LOT WAS EMPTY WHEN WE GOT HERE-- AND SO'S THE BATHROOM.
CRASH!
THERE'S NO ONE IN HERE!
I'M GOING TO TALK TO THAT MANAGER.

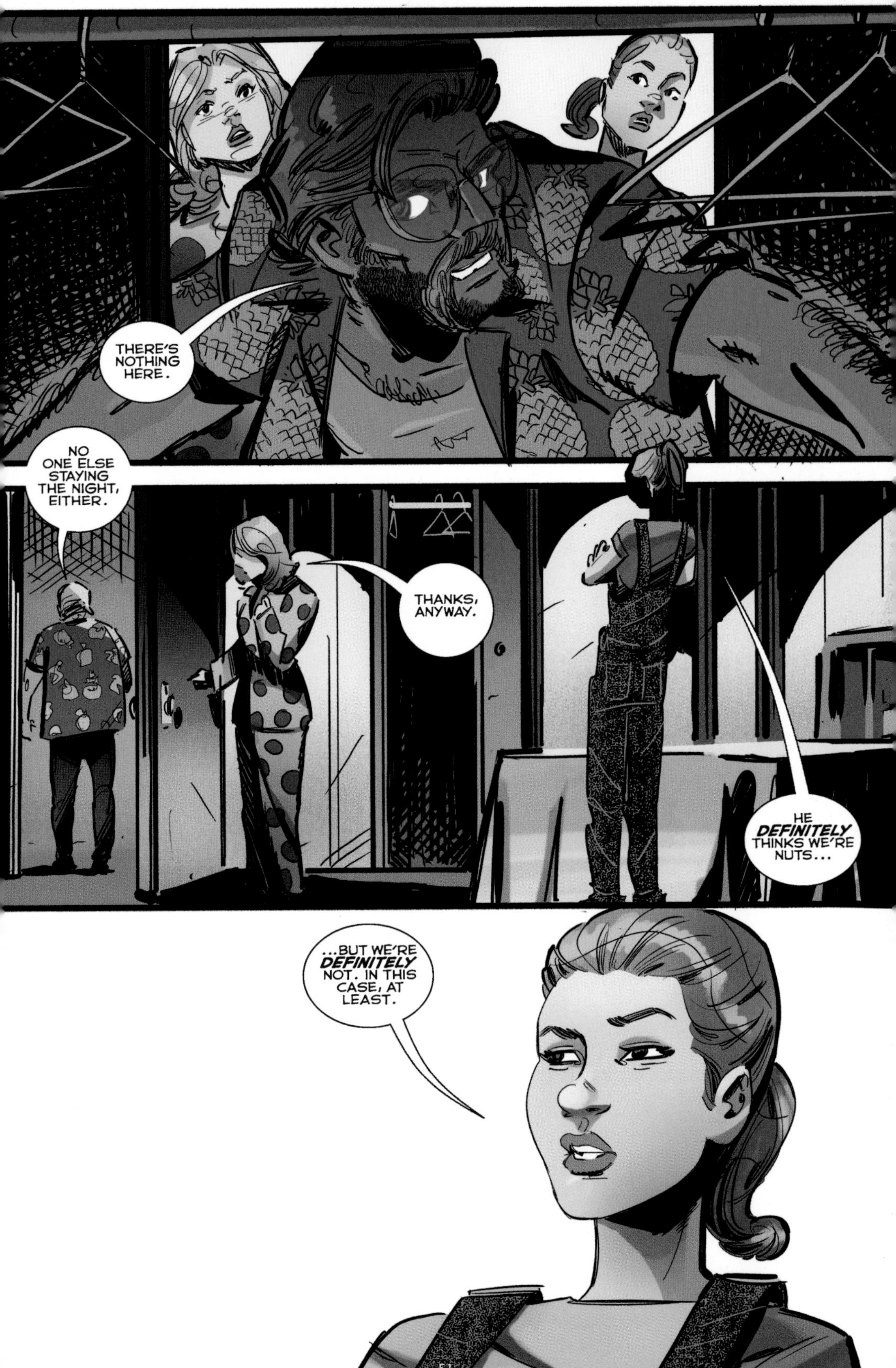

THERE'S NOTHING HERE.
NO ONE ELSE STAYING THE NIGHT, EITHER.
THANKS, ANYWAY.
HE *DEFINITELY* THINKS WE'RE NUTS...
...BUT WE'RE *DEFINITELY* NOT. IN THIS CASE, AT LEAST.

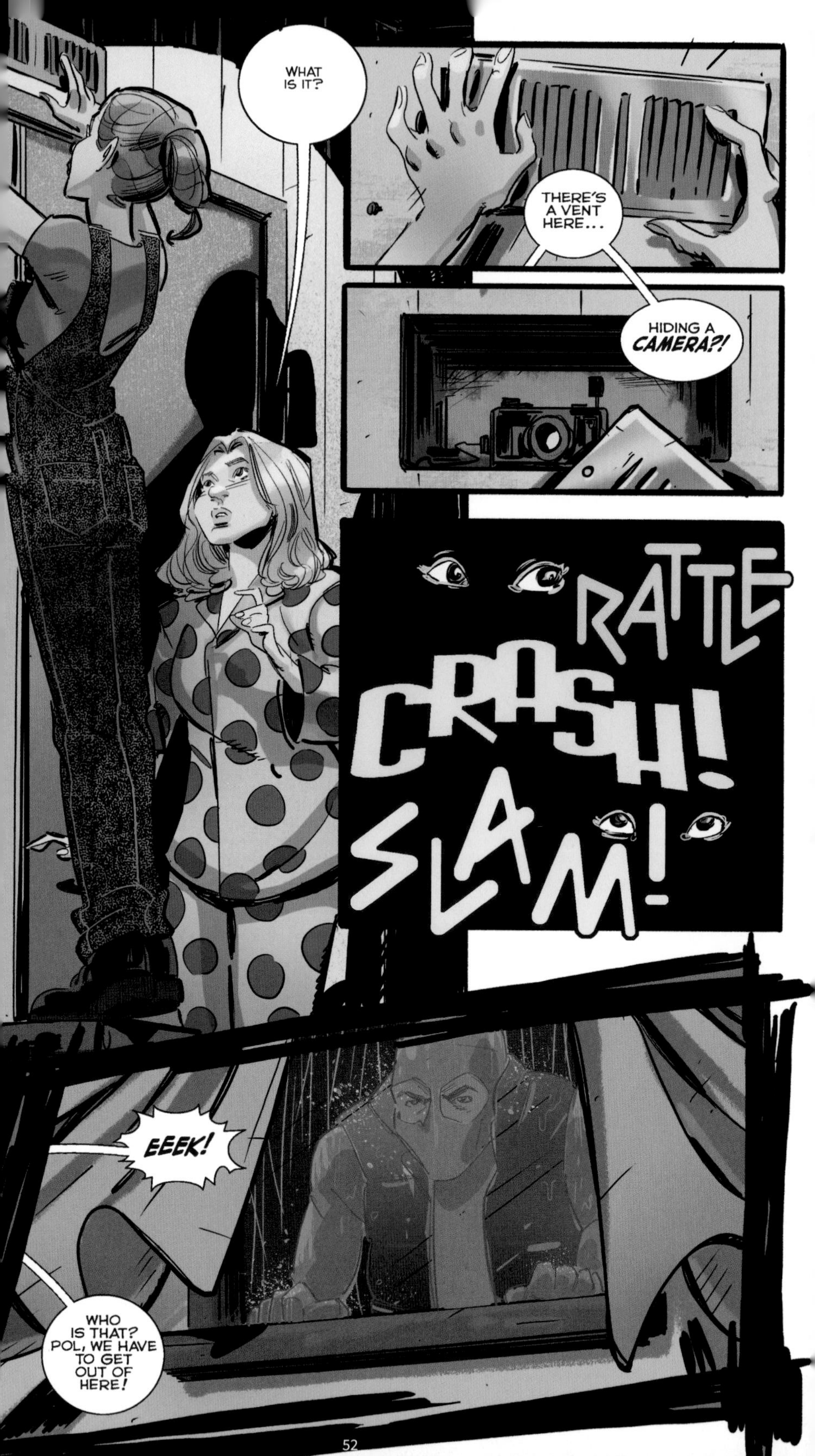

WHAT IS IT?
THERE'S A VENT HERE...
HIDING A CAMERA?!
RATTLE
CRASH!
SLAM!
EEEK!
WHO IS THAT? POL, WE HAVE TO GET OUT OF HERE!

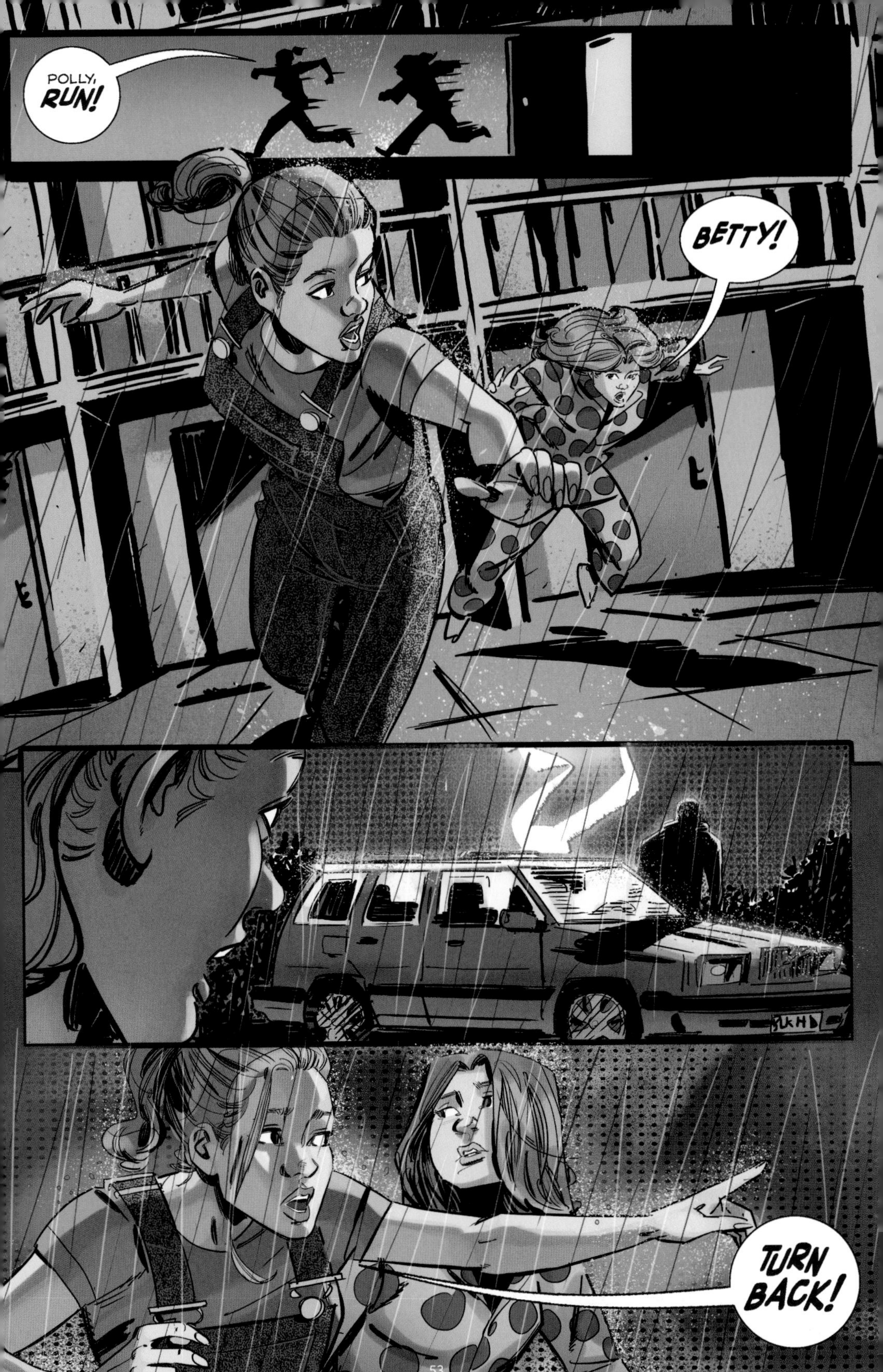
POLLY, RUN!
BETTY!
TURN BACK!

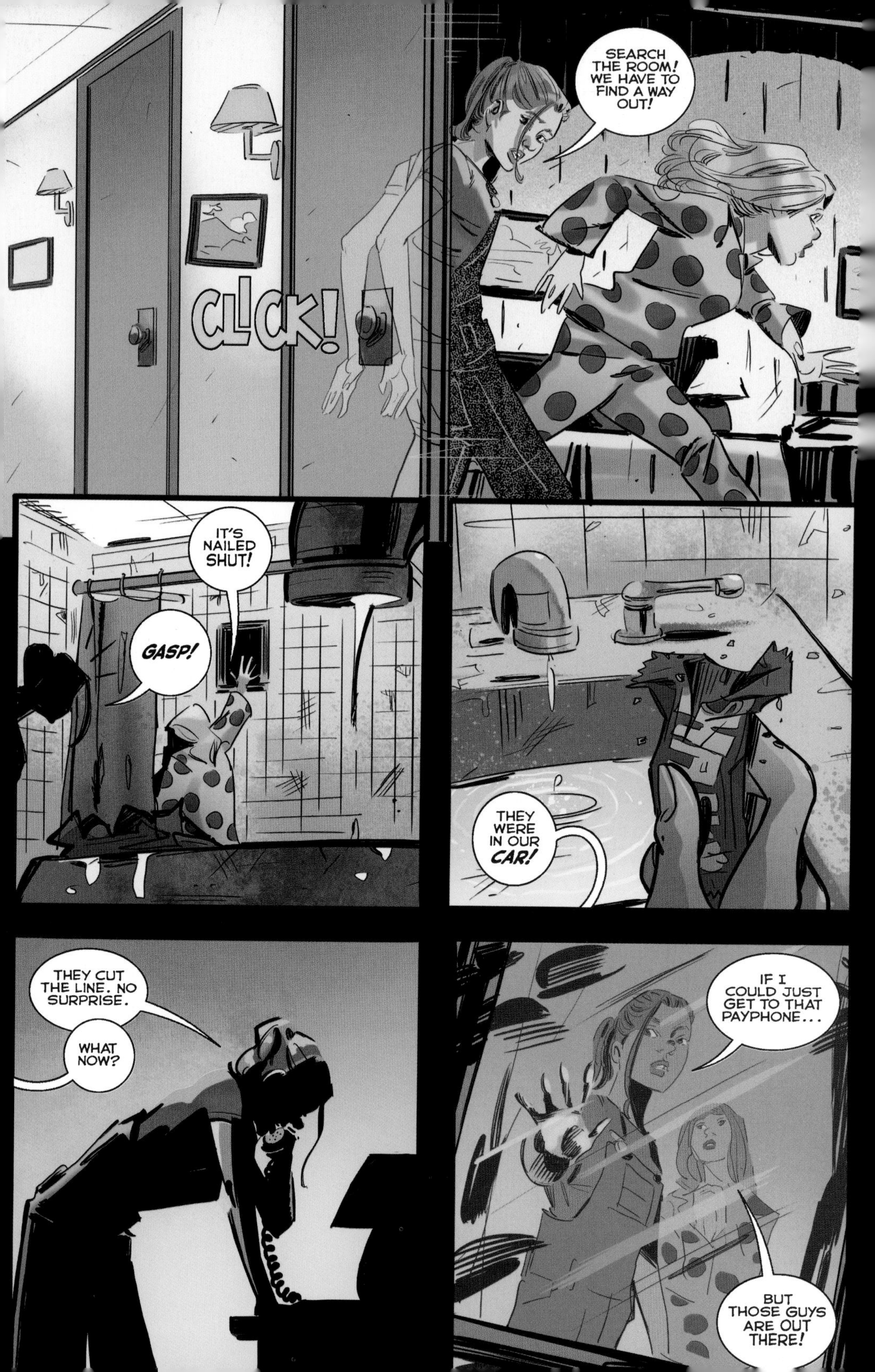
CLICK!
SEARCH THE ROOM! WE HAVE TO FIND A WAY OUT!
IT'S NAILED SHUT!
GASP!
THEY WERE IN OUR CAR!
THEY CUT THE LINE. NO SURPRISE.
WHAT NOW?
IF I COULD JUST GET TO THAT PAYPHONE...
BUT THOSE GUYS ARE OUT THERE!

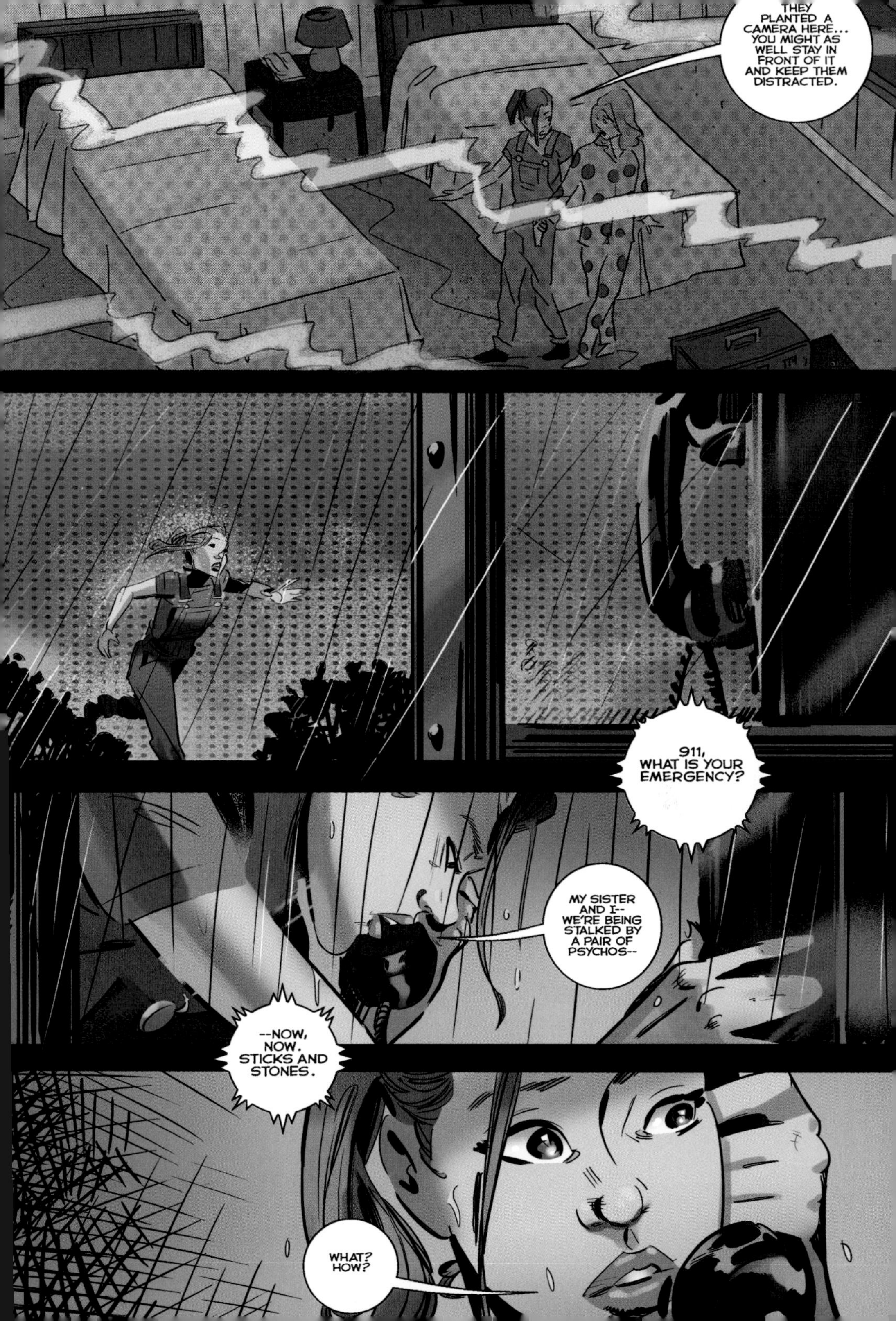
THEY PLANTED A CAMERA HERE... YOU MIGHT AS WELL STAY IN FRONT OF IT AND KEEP THEM DISTRACTED.
911, WHAT IS YOUR EMERGENCY?
MY SISTER AND I-- WE'RE BEING STALKED BY A PAIR OF PSYCHOS--
--NOW, NOW. STICKS AND STONES.
WHAT? HOW?

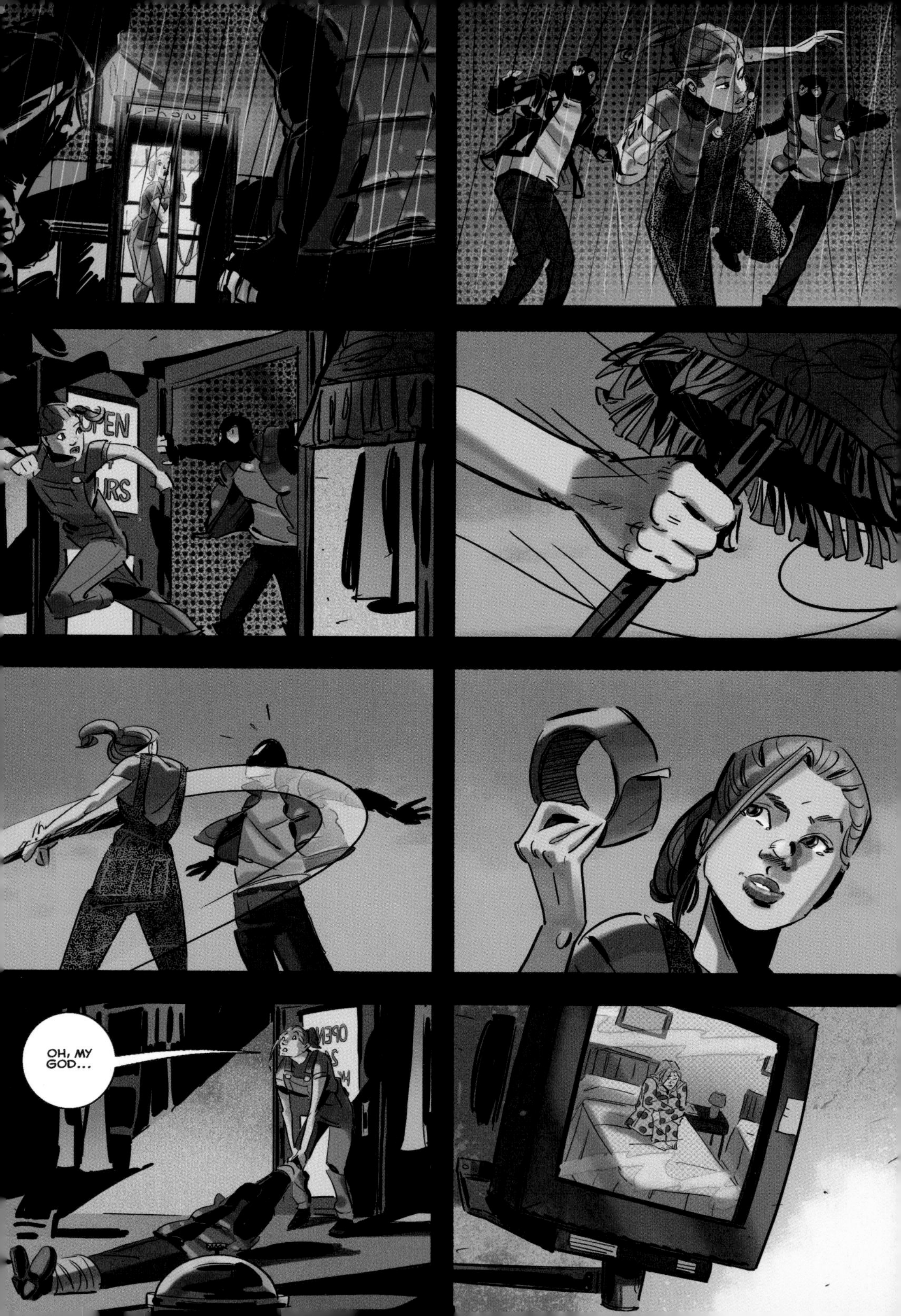
OPEN
OH, MY GOD...

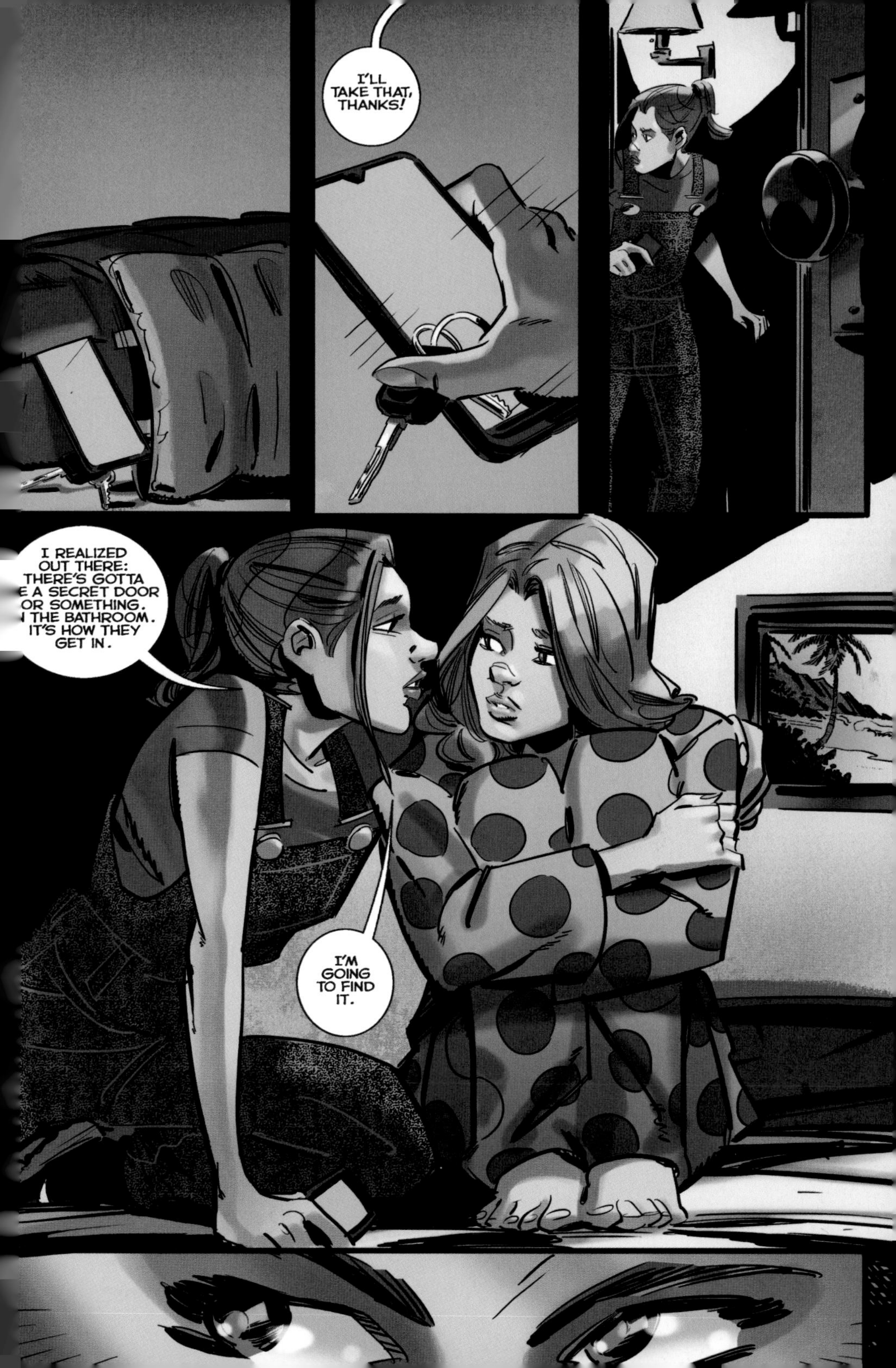
I'LL TAKE THAT, THANKS!
I REALIZED OUT THERE: THERE'S GOTTA
E A SECRET DOOR OR SOMETHING.
N THE BATHROOM. IT'S HOW THEY GET IN.
I'M GOING TO FIND IT.

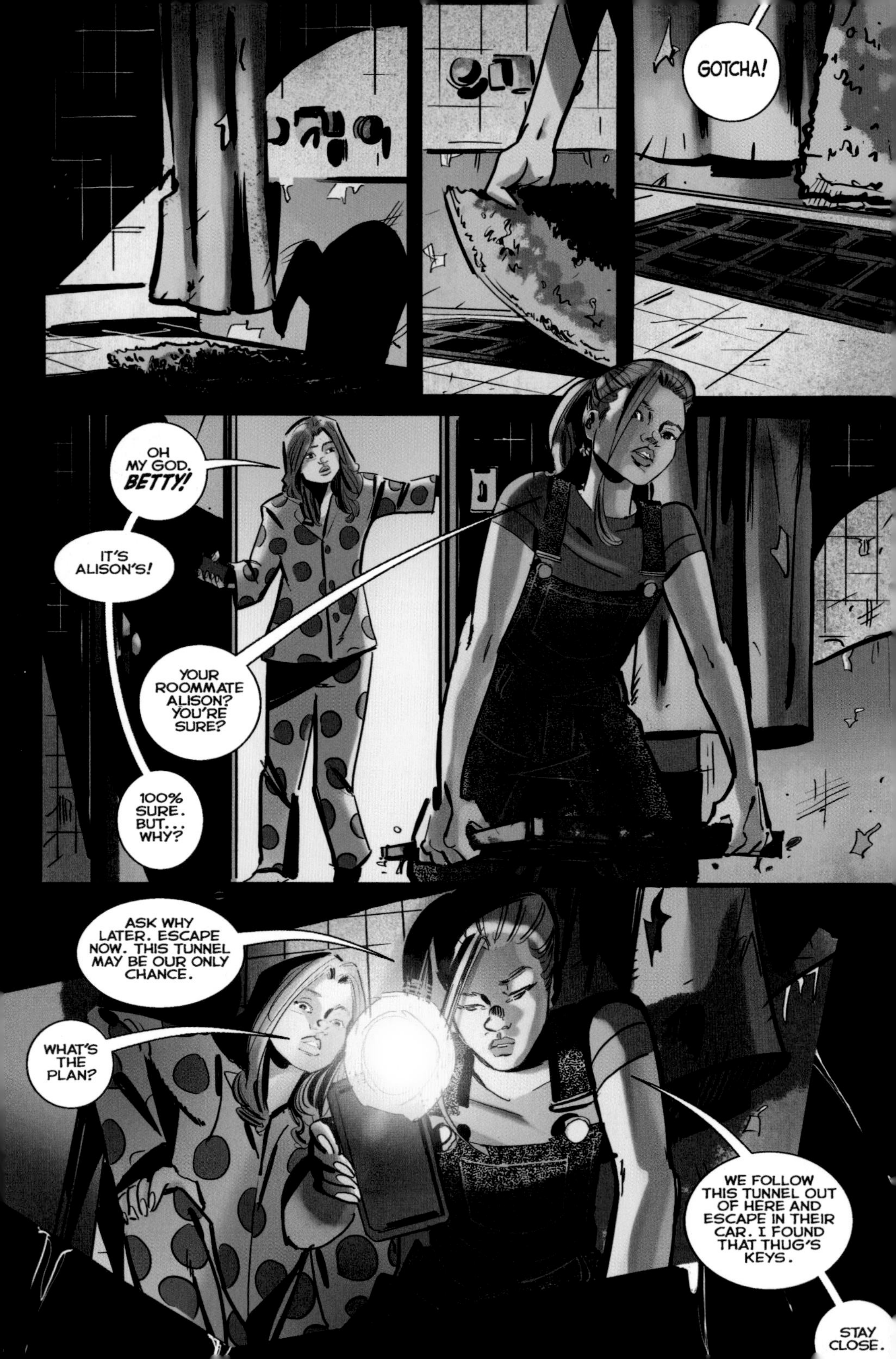
GOTCHA!
OH MY GOD. BETTY!
IT'S ALISON'S!
YOUR ROOMMATE ALISON? YOU'RE SURE?
100% SURE. BUT... WHY?
ASK WHY LATER. ESCAPE NOW. THIS TUNNEL MAY BE OUR ONLY CHANCE.
WHAT'S THE PLAN?
WE FOLLOW THIS TUNNEL OUT OF HERE AND ESCAPE IN THEIR CAR. I FOUND THAT THUG'S KEYS.
STAY CLOSE.

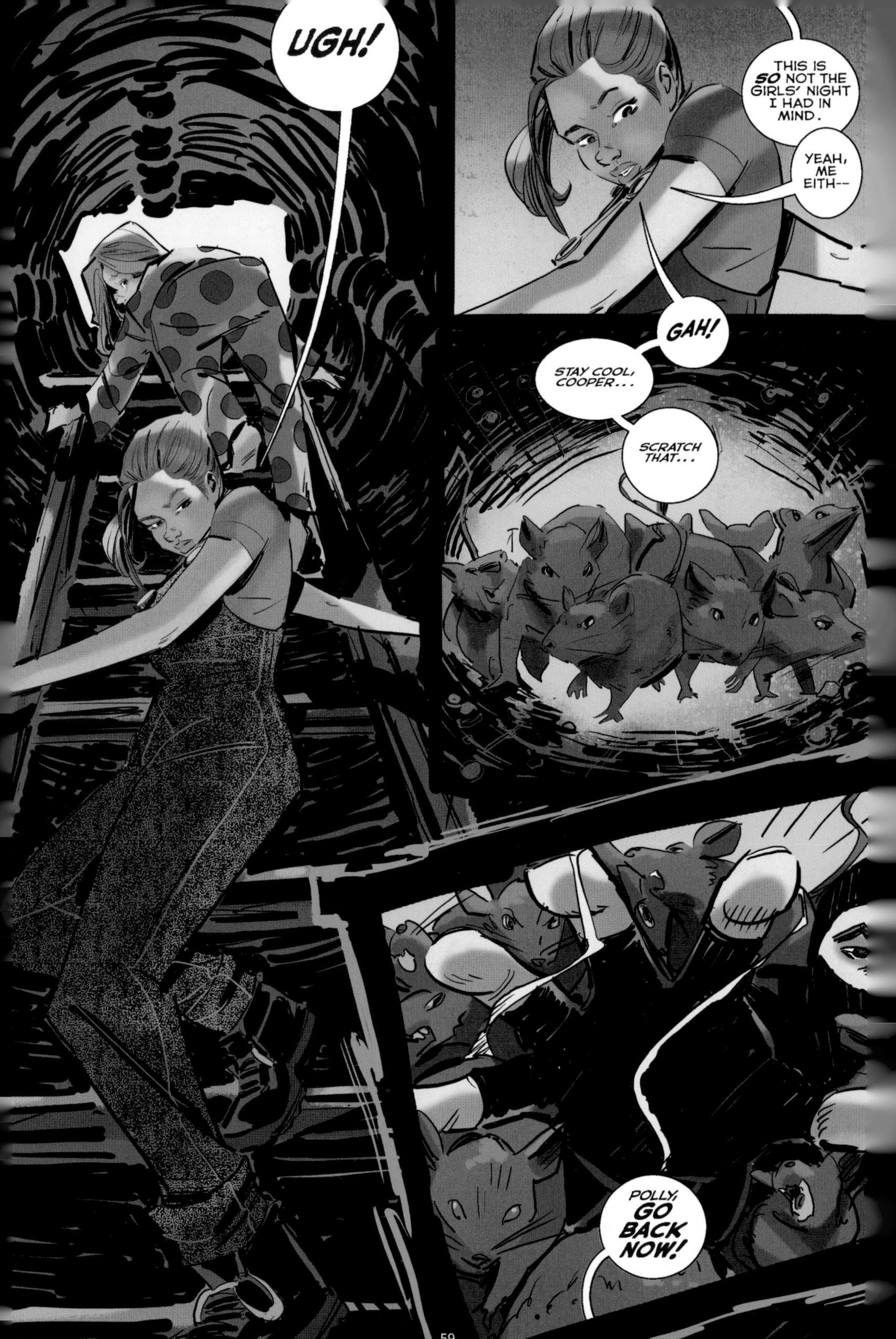
UGH!
THIS IS SO NOT THE GIRLS' NIGHT I HAD IN MIND.
YEAH, ME EITH--
GAH!
STAY COOL, COOPER...
SCRATCH THAT...
POLLY, GO BACK NOW!

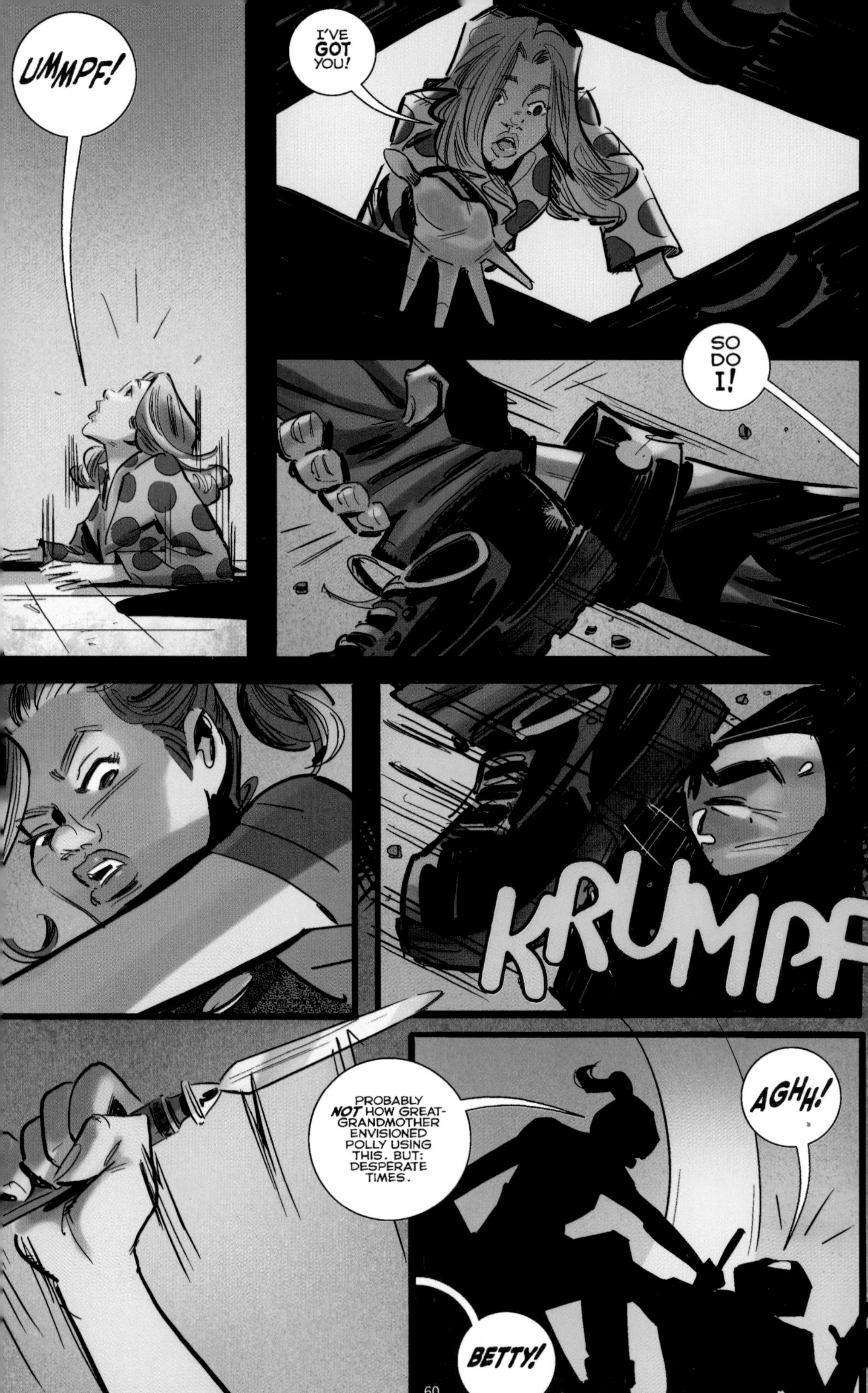
UMMPF!
I'VE GOT YOU!
SO DO I!
KRUMPF
PROBABLY NOT HOW GREAT-GRANDMOTHER ENVISIONED POLLY USING THIS. BUT: DESPERATE TIMES.
AGHH!
BETTY!

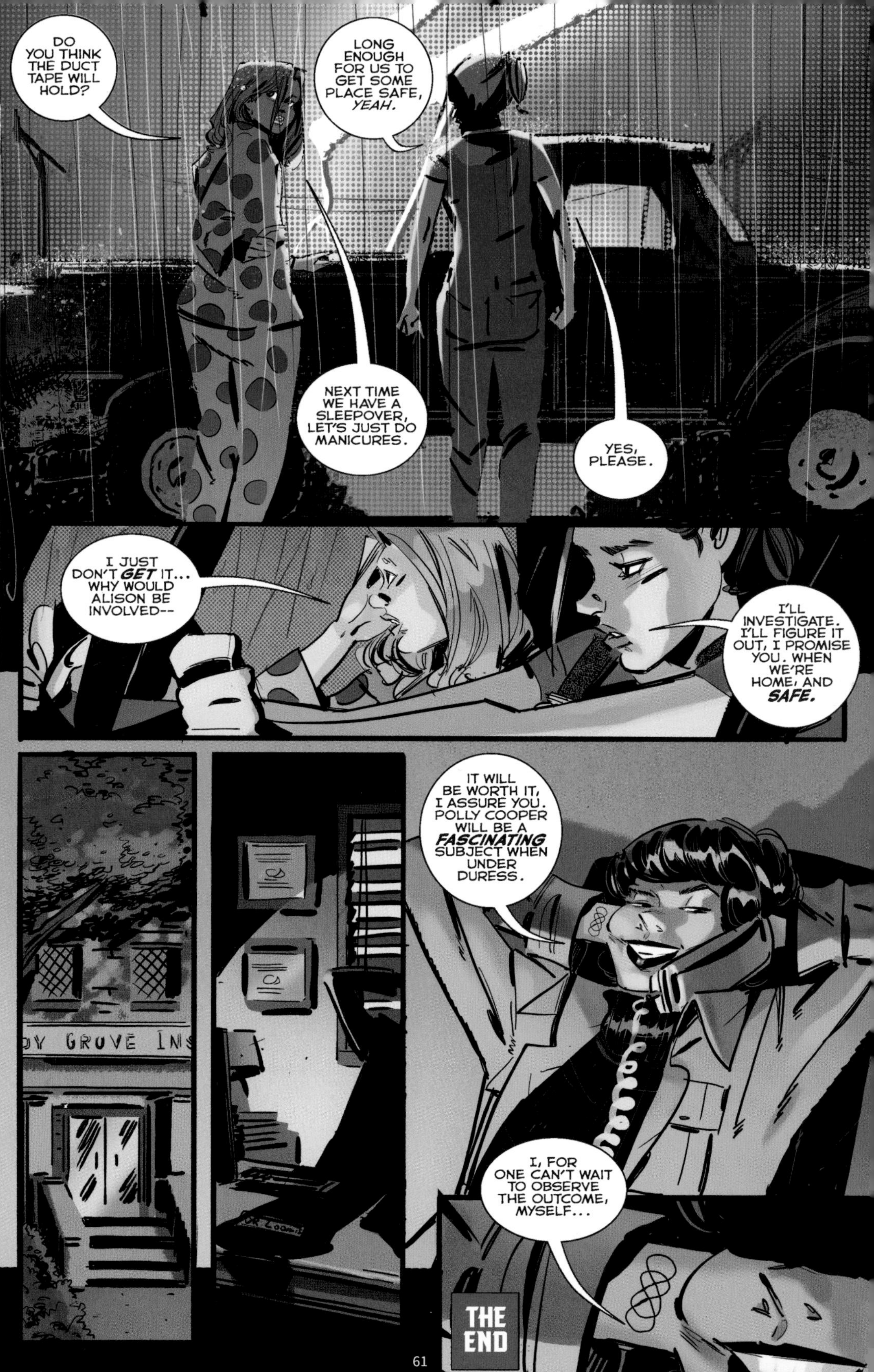
DO YOU THINK THE DUCT TAPE WILL HOLD?
LONG ENOUGH FOR US TO GET SOME PLACE SAFE, *YEAH.*
NEXT TIME WE HAVE A SLEEPOVER, LET'S JUST DO MANICURES.
YES, PLEASE.
I JUST DON'T ***GET*** IT... WHY WOULD ALISON BE INVOLVED--
I'LL INVESTIGATE. I'LL FIGURE IT OUT, I PROMISE YOU. WHEN WE'RE HOME, AND ***SAFE.***
DY GROVE INS
IT WILL BE WORTH IT, I ASSURE YOU. POLLY COOPER WILL BE A ***FASCINATING*** SUBJECT WHEN UNDER DURESS.
I, FOR ONE CAN'T WAIT TO OBSERVE THE OUTCOME, MYSELF...
THE END

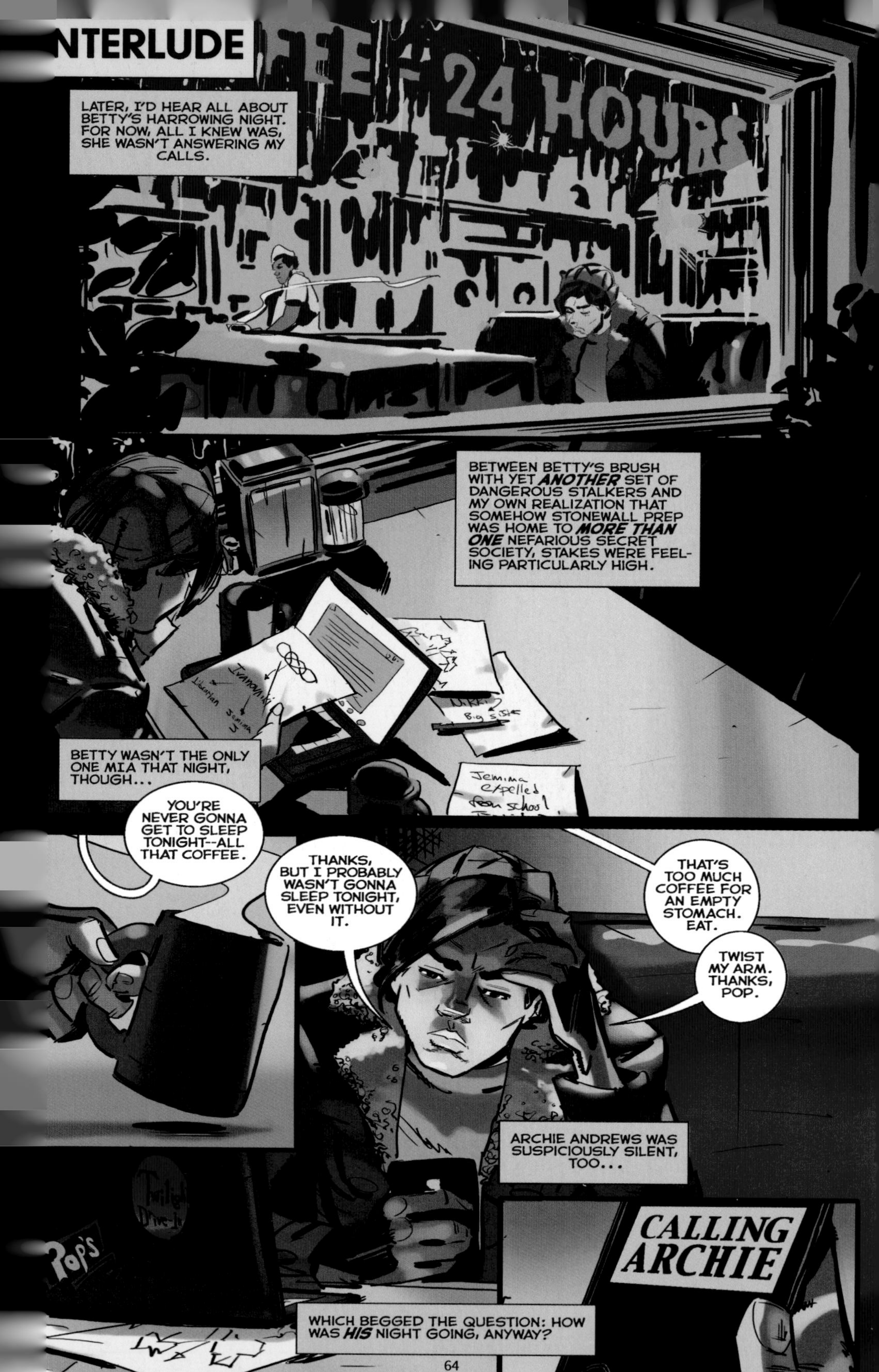
NTERLUDE
24 HOURS
LATER, I'D HEAR ALL ABOUT BETTY'S HARROWING NIGHT. FOR NOW, ALL I KNEW WAS, SHE WASN'T ANSWERING MY CALLS.
BETWEEN BETTY'S BRUSH WITH YET ***ANOTHER*** SET OF DANGEROUS STALKERS AND MY OWN REALIZATION THAT SOMEHOW STONEWALL PREP WAS HOME TO ***MORE THAN ONE*** NEFARIOUS SECRET SOCIETY, STAKES WERE FEELING PARTICULARLY HIGH.
Big Sister
BETTY WASN'T THE ONLY ONE MIA THAT NIGHT, THOUGH...
Jemima expelled from school!
YOU'RE NEVER GONNA GET TO SLEEP TONIGHT--ALL THAT COFFEE.
THANKS, BUT I PROBABLY WASN'T GONNA SLEEP TONIGHT, EVEN WITHOUT IT.
THAT'S TOO MUCH COFFEE FOR AN EMPTY STOMACH. EAT.
TWIST MY ARM. THANKS, POP.
ARCHIE ANDREWS WAS SUSPICIOUSLY SILENT, TOO...
Pop's
CALLING ARCHIE
WHICH BEGGED THE QUESTION: HOW WAS ***HIS*** NIGHT GOING, ANYWAY?

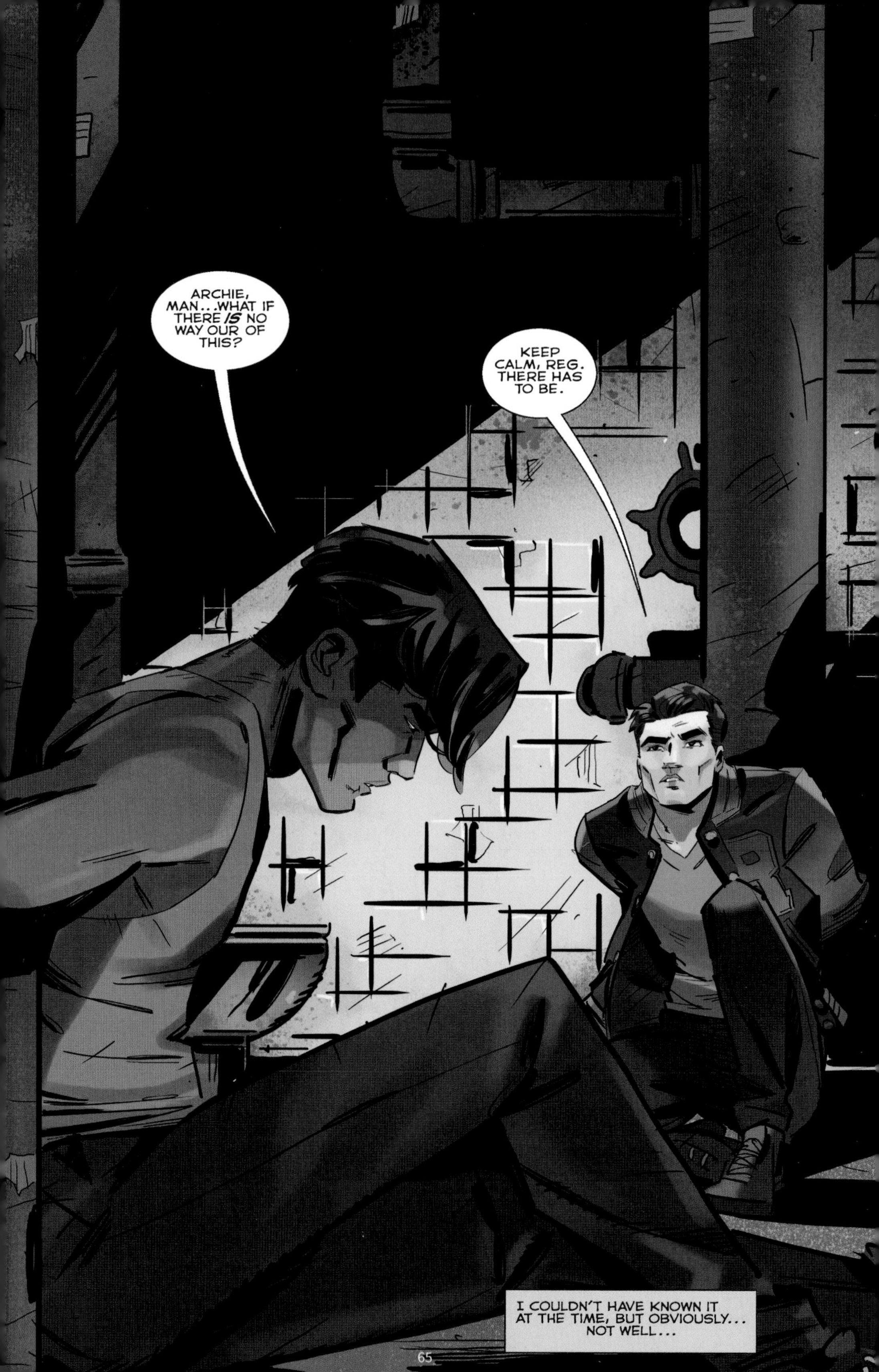

ARCHIE, MAN...WHAT IF THERE IS NO WAY OUR OF THIS?
KEEP CALM, REG. THERE HAS TO BE.
I COULDN'T HAVE KNOWN IT AT THE TIME, BUT OBVIOUSLY... NOT WELL...

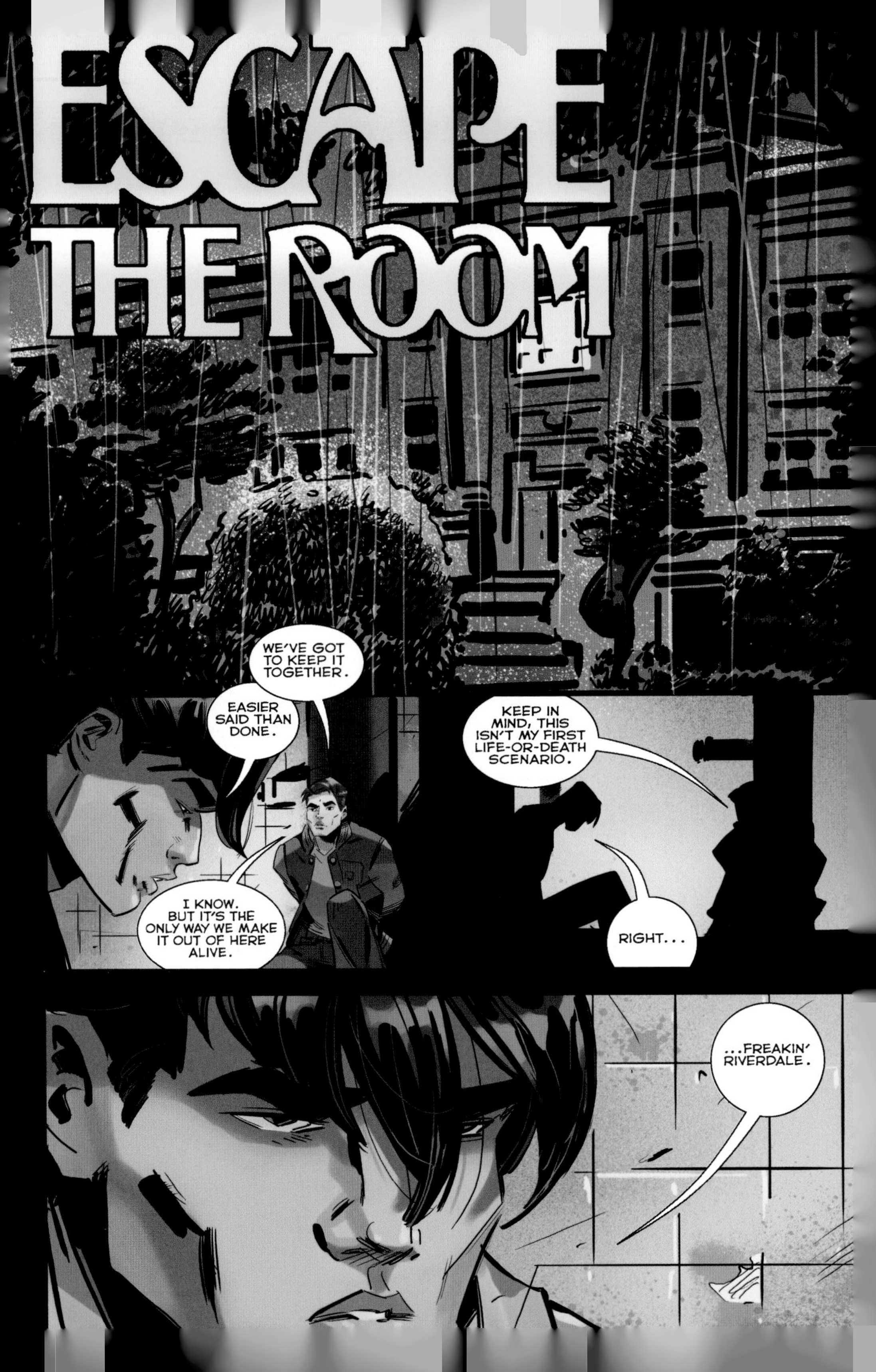
ESCAPE THE ROOM
WE'VE GOT TO KEEP IT TOGETHER.
EASIER SAID THAN DONE.
I KNOW. BUT IT'S THE ONLY WAY WE MAKE IT OUT OF HERE ALIVE.
KEEP IN MIND, THIS ISN'T MY FIRST LIFE-OR-DEATH SCENARIO.
RIGHT...
...FREAKIN' RIVERDALE.

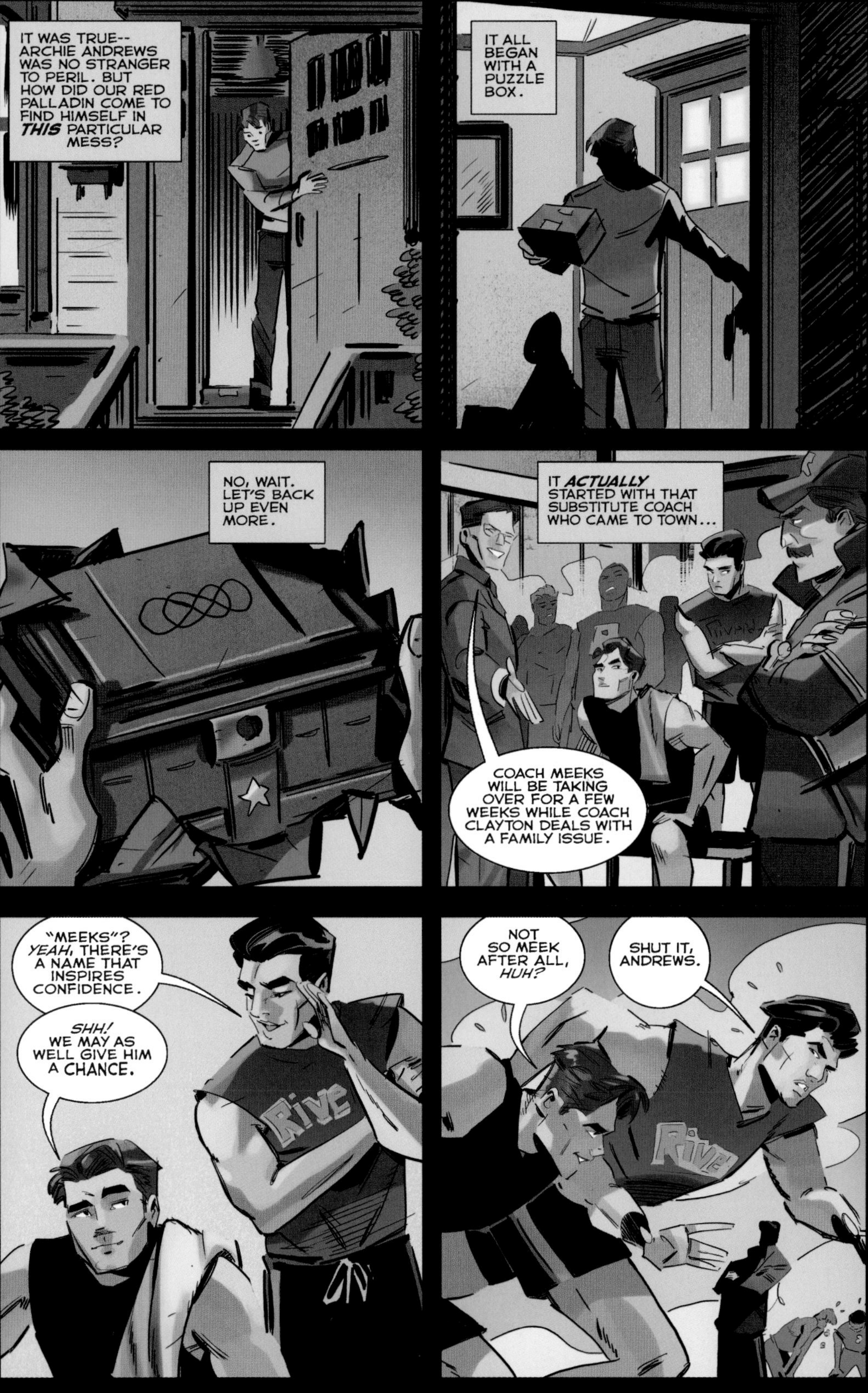
IT WAS TRUE-- ARCHIE ANDREWS WAS NO STRANGER TO PERIL. BUT HOW DID OUR RED PALLADIN COME TO FIND HIMSELF IN *THIS* PARTICULAR MESS?
IT ALL BEGAN WITH A PUZZLE BOX.
NO, WAIT. LET'S BACK UP EVEN MORE.
IT *ACTUALLY* STARTED WITH THAT SUBSTITUTE COACH WHO CAME TO TOWN...
COACH MEEKS WILL BE TAKING OVER FOR A FEW WEEKS WHILE COACH CLAYTON DEALS WITH A FAMILY ISSUE.
"MEEKS"? *YEAH*, THERE'S A NAME THAT INSPIRES CONFIDENCE.
SHH! WE MAY AS WELL GIVE HIM A CHANCE.
NOT SO MEEK AFTER ALL, *HUH?*
SHUT IT, ANDREWS.

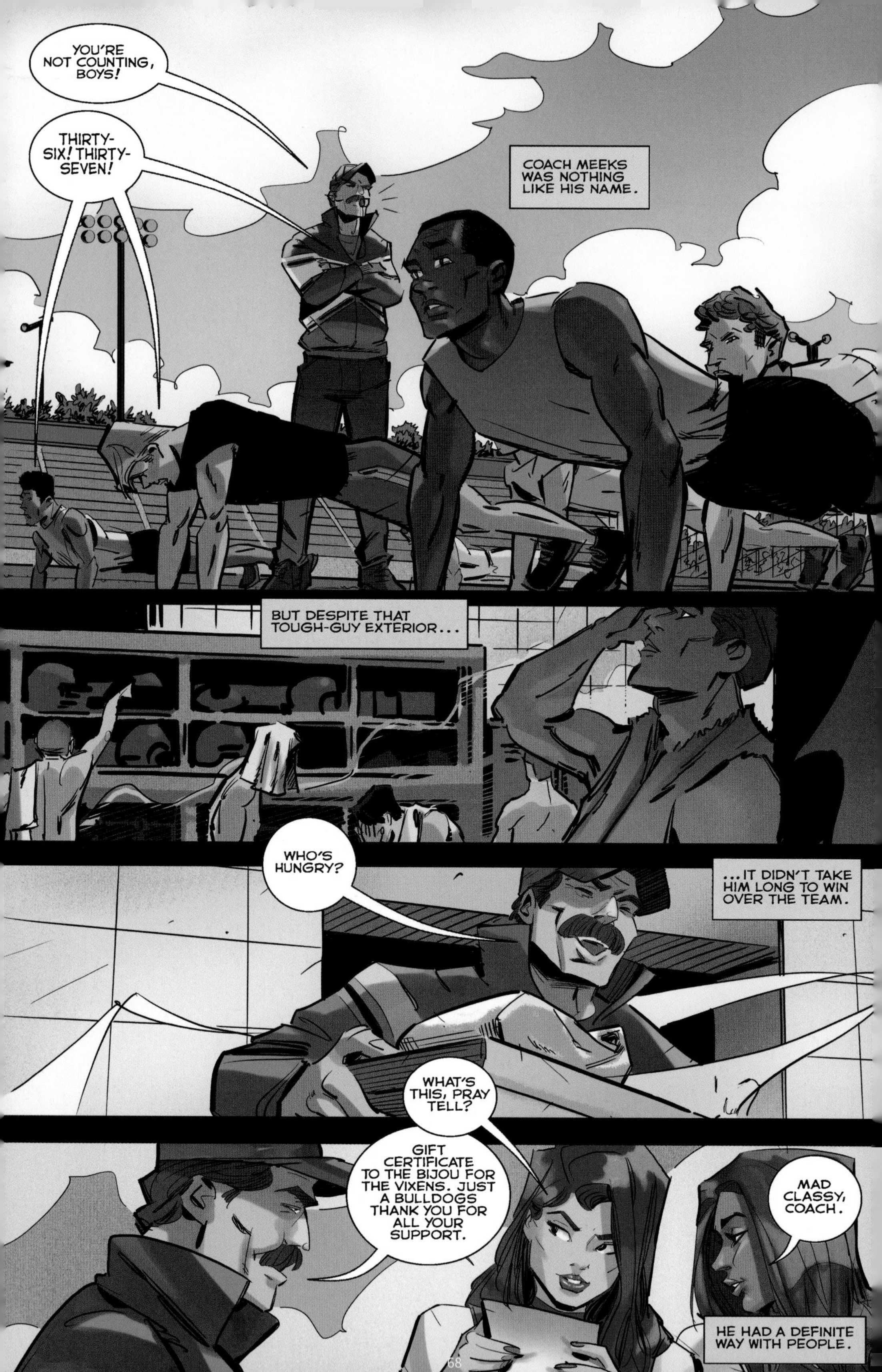
YOU'RE NOT COUNTING, BOYS!
THIRTY-SIX! THIRTY-SEVEN!
COACH MEEKS WAS NOTHING LIKE HIS NAME.
BUT DESPITE THAT TOUGH-GUY EXTERIOR...
WHO'S HUNGRY?
...IT DIDN'T TAKE HIM LONG TO WIN OVER THE TEAM.
WHAT'S THIS, PRAY TELL?
GIFT CERTIFICATE TO THE BIJOU FOR THE VIXENS. JUST A BULLDOGS THANK YOU FOR ALL YOUR SUPPORT.
MAD CLASSY, COACH.
HE HAD A DEFINITE WAY WITH PEOPLE.

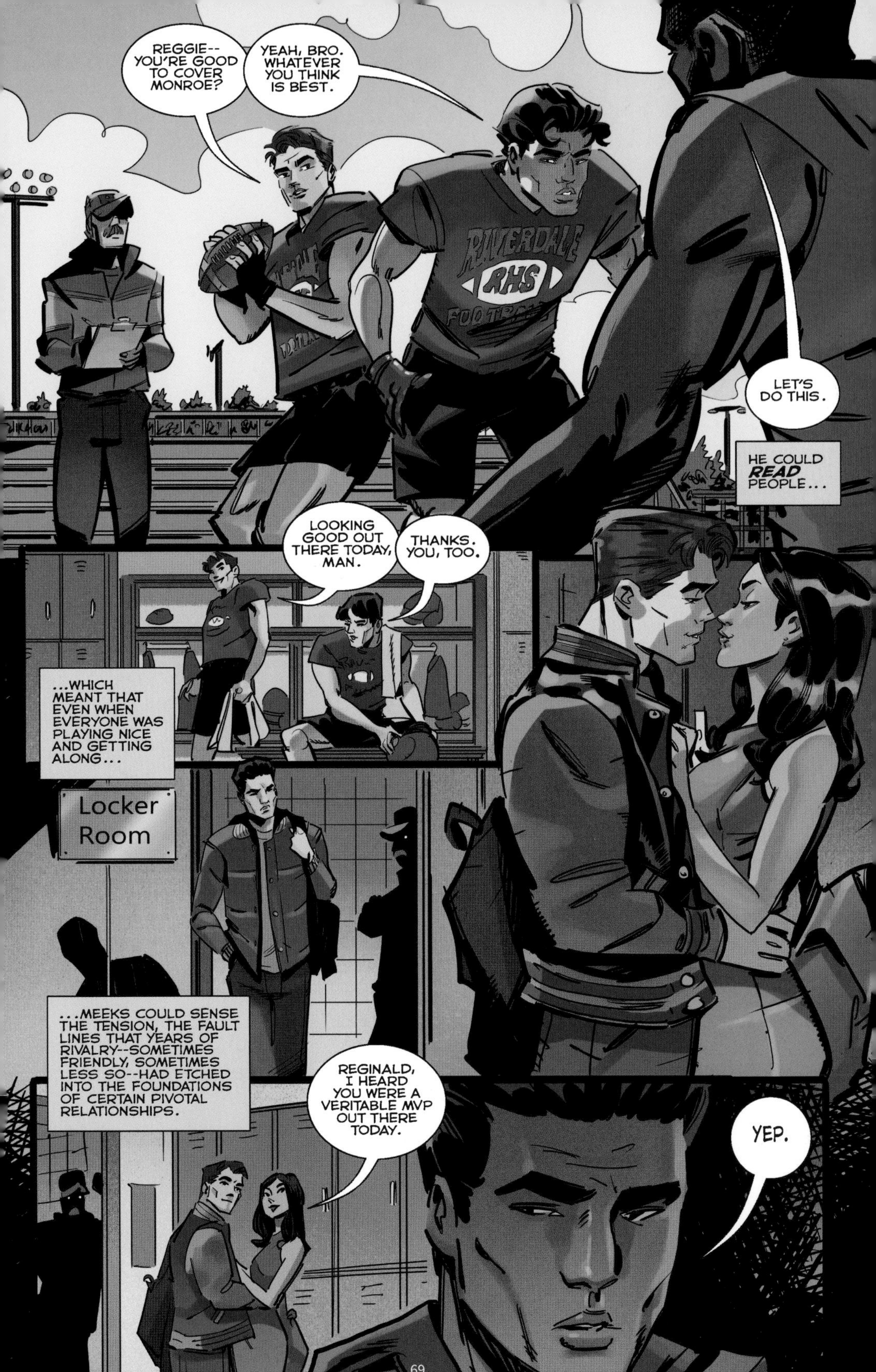
REGGIE-- YOU'RE GOOD TO COVER MONROE?
YEAH, BRO. WHATEVER YOU THINK IS BEST.
RIVERDALE
RHS
LET'S DO THIS.
HE COULD **READ** PEOPLE...
LOOKING GOOD OUT THERE TODAY, MAN.
THANKS. YOU, TOO.
...WHICH MEANT THAT EVEN WHEN EVERYONE WAS PLAYING NICE AND GETTING ALONG...
Locker Room
...MEEKS COULD SENSE THE TENSION, THE FAULT LINES THAT YEARS OF RIVALRY--SOMETIMES FRIENDLY, SOMETIMES LESS SO--HAD ETCHED INTO THE FOUNDATIONS OF CERTAIN PIVOTAL RELATIONSHIPS.
REGINALD, I HEARD YOU WERE A VERITABLE MVP OUT THERE TODAY.
YEP.

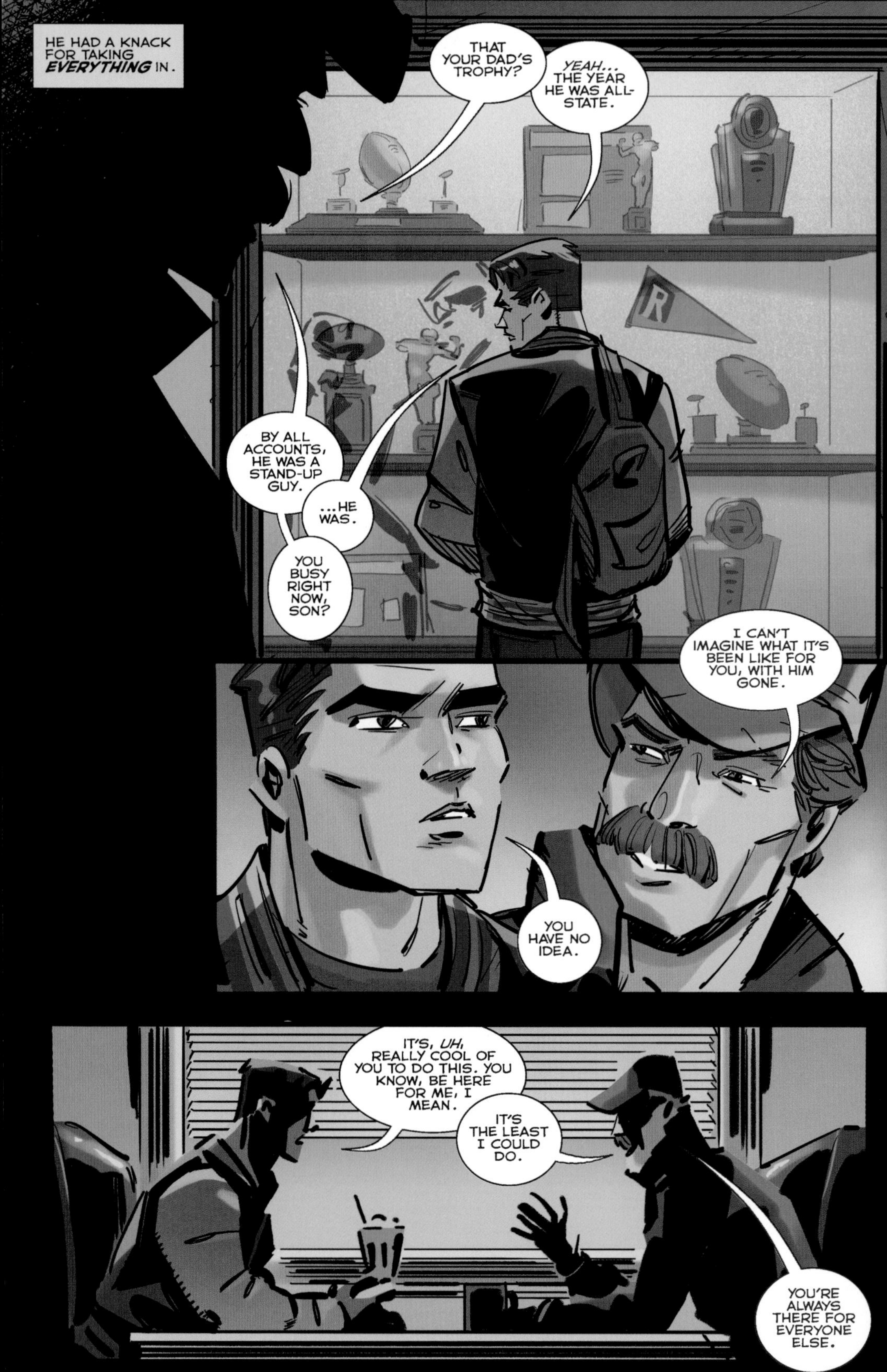
HE HAD A KNACK FOR TAKING *EVERYTHING* IN.
THAT YOUR DAD'S TROPHY?
YEAH... THE YEAR HE WAS ALL-STATE.
BY ALL ACCOUNTS, HE WAS A STAND-UP GUY.
...HE WAS.
YOU BUSY RIGHT NOW, SON?
I CAN'T IMAGINE WHAT IT'S BEEN LIKE FOR YOU, WITH HIM GONE.
YOU HAVE NO IDEA.
IT'S, *UH*, REALLY COOL OF YOU TO DO THIS. YOU KNOW, BE HERE FOR ME, I MEAN.
IT'S THE LEAST I COULD DO.
YOU'RE ALWAYS THERE FOR EVERYONE ELSE.

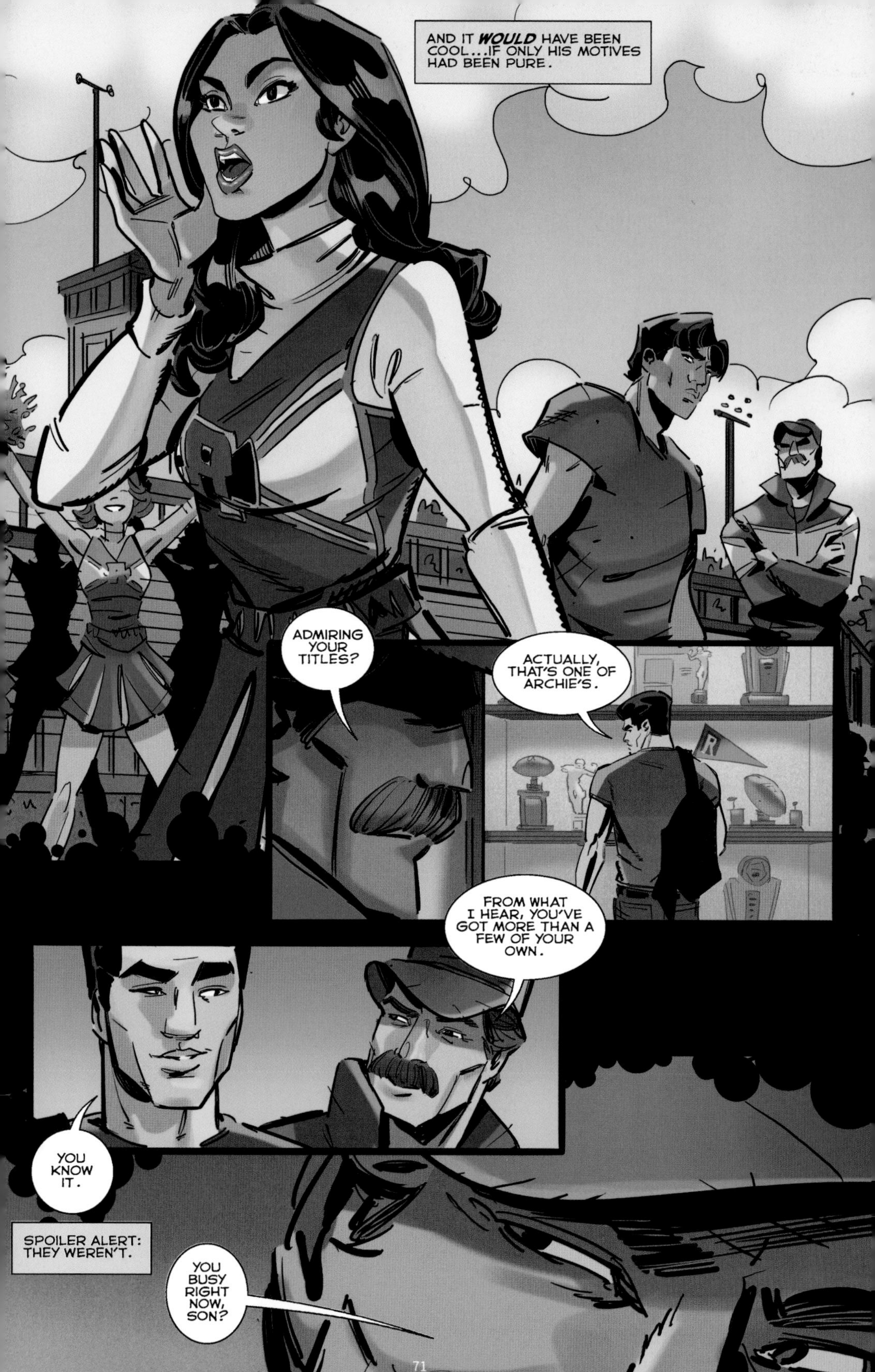
AND IT WOULD HAVE BEEN COOL...IF ONLY HIS MOTIVES HAD BEEN PURE.
ADMIRING YOUR TITLES?
ACTUALLY, THAT'S ONE OF ARCHIE'S.
FROM WHAT I HEAR, YOU'VE GOT MORE THAN A FEW OF YOUR OWN.
YOU KNOW IT.
SPOILER ALERT: THEY WEREN'T.
YOU BUSY RIGHT NOW, SON?

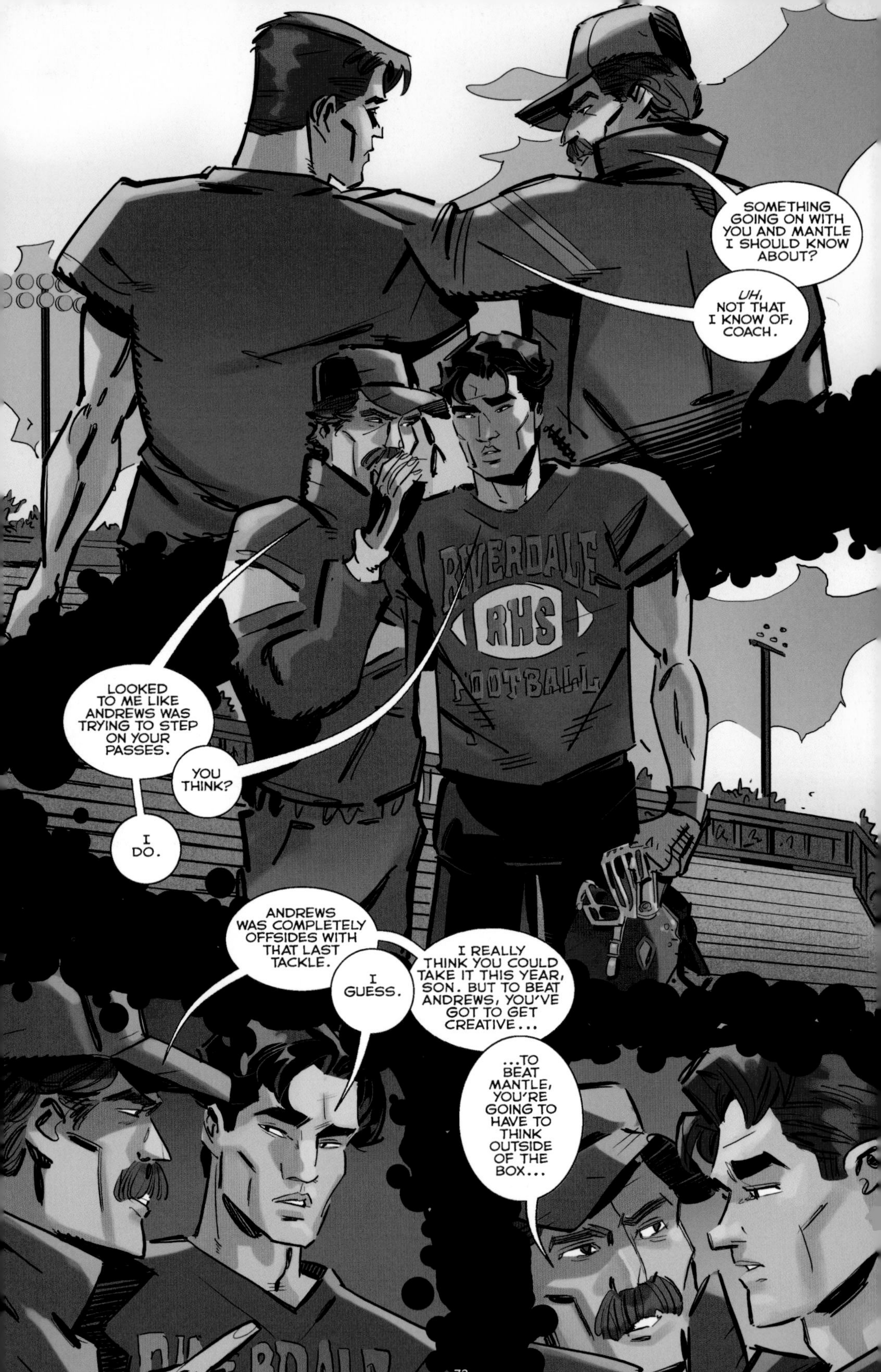
SOMETHING GOING ON WITH YOU AND MANTLE I SHOULD KNOW ABOUT?
UH, NOT THAT I KNOW OF, COACH.
LOOKED TO ME LIKE ANDREWS WAS TRYING TO STEP ON YOUR PASSES.
YOU THINK?
I DO.
ANDREWS WAS COMPLETELY OFFSIDES WITH THAT LAST TACKLE.
I GUESS.
I REALLY THINK YOU COULD TAKE IT THIS YEAR, SON. BUT TO BEAT ANDREWS, YOU'VE GOT TO GET CREATIVE...
...TO BEAT MANTLE, YOU'RE GOING TO HAVE TO THINK OUTSIDE OF THE BOX...

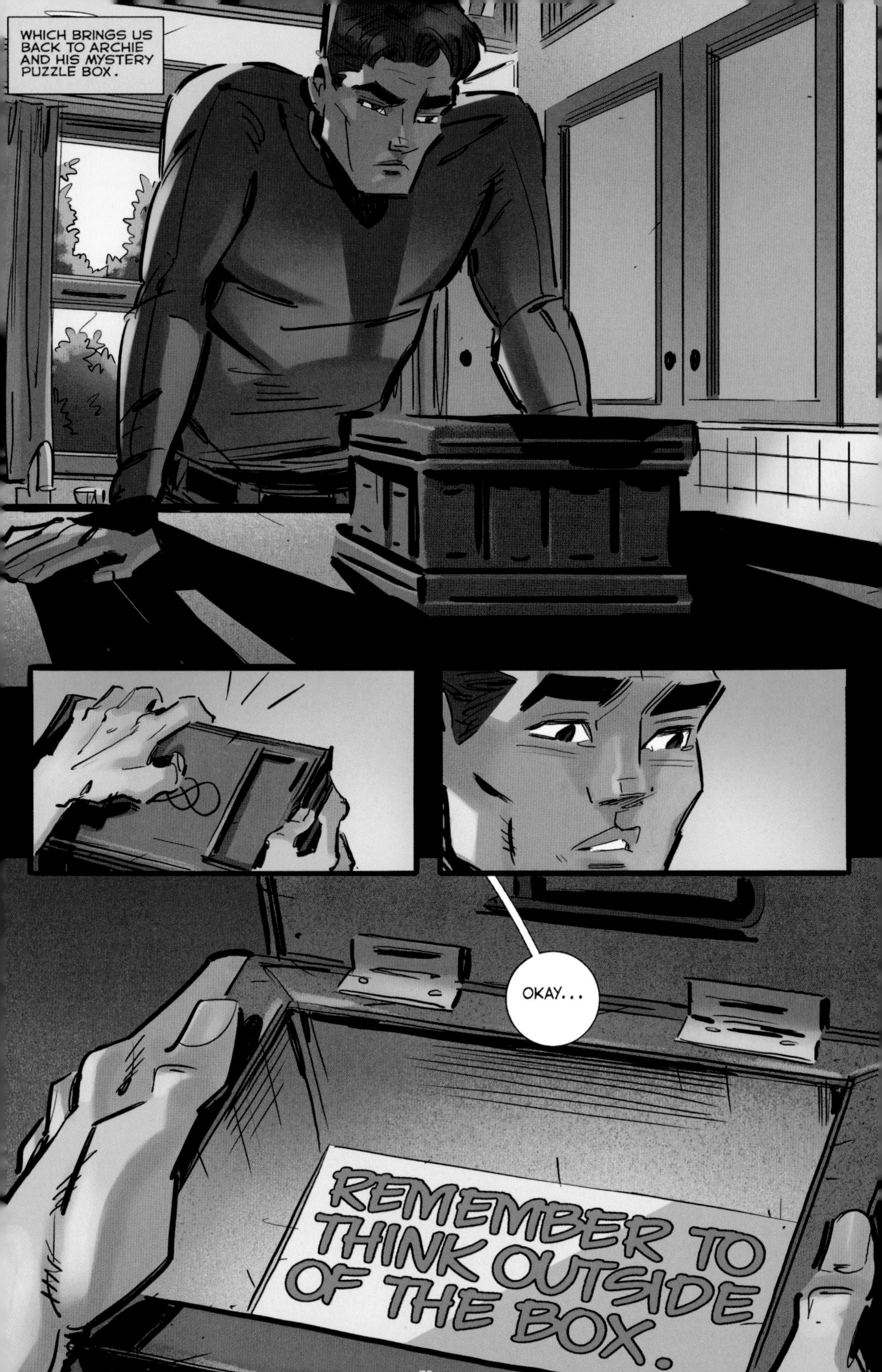
WHICH BRINGS US BACK TO ARCHIE AND HIS MYSTERY PUZZLE BOX.
OKAY...
REMEMBER TO THINK OUTSIDE OF THE BOX.

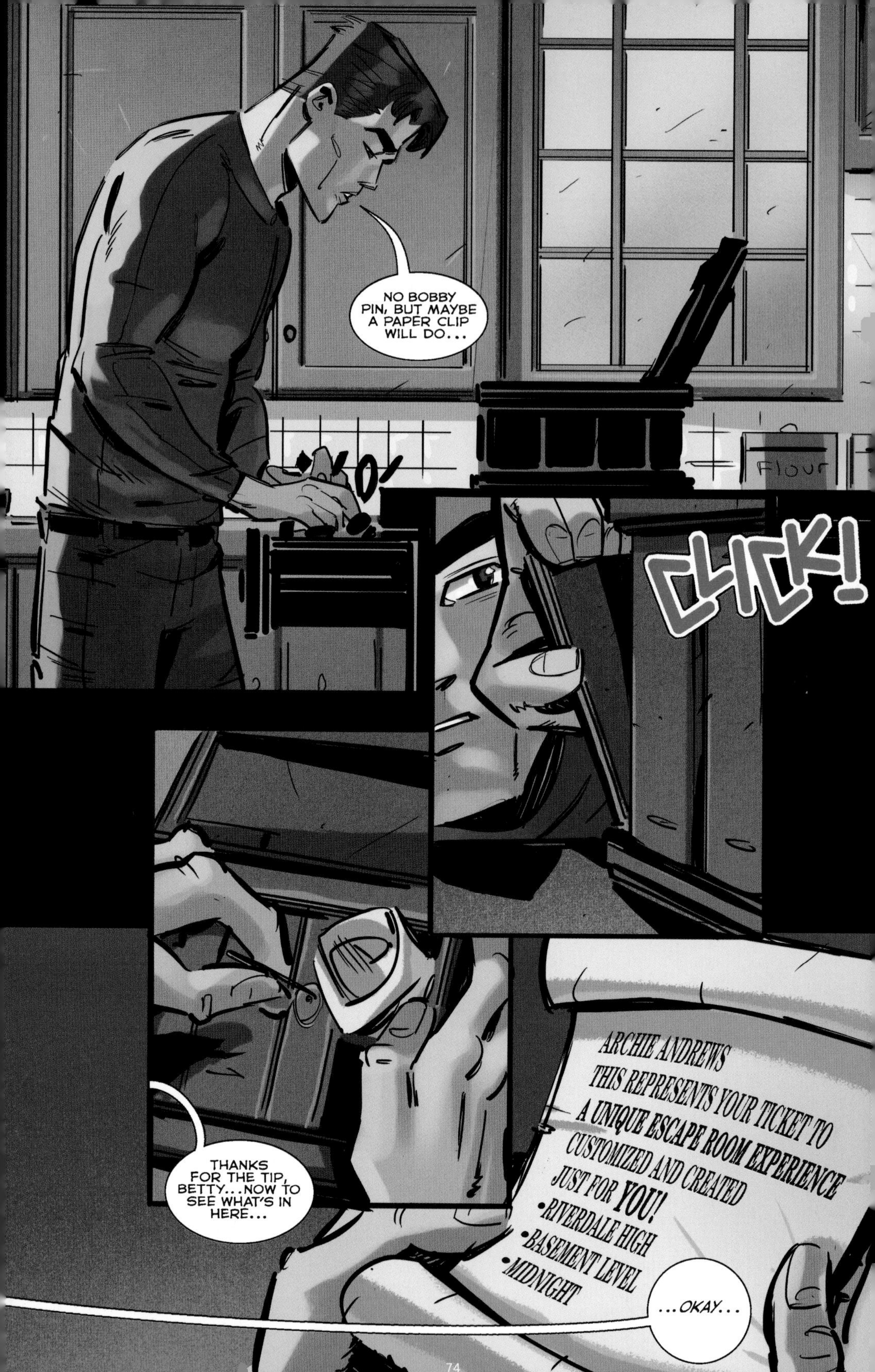

NO BOBBY PIN, BUT MAYBE A PAPER CLIP WILL DO...
CLICK!
THANKS FOR THE TIP, BETTY...NOW TO SEE WHAT'S IN HERE...
ARCHIE ANDREWS
THIS REPRESENTS YOUR TICKET TO
A UNIQUE ESCAPE ROOM EXPERIENCE
CUSTOMIZED AND CREATED
JUST FOR YOU!
•RIVERDALE HIGH
•BASEMENT LEVEL
•MIDNIGHT
...OKAY...

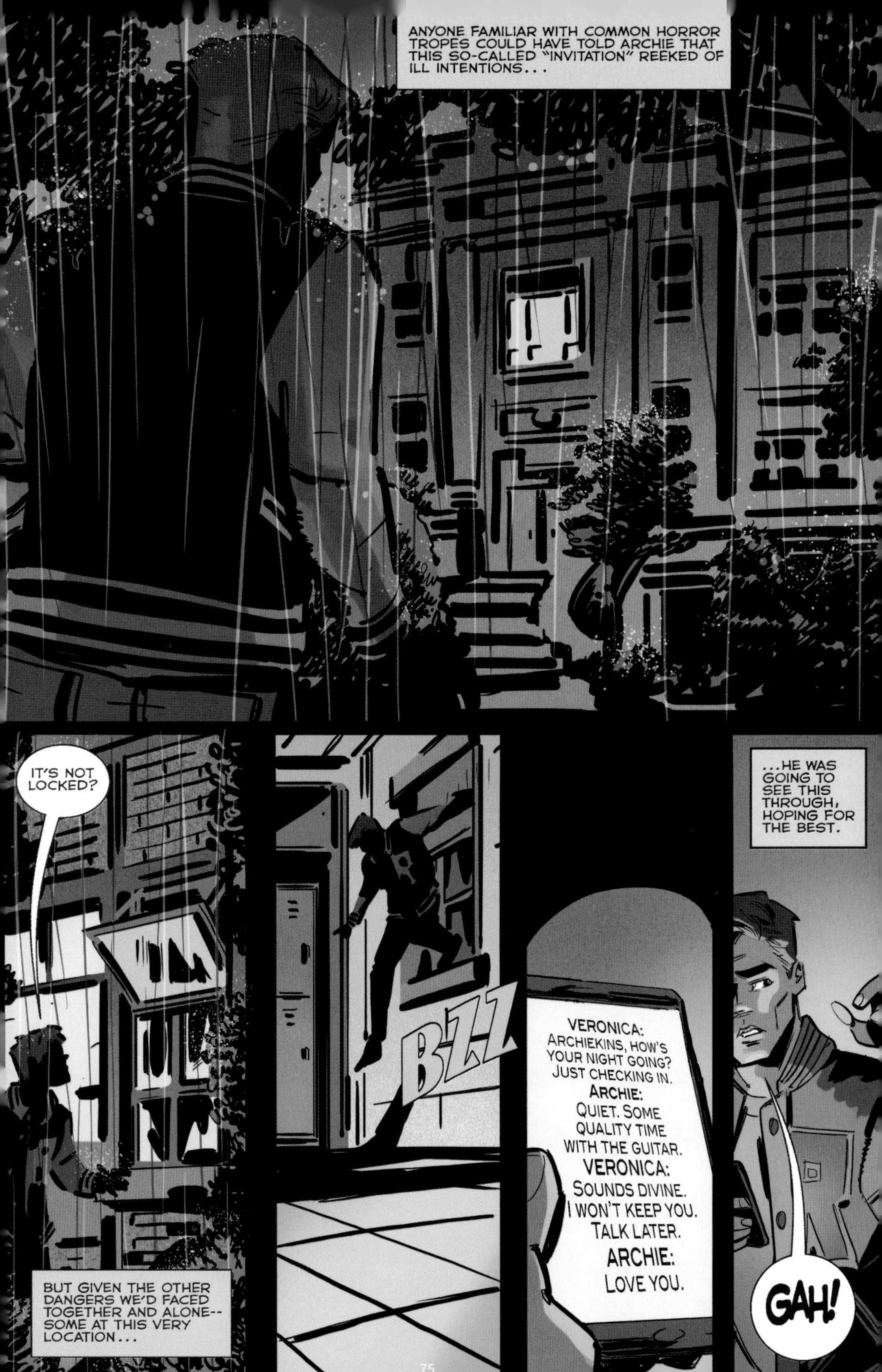

ANYONE FAMILIAR WITH COMMON HORROR TROPES COULD HAVE TOLD ARCHIE THAT THIS SO-CALLED "INVITATION" REEKED OF ILL INTENTIONS...
IT'S NOT LOCKED?
BUT GIVEN THE OTHER DANGERS WE'D FACED TOGETHER AND ALONE-- SOME AT THIS VERY LOCATION...
BZZ
VERONICA: ARCHIEKINS, HOW'S YOUR NIGHT GOING? JUST CHECKING IN.
ARCHIE: QUIET. SOME QUALITY TIME WITH THE GUITAR.
VERONICA: SOUNDS DIVINE. I WON'T KEEP YOU. TALK LATER.
ARCHIE: LOVE YOU.
...HE WAS GOING TO SEE THIS THROUGH, HOPING FOR THE BEST.
GAH!

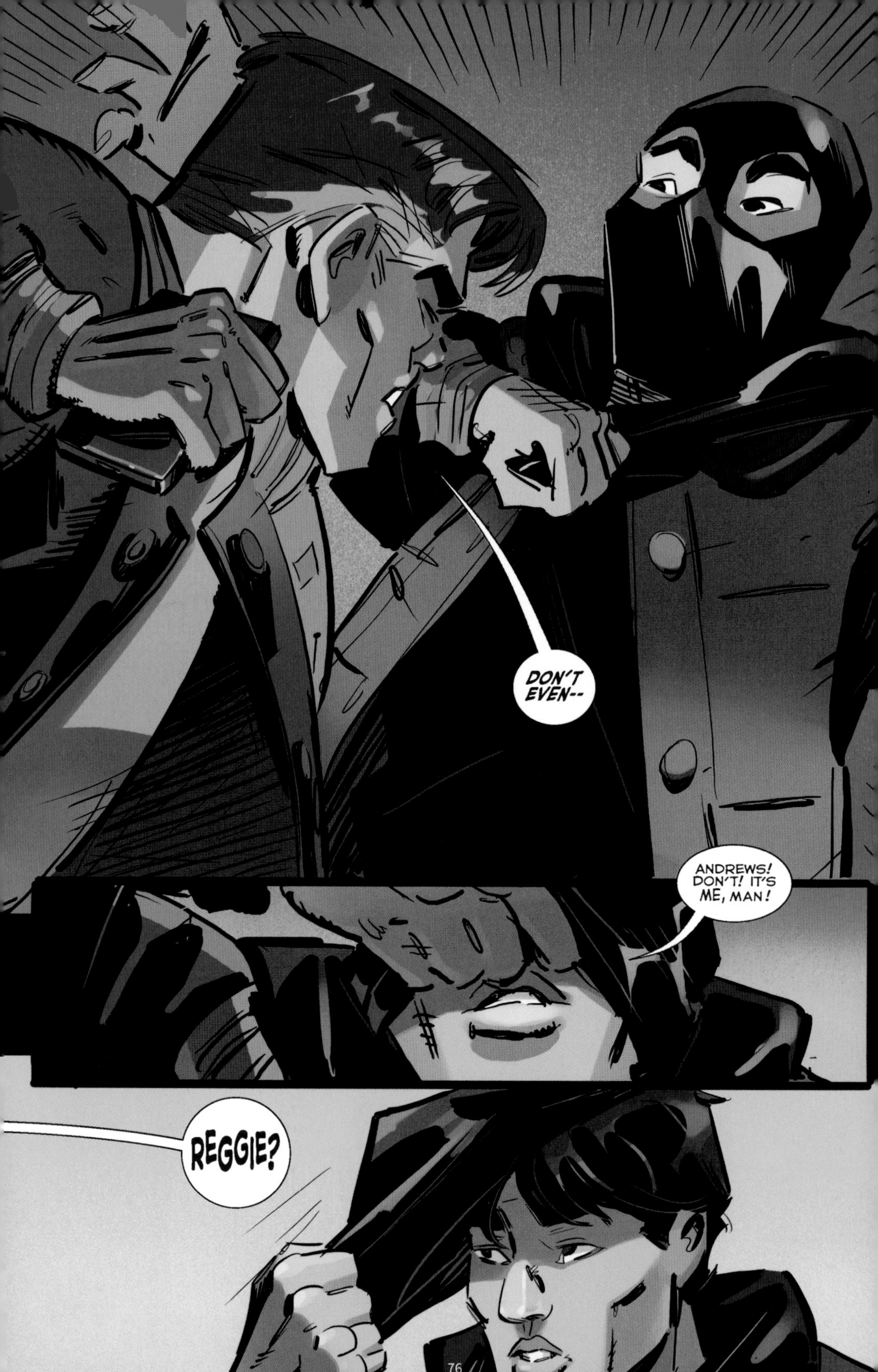
DON'T EVEN--
ANDREWS! DON'T! IT'S ME, MAN!
REGGIE?

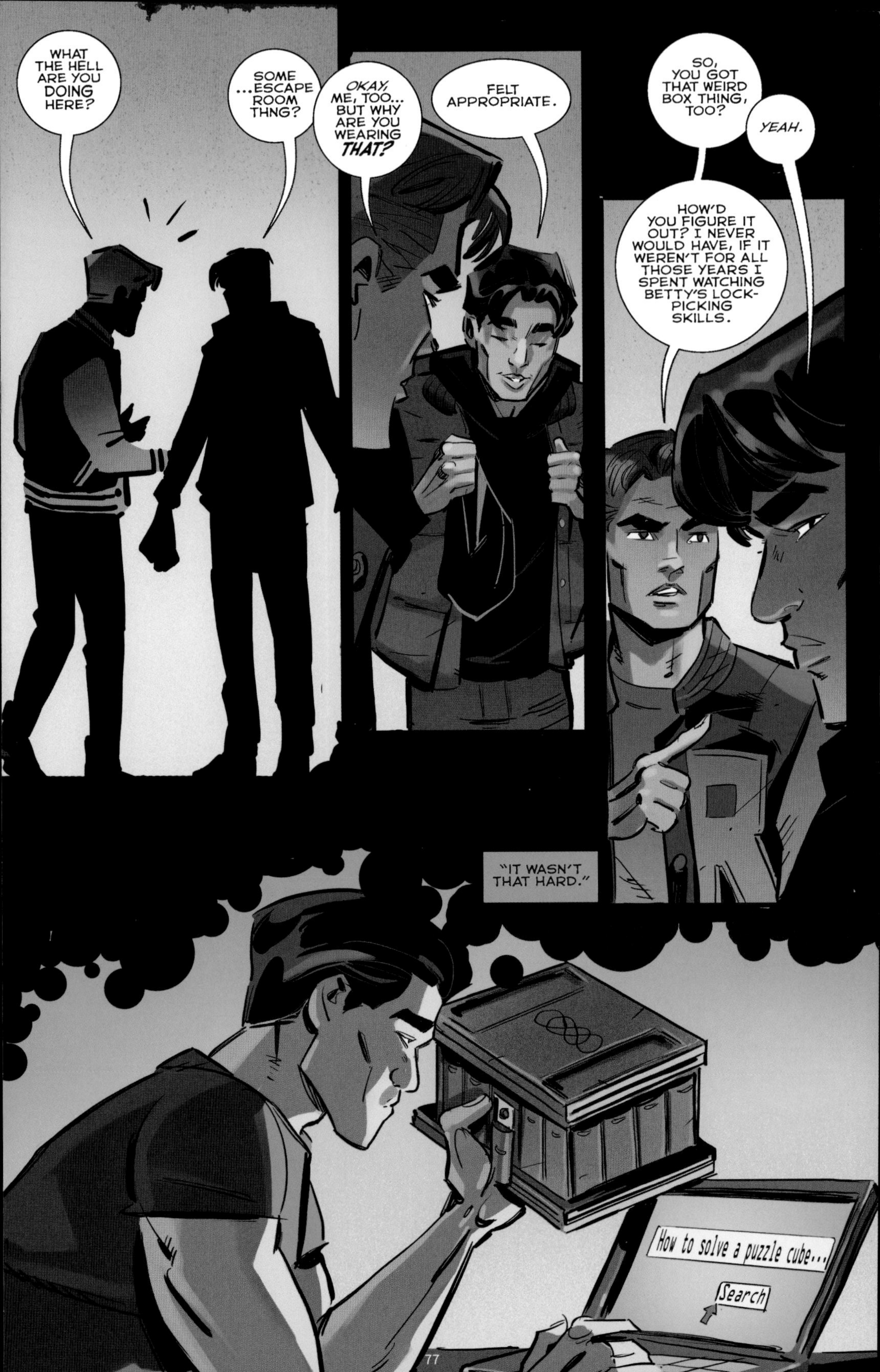
WHAT THE HELL ARE YOU DOING HERE?
SOME ...ESCAPE ROOM THNG?
OKAY, ME, TOO... BUT WHY ARE YOU WEARING THAT?
FELT APPROPRIATE.
SO, YOU GOT THAT WEIRD BOX THING, TOO?
YEAH.
HOW'D YOU FIGURE IT OUT? I NEVER WOULD HAVE, IF IT WEREN'T FOR ALL THOSE YEARS I SPENT WATCHING BETTY'S LOCK-PICKING SKILLS.
"IT WASN'T THAT HARD."
How to solve a puzzle cube...
Search

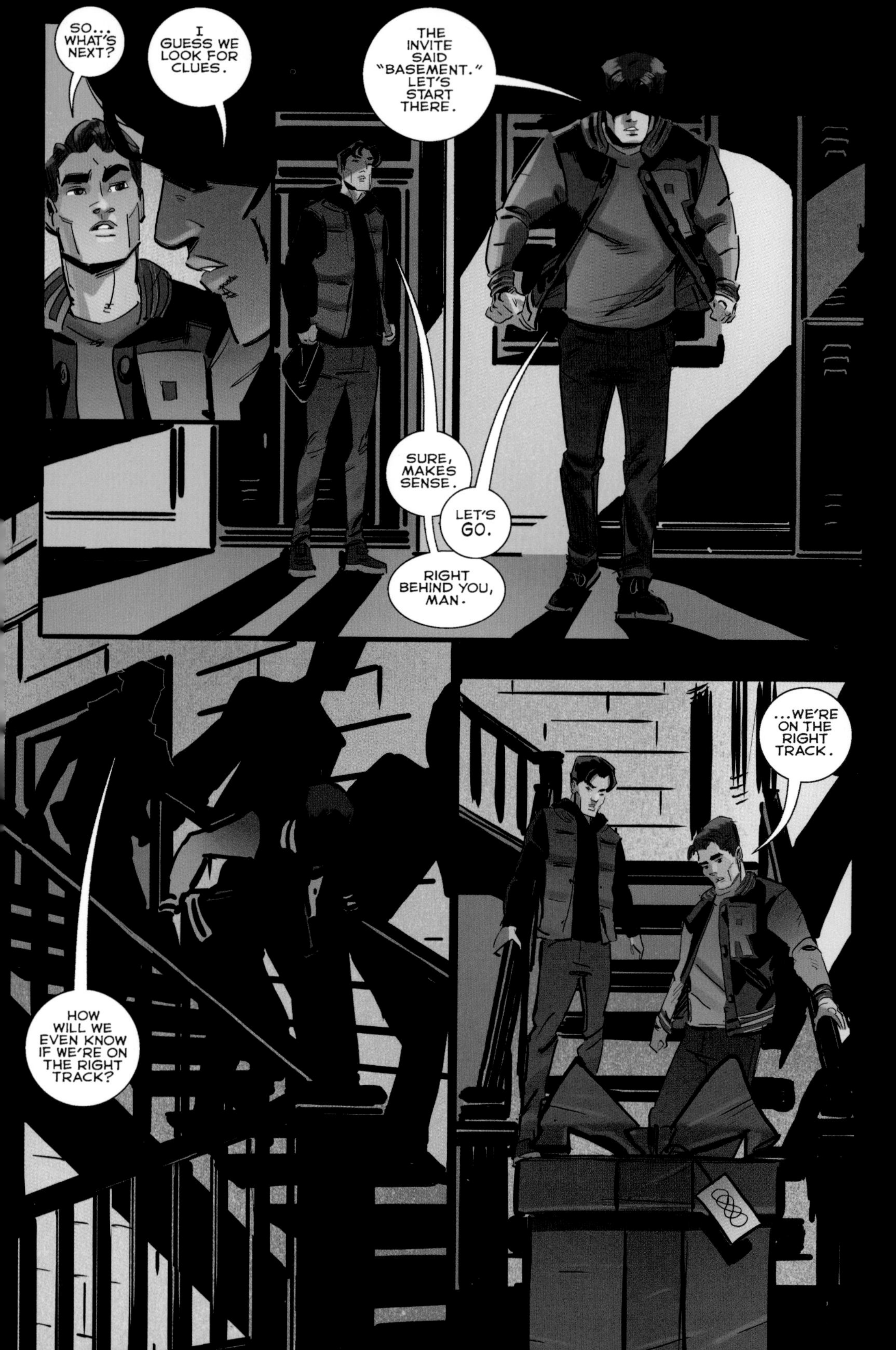
SO... WHAT'S NEXT?
I GUESS WE LOOK FOR CLUES.
THE INVITE SAID "BASEMENT." LET'S START THERE.
SURE, MAKES SENSE.
LET'S GO.
RIGHT BEHIND YOU, MAN.
HOW WILL WE EVEN KNOW IF WE'RE ON THE RIGHT TRACK?
...WE'RE ON THE RIGHT TRACK.

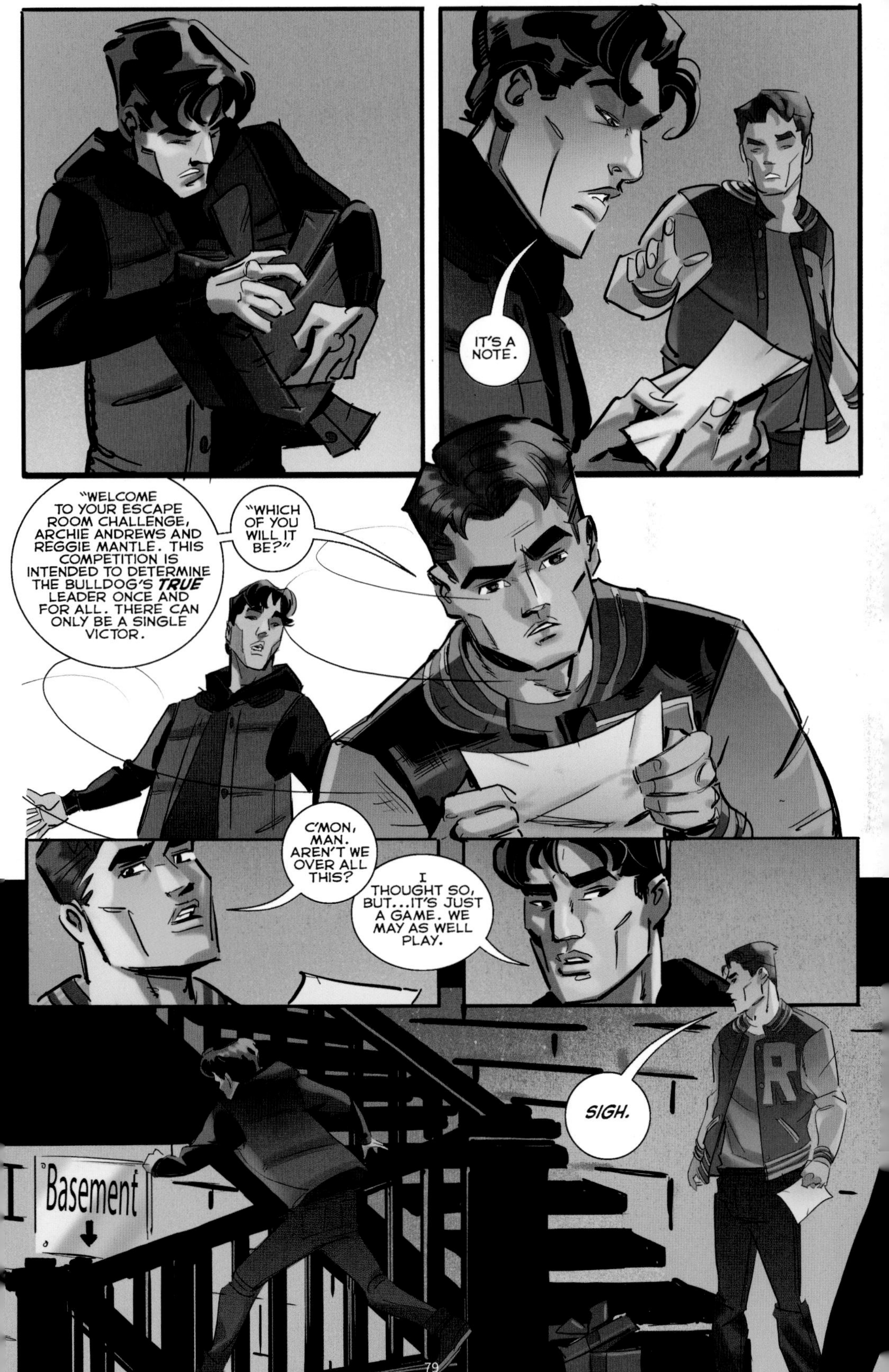
IT'S A NOTE.
"WELCOME TO YOUR ESCAPE ROOM CHALLENGE, ARCHIE ANDREWS AND REGGIE MANTLE. THIS COMPETITION IS INTENDED TO DETERMINE THE BULLDOG'S *TRUE* LEADER ONCE AND FOR ALL. THERE CAN ONLY BE A SINGLE VICTOR.
"WHICH OF YOU WILL IT BE?"
C'MON, MAN. AREN'T WE OVER ALL THIS?
I THOUGHT SO, BUT...IT'S JUST A GAME. WE MAY AS WELL PLAY.
Basement
SIGH.

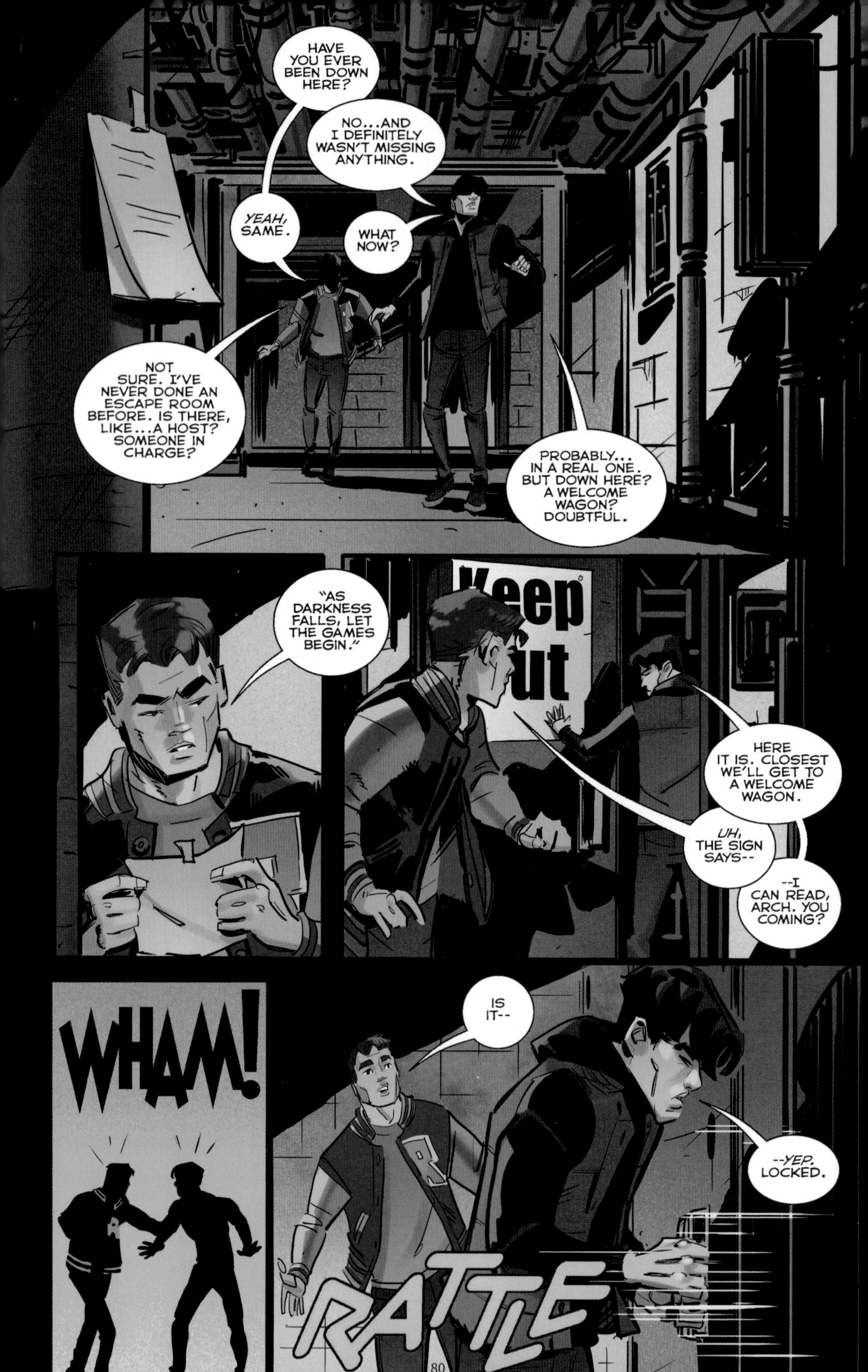
HAVE YOU EVER BEEN DOWN HERE?
NO...AND I DEFINITELY WASN'T MISSING ANYTHING.
YEAH, SAME.
WHAT NOW?
NOT SURE. I'VE NEVER DONE AN ESCAPE ROOM BEFORE. IS THERE, LIKE...A HOST? SOMEONE IN CHARGE?
PROBABLY... IN A REAL ONE. BUT DOWN HERE? A WELCOME WAGON? DOUBTFUL.
"AS DARKNESS FALLS, LET THE GAMES BEGIN."
Keep Out
HERE IT IS. CLOSEST WE'LL GET TO A WELCOME WAGON.
UH, THE SIGN SAYS--
--I CAN READ, ARCH. YOU COMING?
WHAM!
IS IT--
--YEP. LOCKED.
RATTLE

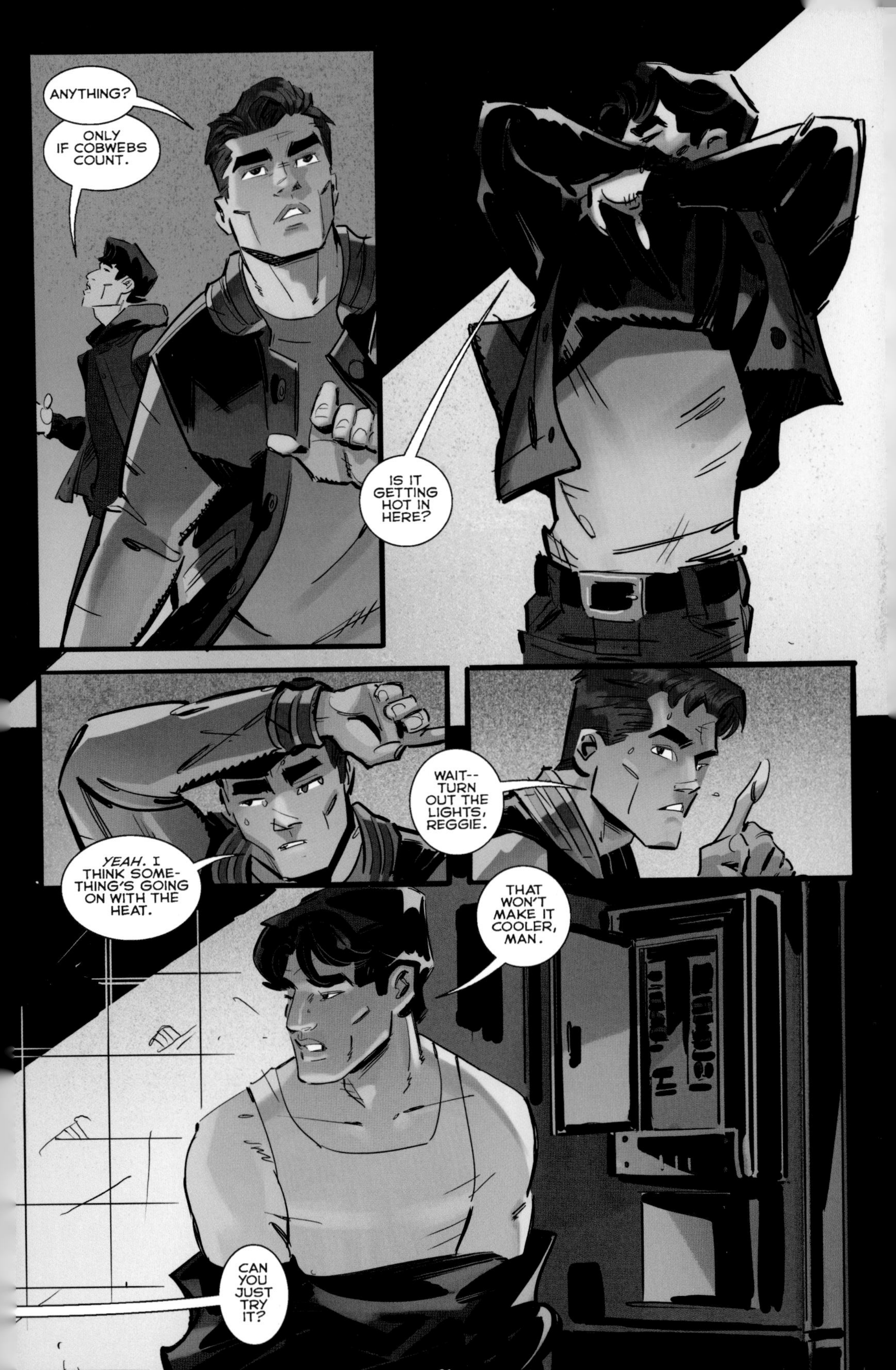
ANYTHING?
ONLY IF COBWEBS COUNT.
IS IT GETTING HOT IN HERE?
YEAH. I THINK SOME-THING'S GOING ON WITH THE HEAT.
WAIT-- TURN OUT THE LIGHTS, REGGIE.
THAT WON'T MAKE IT COOLER, MAN.
CAN YOU JUST TRY IT?

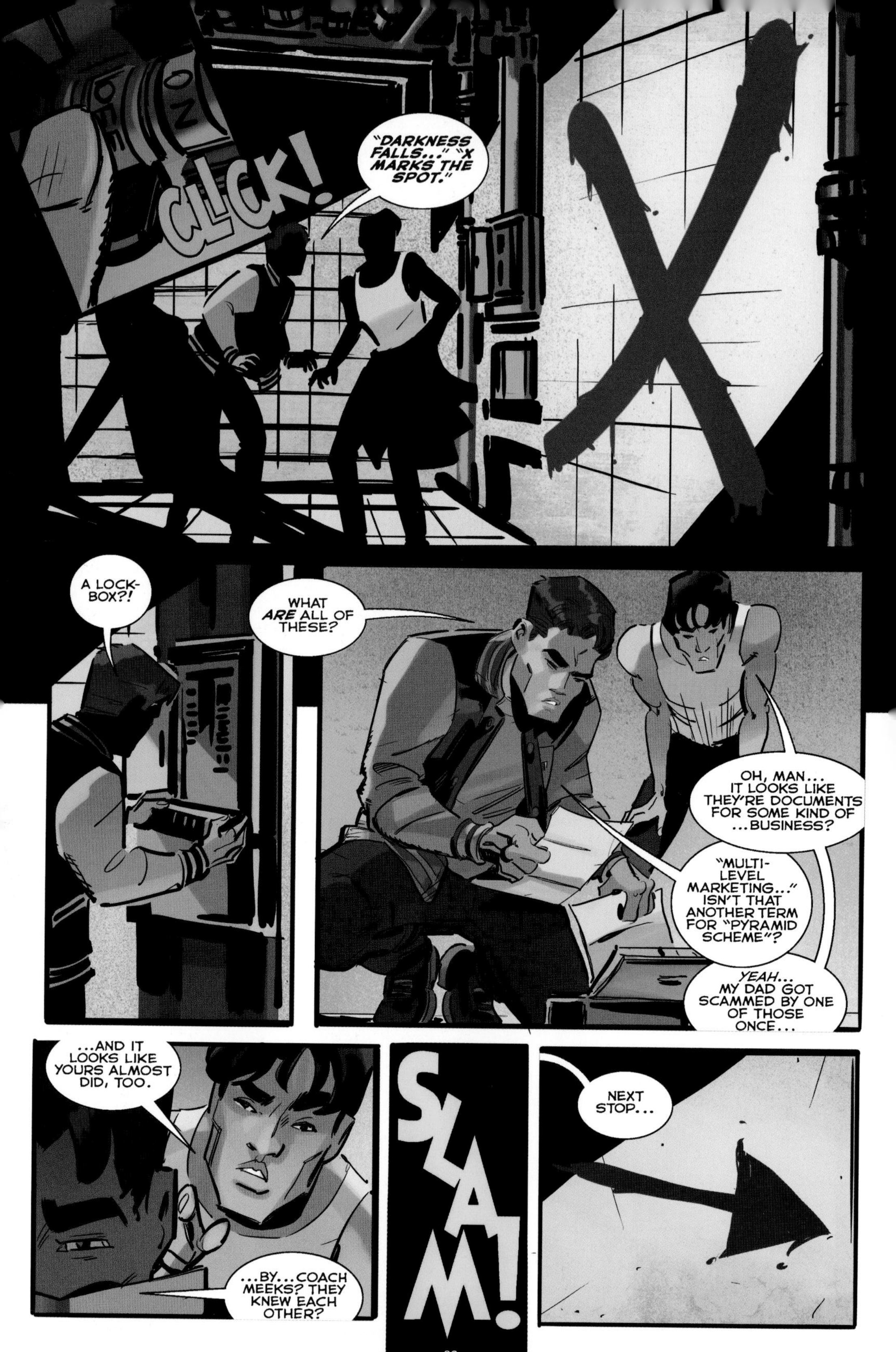
ON
OFF
CLICK!
"DARKNESS FALLS..." "X MARKS THE SPOT."
A LOCK-BOX?!
WHAT *ARE* ALL OF THESE?
OH, MAN... IT LOOKS LIKE THEY'RE DOCUMENTS FOR SOME KIND OF ...BUSINESS?
"MULTI-LEVEL MARKETING..." ISN'T THAT ANOTHER TERM FOR "PYRAMID SCHEME"?
YEAH... MY DAD GOT SCAMMED BY ONE OF THOSE ONCE...
...AND IT LOOKS LIKE YOURS ALMOST DID, TOO.
...BY...COACH MEEKS? THEY KNEW EACH OTHER?
SLAM!
NEXT STOP...

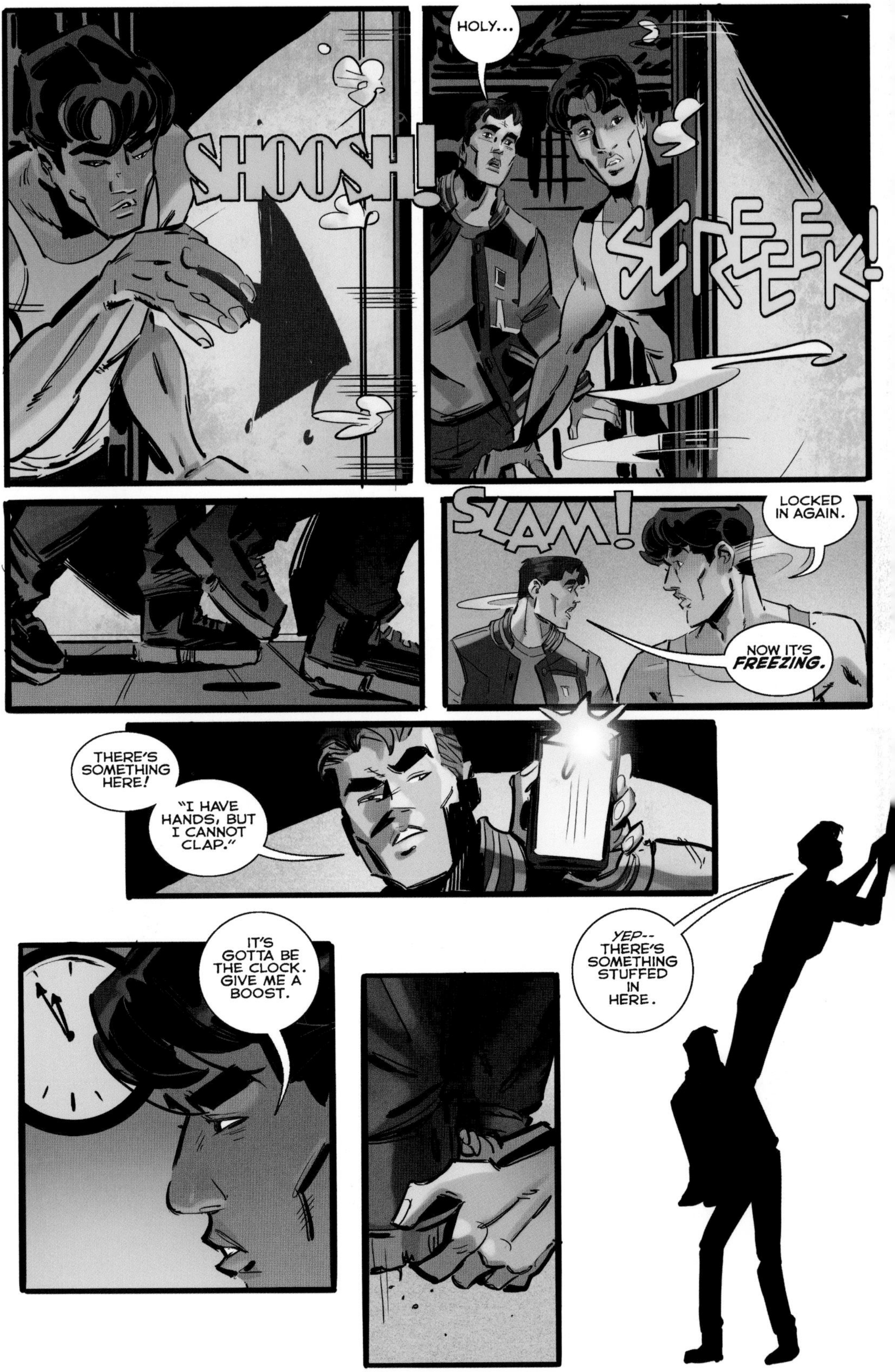
SHOOSH!
HOLY...
SCREEEK!
SLAM!
LOCKED IN AGAIN.
NOW IT'S *FREEZING.*
THERE'S SOMETHING HERE!
"I HAVE HANDS, BUT I CANNOT CLAP."
IT'S GOTTA BE THE CLOCK. GIVE ME A BOOST.
YEP-- THERE'S SOMETHING STUFFED IN HERE.

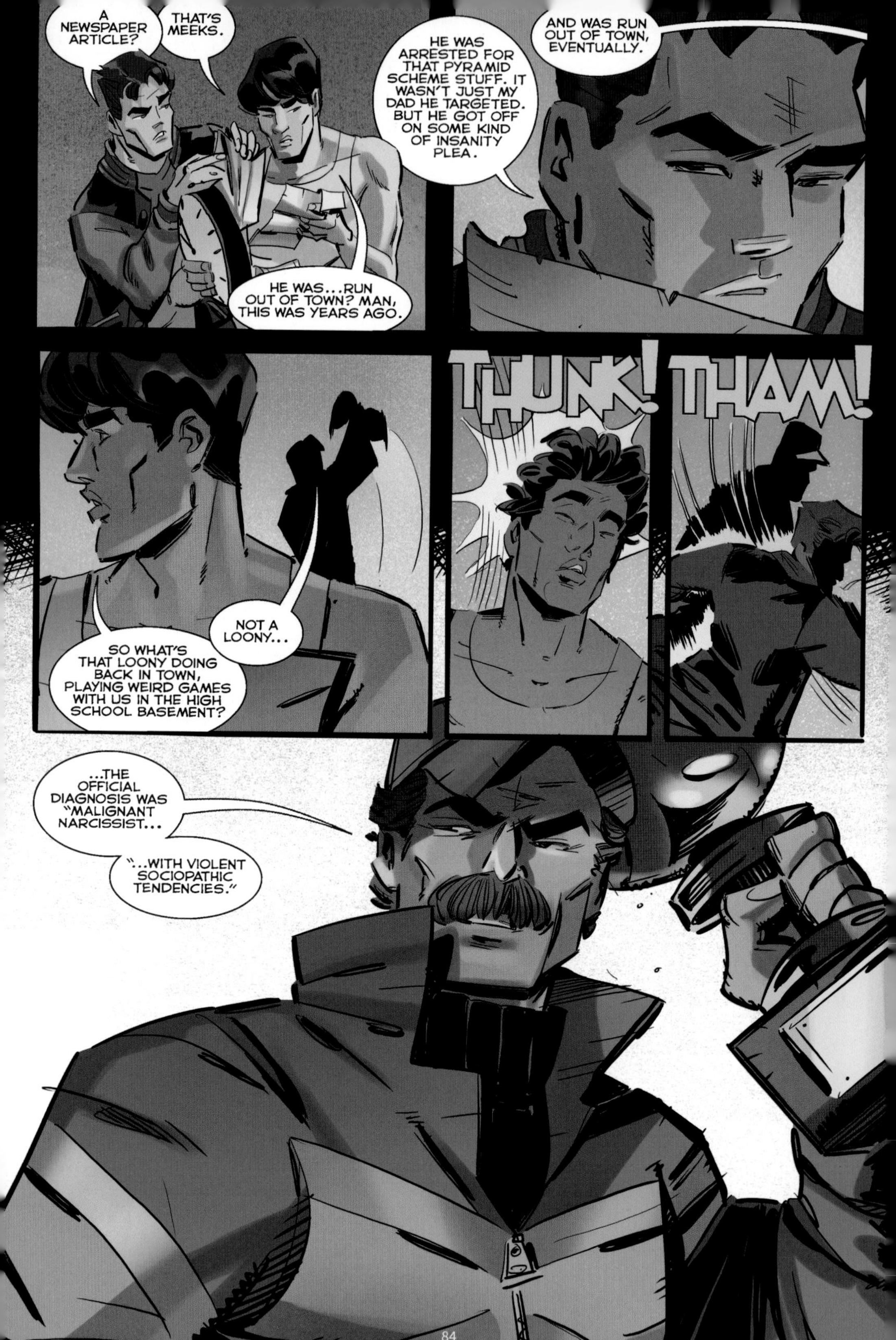
A NEWSPAPER ARTICLE?
THAT'S MEEKS.
HE WAS...RUN OUT OF TOWN? MAN, THIS WAS YEARS AGO.
HE WAS ARRESTED FOR THAT PYRAMID SCHEME STUFF. IT WASN'T JUST MY DAD HE TARGETED. BUT HE GOT OFF ON SOME KIND OF INSANITY PLEA.
AND WAS RUN OUT OF TOWN, EVENTUALLY.
SO WHAT'S THAT LOONY DOING BACK IN TOWN, PLAYING WEIRD GAMES WITH US IN THE HIGH SCHOOL BASEMENT?
NOT A LOONY...
THUNK!
THAM!
...THE OFFICIAL DIAGNOSIS WAS "MALIGNANT NARCISSIST...
"...WITH VIOLENT SOCIOPATHIC TENDENCIES."

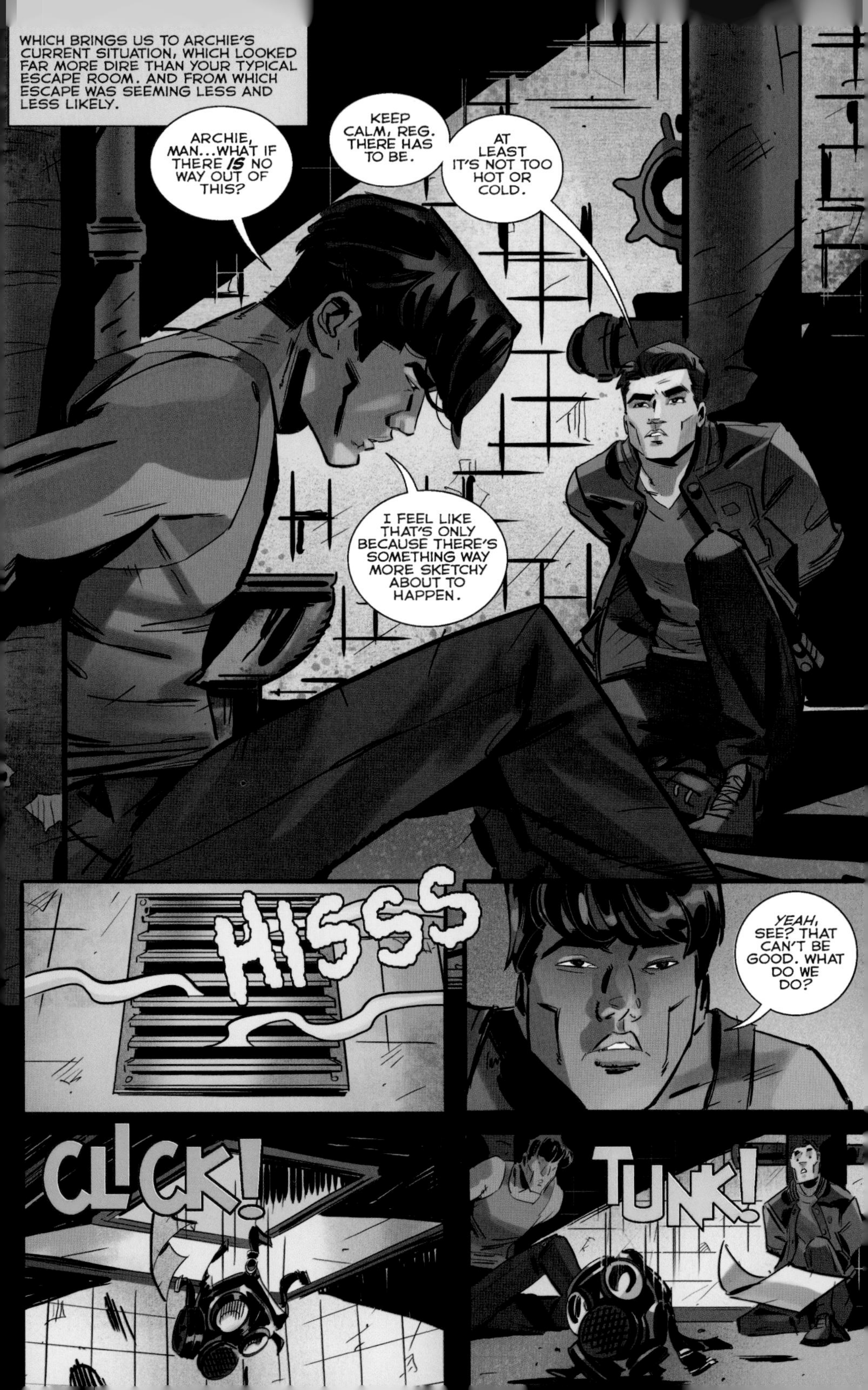
WHICH BRINGS US TO ARCHIE'S CURRENT SITUATION, WHICH LOOKED FAR MORE DIRE THAN YOUR TYPICAL ESCAPE ROOM. AND FROM WHICH ESCAPE WAS SEEMING LESS AND LESS LIKELY.
ARCHIE, MAN...WHAT IF THERE *IS* NO WAY OUT OF THIS?
KEEP CALM, REG. THERE HAS TO BE.
AT LEAST IT'S NOT TOO HOT OR COLD.
I FEEL LIKE THAT'S ONLY BECAUSE THERE'S SOMETHING WAY MORE SKETCHY ABOUT TO HAPPEN.
HISSS
YEAH, SEE? THAT CAN'T BE GOOD. WHAT DO WE DO?
CLICK!
TUNK!

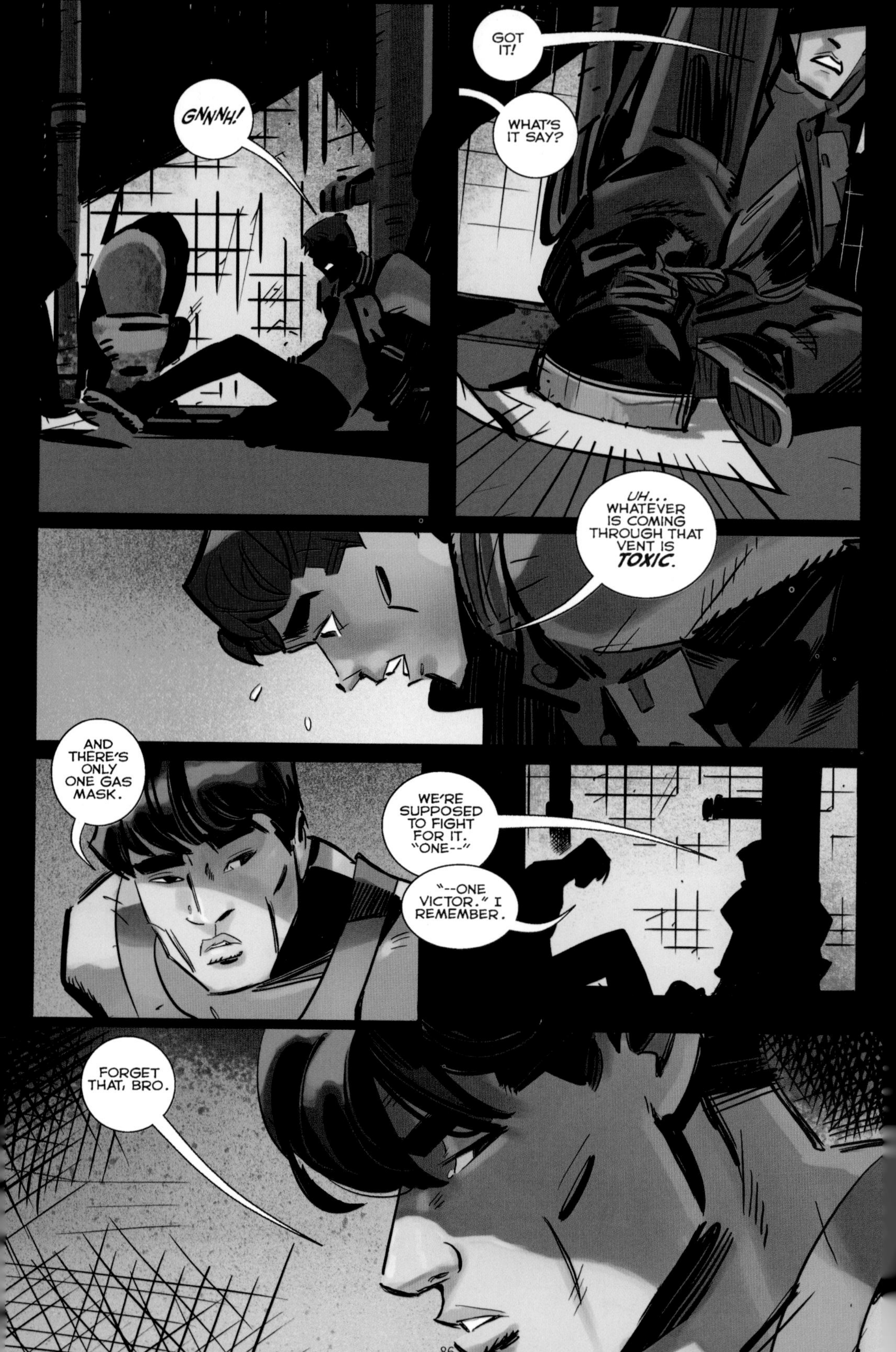
GNNNH!
GOT IT!
WHAT'S IT SAY?
UH... WHATEVER IS COMING THROUGH THAT VENT IS TOXIC.
AND THERE'S ONLY ONE GAS MASK.
WE'RE SUPPOSED TO FIGHT FOR IT. "ONE--"
"--ONE VICTOR." I REMEMBER.
FORGET THAT, BRO.

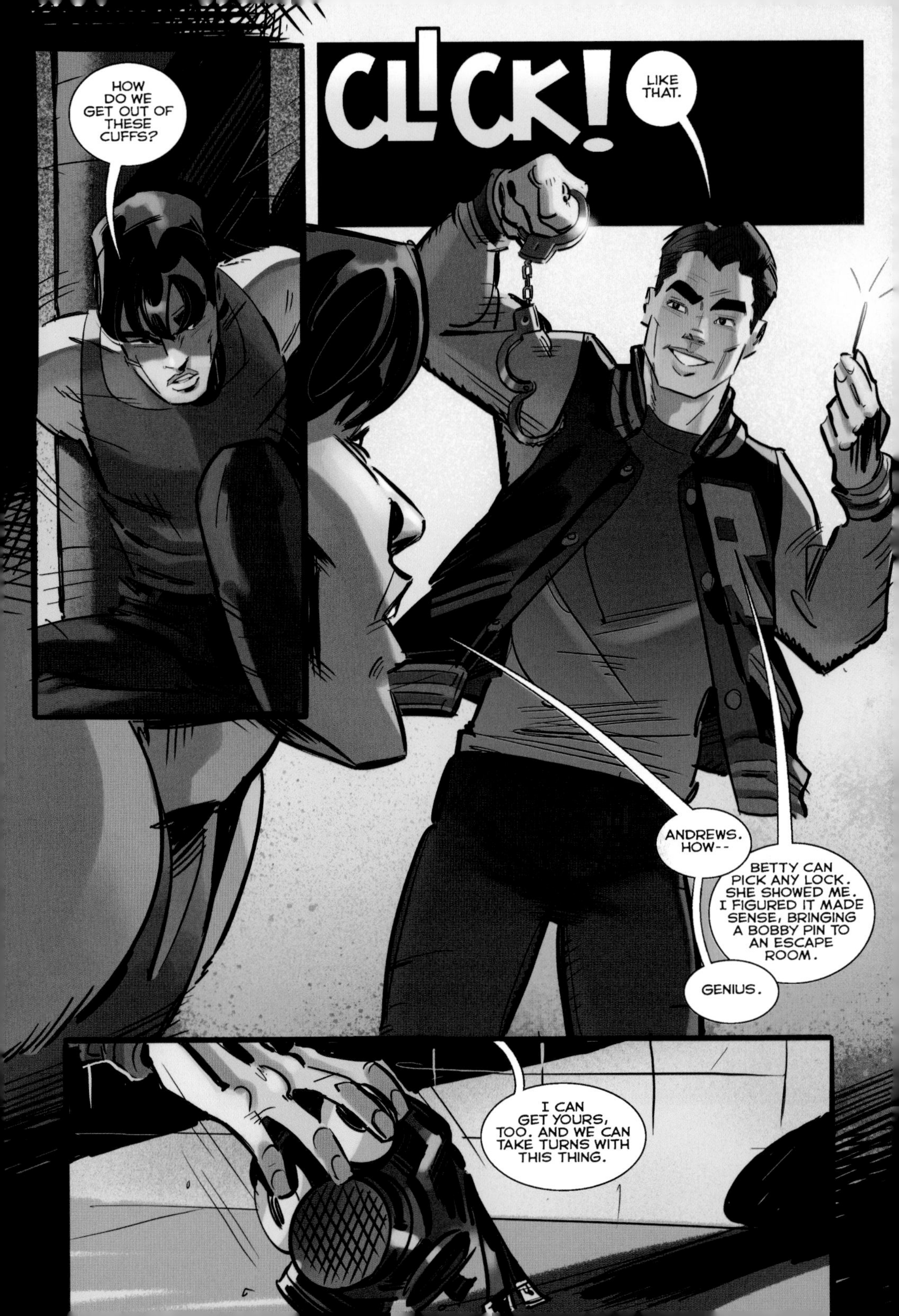
HOW DO WE GET OUT OF THESE CUFFS?
CLICK!
LIKE THAT.
ANDREWS. HOW--
BETTY CAN PICK ANY LOCK. SHE SHOWED ME. I FIGURED IT MADE SENSE, BRINGING A BOBBY PIN TO AN ESCAPE ROOM.
GENIUS.
I CAN GET YOURS, TOO. AND WE CAN TAKE TURNS WITH THIS THING.

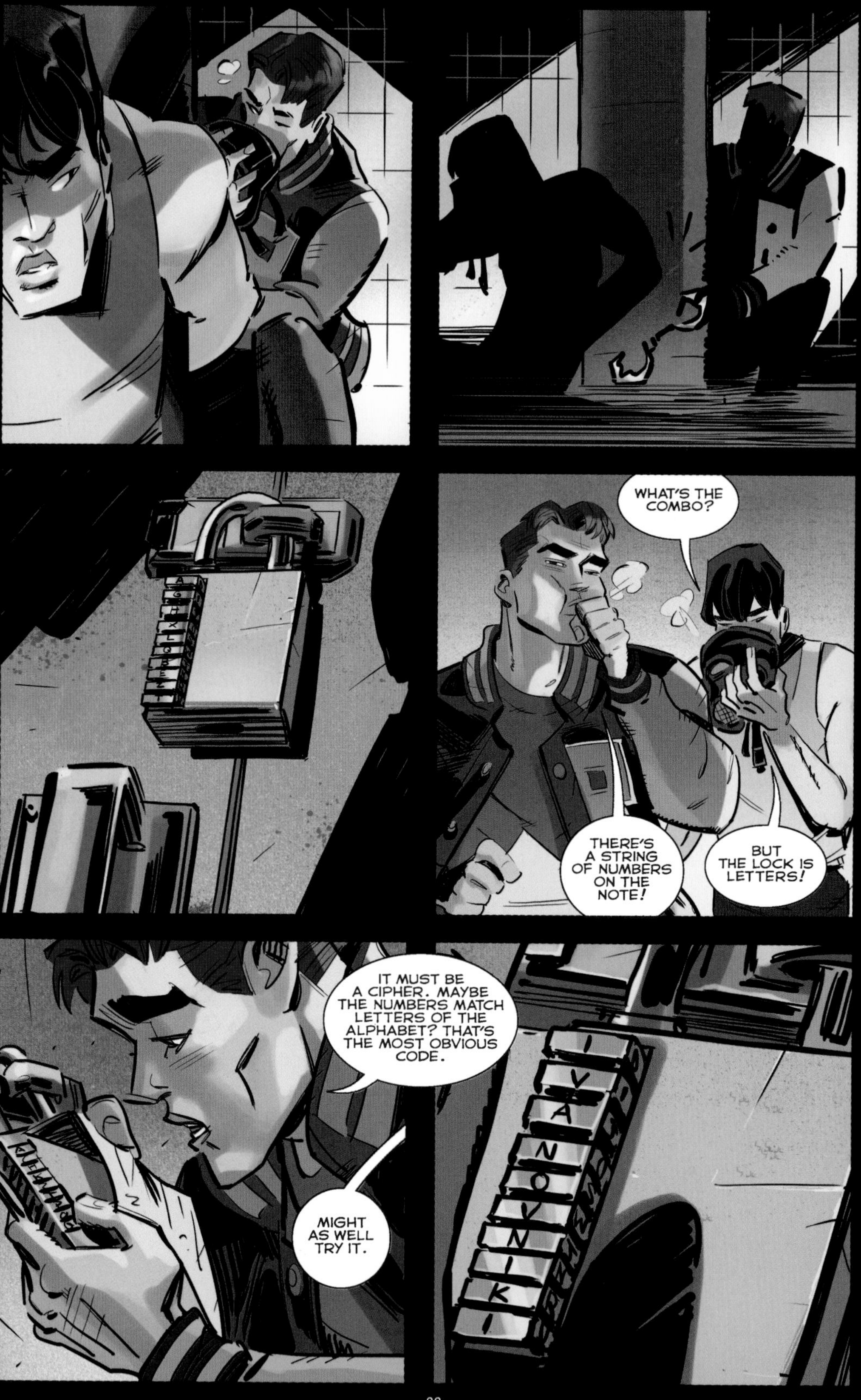
WHAT'S THE COMBO?
THERE'S A STRING OF NUMBERS ON THE NOTE!
BUT THE LOCK IS LETTERS!
IT MUST BE A CIPHER. MAYBE THE NUMBERS MATCH LETTERS OF THE ALPHABET? THAT'S THE MOST OBVIOUS CODE.
MIGHT AS WELL TRY IT.
I
V
A
N
O
V
N
I
K
I

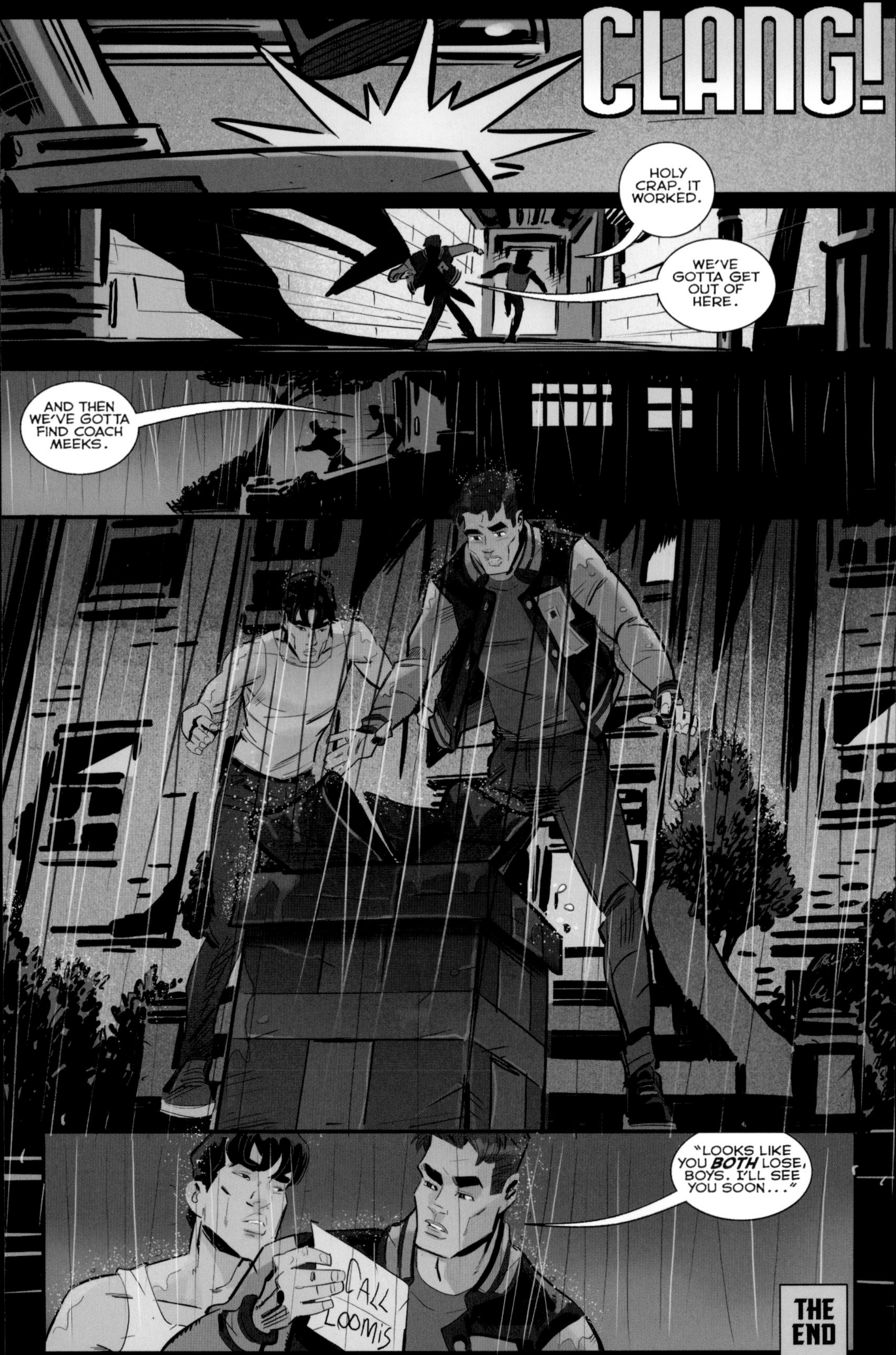
CLANG!
HOLY CRAP. IT WORKED.
WE'VE GOTTA GET OUT OF HERE.
AND THEN WE'VE GOTTA FIND COACH MEEKS.
"LOOKS LIKE YOU **BOTH** LOSE, BOYS. I'LL SEE YOU SOON..."
CALL LOOMIS
THE END

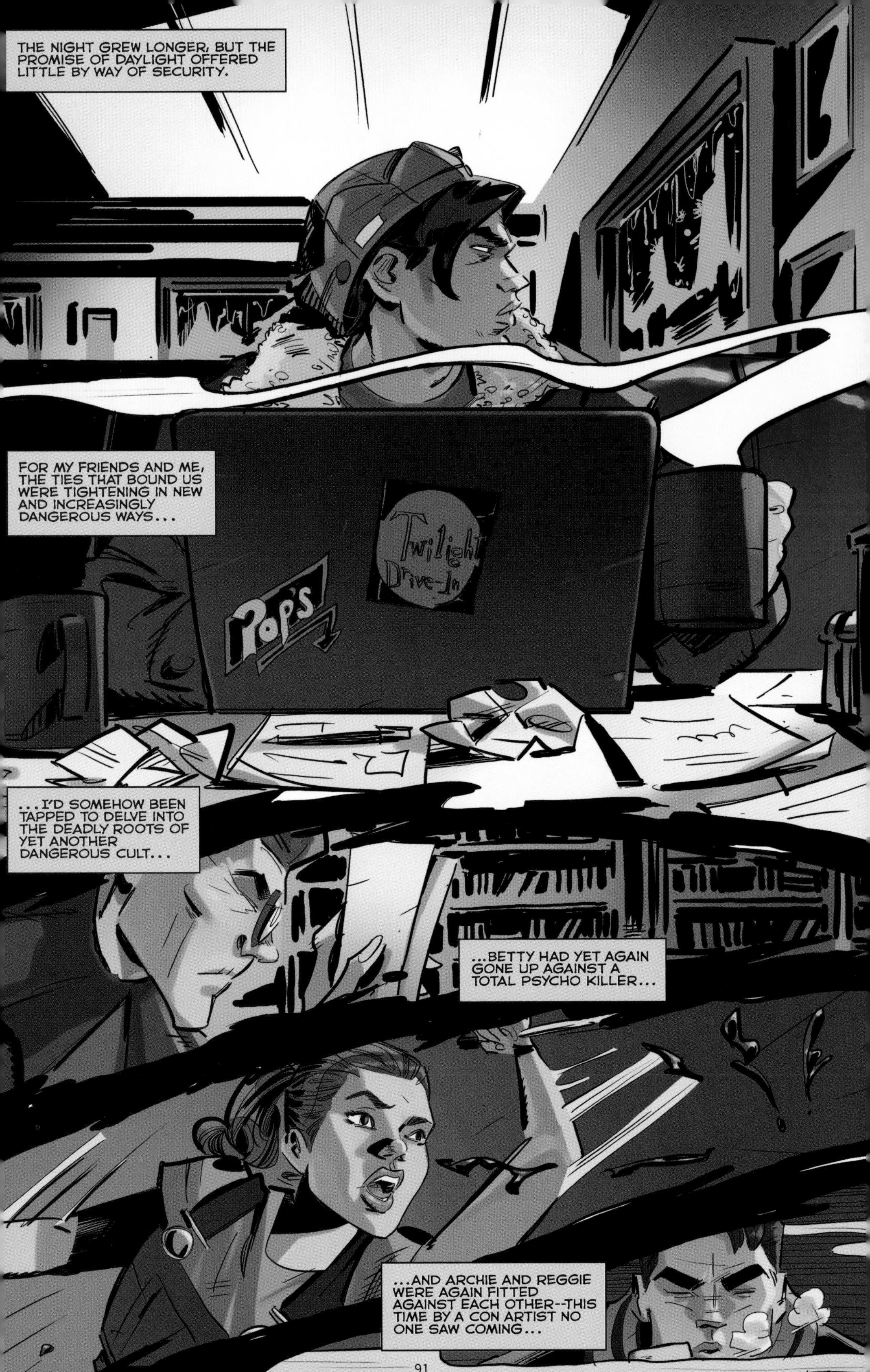
THE NIGHT GREW LONGER, BUT THE PROMISE OF DAYLIGHT OFFERED LITTLE BY WAY OF SECURITY.
FOR MY FRIENDS AND ME, THE TIES THAT BOUND US WERE TIGHTENING IN NEW AND INCREASINGLY DANGEROUS WAYS...
Twilight Drive-In
Pop's
...I'D SOMEHOW BEEN TAPPED TO DELVE INTO THE DEADLY ROOTS OF YET ANOTHER DANGEROUS CULT...
...BETTY HAD YET AGAIN GONE UP AGAINST A TOTAL PSYCHO KILLER...
...AND ARCHIE AND REGGIE WERE AGAIN FITTED AGAINST EACH OTHER--THIS TIME BY A CON ARTIST NO ONE SAW COMING...

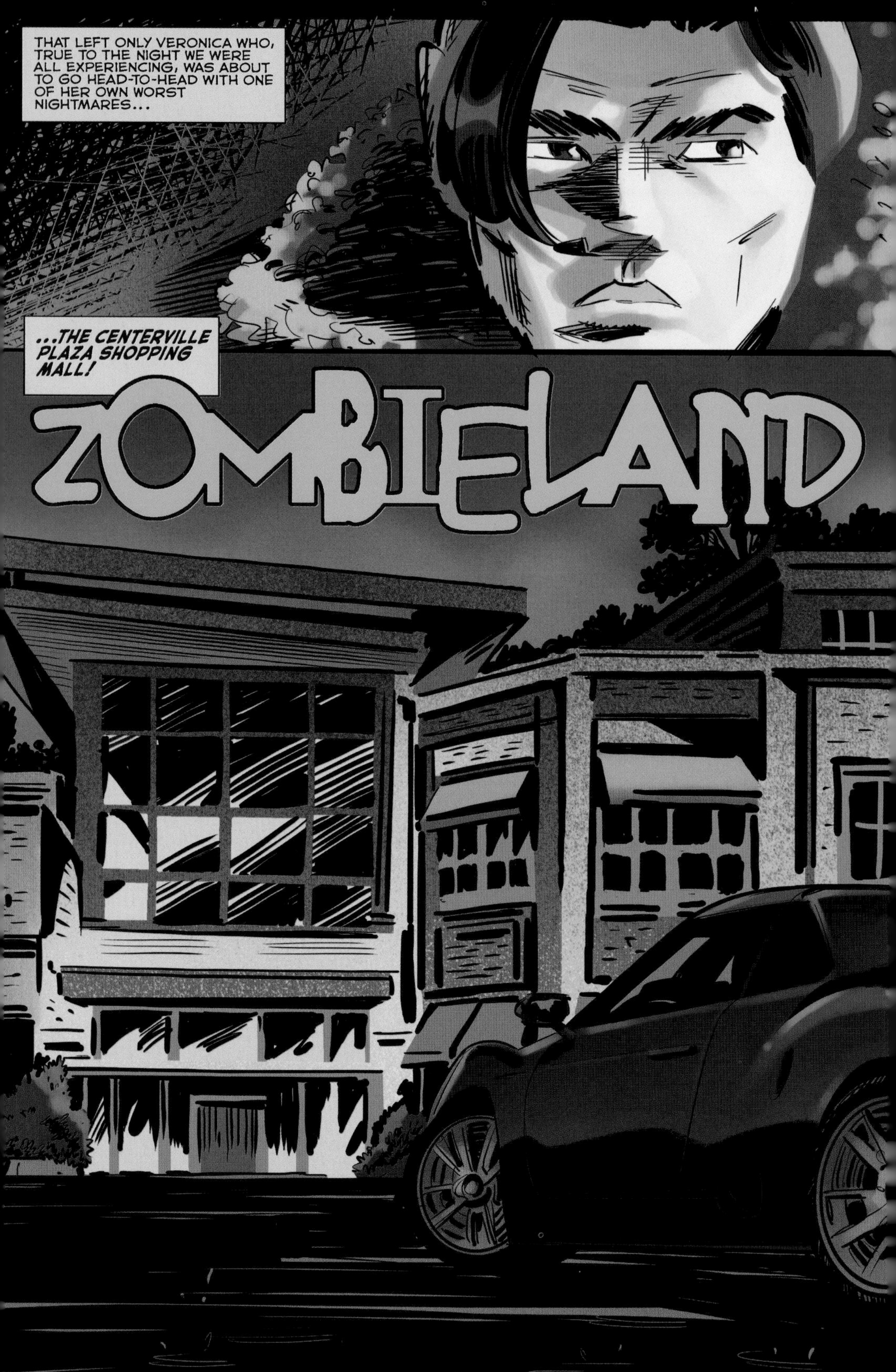
THAT LEFT ONLY VERONICA WHO, TRUE TO THE NIGHT WE WERE ALL EXPERIENCING, WAS ABOUT TO GO HEAD-TO-HEAD WITH ONE OF HER OWN WORST NIGHTMARES...
...THE CENTERVILLE PLAZA SHOPPING MALL!
ZOMBIELAND

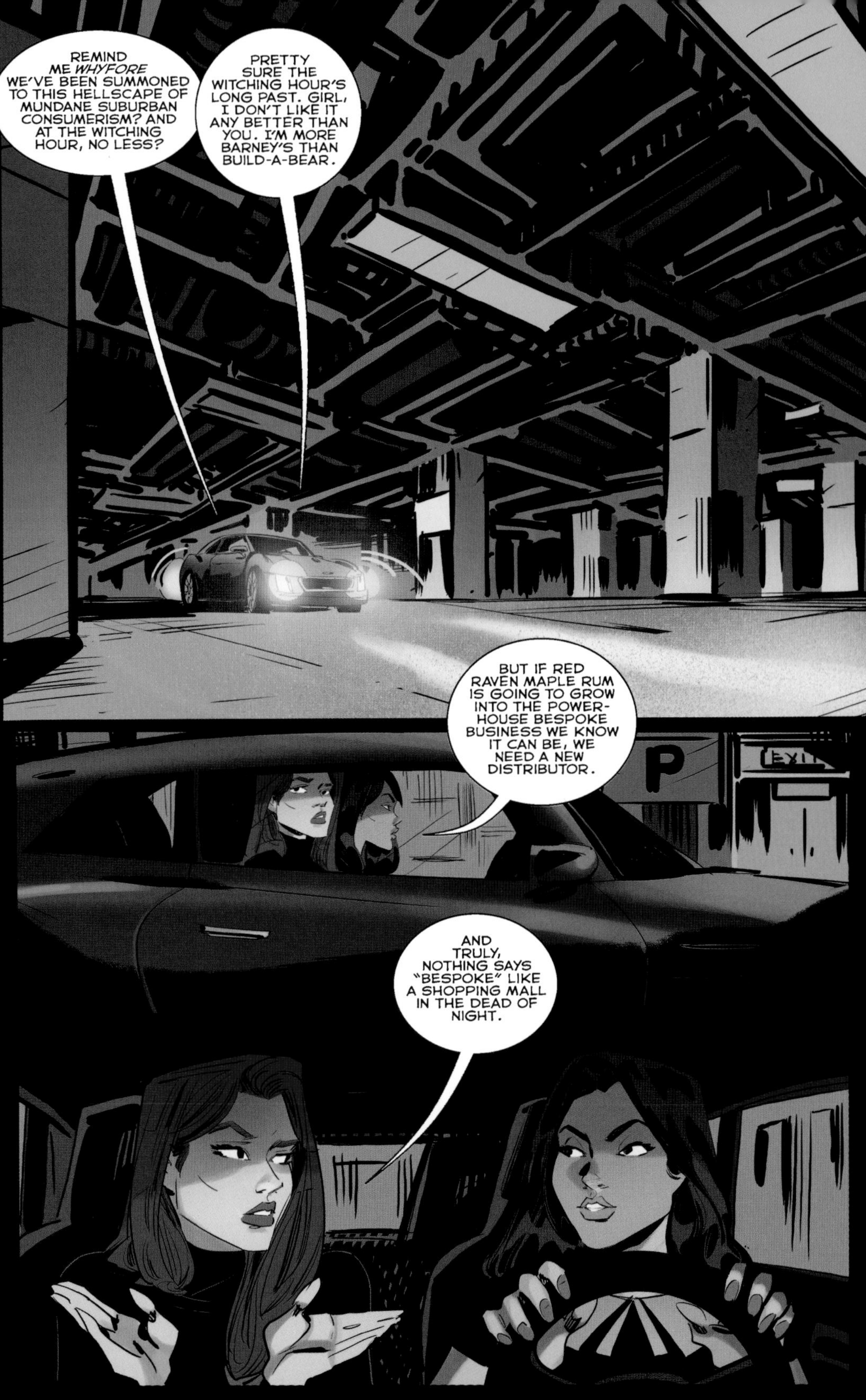
REMIND ME *WHYFORE* WE'VE BEEN SUMMONED TO THIS HELLSCAPE OF MUNDANE SUBURBAN CONSUMERISM? AND AT THE WITCHING HOUR, NO LESS?
PRETTY SURE THE WITCHING HOUR'S LONG PAST. GIRL, I DON'T LIKE IT ANY BETTER THAN YOU. I'M MORE BARNEY'S THAN BUILD-A-BEAR.
BUT IF RED RAVEN MAPLE RUM IS GOING TO GROW INTO THE POWER-HOUSE BESPOKE BUSINESS WE KNOW IT CAN BE, WE NEED A NEW DISTRIBUTOR.
P
AND TRULY, NOTHING SAYS "BESPOKE" LIKE A SHOPPING MALL IN THE DEAD OF NIGHT.

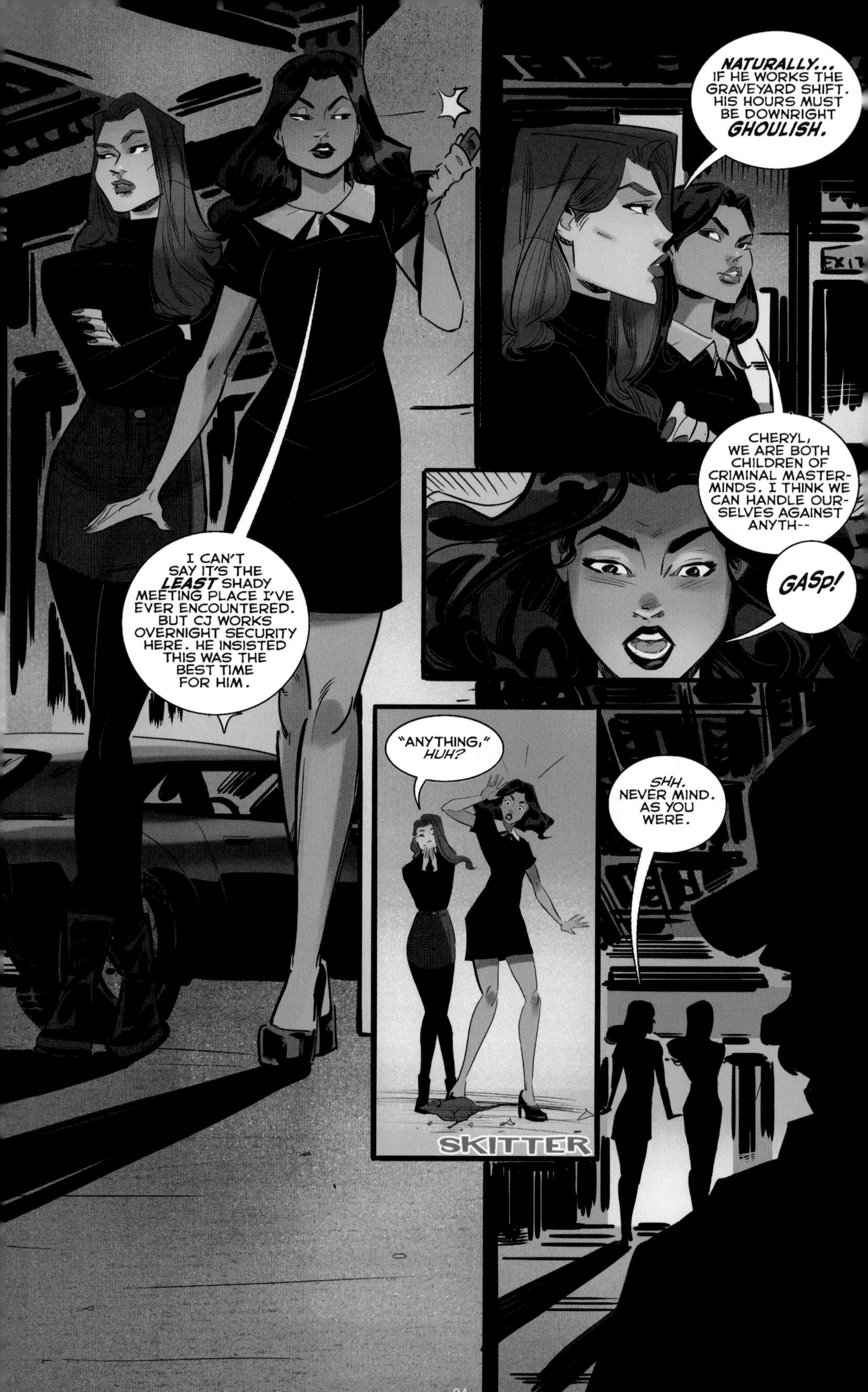

I CAN'T SAY IT'S THE LEAST SHADY MEETING PLACE I'VE EVER ENCOUNTERED. BUT CJ WORKS OVERNIGHT SECURITY HERE. HE INSISTED THIS WAS THE BEST TIME FOR HIM.
NATURALLY... IF HE WORKS THE GRAVEYARD SHIFT. HIS HOURS MUST BE DOWNRIGHT GHOULISH.
EXIT
CHERYL, WE ARE BOTH CHILDREN OF CRIMINAL MASTER-MINDS. I THINK WE CAN HANDLE OUR-SELVES AGAINST ANYTH--
GASp!
"ANYTHING," HUH?
SKITTER
SHH. NEVER MIND. AS YOU WERE.

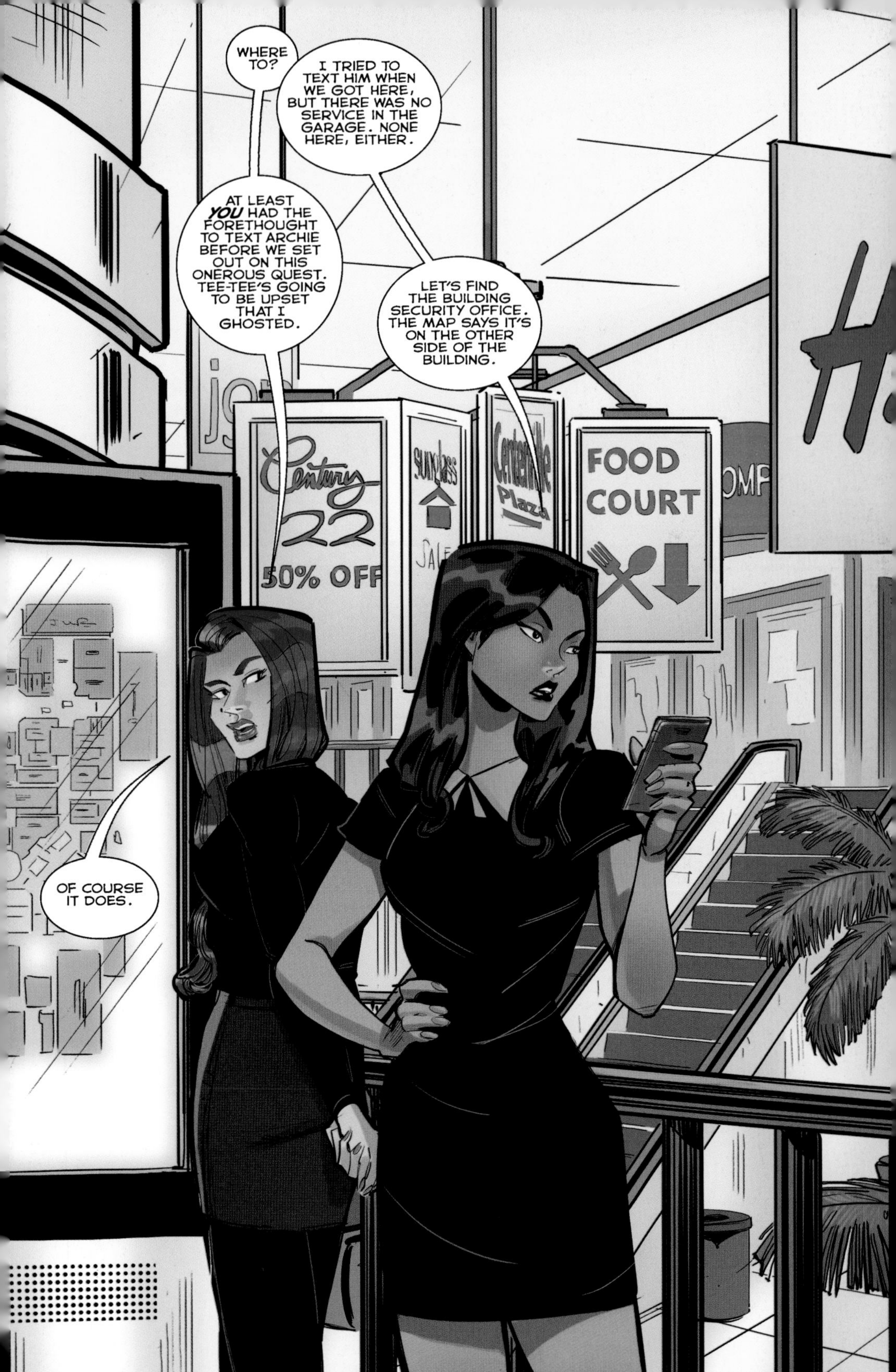
WHERE TO?
I TRIED TO TEXT HIM WHEN WE GOT HERE, BUT THERE WAS NO SERVICE IN THE GARAGE. NONE HERE, EITHER.
AT LEAST YOU HAD THE FORETHOUGHT TO TEXT ARCHIE BEFORE WE SET OUT ON THIS ONEROUS QUEST. TEE-TEE'S GOING TO BE UPSET THAT I GHOSTED.
LET'S FIND THE BUILDING SECURITY OFFICE. THE MAP SAYS IT'S ON THE OTHER SIDE OF THE BUILDING.
OF COURSE IT DOES.
Century 22
50% OFF
Centerville Plaza
FOOD COURT

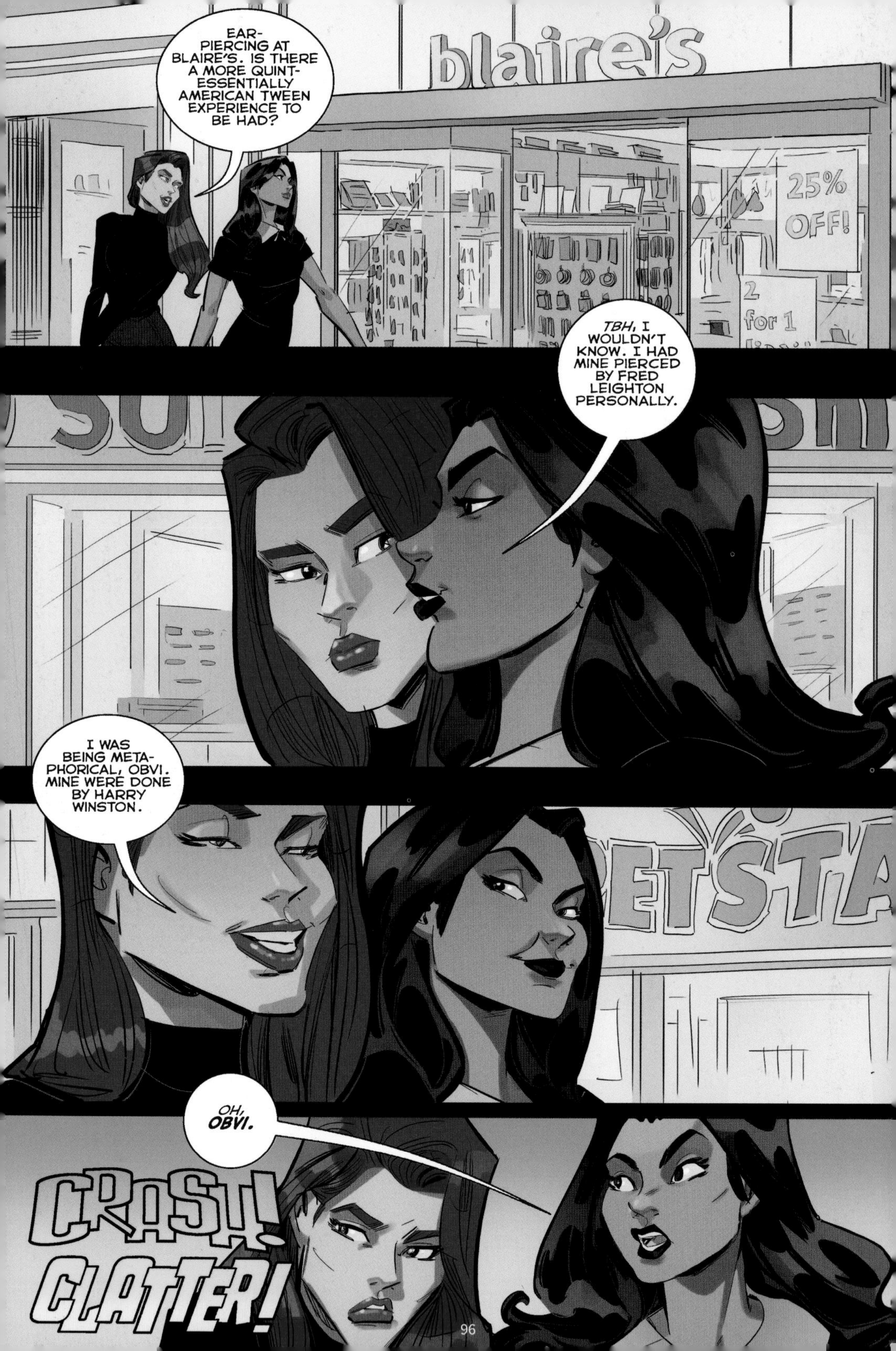
blaire's
EAR-PIERCING AT BLAIRE'S. IS THERE A MORE QUINT-ESSENTIALLY AMERICAN TWEEN EXPERIENCE TO BE HAD?
25% OFF!
2 for 1
TBH, I WOULDN'T KNOW. I HAD MINE PIERCED BY FRED LEIGHTON PERSONALLY.
I WAS BEING META-PHORICAL, OBVI. MINE WERE DONE BY HARRY WINSTON.
OH, ***OBVI.***
CRASH!
CLATTER!

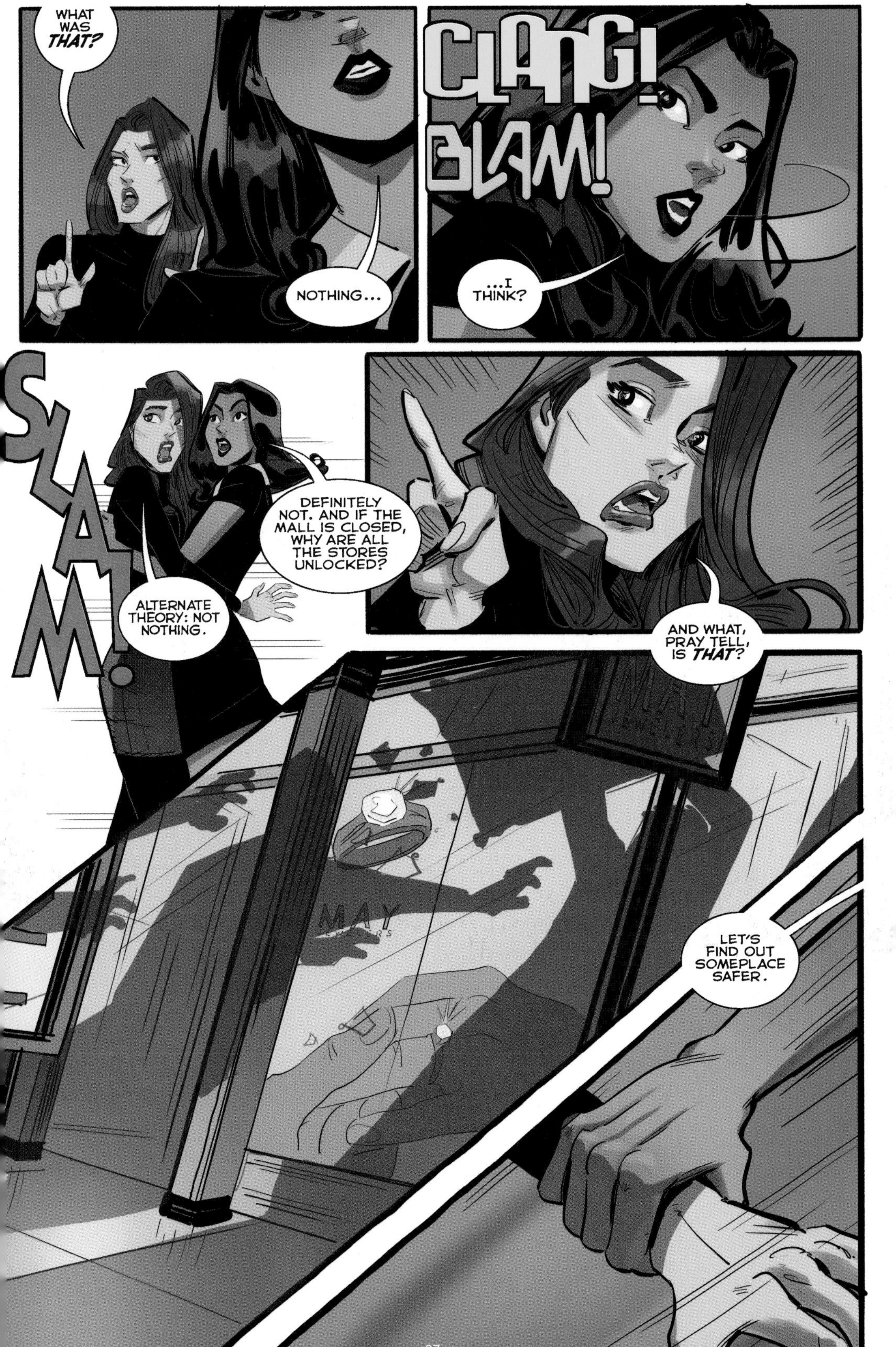
WHAT WAS THAT?
NOTHING...
CLANG!
BLAM!
...I THINK?
SLAM!
ALTERNATE THEORY: NOT NOTHING.
DEFINITELY NOT. AND IF THE MALL IS CLOSED, WHY ARE ALL THE STORES UNLOCKED?
AND WHAT, PRAY TELL, IS THAT?
MAY
LET'S FIND OUT SOMEPLACE SAFER.

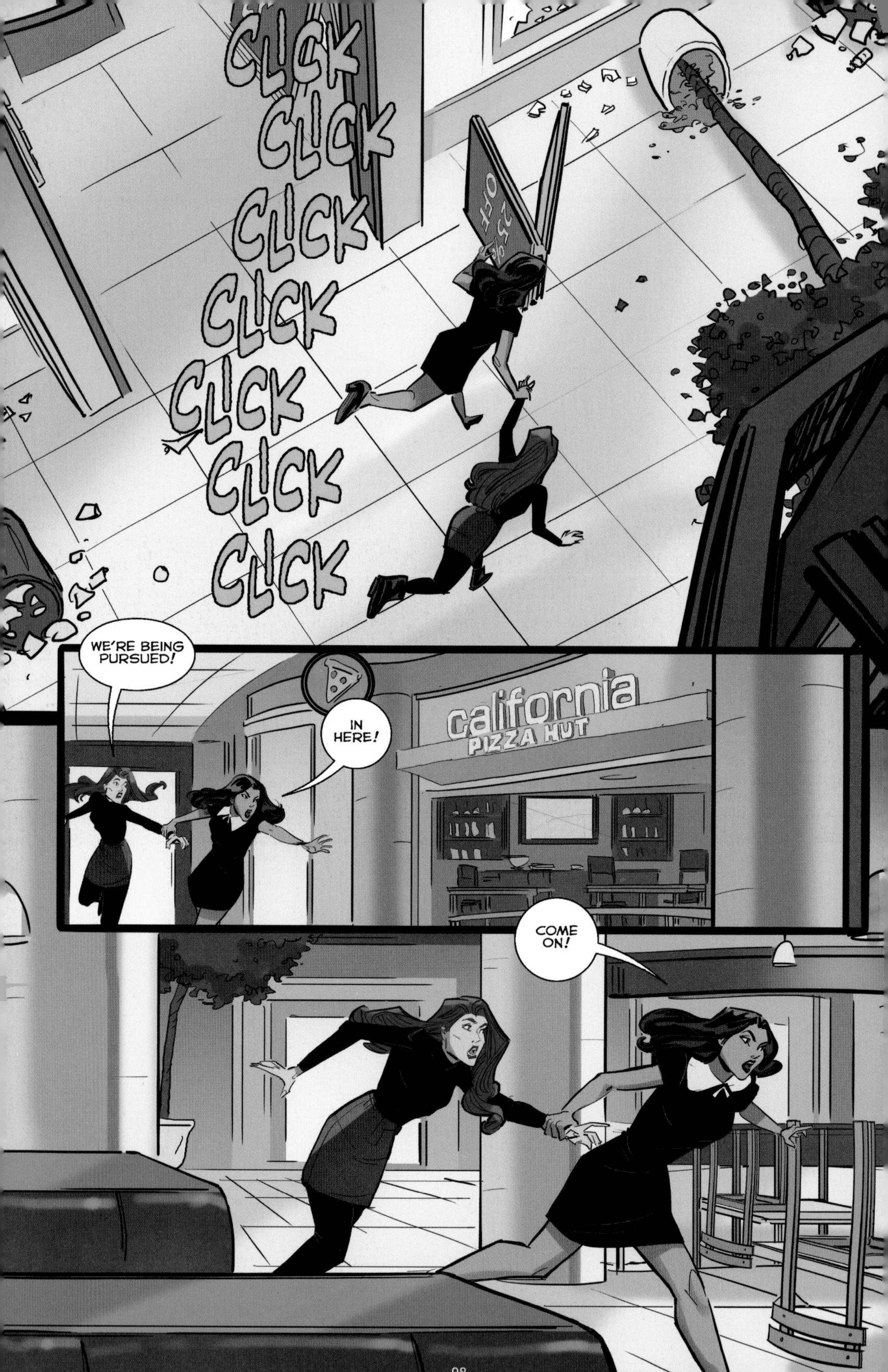
CLICK
CLICK
CLICK
CLICK
CLICK
CLICK
CLICK
25% OFF
WE'RE BEING PURSUED!
IN HERE!
california
PIZZA HUT
COME ON!

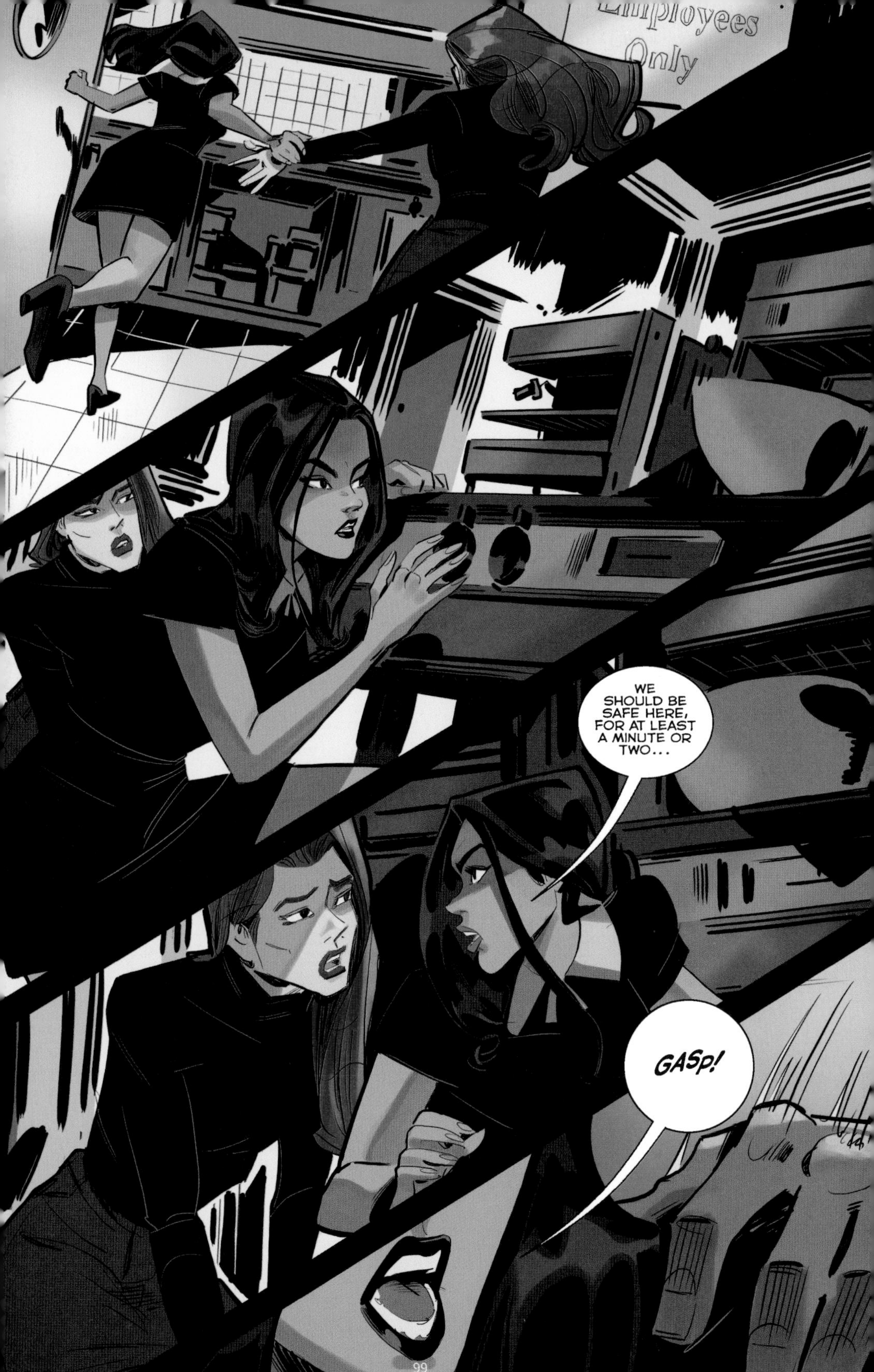
Employees Only
WE SHOULD BE SAFE HERE, FOR AT LEAST A MINUTE OR TWO...
GASp!

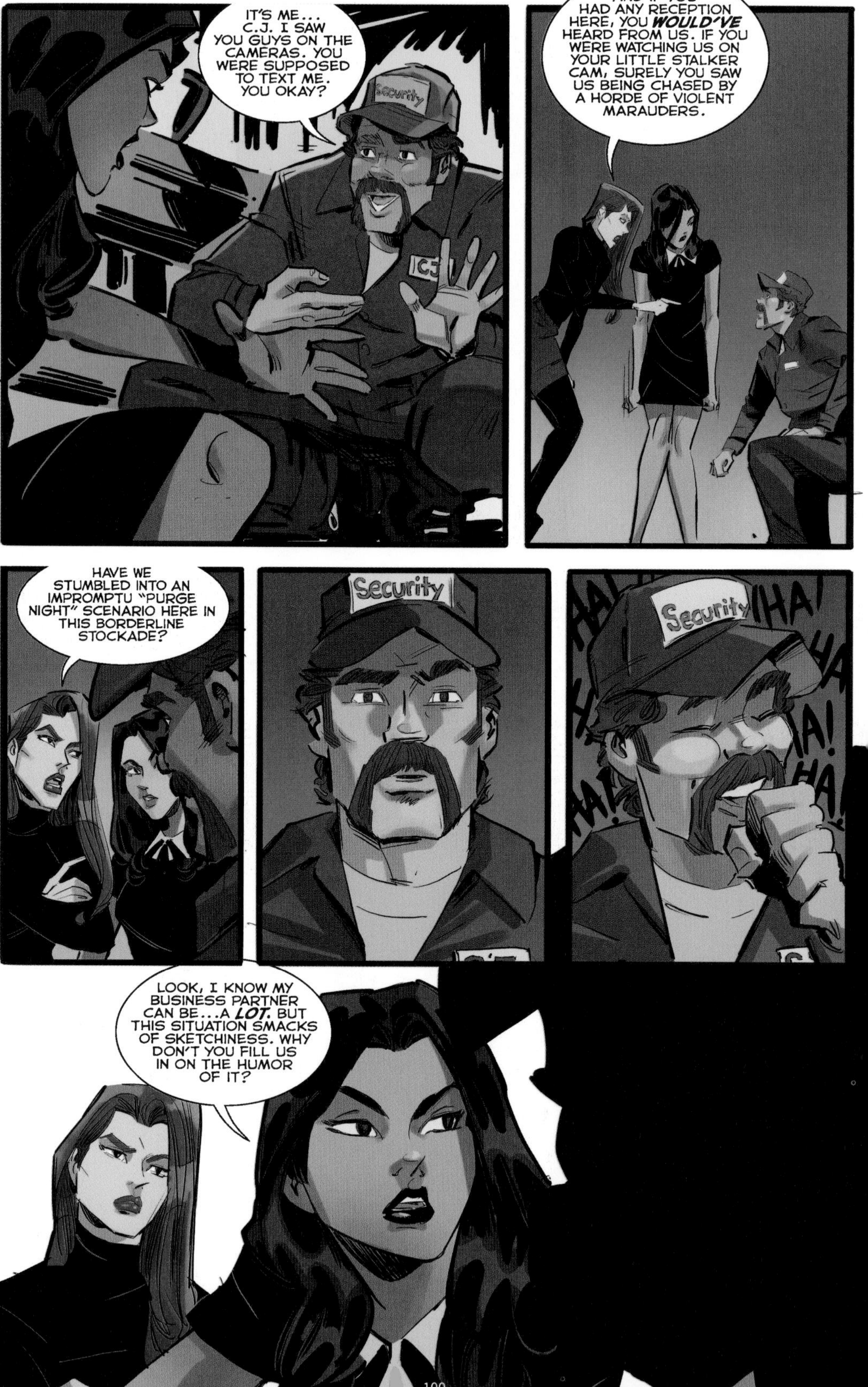
IT'S ME... C.J. I SAW YOU GUYS ON THE CAMERAS. YOU WERE SUPPOSED TO TEXT ME. YOU OKAY?
Security
AND IF YOU HAD ANY RECEPTION HERE, YOU ***WOULD'VE*** HEARD FROM US. IF YOU WERE WATCHING US ON YOUR LITTLE STALKER CAM, SURELY YOU SAW US BEING CHASED BY A HORDE OF VIOLENT MARAUDERS.
HAVE WE STUMBLED INTO AN IMPROMPTU "PURGE NIGHT" SCENARIO HERE IN THIS BORDERLINE STOCKADE?
Security
Security
HA! HA! HA! HA! HA! HA! HA!
LOOK, I KNOW MY BUSINESS PARTNER CAN BE...A ***LOT.*** BUT THIS SITUATION SMACKS OF SKETCHINESS. WHY DON'T YOU FILL US IN ON THE HUMOR OF IT?

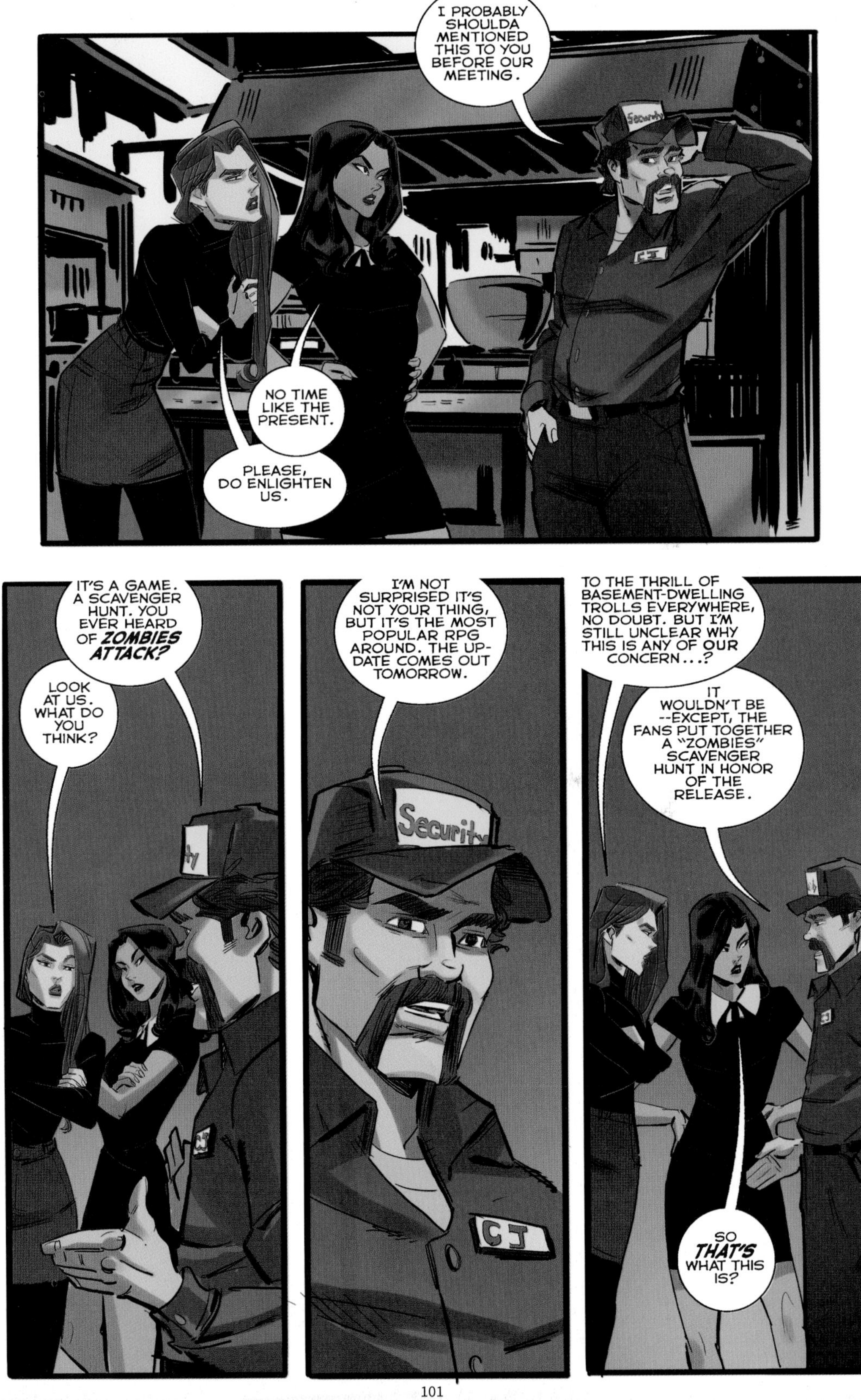
I PROBABLY SHOULDA MENTIONED THIS TO YOU BEFORE OUR MEETING.
Security
NO TIME LIKE THE PRESENT.
PLEASE, DO ENLIGHTEN US.
IT'S A GAME. A SCAVENGER HUNT. YOU EVER HEARD OF ***ZOMBIES ATTACK?***
LOOK AT US. WHAT DO YOU THINK?
I'M NOT SURPRISED IT'S NOT YOUR THING, BUT IT'S THE MOST POPULAR RPG AROUND. THE UPDATE COMES OUT TOMORROW.
Security
CJ
TO THE THRILL OF BASEMENT-DWELLING TROLLS EVERYWHERE, NO DOUBT. BUT I'M STILL UNCLEAR WHY THIS IS ANY OF **OUR** CONCERN...?
IT WOULDN'T BE --EXCEPT, THE FANS PUT TOGETHER A "ZOMBIES" SCAVENGER HUNT IN HONOR OF THE RELEASE.
SO ***THAT'S*** WHAT THIS IS?

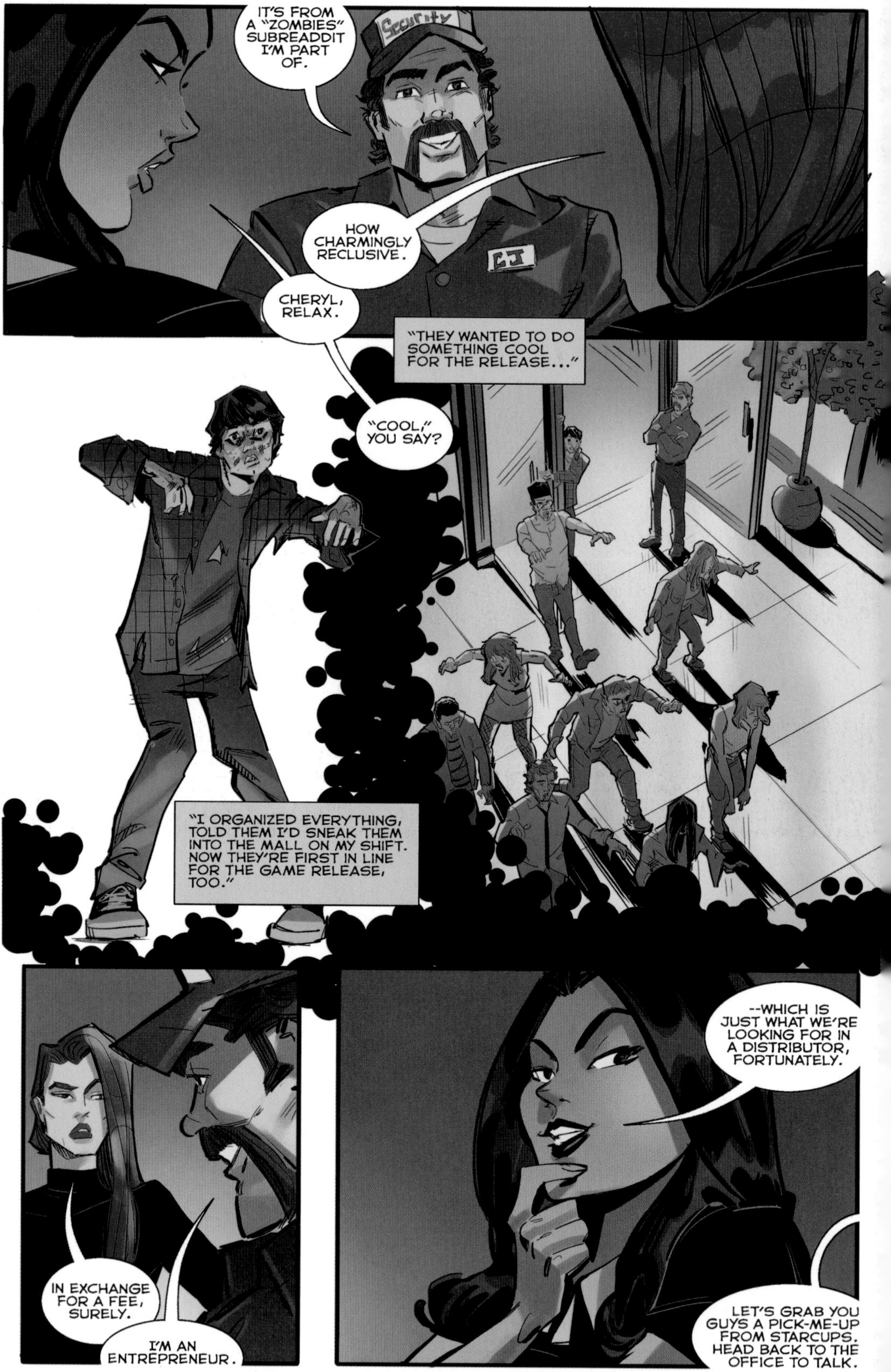
IT'S FROM A "ZOMBIES" SUBREADDIT I'M PART OF.
HOW CHARMINGLY RECLUSIVE.
CHERYL, RELAX.
"THEY WANTED TO DO SOMETHING COOL FOR THE RELEASE..."
"COOL," YOU SAY?
"I ORGANIZED EVERYTHING, TOLD THEM I'D SNEAK THEM INTO THE MALL ON MY SHIFT. NOW THEY'RE FIRST IN LINE FOR THE GAME RELEASE, TOO."
IN EXCHANGE FOR A FEE, SURELY.
I'M AN ENTREPRENEUR.
--WHICH IS JUST WHAT WE'RE LOOKING FOR IN A DISTRIBUTOR, FORTUNATELY.
LET'S GRAB YOU GUYS A PICK-ME-UP FROM STARCUPS. HEAD BACK TO THE OFFICE TO TALK.

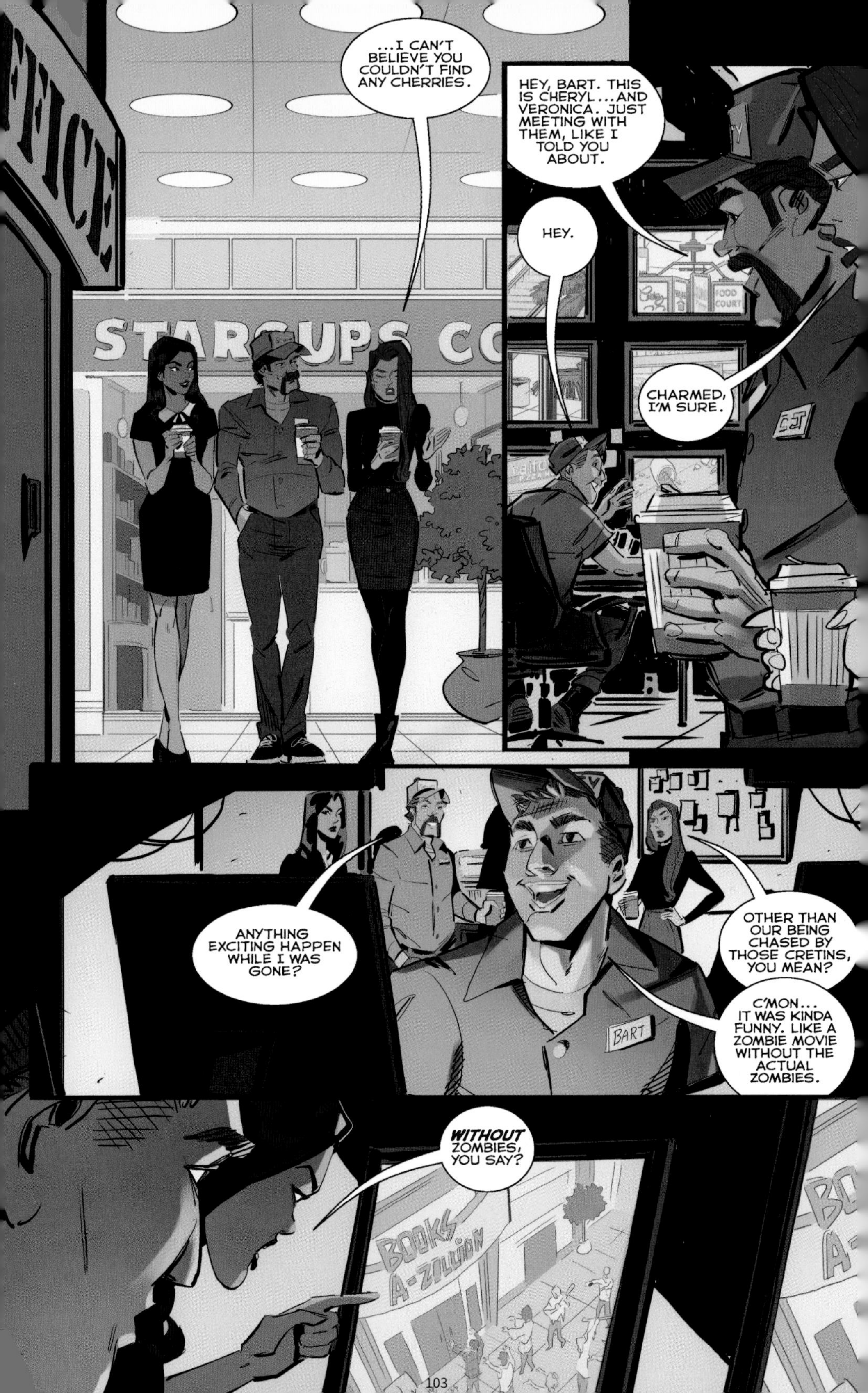

FFICE
STARCUPS CO
...I CAN'T BELIEVE YOU COULDN'T FIND ANY CHERRIES.
HEY, BART. THIS IS CHERYL...AND VERONICA. JUST MEETING WITH THEM, LIKE I TOLD YOU ABOUT.
HEY.
FOOD COURT
CHARMED, I'M SURE.
ANYTHING EXCITING HAPPEN WHILE I WAS GONE?
OTHER THAN OUR BEING CHASED BY THOSE CRETINS, YOU MEAN?
BART
C'MON... IT WAS KINDA FUNNY. LIKE A ZOMBIE MOVIE WITHOUT THE ACTUAL ZOMBIES.
WITHOUT ZOMBIES, YOU SAY?
BOOKS A-ZILLION

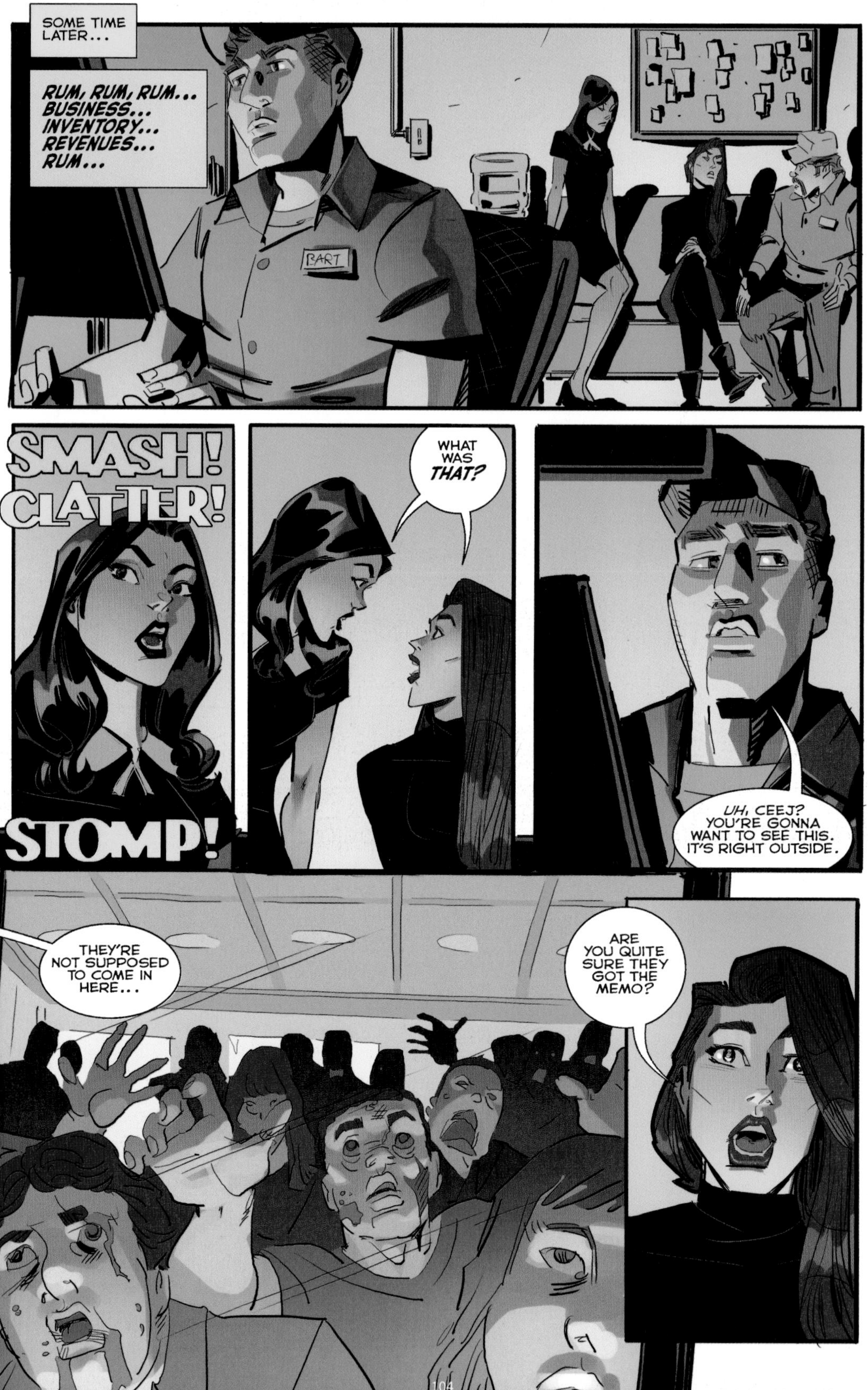
SOME TIME LATER...
RUM, RUM, RUM... BUSINESS... INVENTORY... REVENUES... RUM...
BART
SMASH! CLATTER!
STOMP!
WHAT WAS THAT?
UH, CEEJ? YOU'RE GONNA WANT TO SEE THIS. IT'S RIGHT OUTSIDE.
THEY'RE NOT SUPPOSED TO COME IN HERE...
ARE YOU QUITE SURE THEY GOT THE MEMO?

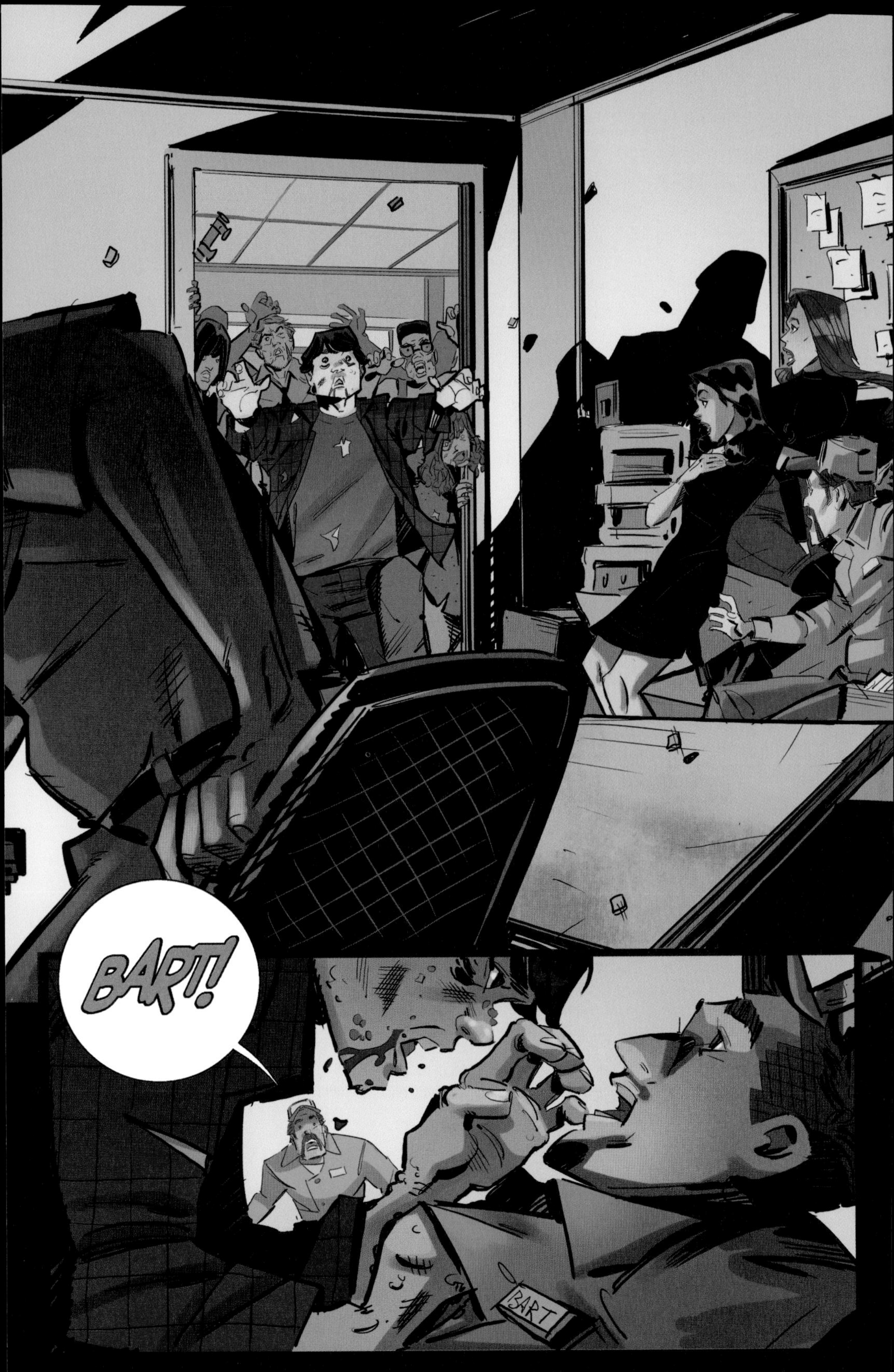
BART!
BART

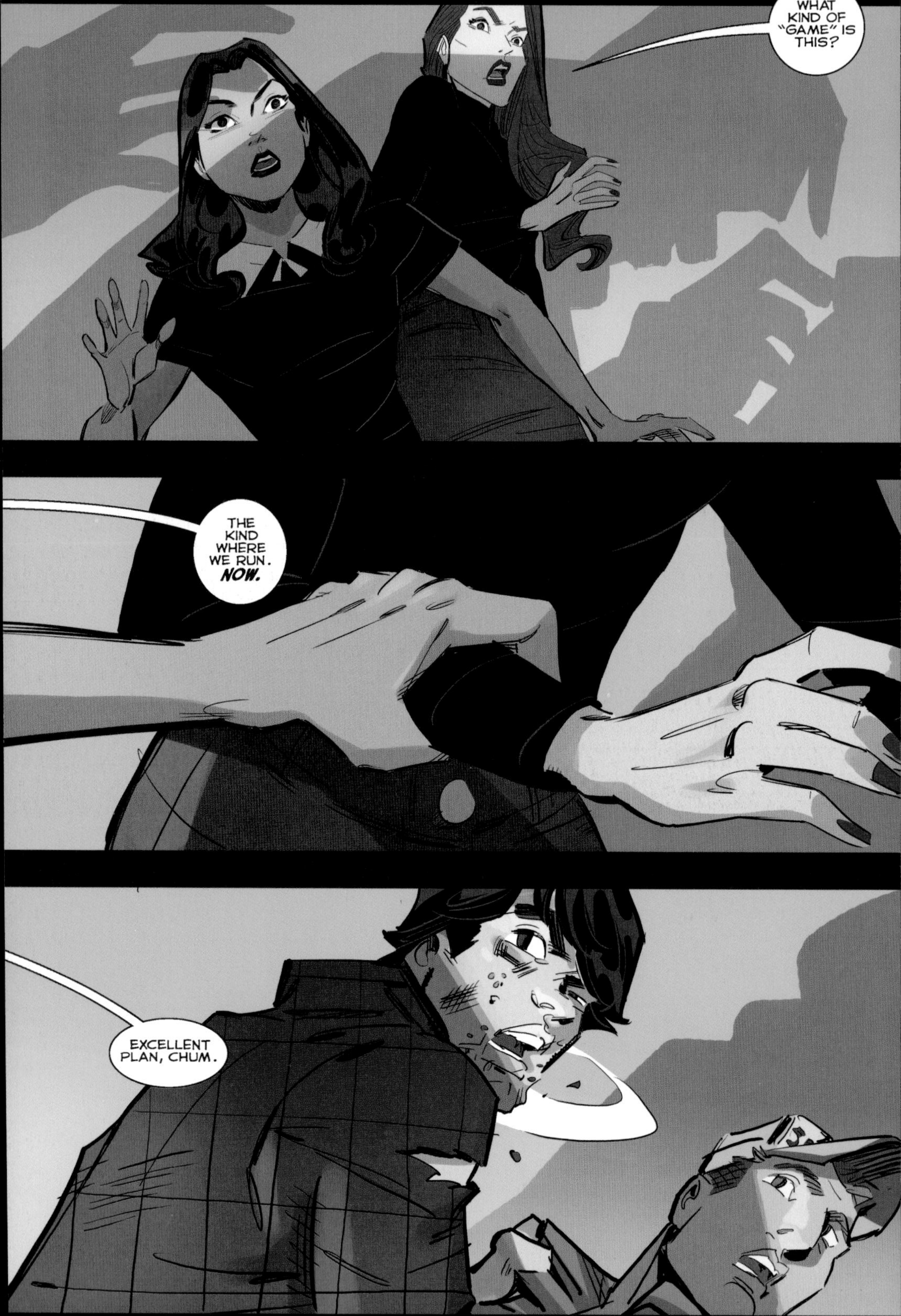
WHAT KIND OF "GAME" IS THIS?
THE KIND WHERE WE RUN. NOW.
EXCELLENT PLAN, CHUM.

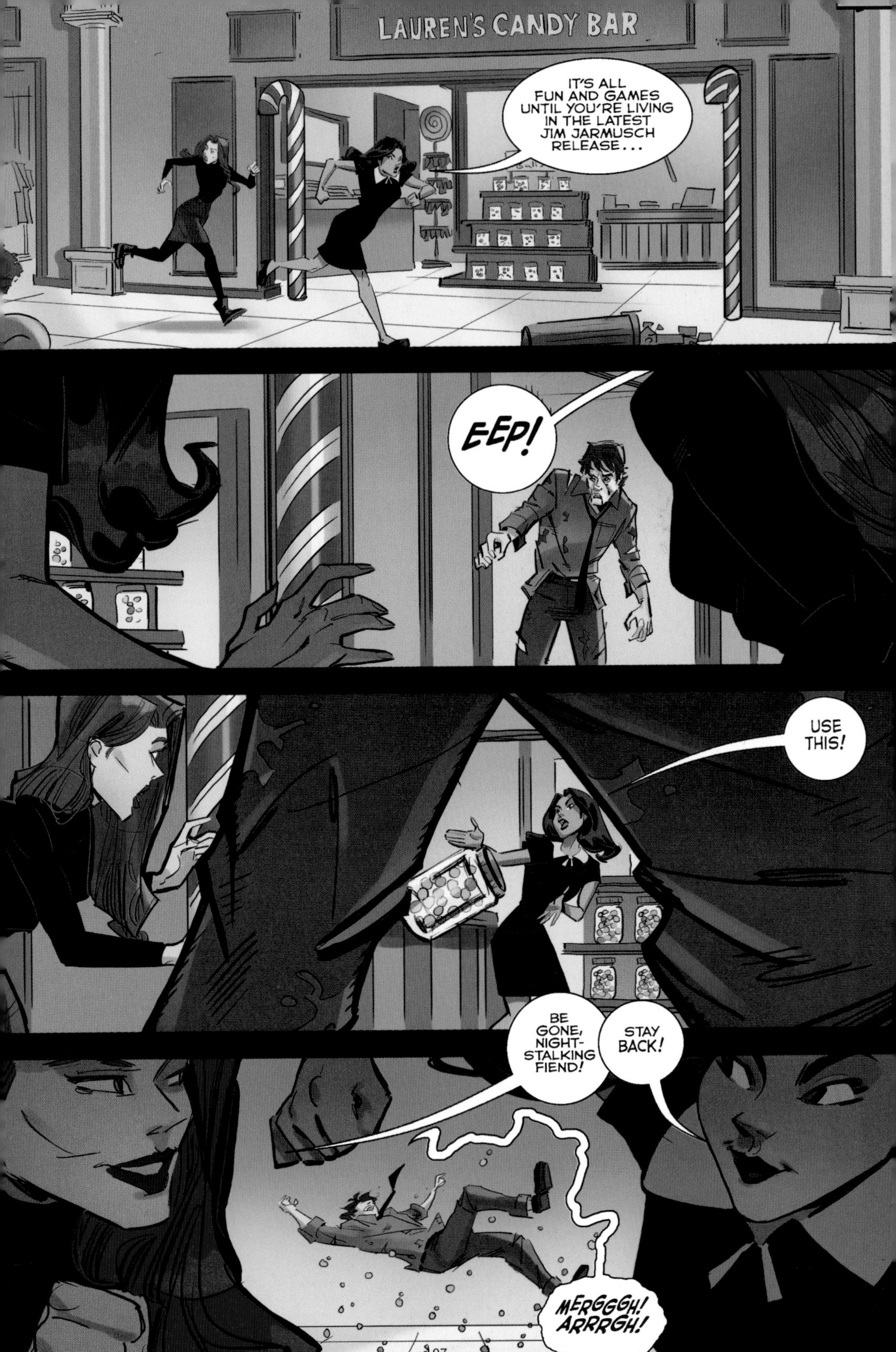
LAUREN'S CANDY BAR
IT'S ALL FUN AND GAMES UNTIL YOU'RE LIVING IN THE LATEST JIM JARMUSCH RELEASE...
EEP!
USE THIS!
BE GONE, NIGHT-STALKING FIEND!
STAY BACK!
MERGGGH! ARRRGH!

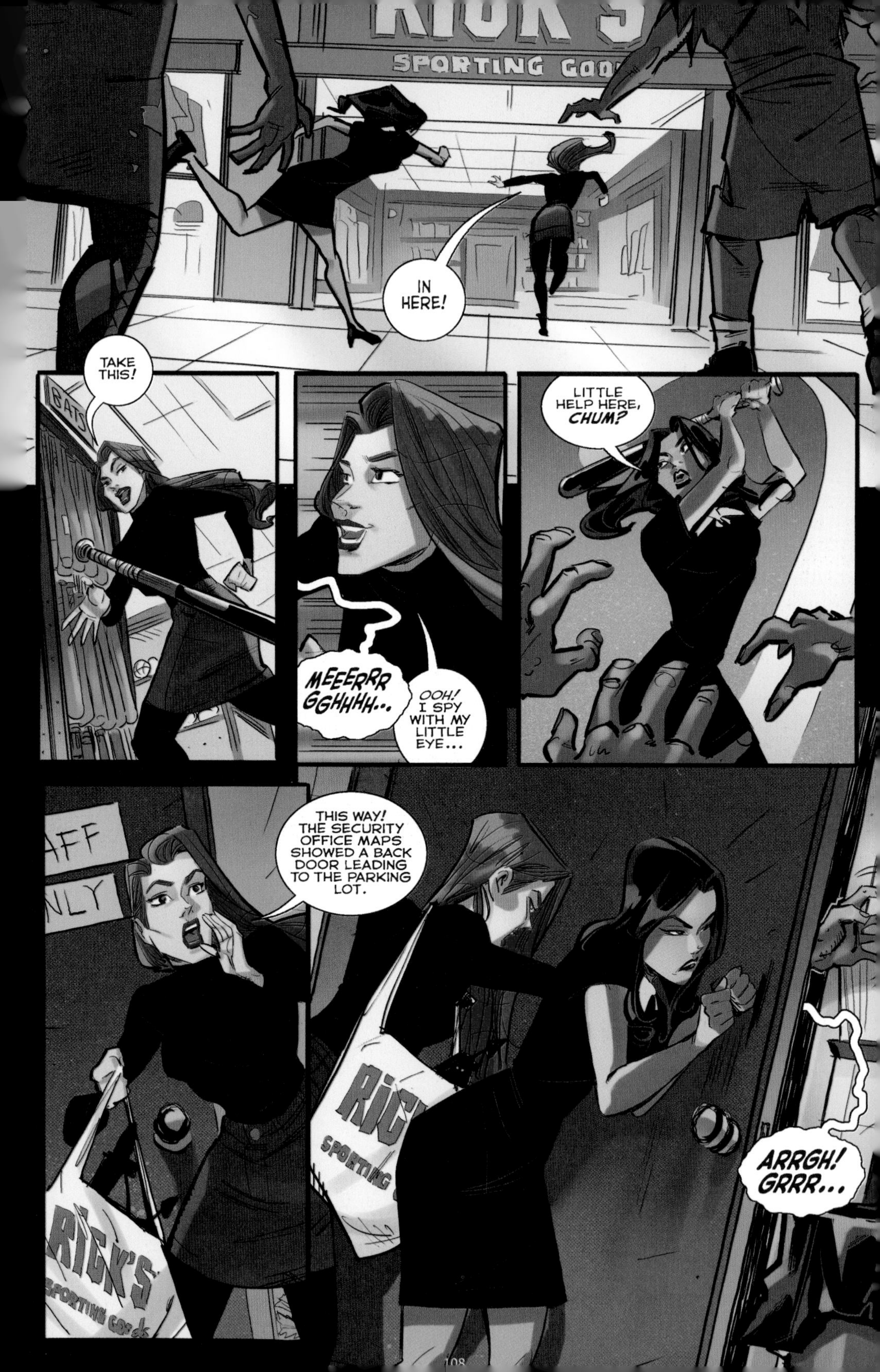
RICK'S
SPORTING GOO
IN HERE!
TAKE THIS!
BATS
MEEERRR GGHHHH...
OOH! I SPY WITH MY LITTLE EYE...
LITTLE HELP HERE, CHUM?
AFF
NLY
THIS WAY! THE SECURITY OFFICE MAPS SHOWED A BACK DOOR LEADING TO THE PARKING LOT.
ARRGH! GRRR...

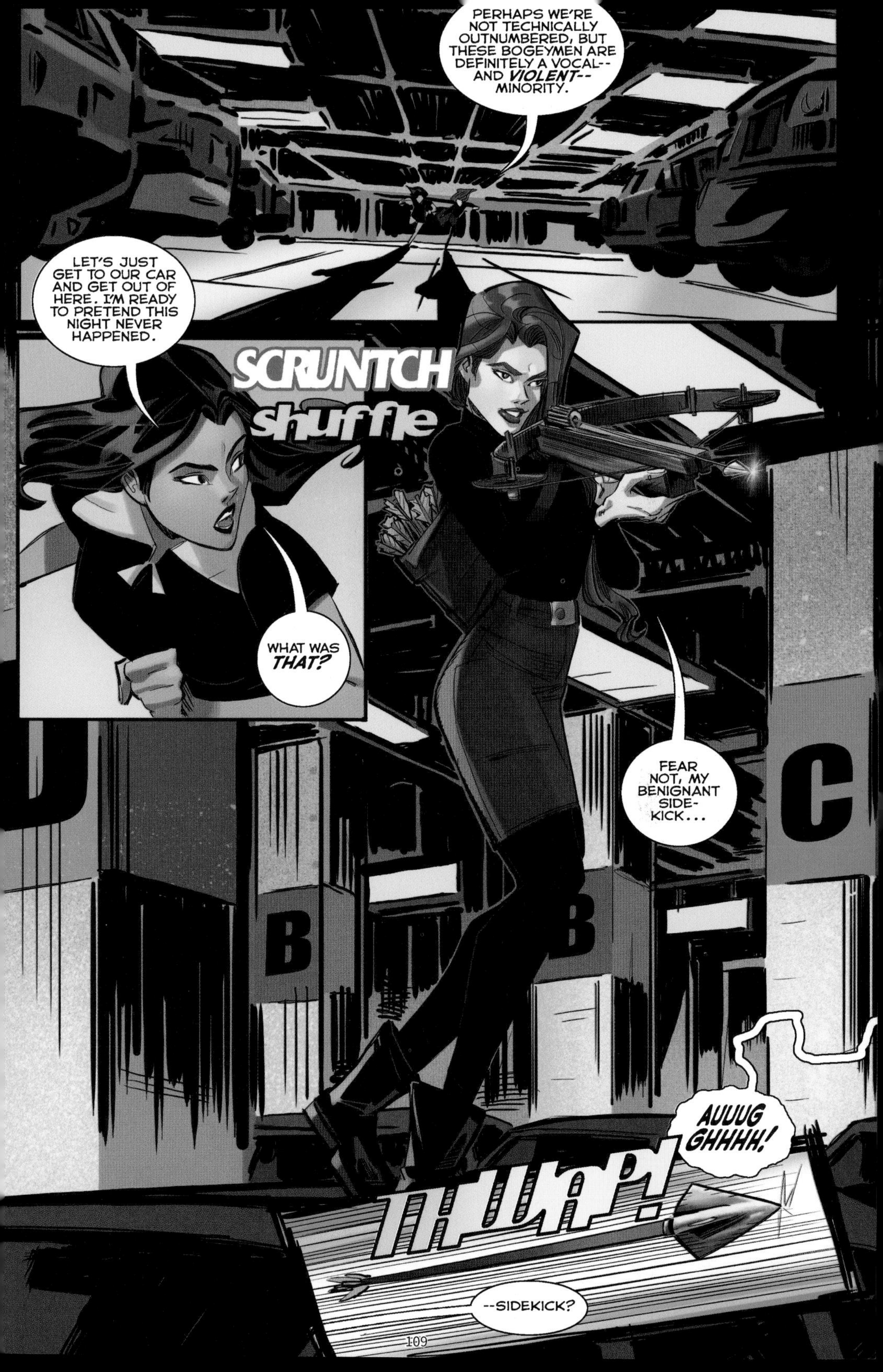

PERHAPS WE'RE NOT TECHNICALLY OUTNUMBERED, BUT THESE BOGEYMEN ARE DEFINITELY A VOCAL-- AND VIOLENT-- MINORITY.
LET'S JUST GET TO OUR CAR AND GET OUT OF HERE. I'M READY TO PRETEND THIS NIGHT NEVER HAPPENED.
SCRUNTCH
shuffle
WHAT WAS THAT?
FEAR NOT, MY BENIGNANT SIDE-KICK...
C
B
B
AUUUG GHHHH!
THUNP!
--SIDEKICK?

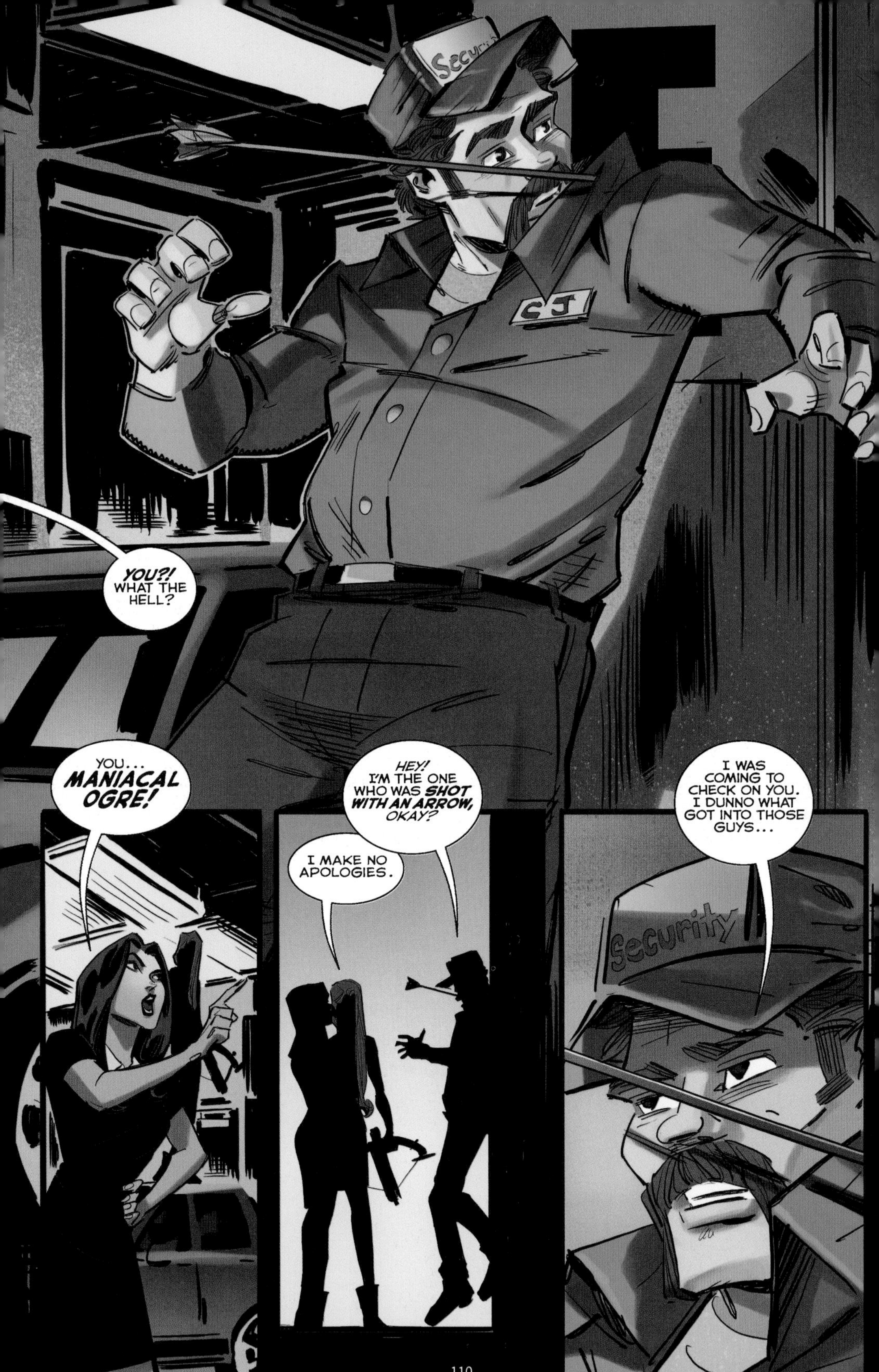
Security
CJ
YOU?! WHAT THE HELL?
YOU... MANIACAL OGRE!
HEY! I'M THE ONE WHO WAS SHOT WITH AN ARROW, OKAY?
I MAKE NO APOLOGIES.
I WAS COMING TO CHECK ON YOU. I DUNNO WHAT GOT INTO THOSE GUYS...
Security

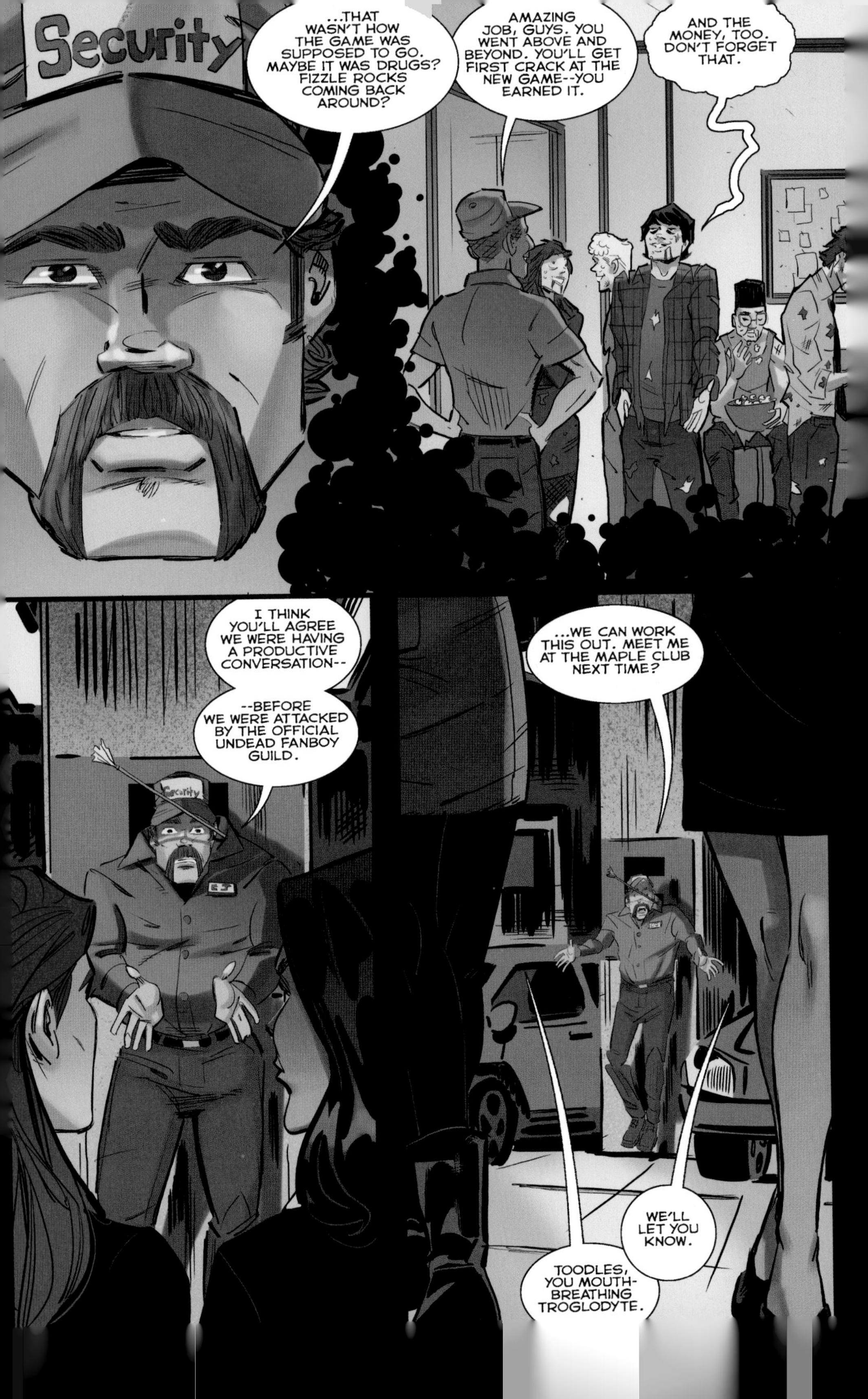
...THAT WASN'T HOW THE GAME WAS SUPPOSED TO GO. MAYBE IT WAS DRUGS? FIZZLE ROCKS COMING BACK AROUND?
AMAZING JOB, GUYS. YOU WENT ABOVE AND BEYOND. YOU'LL GET FIRST CRACK AT THE NEW GAME--YOU EARNED IT.
AND THE MONEY, TOO. DON'T FORGET THAT.
Security
I THINK YOU'LL AGREE WE WERE HAVING A PRODUCTIVE CONVERSATION--
--BEFORE WE WERE ATTACKED BY THE OFFICIAL UNDEAD FANBOY GUILD.
...WE CAN WORK THIS OUT. MEET ME AT THE MAPLE CLUB NEXT TIME?
WE'LL LET YOU KNOW.
TOODLES, YOU MOUTH-BREATHING TROGLODYTE.

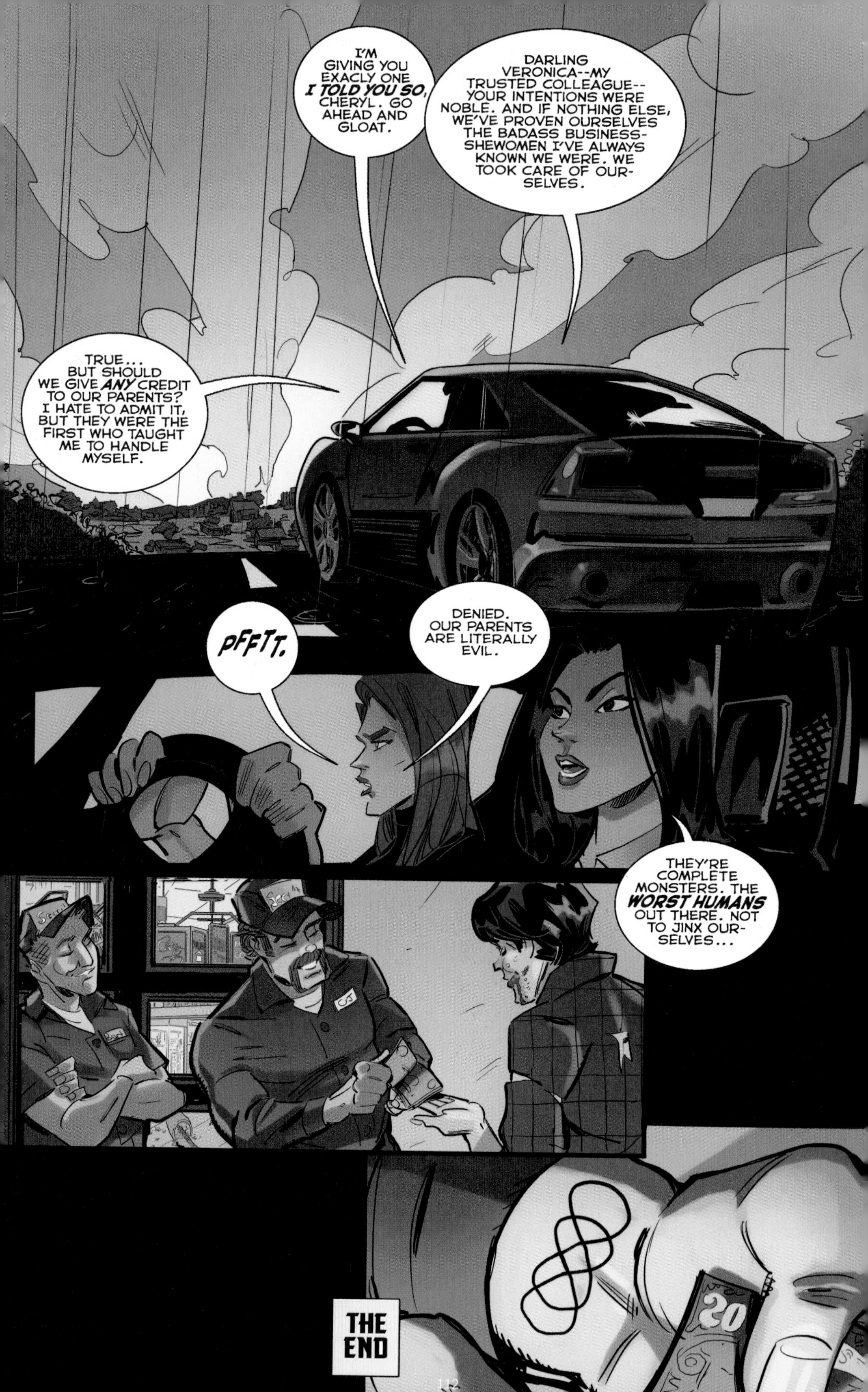
I'M GIVING YOU EXACLY ONE I TOLD YOU SO, CHERYL. GO AHEAD AND GLOAT.
DARLING VERONICA--MY TRUSTED COLLEAGUE--YOUR INTENTIONS WERE NOBLE. AND IF NOTHING ELSE, WE'VE PROVEN OURSELVES THE BADASS BUSINESS-SHEWOMEN I'VE ALWAYS KNOWN WE WERE. WE TOOK CARE OF OUR-SELVES.
TRUE... BUT SHOULD WE GIVE ANY CREDIT TO OUR PARENTS? I HATE TO ADMIT IT, BUT THEY WERE THE FIRST WHO TAUGHT ME TO HANDLE MYSELF.
PFFTT.
DENIED. OUR PARENTS ARE LITERALLY EVIL.
THEY'RE COMPLETE MONSTERS. THE WORST HUMANS OUT THERE. NOT TO JINX OUR-SELVES...
THE END

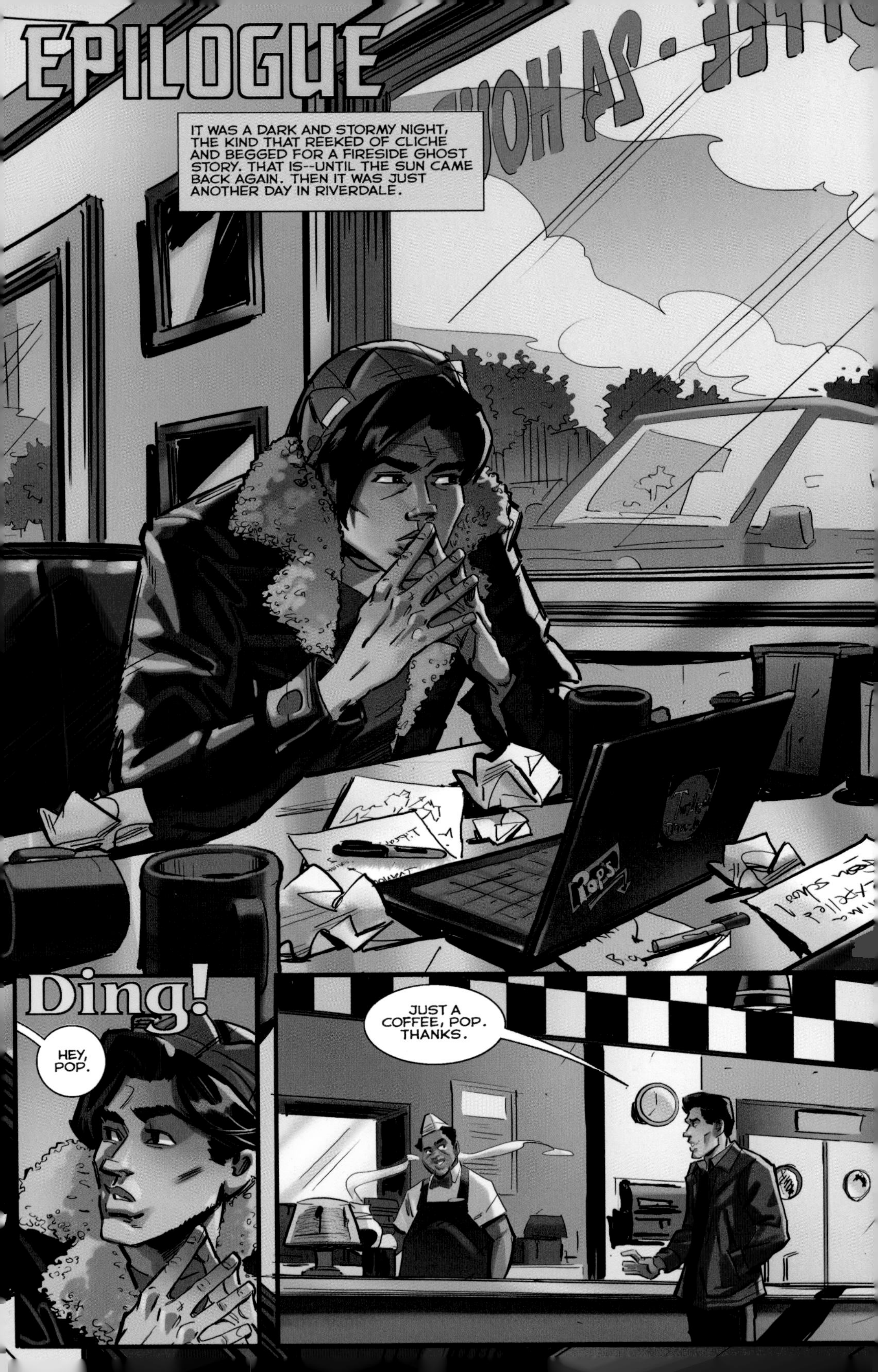
EPILOGUE
IT WAS A DARK AND STORMY NIGHT, THE KIND THAT REEKED OF CLICHE AND BEGGED FOR A FIRESIDE GHOST STORY. THAT IS--UNTIL THE SUN CAME BACK AGAIN. THEN IT WAS JUST ANOTHER DAY IN RIVERDALE.
Pop's
Ding!
HEY, POP.
JUST A COFFEE, POP. THANKS.

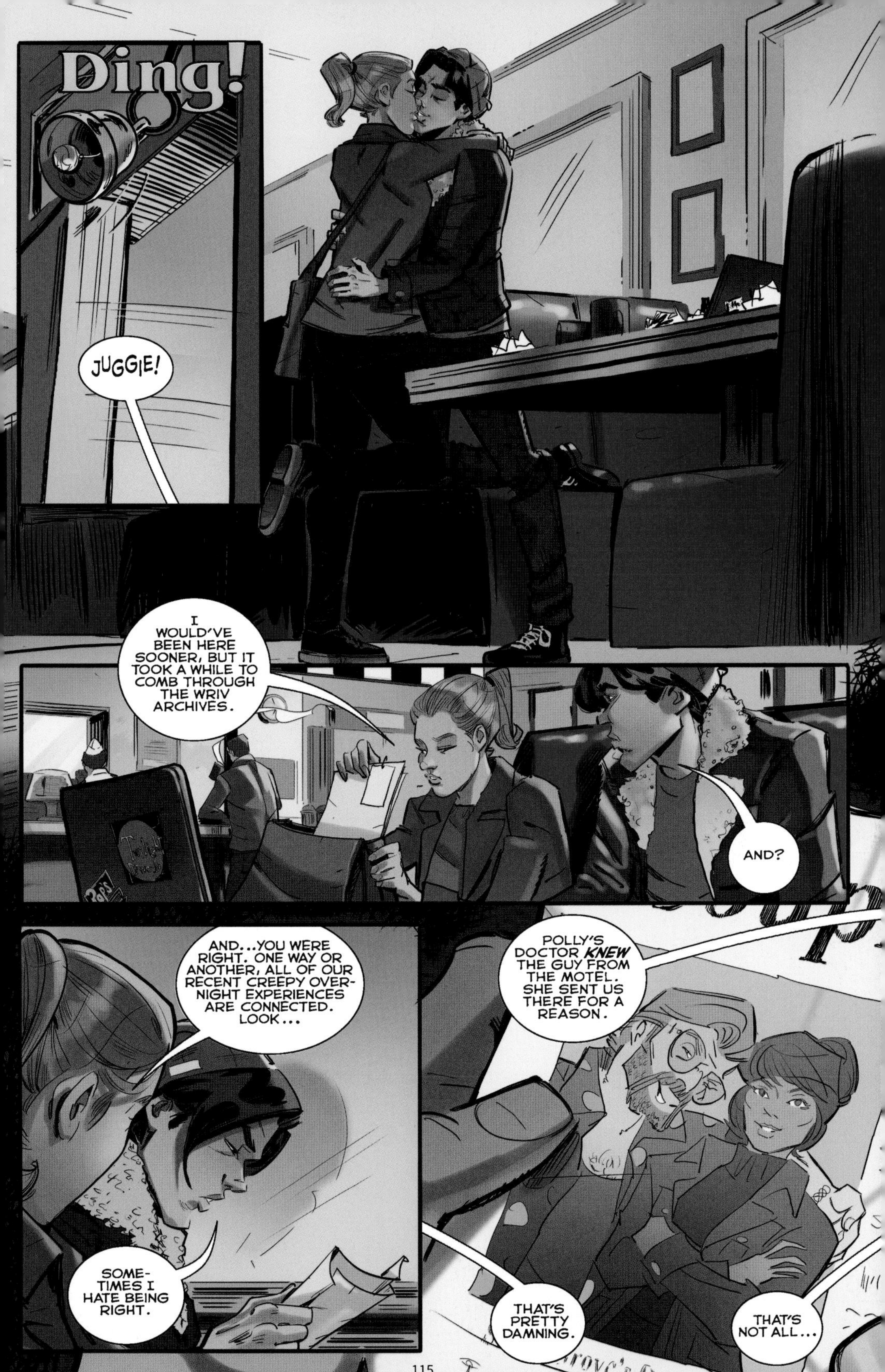
Ding!
JUGGIE!
I WOULD'VE BEEN HERE SOONER, BUT IT TOOK A WHILE TO COMB THROUGH THE WRIV ARCHIVES.
AND?
AND...YOU WERE RIGHT. ONE WAY OR ANOTHER, ALL OF OUR RECENT CREEPY OVER-NIGHT EXPERIENCES ARE CONNECTED. LOOK...
SOME-TIMES I HATE BEING RIGHT.
POLLY'S DOCTOR KNEW THE GUY FROM THE MOTEL. SHE SENT US THERE FOR A REASON.
THAT'S PRETTY DAMNING.
THAT'S NOT ALL...

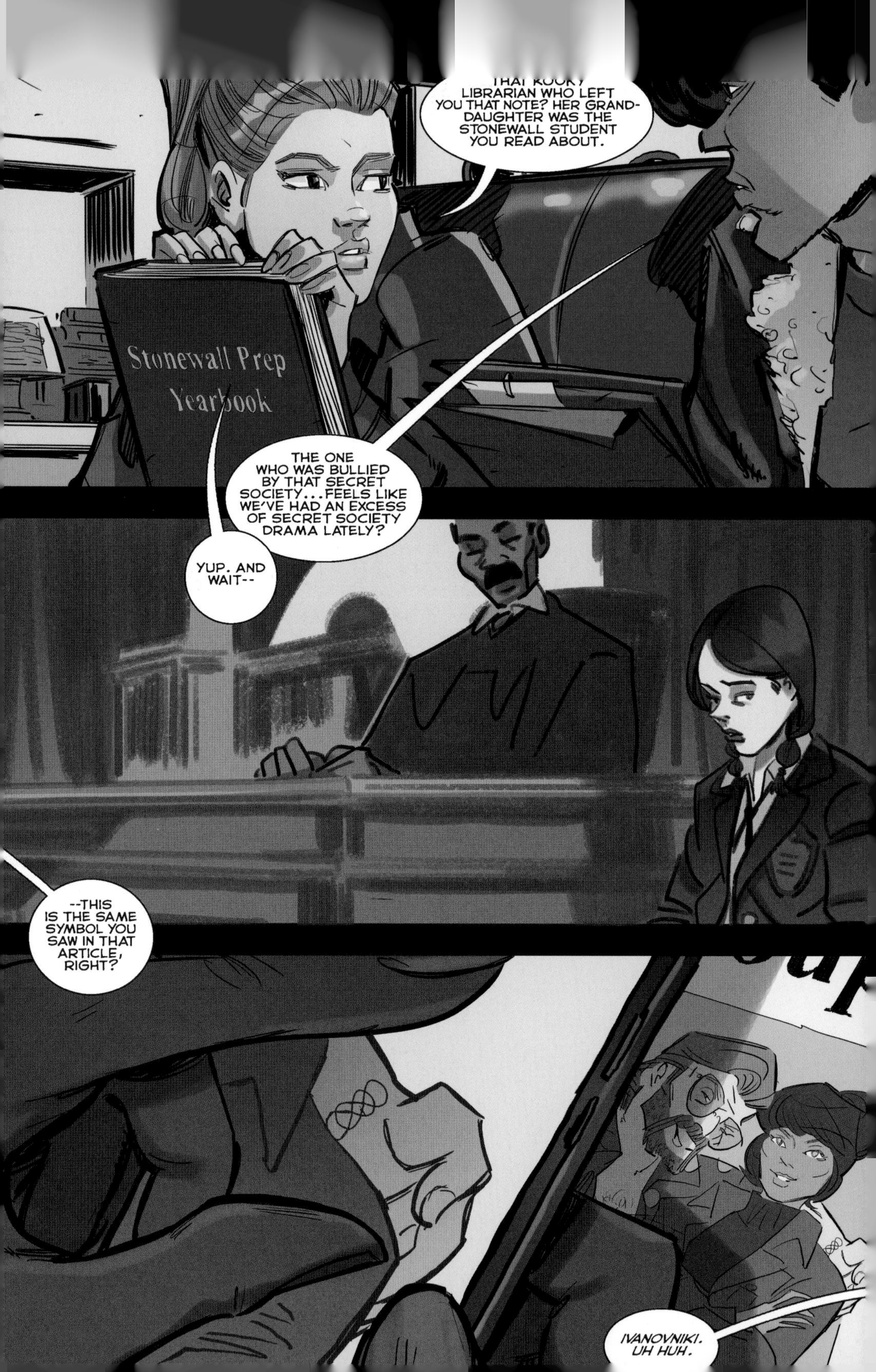
THAT KOOKY LIBRARIAN WHO LEFT YOU THAT NOTE? HER GRAND-DAUGHTER WAS THE STONEWALL STUDENT YOU READ ABOUT.
Stonewall Prep Yearbook
THE ONE WHO WAS BULLIED BY THAT SECRET SOCIETY...FEELS LIKE WE'VE HAD AN EXCESS OF SECRET SOCIETY DRAMA LATELY?
YUP. AND WAIT--
--THIS IS THE SAME SYMBOL YOU SAW IN THAT ARTICLE, RIGHT?
IVANOVNIKI. UH HUH.

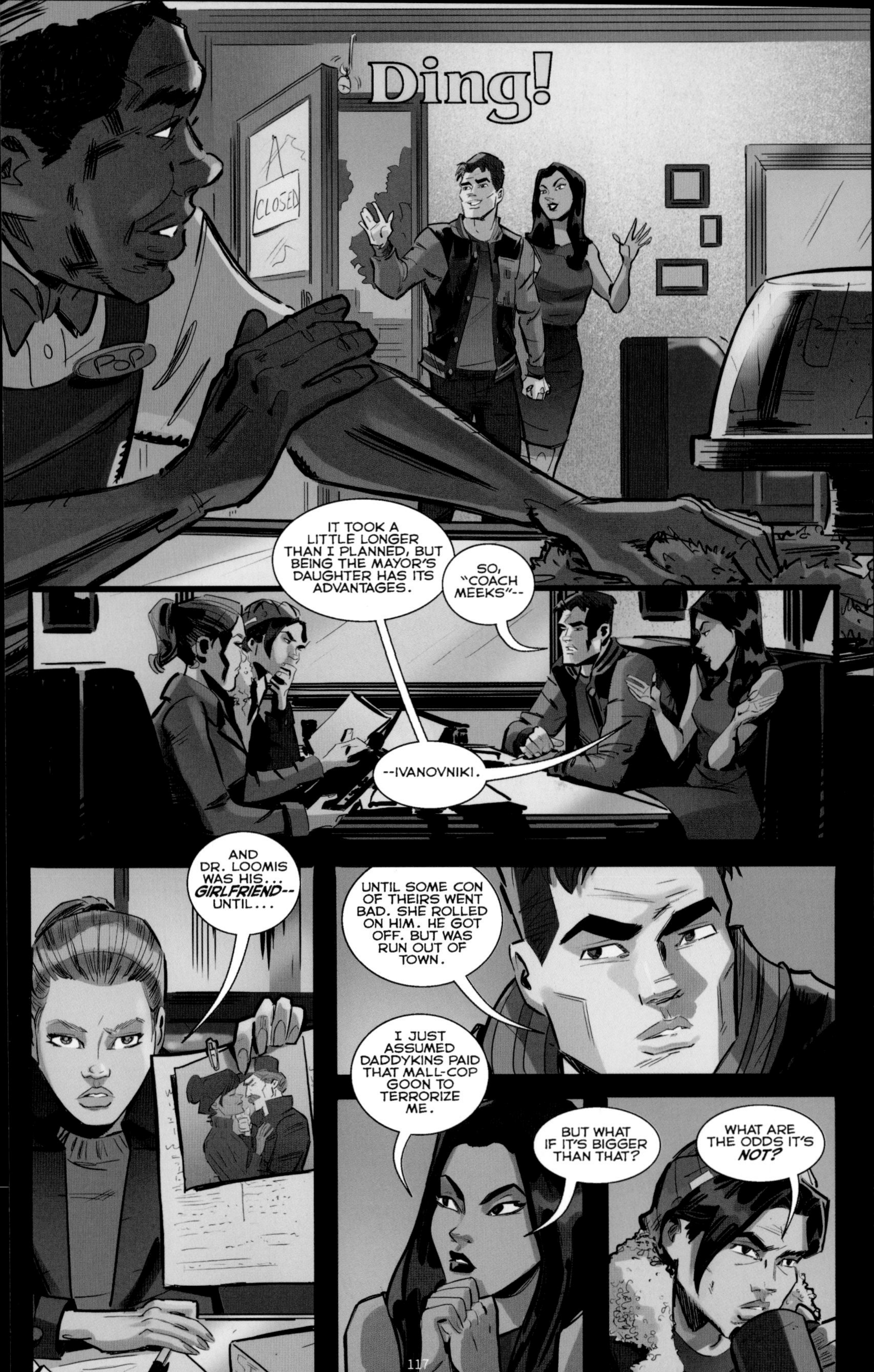
Ding!
CLOSED
POP
IT TOOK A LITTLE LONGER THAN I PLANNED, BUT BEING THE MAYOR'S DAUGHTER HAS ITS ADVANTAGES.
SO, "COACH MEEKS"--
--IVANOVNIKI.
AND DR. LOOMIS WAS HIS... *GIRLFRIEND*-- UNTIL...
UNTIL SOME CON OF THEIRS WENT BAD. SHE ROLLED ON HIM. HE GOT OFF. BUT WAS RUN OUT OF TOWN.
I JUST ASSUMED DADDYKINS PAID THAT MALL-COP GOON TO TERRORIZE ME.
BUT WHAT IF IT'S BIGGER THAN THAT?
WHAT ARE THE ODDS IT'S ***NOT?***

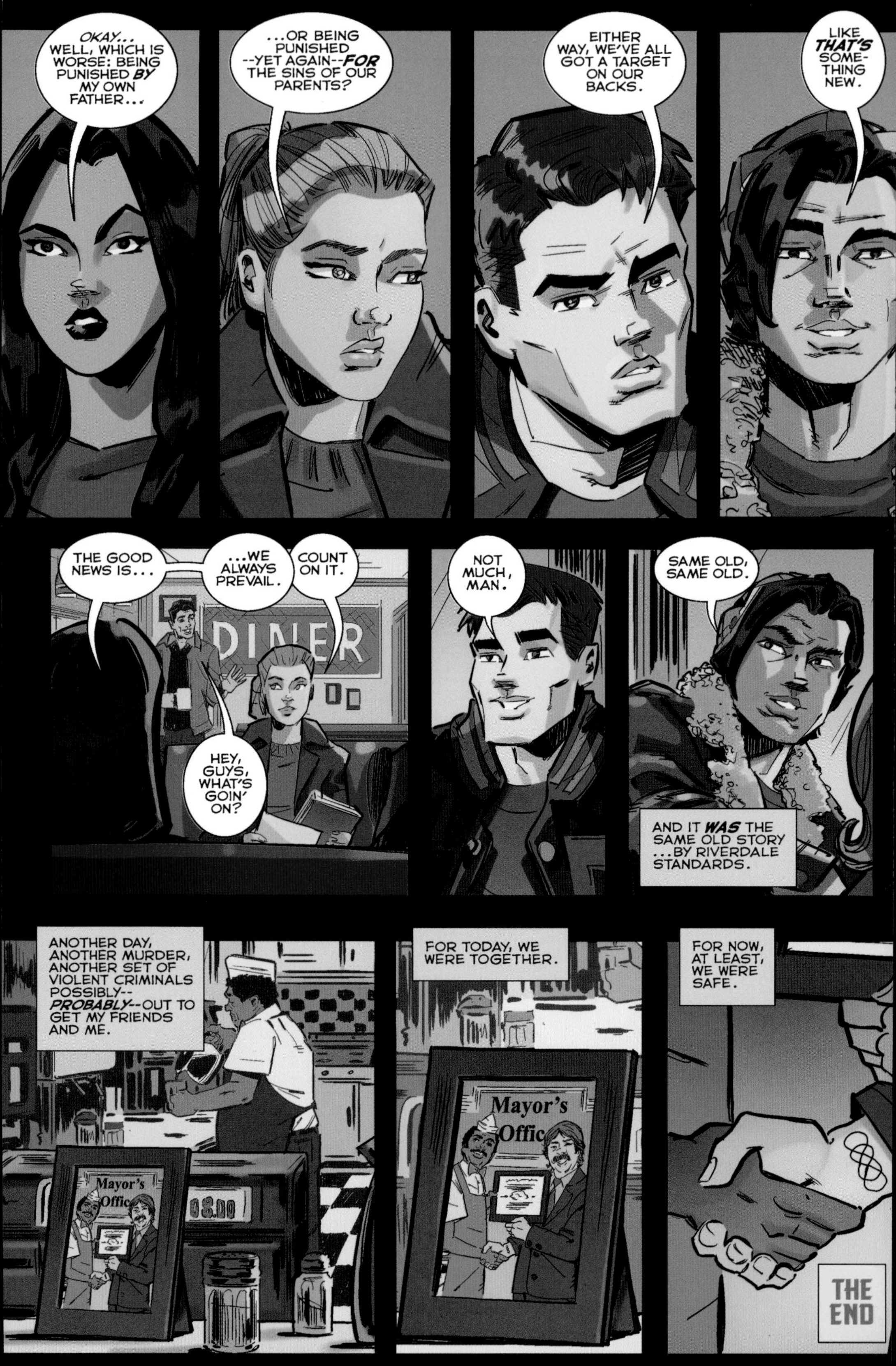
OKAY... WELL, WHICH IS WORSE: BEING PUNISHED BY MY OWN FATHER...
...OR BEING PUNISHED --YET AGAIN--FOR THE SINS OF OUR PARENTS?
EITHER WAY, WE'VE ALL GOT A TARGET ON OUR BACKS.
LIKE THAT'S SOMETHING NEW.
THE GOOD NEWS IS...
...WE ALWAYS PREVAIL.
COUNT ON IT.
DINER
HEY, GUYS, WHAT'S GOIN' ON?
NOT MUCH, MAN.
SAME OLD, SAME OLD.
AND IT WAS THE SAME OLD STORY ...BY RIVERDALE STANDARDS.
ANOTHER DAY, ANOTHER MURDER, ANOTHER SET OF VIOLENT CRIMINALS POSSIBLY--PROBABLY--OUT TO GET MY FRIENDS AND ME.
Mayor's Offic
FOR TODAY, WE WERE TOGETHER.
Mayor's Offic
FOR NOW, AT LEAST, WE WERE SAFE.
THE END

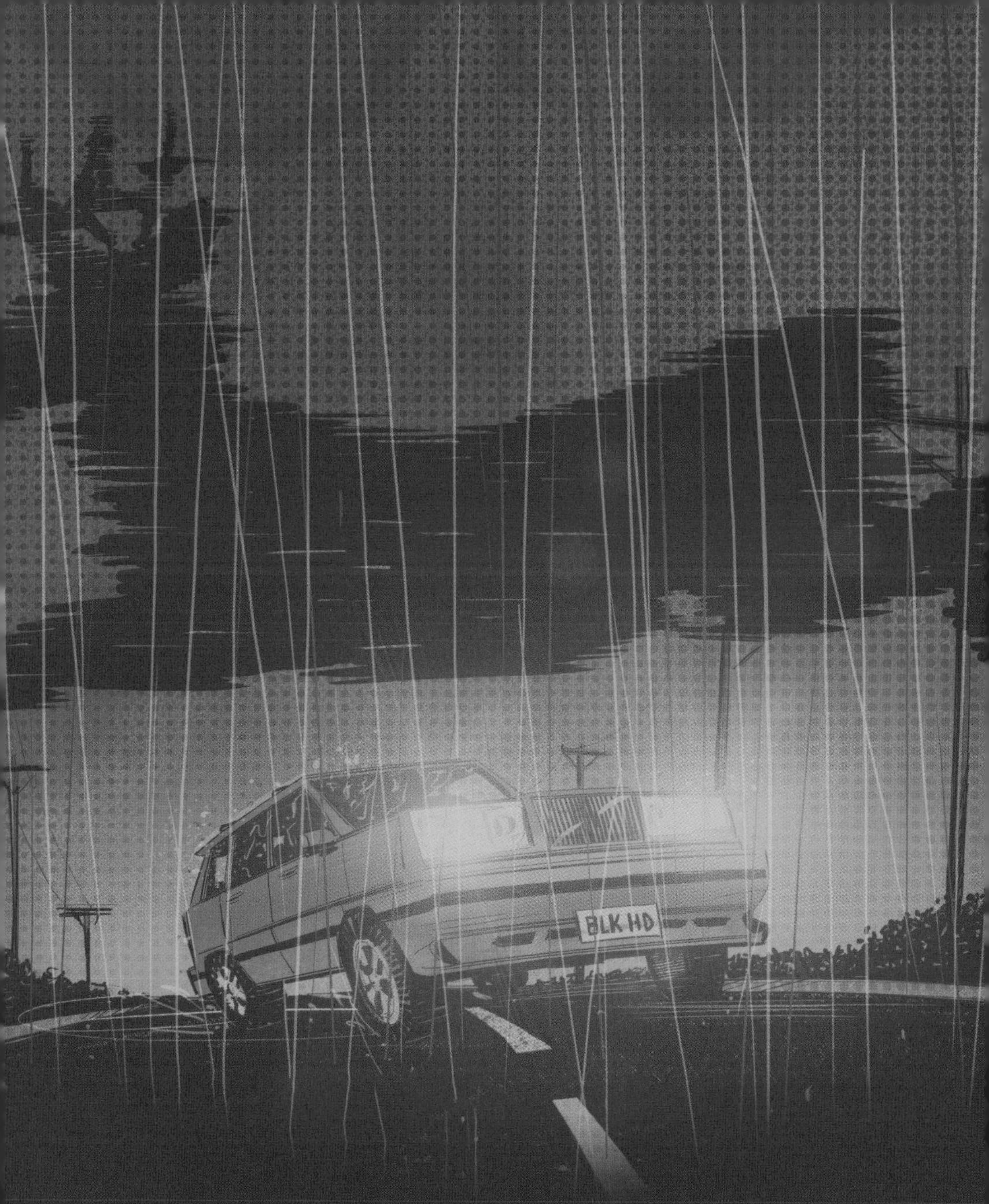
BLK HD

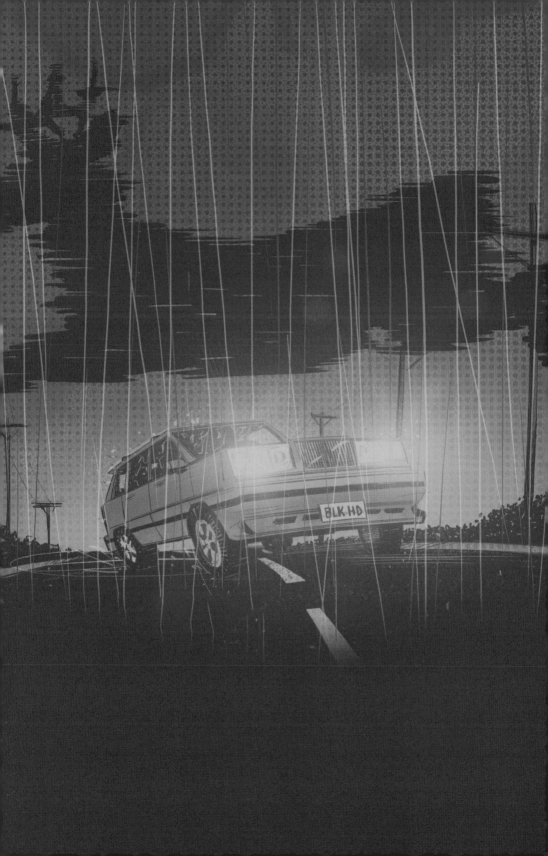

The distance between turning in a draft and seeing a book come to life can be vast.

It's always surreal to me as an author, to look over final typeset proofs and think back to the specific writing process of the project in question. Inevitably I can recall *exactly* where I was—what I ate, how I was feeling, what the weather was like that day—when I wrote a specific scene or story, and it's a sudden, hazy side trip into the experience of writing the book all over again for better or for worse. (Usually for the better.)

When Alex Segura and Jamie Rotante first approached Thomas and me about an original graphic novel for Season 4 of *Riverdale*, it was summer of 2019. I was thrilled to jump on board. We knew, as always, that our plots would have to exist parallel to the story arcs of the TV show so as not to disrupt one another. And I was prepared, as always, to watch a small gulf unfold between the narratives that Thomas and I wove early that summer, and the direction the show took as it followed its season's trajectory. I knew that revisiting this graphic novel would be a bit like opening a time capsule, eventually.

Ha.

Of course, I couldn't have possibly foreseen how *much* would change from first pitch, to outline, to sketches, to page proofs. In the world of Archie and *Riverdale*, yes—as of this writing our characters have jumped ahead seven years on our beloved show. Betty's in the FBI. Archie's in the army. Jughead's a published author. Veronica is married. If you're watching it (and of course you're watching it), you know—Riverdale's changed.

But it's more than that. A *lot* of things have changed, for so many of us, since 2019. It's safe to say the circumstances surrounding the creation of this book were (for me, at least) previously unimaginable. It's been a long process with crazy curveballs and endless uncertainty. When I was asked to have a look at the final pages of this book, I hesitated, because I wasn't sure what feelings it would dredge up.

As it turns out? *All* of them.

I'm so in love with the wild and sophisticated new direction the show's taken, but wow, was it nice to see our Core Four back on familiar—if ever-perilous—high school territory. Stonewall Prep. Riverdale High. Red Raven Maple Rum. Even a throwaway Gargoygle King reference? How quaint. How comforting.

And isn't that why we love Archie and his pals in the first place? Ask any Archie reader how long they've been a fan and no matter their age, chances are they'll say: forever. Archie's (and *Archie's*) ability to evolve and react to contemporary contexts while still keeping one foot rooted in nostalgia is truly a feat.

So yes, in looking back at this book, I'll remember having moments of wondering if spring 2020 was *really* the best time to be writing a story loosely inspired by a Romero apocalypse movie, among other things (it was very cathartic!). But Thomas Pitilli's bold, articulate illustrations are so engaging, it's hard for me to worry about anything else while I'm taking them in. And any time I struggled with a panel or a layout, his artistic vision always paved the way.

This book was written a lifetime ago. But these characters are timeless, and I'm always happy to hang with them for a while. I'm so lucky to get to work with Alex, Jamie, and Thomas. And endless thanks too to Andre Szymanowicz for his spectacular coloring work capturing the moody hues of our peppy town, and to John Workman for his dynamic lettering.

It was fun to revisit this graphic novel—and some old-school *Riverdale*—again, and I so hope it's fun for you to come join us in its world for a bit! I think we can agree, we all deserve a little escape to Riverdale, any time.

- MICOL OSTOW

ABOUT THE AUTHOR

Micol Ostow has written approximately seven zillion books for readers of all ages, including novels based on iconic characters like Nancy Drew, Buffy the Vampire Slayer, and the infamous Plastics of *Mean Girls*. She is thrilled to add Archie and his pals to her resume. In addition to *Riverdale* comics and graphic novels, Micol has written several bestselling novels based on the smash hit tv show for Scholastic. She lives in Brooklyn with her husband, her two daughters, and an angsty beagle mix named Peter Parker.

Visit Micol online at: www.micolostow.com

ABOUT THE ARTIST

Thomas Pitilli is an illustrator and comic book artist who has illustrated various comic projects for Archie Comics, including the *Riverdale* monthly series. He is also known for his illustration work on the graphic novel *Gotham High* for DC Comics. In addition to his comic work, Thomas also contributes illustrations to Scholastic, *Wall Street Journal*, *Entertainment Weekly*, as well as many others. When not making art, Thomas enjoys music, museums, and long walks while daydreaming.

ABOUT THE COLORIST

Andre Szymanowicz is an artist and designer living in New Jersey, who, like most, has read and loved Archie digests growing up. He spends his time trying not to get real paint on his computer screen while struggling to remember he can't Ctrl+Z a canvas.

ABOUT THE LETTERER

John Workman managed to turn a love for the comics form into a career. During the past five decades, he has held the positions of editor, writer, art director, penciler, inker, colorist, letterer, production director, and book designer for various companies. He created (with some help from Bhob Stewart and Bob Smith) the offbeat stories in *Wild Things* and both wrote and drew the comics series *Sindy*, *Fallen Angels*, and *Roma*. He continues to write and draw and to do a whole lot of lettering for a number of comics companies on an international level.

CHARACTER
SKETCHES

THOMAS PITILLI'S CONCEPT DESIGN FOR COACH MEEKS

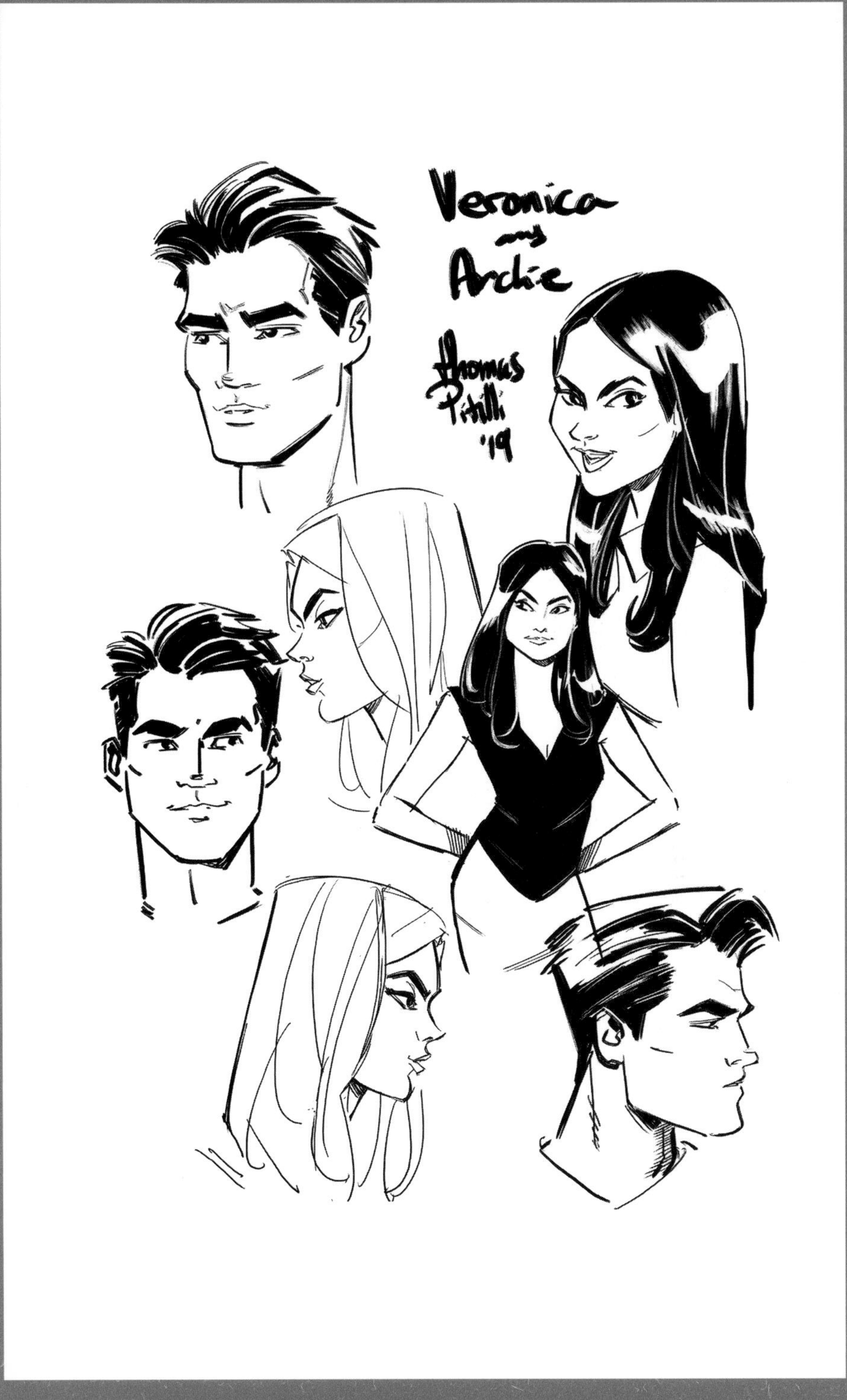
Veronica
and
Archie
thomas
Pitilli
'19

THOMAS PITILLI'S UPDATED DESIGNS FOR ARCHIE AND VERONICA

SCRIPT & ART
PROCESS

RIVERDALE
Season 4OGN: THE TIES THAT BIND

Part 1: _NIGHTCRAWLERS_
11.19.19
by Micol Ostow

PAGE 1

PROLOGUE

*(Note that this is the wraparound story of Jug relaying the Core Four's respective adventures, so however you want to format that is a-ok!)

Panel 1. EXT. ROAD TO RIVERDALE — NIGHT — Panoramic panel, maybe the top third of the page? We're looking toward the town, pine trees in the distance, the iconic sign reading 'Welcome to Riverdale — the town with PEP!'. It's a dark and stormy night, the whole noir cliché, which JUGHEAD is about to reinforce.

                       JUGHEAD (NARRATION)
             IT WAS A DARK AND STORMY NIGHT, THE KIND THAT
             REEKED OF CLICHÉ AND BEGGED FOR A FIRESIDE GHOST
             STORY.

Panel 2. (INSET) EXT. POP'S DINER — CLOSE on the neon sign.

                       JUGHEAD (NARRATION)
             I DIDN'T HAVE THE FIREPLACE, BUT CREEPY STORIES?
             NEVER IN SHORT SUPPLY.

Panel 3. INT. POP'S DINER — JUG walks in, soggy from the storm, bag (with his laptop) under his shoulder. POP is behind the count‹

                   POP

          HEY, JUGHEAD? HOME FOR A VISIT?

                   JUG

          YUP.

                   POP

          ANYWHERE YOU LIKE.

SCRIPT BY MICOL OSTOW

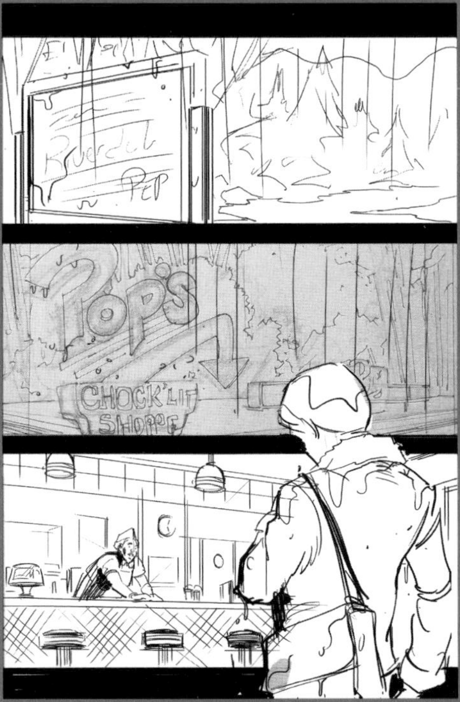
CHOCK'LIT
SHOPPE

LAYOUTS BY THOMAS PITILLI

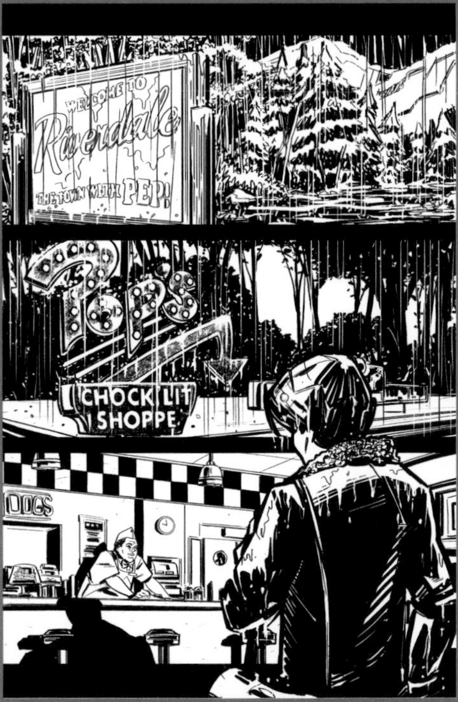
WELCOME TO
Riverdale
THE TOWN WITH PEP!
CHOCK'LIT
SHOPPE
DOGS

INKS BY THOMAS PITILLI

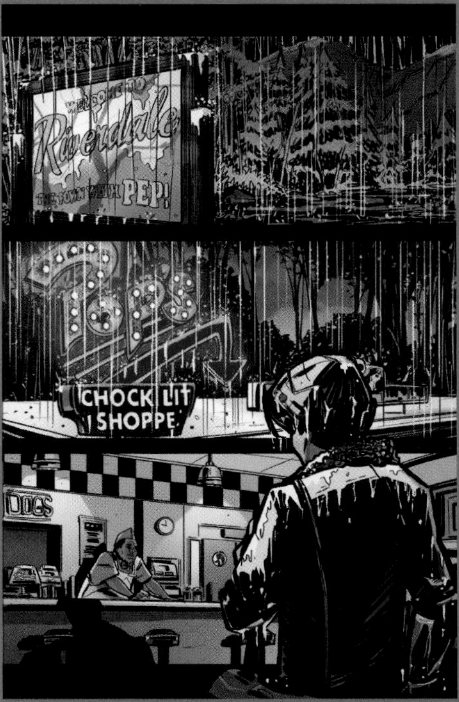
WELCOME TO
Riverdale
THE TOWN WITH PEP!
CHOCK'LIT
SHOPPE
DOGS

COLORS BY ANDRE SYZMANOWICZ

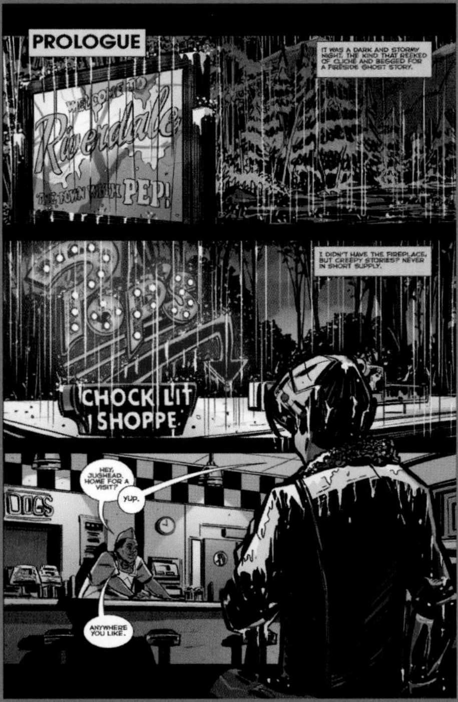
PROLOGUE
IT WAS A DARK AND STORMY NIGHT. THE KIND THAT REEKED OF CLICHÉ AND BEGGED FOR A FIRESIDE GHOST STORY.
I DIDN'T HAVE THE FIREPLACE. BUT CREEPY STORIES? NEVER IN SHORT SUPPLY.
WELCOME TO
Riverdale
THE TOWN WITH PEP!
CHOCK'LIT
SHOPPE
HEY, JUGHEAD. HOME FOR A VISIT?
YUP.
ANYWHERE YOU LIKE.

LETTERS BY JOHN WORKMAN

BETTY & VERONICA
THE BOND OF FRIENDSHIP

Archie's first-ever original young adult graphic novel, starring everyone's favorite BFFs Betty and Veronica! There are a number of truths in Riverdale—Archie Andrews will forever be clumsy and love-struck, Jughead Jones has an appetite that can never be satiated, Pop's will always serve the best burgers and shakes and Betty and Veronica will be best friends no matter what comes between them. But when a career day at Riverdale High has the two BFFs examining their futures, they start to wonder just where they'll end up—and how their lives may take very different paths. This original graphic novel explores the unbreakable bond that allows Betty and Veronica's friendship to withstand the tests of space and time.

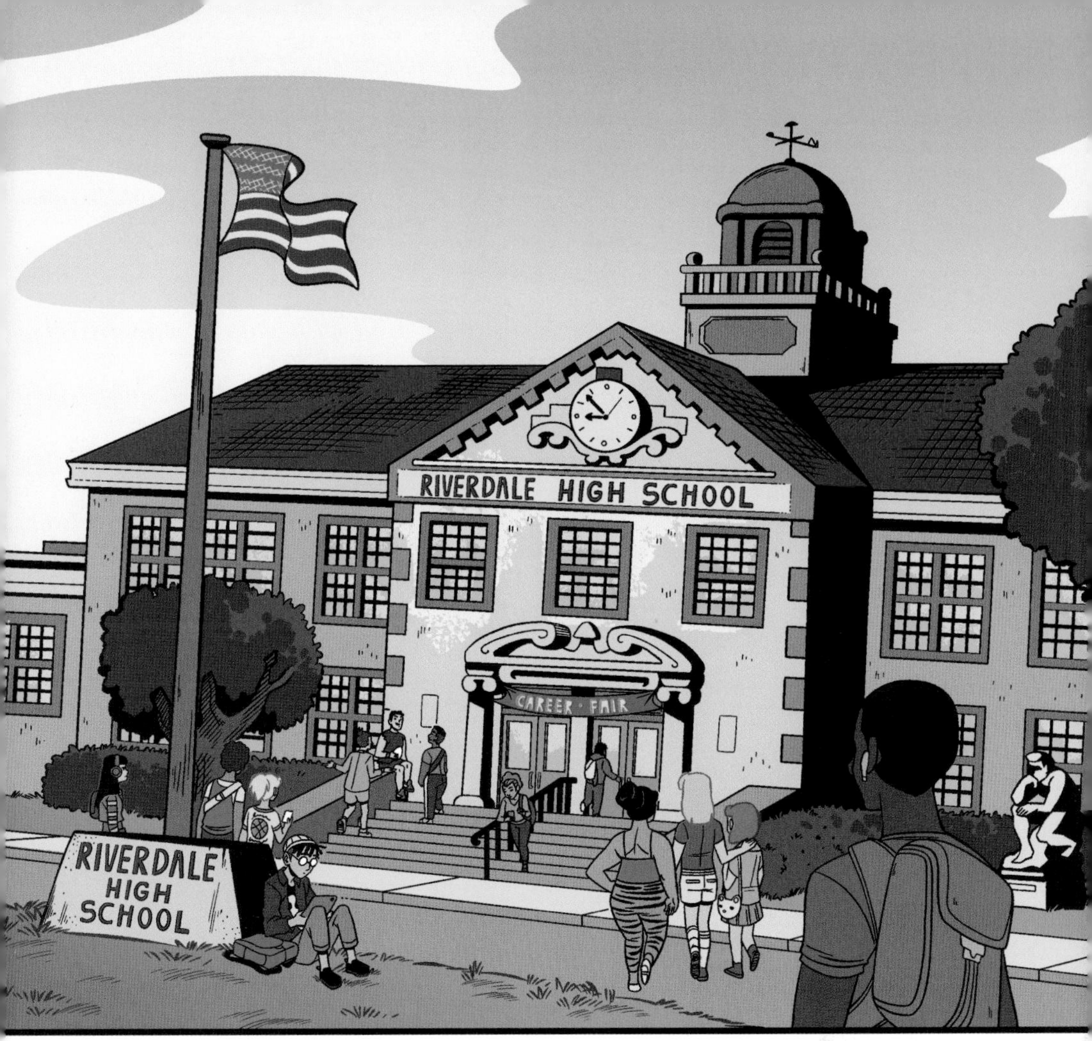
RIVERDALE HIGH SCHOOL
CAREER · FAIR
RIVERDALE HIGH SCHOOL

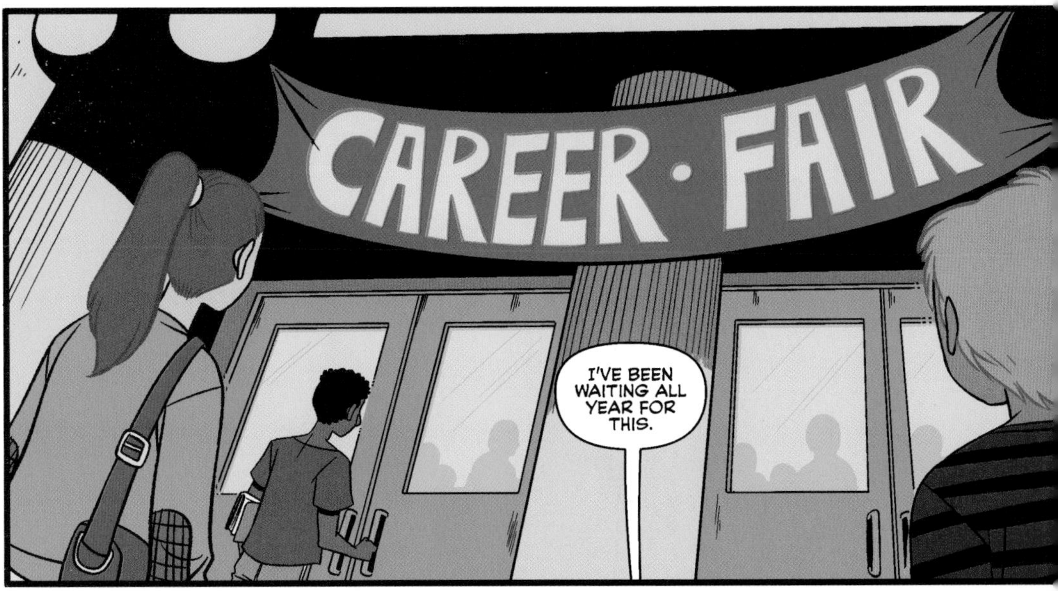
CAREER · FAIR
I'VE BEEN WAITING ALL YEAR FOR THIS.

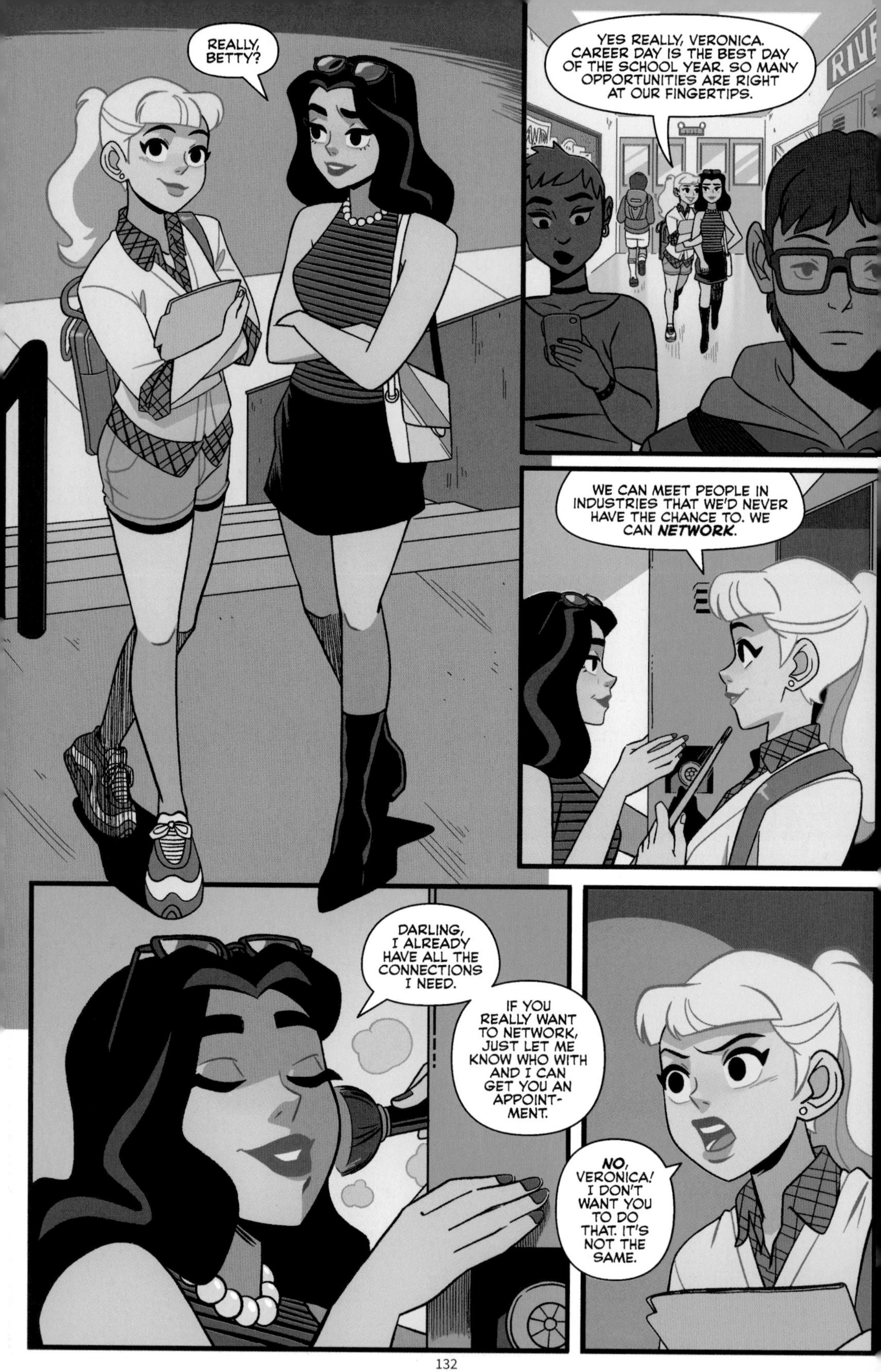
REALLY, BETTY?
YES REALLY, VERONICA. CAREER DAY IS THE BEST DAY OF THE SCHOOL YEAR. SO MANY OPPORTUNITIES ARE RIGHT AT OUR FINGERTIPS.
WE CAN MEET PEOPLE IN INDUSTRIES THAT WE'D NEVER HAVE THE CHANCE TO. WE CAN ***NETWORK***.
DARLING, I ALREADY HAVE ALL THE CONNECTIONS I NEED.
IF YOU REALLY WANT TO NETWORK, JUST LET ME KNOW WHO WITH AND I CAN GET YOU AN APPOINT-MENT.
NO, VERONICA! I DON'T WANT YOU TO DO THAT. IT'S NOT THE SAME.

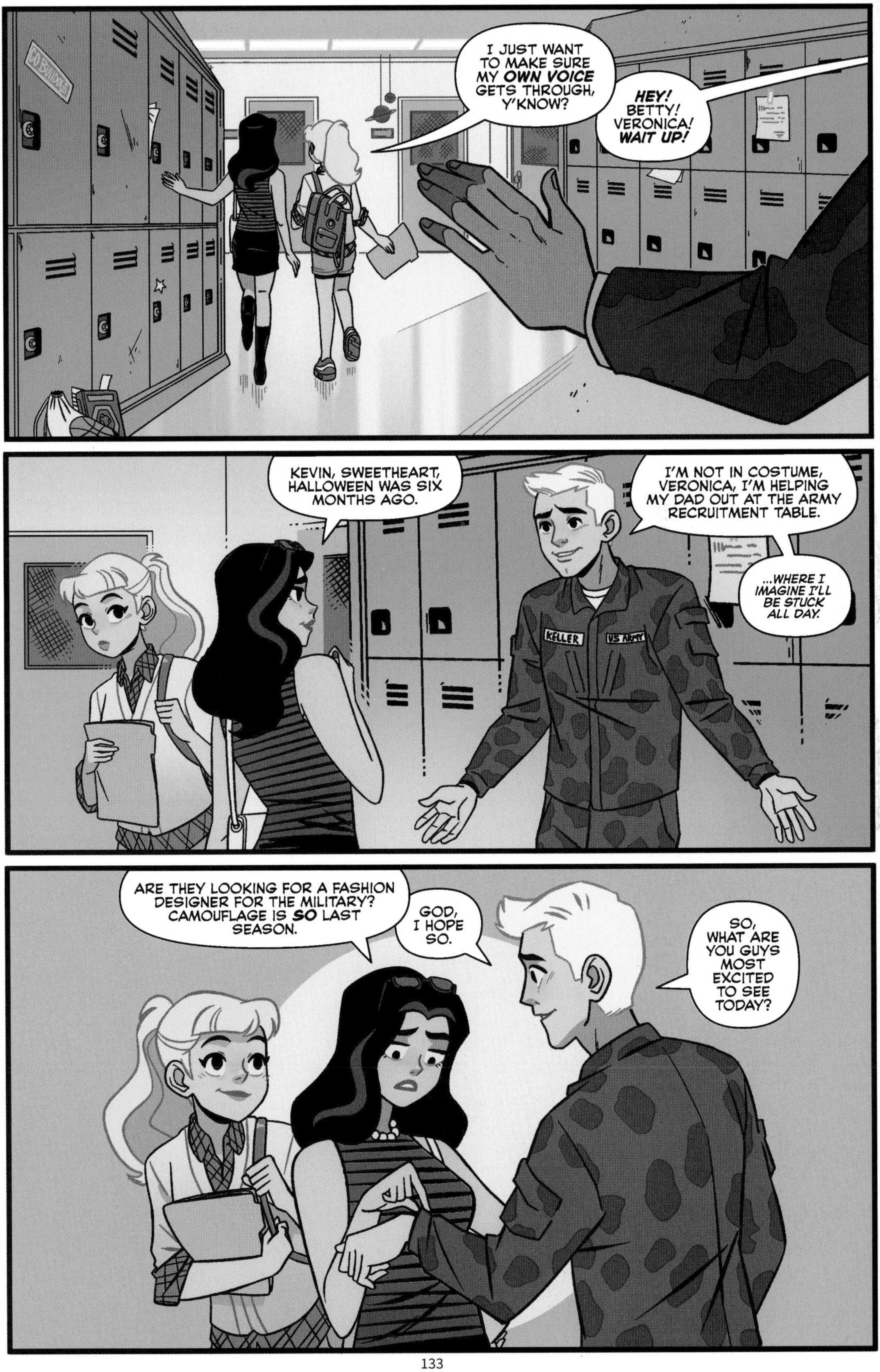
GO BULLDOGS
I JUST WANT TO MAKE SURE MY **OWN VOICE** GETS THROUGH, Y'KNOW?
HEY! *BETTY! VERONICA!* ***WAIT UP!***
KEVIN, SWEETHEART, HALLOWEEN WAS SIX MONTHS AGO.
I'M NOT IN COSTUME, VERONICA, I'M HELPING MY DAD OUT AT THE ARMY RECRUITMENT TABLE.
...WHERE I IMAGINE I'LL BE STUCK ALL DAY.
KELLER
US ARMY
ARE THEY LOOKING FOR A FASHION DESIGNER FOR THE MILITARY? CAMOUFLAGE IS ***SO*** LAST SEASON.
GOD, I HOPE SO.
SO, WHAT ARE YOU GUYS MOST EXCITED TO SEE TODAY?

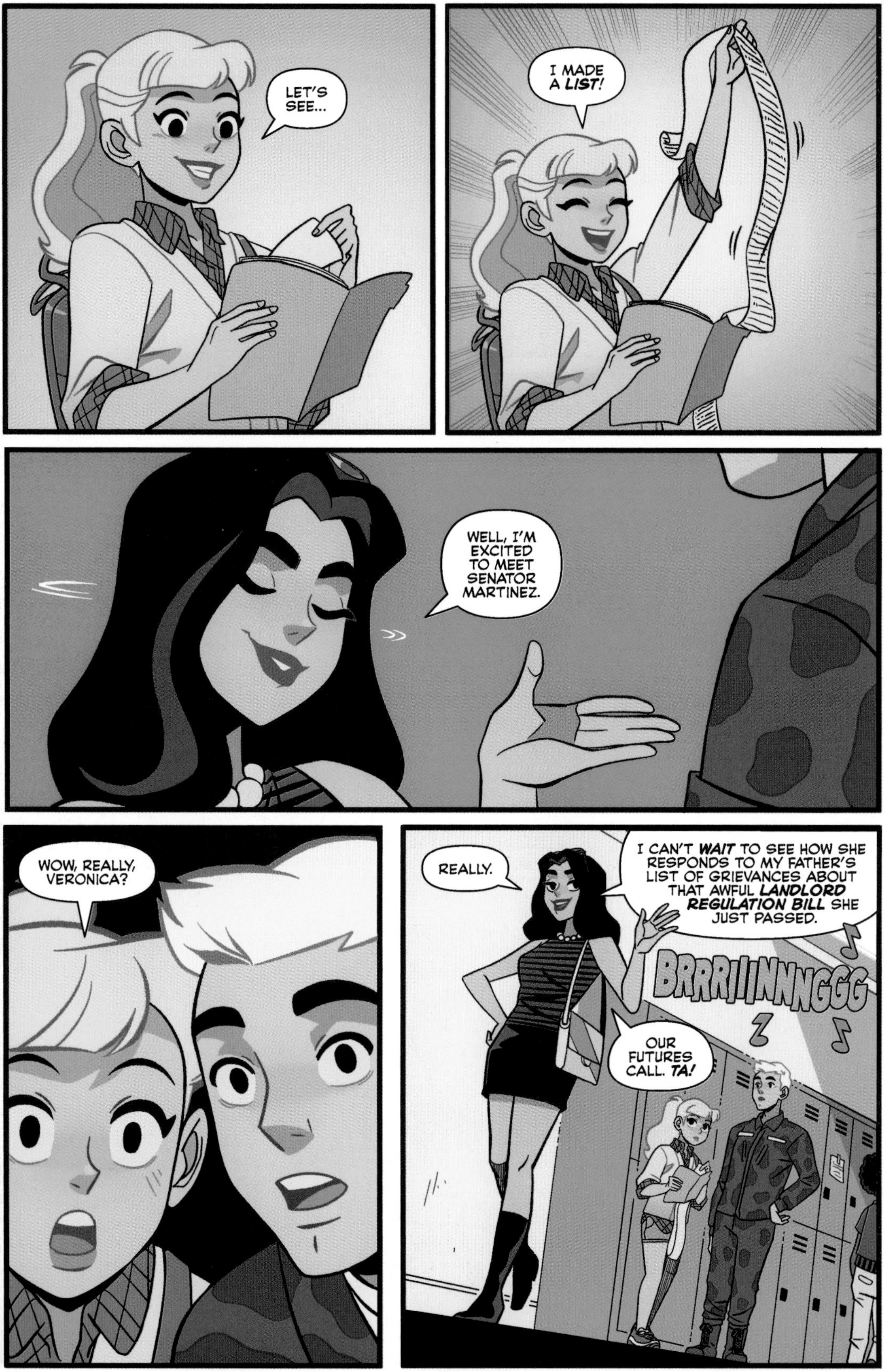
LET'S SEE...
I MADE A **LIST**!
WELL, I'M EXCITED TO MEET SENATOR MARTINEZ.
WOW, REALLY, VERONICA?
REALLY.
I CAN'T **WAIT** TO SEE HOW SHE RESPONDS TO MY FATHER'S LIST OF GRIEVANCES ABOUT THAT AWFUL **LANDLORD REGULATION BILL** SHE JUST PASSED.
BRRRIIINNNGGG
OUR FUTURES CALL. **TA**!

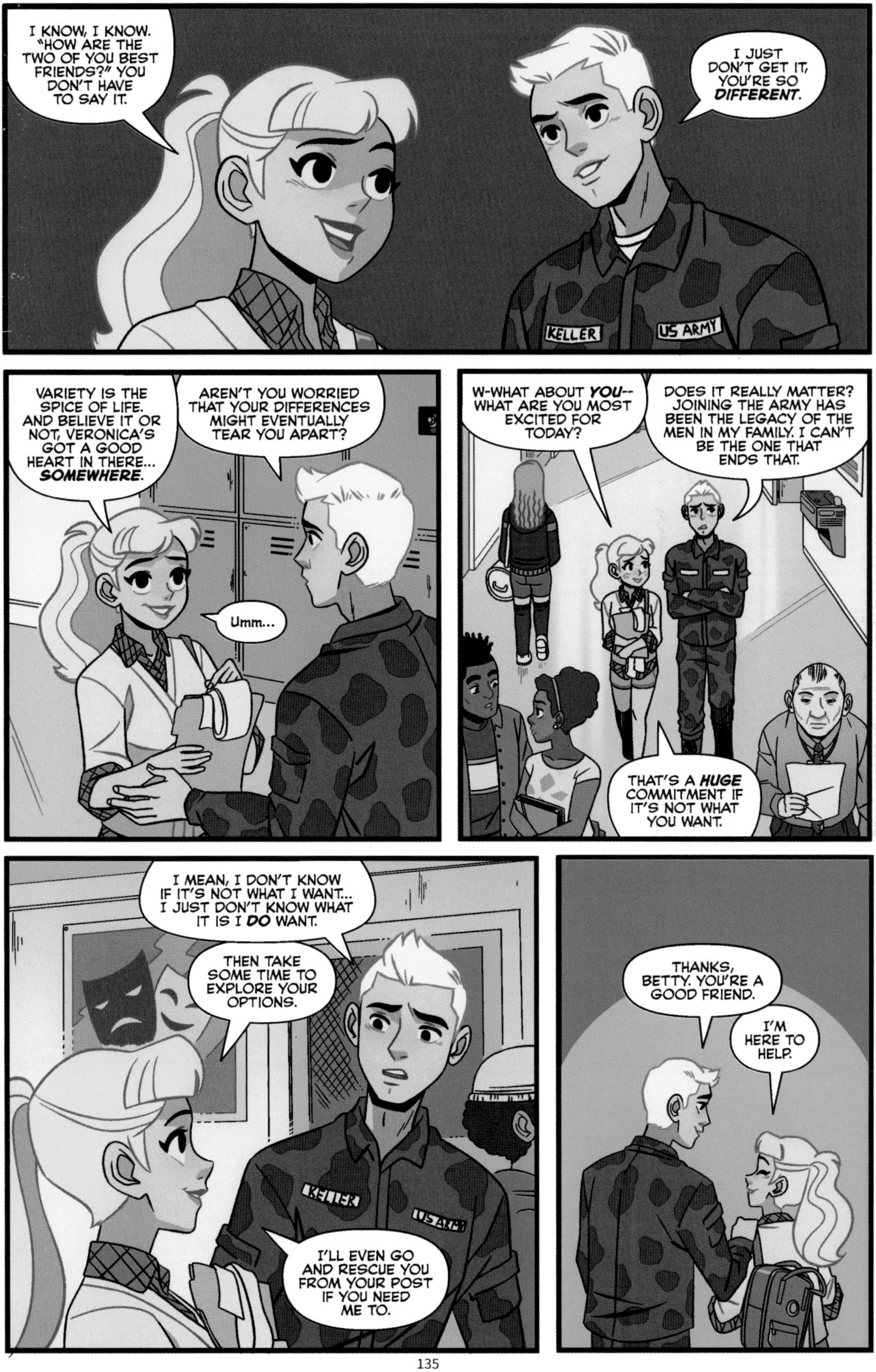
I KNOW, I KNOW. "HOW ARE THE TWO OF YOU BEST FRIENDS?" YOU DON'T HAVE TO SAY IT.
I JUST DON'T GET IT, YOU'RE SO *DIFFERENT*.
KELLER
US ARMY
VARIETY IS THE SPICE OF LIFE. AND BELIEVE IT OR NOT, VERONICA'S GOT A GOOD HEART IN THERE... ***SOMEWHERE***.
AREN'T YOU WORRIED THAT YOUR DIFFERENCES MIGHT EVENTUALLY TEAR YOU APART?
Umm...
W-WHAT ABOUT ***YOU***-- WHAT ARE YOU MOST EXCITED FOR TODAY?
DOES IT REALLY MATTER? JOINING THE ARMY HAS BEEN THE LEGACY OF THE MEN IN MY FAMILY. I CAN'T BE THE ONE THAT ENDS THAT.
THAT'S A ***HUGE*** COMMITMENT IF IT'S NOT WHAT YOU WANT.
I MEAN, I DON'T KNOW IF IT'S NOT WHAT I WANT... I JUST DON'T KNOW WHAT IT IS I ***DO*** WANT.
THEN TAKE SOME TIME TO EXPLORE YOUR OPTIONS.
KELLER
US ARMY
I'LL EVEN GO AND RESCUE YOU FROM YOUR POST IF YOU NEED ME TO.
THANKS, BETTY. YOU'RE A GOOD FRIEND.
I'M HERE TO HELP.

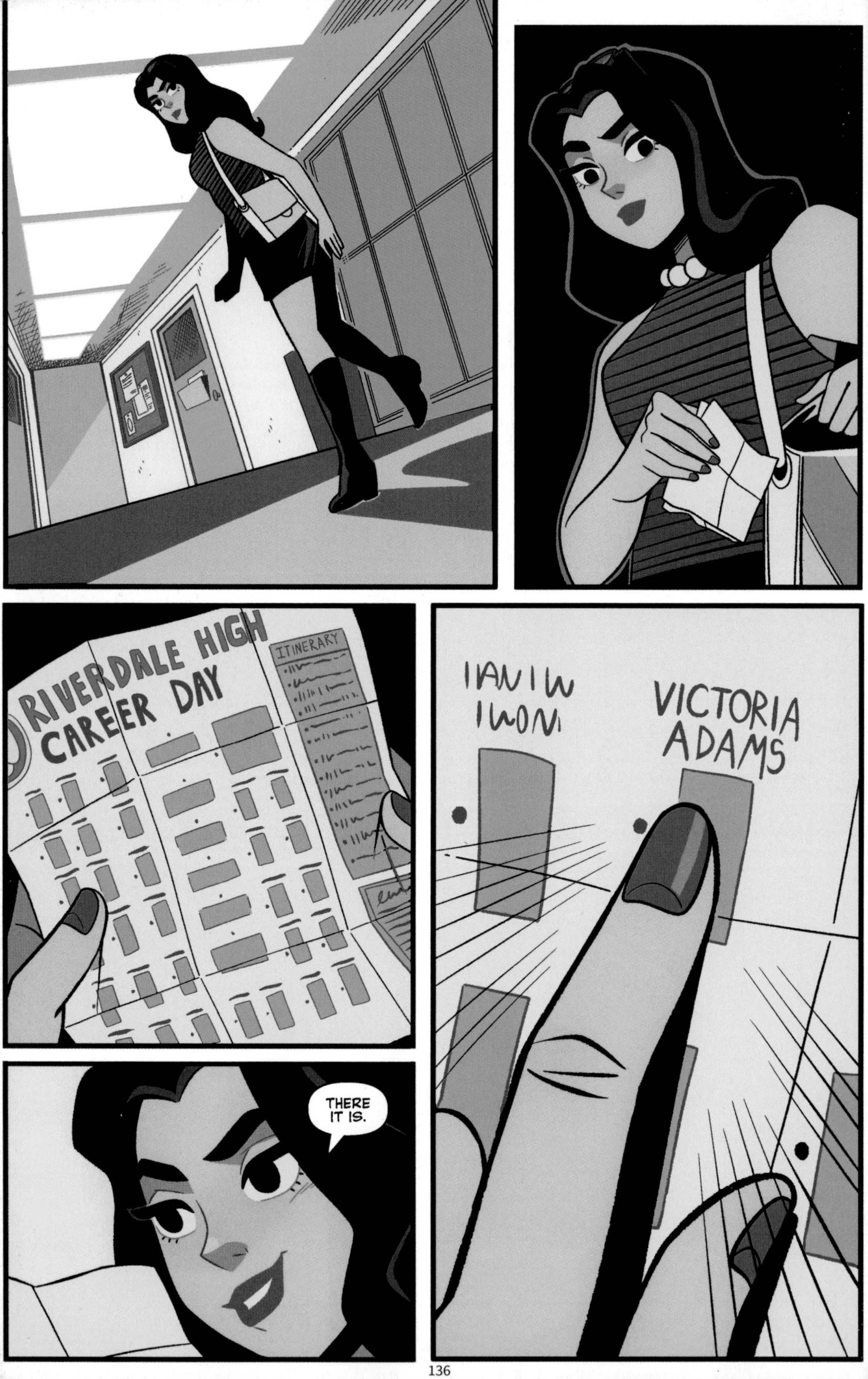
RIVERDALE HIGH
CAREER DAY
ITINERARY
VICTORIA
ADAMS
THERE IT IS.

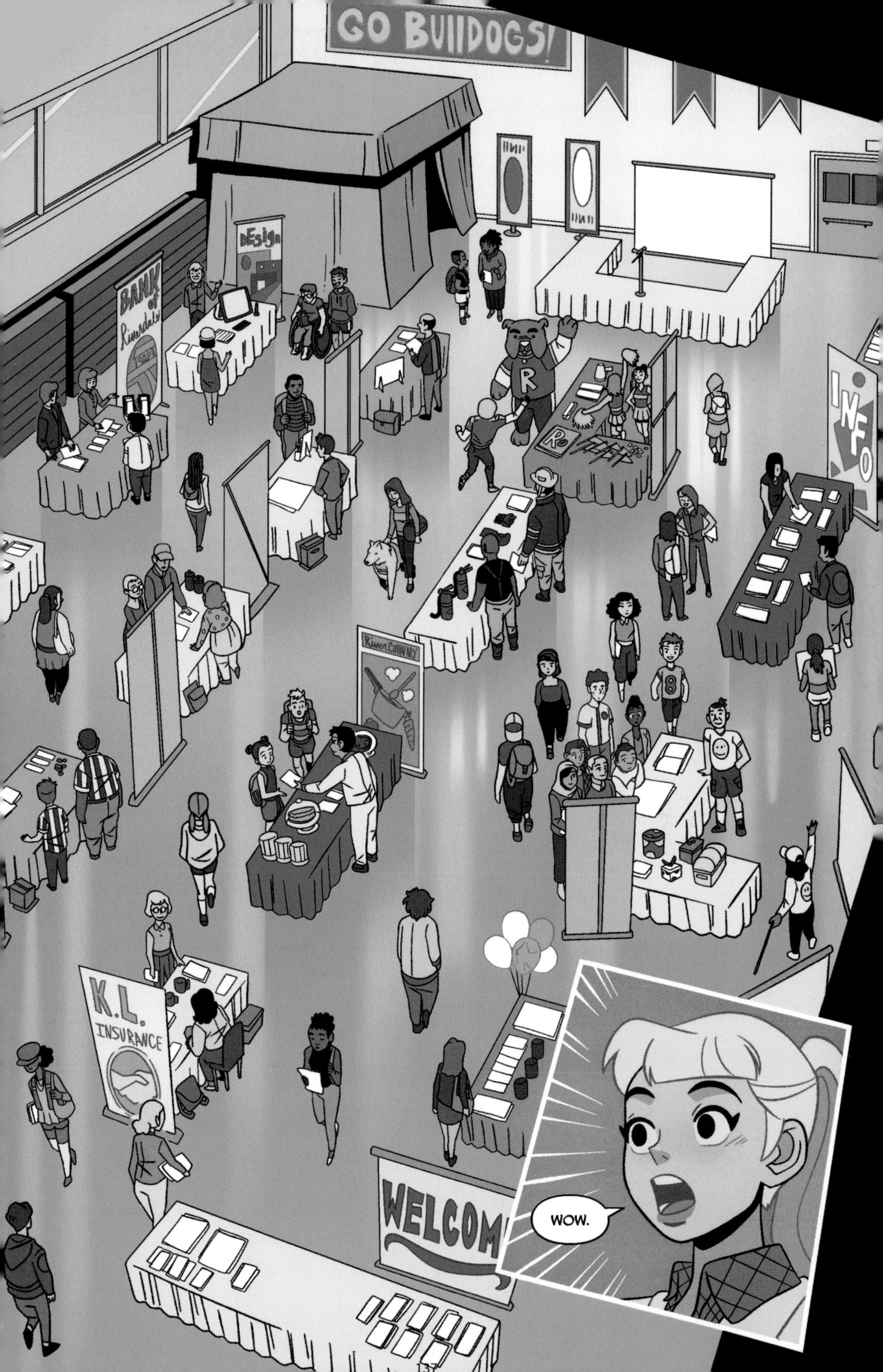
GO BULLDOGS!
DESIGN
BANK of Riverdale
INFO
River CULINARY
K.L. INSURANCE
WELCOM
WOW.

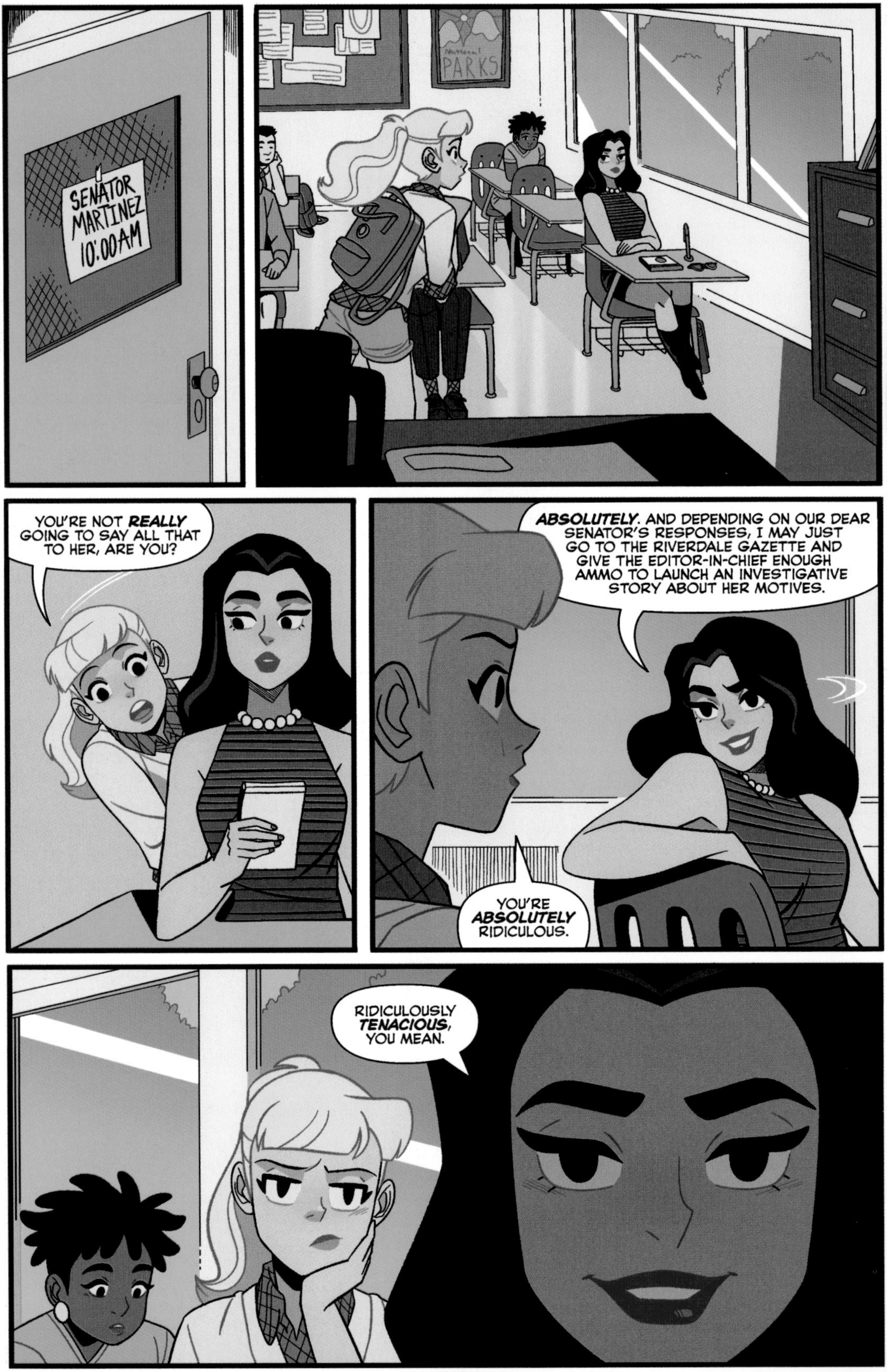
SENATOR MARTINEZ 10:00AM
PARKS
YOU'RE NOT **REALLY** GOING TO SAY ALL THAT TO HER, ARE YOU?
ABSOLUTELY. AND DEPENDING ON OUR DEAR SENATOR'S RESPONSES, I MAY JUST GO TO THE RIVERDALE GAZETTE AND GIVE THE EDITOR-IN-CHIEF ENOUGH AMMO TO LAUNCH AN INVESTIGATIVE STORY ABOUT HER MOTIVES.
YOU'RE **ABSOLUTELY** RIDICULOUS.
RIDICULOUSLY **TENACIOUS**, YOU MEAN.

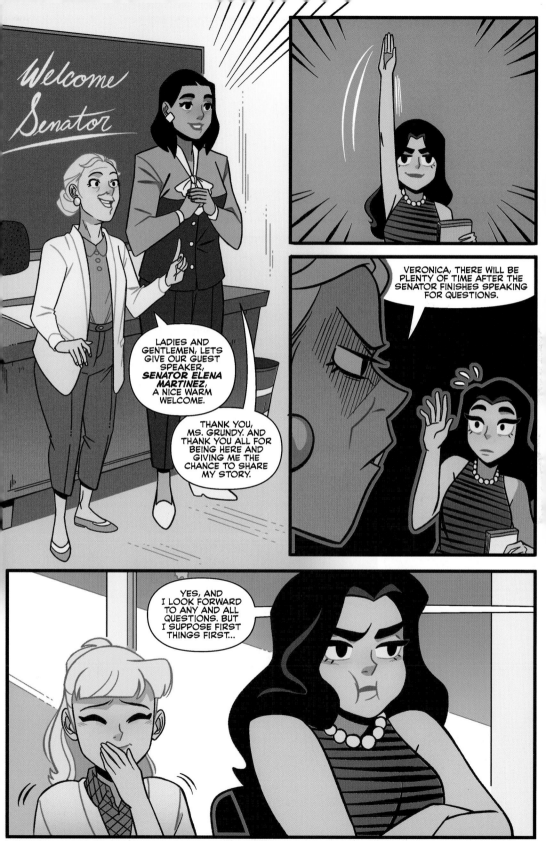

LADIES AND GENTLEMEN, LETS GIVE OUR GUEST SPEAKER, **SENATOR ELENA MARTINEZ,** A NICE WARM WELCOME.

THANK YOU, MS. GRUNDY. AND THANK YOU ALL FOR BEING HERE AND GIVING ME THE CHANCE TO SHARE MY STORY.

VERONICA, THERE WILL BE PLENTY OF TIME AFTER THE SENATOR FINISHES SPEAKING FOR QUESTIONS.

YES, AND I LOOK FORWARD TO ANY AND ALL QUESTIONS. BUT I SUPPOSE FIRST THINGS FIRST...

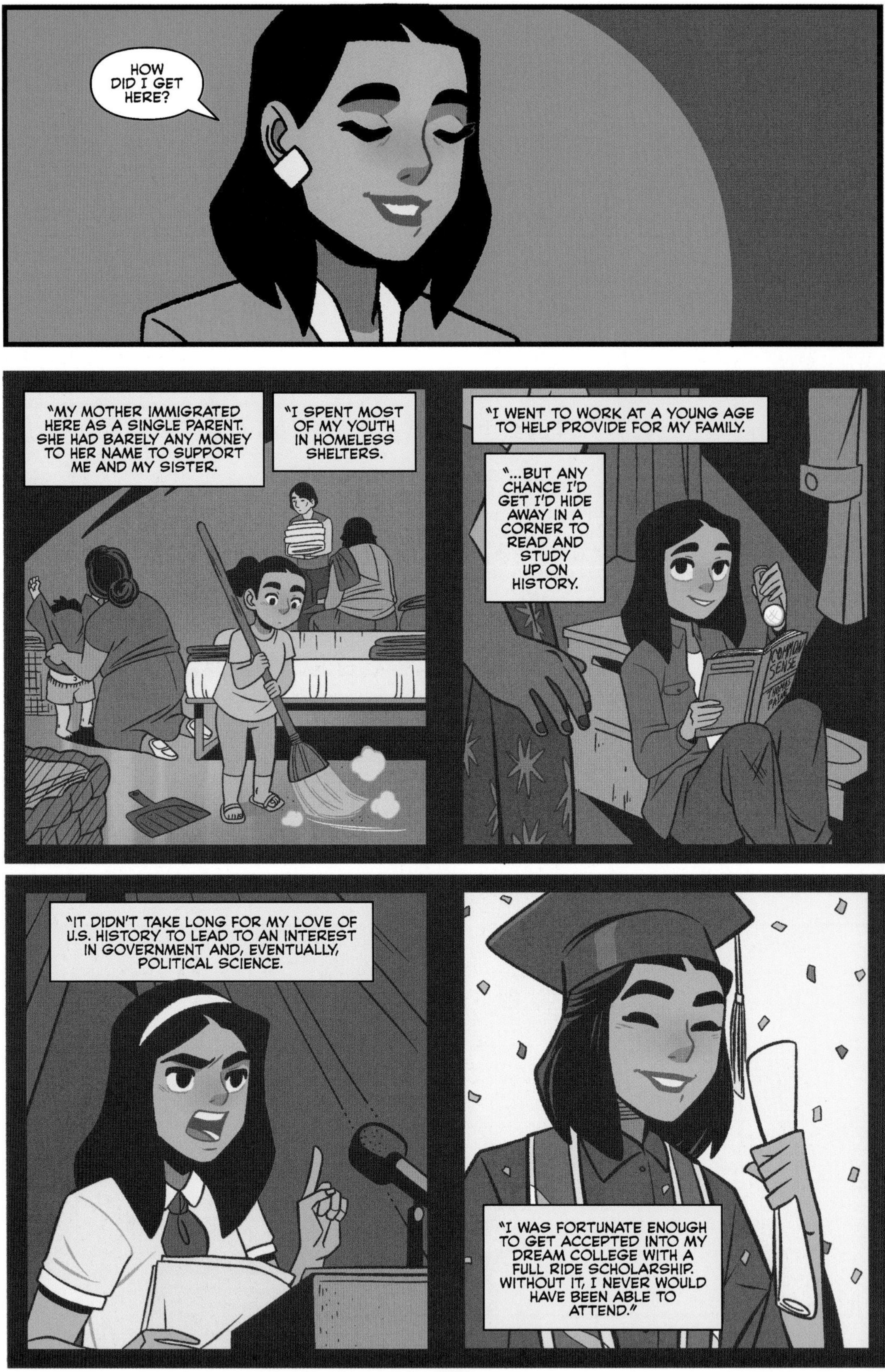
HOW DID I GET HERE?
"MY MOTHER IMMIGRATED HERE AS A SINGLE PARENT. SHE HAD BARELY ANY MONEY TO HER NAME TO SUPPORT ME AND MY SISTER.
"I SPENT MOST OF MY YOUTH IN HOMELESS SHELTERS.
"I WENT TO WORK AT A YOUNG AGE TO HELP PROVIDE FOR MY FAMILY.
"...BUT ANY CHANCE I'D GET I'D HIDE AWAY IN A CORNER TO READ AND STUDY UP ON HISTORY.
"IT DIDN'T TAKE LONG FOR MY LOVE OF U.S. HISTORY TO LEAD TO AN INTEREST IN GOVERNMENT AND, EVENTUALLY, POLITICAL SCIENCE.
"I WAS FORTUNATE ENOUGH TO GET ACCEPTED INTO MY DREAM COLLEGE WITH A FULL RIDE SCHOLARSHIP. WITHOUT IT, I NEVER WOULD HAVE BEEN ABLE TO ATTEND."

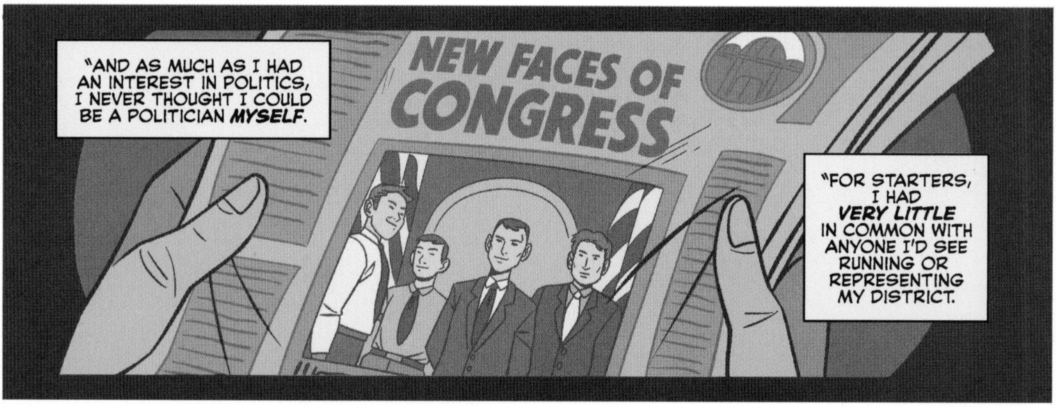
"AND AS MUCH AS I HAD AN INTEREST IN POLITICS, I NEVER THOUGHT I COULD BE A POLITICIAN *MYSELF*.
NEW FACES OF CONGRESS
"FOR STARTERS, I HAD *VERY LITTLE* IN COMMON WITH ANYONE I'D SEE RUNNING OR REPRESENTING MY DISTRICT.

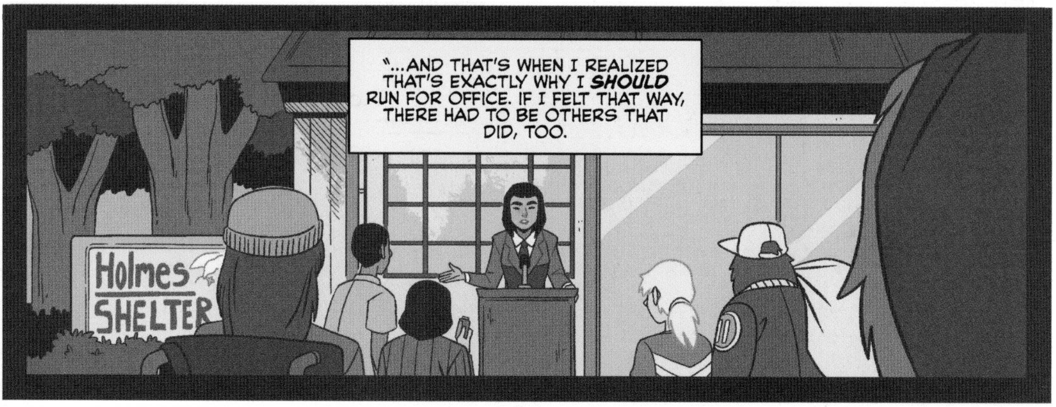
"...AND THAT'S WHEN I REALIZED THAT'S EXACTLY WHY I *SHOULD* RUN FOR OFFICE. IF I FELT THAT WAY, THERE HAD TO BE OTHERS THAT DID, TOO.
Holmes SHELTER

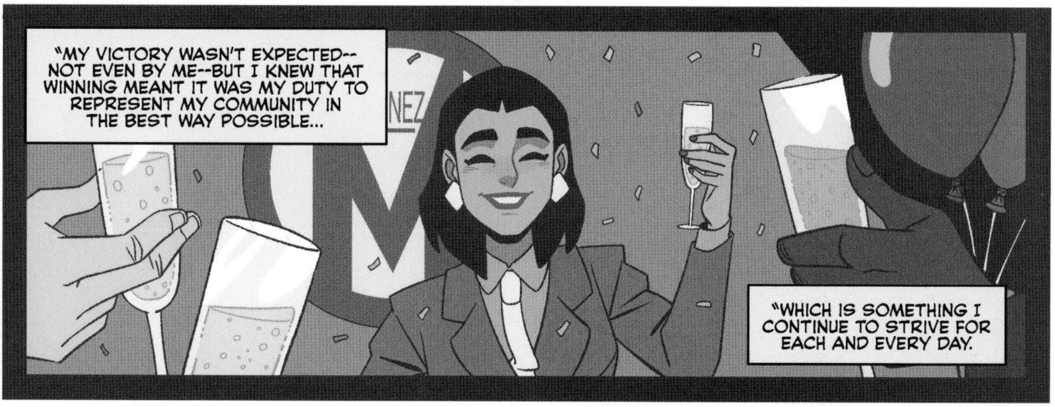
"MY VICTORY WASN'T EXPECTED--NOT EVEN BY ME--BUT I KNEW THAT WINNING MEANT IT WAS MY DUTY TO REPRESENT MY COMMUNITY IN THE BEST WAY POSSIBLE...
"WHICH IS SOMETHING I CONTINUE TO STRIVE FOR EACH AND EVERY DAY.

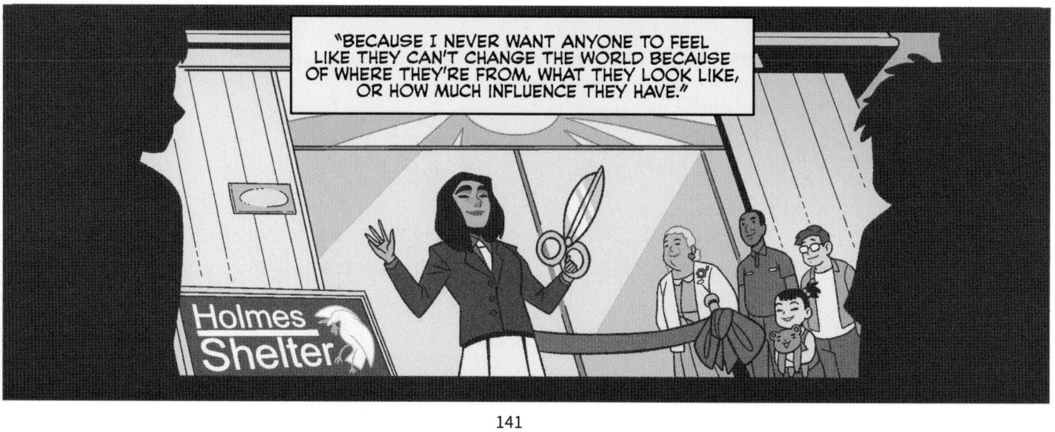
"BECAUSE I NEVER WANT ANYONE TO FEEL LIKE THEY CAN'T CHANGE THE WORLD BECAUSE OF WHERE THEY'RE FROM, WHAT THEY LOOK LIKE, OR HOW MUCH INFLUENCE THEY HAVE."
Holmes Shelter

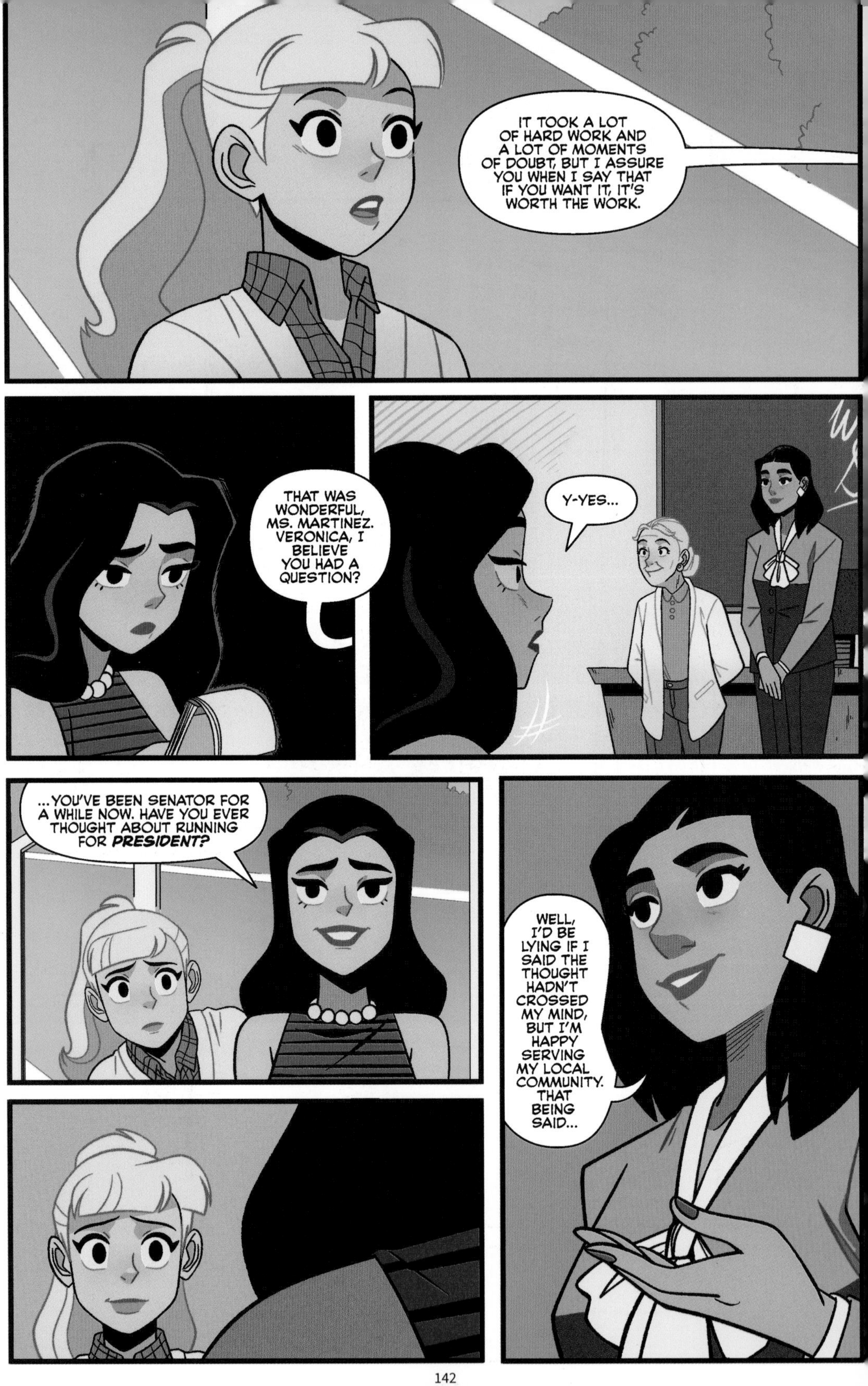
IT TOOK A LOT OF HARD WORK AND A LOT OF MOMENTS OF DOUBT, BUT I ASSURE YOU WHEN I SAY THAT IF YOU WANT IT, IT'S WORTH THE WORK.
THAT WAS WONDERFUL, MS. MARTINEZ. VERONICA, I BELIEVE YOU HAD A QUESTION?
Y-YES...
...YOU'VE BEEN SENATOR FOR A WHILE NOW. HAVE YOU EVER THOUGHT ABOUT RUNNING FOR ***PRESIDENT?***
WELL, I'D BE LYING IF I SAID THE THOUGHT HADN'T CROSSED MY MIND, BUT I'M HAPPY SERVING MY LOCAL COMMUNITY. THAT BEING SAID...